To Mike +

Love

Dow

On the Other Side
of Death Mountain
A Jay Mountain Healing Novel

by Douglass N. Powell, M.D.

DORRANCE
PUBLISHING CO
EST. 1920
PITTSBURGH, PENNSYLVANIA 15238

Dorrance Publishing Co
585 Alpha Drive
Suite 103
Pittsburgh, PA 15238
Visit our website at www.dorrancebookstore.com

ISBN: 978-1-6442-6948-0
eISBN: 978-1-6442-6301-3

Acknowledgements

I would like to sincerely thank everyone who had a hand in helping me write this book. First and foremost are my family and friends. They have been interested and supportive for the whole project. I could not have completed this without their kind, loving encouragement. My father took me hunting each fall for over three decades in the mountains around Jay, New York, teaching me the traditions and lore of the area. My wife, Cathy allowed me the time to write and explore the inner worlds of these novels. She is my light.

This is the third book in a series called *Jay Mountain Healing Novels*. All of my books have been edited and critiqued by Liz Dodd of Juneau, Alaska. She has proven to be a kindred soul who gets me and my writing. She has helped me hone my skills and craft. If this book is easily readable, it is due to her efforts. I thank her.

I also want to thank Dr. Joseph M. Helms, the father of Medical Acupuncture. He and his band of eccentric teachers taught me the kind, contemplative arts of acupuncture and gave me a new lease on life when I had burned out with a busy medical practice. He gave me another career to pursue, a purpose and deeply moving spiritual practice, and the energy to pick up my computer and finish my first novel. From there, it has become a downhill course, indeed. Special thanks to all the preceptors, and, Pam Sinclair and Linda Yemoto.

The proceeds of the sale of this book will be donated to the ACUS Foundation, started by Dr. Helms to provide teaching of Medical Acupuncture to military physicians. Through their efforts, our active duty and retired military personnel and their dependents can get Medical Acupuncture—a timeless healing without drugs or their side effects. Please join me in supporting their ambitious and labor intensive endeavor.

To my readers: Please enjoy this and the five others in the series.

1

Jim Tower stared at his fingernails. About a decade ago, he had finally been able to stop chewing them until they bled. At that time, his arch-rival, Demian Listing, had made amends for his family's mistreatment of Jim's less fortunate forebears. Subsequently, Jim's multitude of health issues spontaneously resolved. Even his complexion cleared up. Demian proceeded to establish a new research center for Jim to direct, then funded research concerning the lifestyles of the people of the Adirondacks. Three research assistants were hired, and they went on to publish multiple authentic descriptions of the harsh daily work settlers had to perform to subsist in the mountains. Jim continued as the publisher of the only weekly newspaper for the Lake Placid area as he became the endowed curator of the Jay Mountain History and Research Center and director of the Jay Mountain Museum and Demonstration Center.

While he waited for his long-time friend, Sheriff Todd Wilkins, to respond to his call, his index finger's nail looked too inviting. Jim's secretary had mentioned that three men had been asking questions about the area around the lands previously owned by the Listing family on Jay Mountain. They had also been to the deeds office and had copies of surveyor's maps made. This had quickly aroused her suspicions, and Jim's call to the sheriff followed.

Todd drove up in the sheriff's patrol vehicle, got out, and entered Jim's office. "Hi, Jim. Good to see you. What's up?" the sheriff asked.

"I don't *know* that anything is up, but I am concerned," Jim replied.

The sheriff took off his hat, wiped his brow and waited. "Staring at your fingernails is not going to tell me what the problem is." Todd laughed. "Just take your time and tell me. Do I need to sit down?"

"Yeah." Jim pointed to his office. They found chairs in front of his marble-topped antique desk in the center of the room. This large area also had an old roll-top desk with papers, envelopes, pens, and pipes sticking out of most of the slots in the desk top. An antique writing quill and ink set rested alone on the top of the desk, making it the focal point of that half of the space.

"I haven't been in your office before—it's really nice. The antiques match the rest of the historical center. Really nice." Todd looked around slowly, using his trained eye to notice the small touches that made the room's décor work. Most of the available space had something in or on it—pictures, statutes, floor stands, and collections of tools and watches—arranged in groupings that drew in the onlooker's eyes.

"Thanks. I truly love the history of the area and have tried to recreate a little of it here."

"You've succeeded, for sure." Todd paused. "Now, what's on your mind?"

"Lake Placid gets its share of visitors—most people, just like you and me, are out to enjoy the mountains, lakes, hikes, history and slower pace up around here."

"The slower pace is what I'm getting now, right?" He laughed.

"OK, to get to the point, after the trial of that shit, Gary Canig, maybe my suspicions are heightened, or maybe not...." Jim continued to stare at his nails.

"What's going on?" Todd understood the gravity of the situation. He had participated in the arrest of Gary Canig and understood how malicious he was.

"Three foreigners with German accents came into the deeds office and wanted to look up deeds around the Listing family's old spread up on Jay Mountain. They also spent several days at the library looking up local newspapers going back twenty years. My secretary, who also works part-time at the library, told me about them. They spoke to no one. They came and left. That's it."

"Anything else bother her about the men or their actions?"

"She deals with the public every day. She said they unnerved her and she couldn't say why." Jim put his hands in his pockets quickly, the arms of his chair making it a tight squeeze. "Anyway, after the trial, I just don't know. Mirror Lake is cleaning itself up, the town is getting back to normal, Gary Canig is in jail for life, and I should be happy that all is well—but I just don't have that feeling anymore. I can't trust that things are all right. *I don't know.*"

"When were the men doing all that research?"

"Up until yesterday."

"I'll drop by and talk to your secretary at the library. I'll do my best job of snooping around. I'll find out from her if they left any addresses or gave any ID or anything else that might be relevant. I can think of quite a few legitimate reasons why the men might have been here, including they might be reporters and such. But I'll keep an eye out and look into it for you."

"Thanks, Todd. If in a few days you tell me I was just a little too paranoid, I'll be very happy—I'll buy us a few beers for your trouble."

"I'll let you know. This area has had enough turmoil. I'm glad to be fore-warned if there might be something else brewing."

They both stood, understanding that the sheriff had places to be and people to talk to. "Thanks for being here. Watch your back," Jim warned.

"As always."

As historian of the area, Jim knew there were no other episodes like the recent attack on Lake Placid by Gary Canig. This CIA agent had devised a weapon that was inserted via hip implants, causing an electromagnetic pulse. The weapon fired and essentially fused all the electronic equipment within a five-mile radius of Mirror Lake, paralyzing the village of Lake Placid, killing the fish and birds in the area, and nearly killing the unsuspecting man who had had the implants inserted, sending him to the neurosurgical intensive care unit. It displaced the whole population of the village for weeks as clean up and restoration proceeded. A dozen older patients with computerized medication pumps for insulin died due to the malfunction of the pumps. Patients with pacemakers could feel their unprotected hearts slow, and they reported to hospitals for replacements of their units.

Demian Listing, the richest man in northern New York State, stepped in financially to offer assistance for the rebuilding of the town and businesses and to help people get back on their feet. Mother Nature would restore Mirror Lake to its pristine clear waters. The birds would come back, and the fish could be restocked, if needed.

But something sinister gnawed at the back of Jim's mind about Gary Canig. It took four men—Sheriff Wilkins, Demian, Will Williams, and Bennie—to successfully subdue the rogue CIA agent. This man had murdered, ruined lives, stolen huge amounts of money, and worked the system to his advantage before. He would not hesitate to do so again.

2

Jenn thought about the day. Combing her hair had hurt. Getting dressed had taken about an hour. The same as always.

Bennie came by to chat. When he was in town, he came at 11:00 AM, sharp. She wondered if he had nowhere else to be. She had given up telling him not to come.

Bennie had befriended the owner of a small local motel situated on a deserted road leading to nowhere in particular—it had difficulty filling even two or three of its twenty rooms on most nights. The end room, being the last one on the renovation list, never rented out. The lock didn't work, the light bulbs had all blown, and the air conditioner hummed loudly and stank of old mustiness. At best, it only cooled the room slightly. Bennie came and went as he pleased, knowing the owner liked him being around to keep the locals from drinking in the parking lot and urinating in the flowerbeds. The roses couldn't grow well in that environment. When he stayed in town, he took that end room to watch over the place.

"All in all, it's a beautiful day. Why don't we go to the river and lay in the sun?" Bennie's tone was light as if asking about the weather report. He knew what Jenn's response to the question would be.

"Even walking three steps would make my feet ache. You know that."

"I do. I was just hopeful."

"Why don't you give up on me and leave me alone?" she moaned. Simply breathing enough to speak caused her pain in her ribs and the muscles running down her sides.

"I don't give up on anything that's worthwhile." He paused. "When I was away for the last few days, I traveled up north to help out an old friend. I met some amazing healers. They could help you. I would take you there, if you'd let me."

"Yeah. Like I haven't heard that before." Her voice had a groaning quality.

"You haven't heard that from me. I mean what I say and I say what I mean." He looked offended. His word was his bond since his Military Academy days.

"I can't even think about riding in a car for very long. It hurts too much." She looked to the floor of her small apartment. "I gave up thinking that I'll ever feel better."

"I've given up a lot of things too. I gave up thinking that I'll be normal and have a normal life. I only have a few friends. When they call, I go running. I'm off the grid—which I sometimes like—no telemarketers, spam, and so forth. My only other friends are online. I've never seen them in person and don't think I ever will."

"Why can't you have a normal life? You don't have this chronic pain that the doctors can't figure out," she asked.

He looked out the window and then around the small apartment. "I don't know. I just don't fit in anymore." Bennie recalled the inscription in marble at the entrance to the Wounded Warrior Center of Excellence, National Naval Medical Center: "*Some scars go deeper than what you can see.*" When he had been treated there, he couldn't allow the therapists and doctors to help him. He was still too wounded to trust. Now, he just didn't know.

"Why?"

Bennie thought about this role reversal. He was usually the one who tried to cheer her up. Now she asked the tough questions. "I've seen too many things and done too many things in my life." He let that linger.

"If you bring your car around to the front door, maybe I could ride for a while. Watch the bumps, though." She looked resigned, not at all excited.

"It's a deal." He offered his arm to help her up. She took it and got to her feet with a moan. He stood about six feet tall, had broad shoulders and was very fit. His muscles rippled under his shirt, and Jenn could feel their definition as he ushered her along. She thought that he could be a movie double for Kevin Costner, but darker, with brown hair and eyes. Bennie was in better condition than the actor. He could seriously model if he wanted to.

Jenn wobbled to the door and thought back to when she was fourteen. Up until that day, she had led an ordinary life. She had run and played. She had hoped to become a nationally acclaimed gymnast and had won a spot on the local high school team. She had competed on the balance beam and had perfected her standing backflip, landing with a perfect grip on the beam. *Wow.* That had taken *years* of hard work. Now, all that effort became moot.

After that day, everything began to hurt. Everything. Her hair hurt to comb or brush. Her scalp hurt to part her hair in the style that so many girls were using—low on the side and pulled back into a tight braid. Her fingers hurt to run them through her hair.

She could no longer be that carefree girl. She no longer had a bright future in gymnastics. She couldn't bring herself to envision her future at all because of her continuously aching and painful present. Even her thoughts and emotions hurt, giving rise to a deep ache and dullness in the center of her head. *Jesus.*

The long line of doctors, healers, therapists and charlatans she and her parents had consulted numbered in the thirties. None of them had helped. All of them were expensive. Jenn's parents essentially bankrupted themselves trying to find a future for their daughter until they died. Her mother developed breast cancer at the age of forty. Her father developed pancreatic cancer shortly thereafter. They both died within a month of each other. They had provided for their daughter with life insurance policies, but those policies did not bring her joy or relief from the pain.

The first series of doctors did test after grueling test. Then they referred her to even more refined specialists. These super doctors did more and more invasive tests, causing even more pain. Their tests always involved a biopsy of something or a needle sample of something else. She suffered through test injections, unproven therapies, psychotherapies, ice baths and shock therapies. Her body wore the scars of these attempts to diagnose her illness. Those scars themselves became even more inflamed and tender as the years wore on. They became a deep purplish red and had swollen over time enough to restrict her joint's motions. Now her wrists, knees and ankles only bent reluctantly—incompletely, painfully and slowly. She felt her skin had a layer of cardboard underneath. It crinkled achingly as she bent a joint.

Finally, Jenn refused to go to any more consultants. She refused to take any more medication. None of that had helped her in the least. She came to believe she was unworthy of feeling well.

Jenn wore loose clothing in neutral or light pastel colors with large, clunky athletic shoes. She slowly settled into the front seat of Bennie's old BMW. The bucket seat fit well, cradling her whole back, neck, and thighs, but everywhere it touched her body, she burned. She winced just at the start of the motor. Her ears hurt listening to the exhaust. She finally asked, "Tell me about you. Why do you come around? Why do you waste your time on me?"

"I hardly think it's a waste of time." He deliberately slowed down to cross the short curb separating the parking lot from the highway. "What do you want to know? And do you want it all to be the truth?" It surprised him that he had asked her that; it came out before he could stop himself.

"No. First make up a real story for me. Make it a fanciful story about nothing like the modern days. And make it good to distract me from this misery."

"You're not too demanding, are you?"

"You asked," she quickly responded. "Yes. And then I want the truth. I want to hear all about your life. I mean it."

Bennie raised his eyebrows. "I have to make up a story on the spot? It can't be something I've read or heard along the way?"

"On the spot. Right now. Make it good. And quick, too."

"Jesus." He smiled at the challenge, thinking he had not had such an opportunity before and knowing he had only one chance to distract his young friend.

"I'm waiting." Jenn drummed her fingers in a display of impatience, although it hurt her to do so. She felt electric shocks from her fingertips all the way up her elbows to her shoulders while she tapped on the leather dashboard.

"I'm glad you're here with me. This is the first time you've let me drive you anywhere." He thought as he shifted and drove. "I would like to tell you about an idyllic place that I visited just last week. OK?" Bennie quickly surveyed his surroundings methodically. No one followed. His eyes flew to the mirrors every few seconds to confirm they were safe.

"I guess you can default to some real-life experience, if you have to," Jenn sighed.

"I visited a truly magical place. It's in the Adirondacks, outside a small village named Jay, New York. I was there visiting my oldest and dearest friend. I haven't seen him in about ten years. That's a whole different story, though."

"Yeah?"

"Don't interrupt. You don't want to rush me, do you?" He rolled his eyes in an exaggerated manner.

She glared at him, wincing as the next bump passed. He instinctively slowed down.

"So, there we were. A few of his friends have a place on Jay Mountain. It's one of the high peaks. The other surrounding mountains are Death Mountain, Bitch Mountain, and Arnold Mountain—it was named after Benedict—it's a traitorous mountain. There are others, but, from the names, you get the picture."

"I'm waiting...." Jenn sounded exasperated but actually enjoyed seeing Bennie squirm under the pressure of producing a new story on the spot. She smiled for the first time in years—until her cheeks hurt.

"I'm working on it. Jesus. Give me a break." He took a breath, his thoughts focused on the far-away mountain, and he continued. "We went to a place called the Beaver Dams. Because guess what? There were indeed beaver dams and lakes and streams and hills and mountains and trees. Beautiful, really."

They turned the corner and passed several fast food joints, gas stations, hair salons, and an ice cream stand.

"Yeah?"

"Well, the legend goes back to the Civil War. There is the legend that somewhere in the Adirondacks there is buried gold. Do you know what? My friends figured it out and proved the existence of a nephew of General Robert E. Lee. The general, himself, sent his nephew to the North to rob all the gold he could from the payrolls shipped by railroad before the Civil War. These supplied the huge mining, lumbering, and manufacturing concerns in the Adirondacks in those days. They all shipped their money—mostly gold—by train because it proved most efficient to do so. This nephew also intended to steal repeating rifles to bring to the South to use against the North. The bigger arms manufacturers located their plants in the north. Gunpowder, as it was formulated in those days, was too unstable to be used in large quantities in the heat of the south, and after too many accidental explosions, they had moved their operations to the North."

Jenn showed a quizzical expression.

"One thing led to another. The nephew married a local girl. She got pregnant but died in childbirth. He killed the physician looking after the delivery, was jailed, hung himself or was killed by his men to protect the mission—and the gold remained buried."

"Huh?"

"Yeah. So, talk about shit luck. You get married, try to have a baby, your wife dies in childbirth, you lose your baby, you hang yourself or your men off you and the gold and rifles you pledged your uncle—none other than General Robert E. Lee—never get to the South. Who knows? Could the South have been able to hold off the North with more money and repeating arms? Who knows? This life would certainly be a whole lot different if the South won the war. Even if there was a truce and no one claimed victory."

"Wow. Is that the story?" Jenn asked.

"No way. You asked for a story. That's just the preamble." He turned onto the highway. "I thought the road would be smoother here. Mind if we just drive? When you want, tell me and we'll head home."

"I want to hear the rest of the story. You're hot, and I don't want to derail this tale."

"So my friend and his group figured it out. Seems that there were five guys staying at the small hunting camp in the Jay Mountain area. They all figured out a small bit of the story, individually, and after adding it up, they went on to find the gold. They also had help from a local healer named Madison. She taught one of the men how to meditate and that led him to find the final clue in a meditation."

He shifted to pass a large oil truck. Jenn's head tilted back as he accelerated. She grimaced.

"Sorry. I had to pass him to get out of the way of the group of cars following us. Not safe to get caught in a posse of cars." Bennie continued to keep track of all the surrounding cars. Like always. None of the cars seemed intent on tailing them, though. He didn't register any of the cars more than once, so he could be confident that pursuers were not doing a multiple car surveillance.

"Whatever. Get on with the story."

"As I was saying…I visited the same site where they had found evidence of the prior Civil War troops. The troops had left two stone pyramids with engravings as maps of the Beaver Dams area. These could be superimposed on each other to mark out the location of the buried gold. I went through the drawings and found that one of the maps had an error by comparing it to the mountains and especially the beaver's streams. At the academy, we were taught that such errors pointed in the direction of the map's other markings. It was a subterfuge to mislead an enemy who might have fallen into possession of secret communiqués."

"Academy? What academy?"

"West Point. I graduated about twenty years ago."

"What?" Her voice pronounced her amazement.

"Yeah. Then I did two tours in Iraq."

"I never knew…."

"I didn't tell you. Wasn't germane to my current life." He pulled onto the Northway.

"So?"

"So the original person who followed the map's markings didn't know about the trick taught at the academy. He didn't reverse his directions. He didn't find the gold. I did."

"What?"

"Yeah. I did." His tone was matter of fact.

"How much gold?" she persisted.

"Don't know. I haven't dug it up yet."

"So you found a cache of Civil War gold and you haven't bothered to dig it up yet?"

"It's not that simple, you know?" He shifted to keep the car from jerking.

"Shit. Damn. Is this true or all made up?" Jenn looked at him in amazement.

"Both. Just like you asked." He looked smug.

"You bastard." She settled into the seat just a little further. "It did take my mind off my pain for a little while, though."

"I'm glad of that."

They passed the exits of Saratoga Springs, Gore Mountain, and Lake George. Bennie pulled off at a rest area. "Why don't we get out to rest a little?" He continued until they overlooked a beautiful mountain vista, with lakes, forests, and mists in the distance. The bright light of the midday sun made them both squint. Bennie bought Jenn a cheap pair of sunglasses in a small kiosk selling sun protection products. He saw that even the bright sun caused her discomfort, making her squint and causing her forehead muscles to ache.

"Thank you for this short respite from the pain. The distraction was pleasant. And you do tell a good story—or is it the truth?"

"Well, why don't we see? I'll take you there."

"No. I've got to rest. If I travel, I can only go a few minutes. If I go further, I pay for it for days." She rubbed her elbows and then her low back.

"I get it. But if I could ever show you the area around Lake Placid, I know you could somehow feel better. My friends would all see you and see how to help you…."

"I don't trust that anyone can ever help me feel better. I'm just cursed to live this life."

Bennie stared off in the distance. He knew in his heart that Madison, Gunner and Marion would stop at nothing to try to help her. Then he looked at Jenn. She had red hair, cut short, a pale complexion and always wore loose clothing that was not too revealing. She was thin but still curvaceous, like the popular models of the 1970s. If she smiled, her mouth didn't quite turn up at the corners. There was always something lurking there that didn't allow her to feel joy.

3

The next day, Bennie arrived at 11:00 AM, on the dot. He knocked, and Jenn called to him to let himself in.

"I really want to thank you for the drive yesterday. I had to rest the remainder of the day, but it was beautiful," Jenn sighed.

"My pleasure. My car didn't fare so well. It's used to driving like hell and revving to the red line in all the gears. It probably won't ever forgive me for driving so slow…" he laughed.

"What part of that story you told me is true? Or did you just stretch the truth? How about old-fashioned hyperbole? How about prevarication? Any of that yesterday?"

He laughed at her list of sayings covering the fine art of subterfuge. "You know? I told you that the only way to really find out is to go to that area and see for yourself."

"No way. I hurt too much." Jenn sounded resolute.

"What do you think you could do if I distract you? I'd like to try." Bennie sounded genuine.

"I really don't know." She looked out the window to her small apartment. "I am intrigued about your story. What part was true?"

"Pretty much all of it, unfortunately. I didn't want to fail with distracting you, and I was driving, so I had to partly pay attention to the road. That really put me on the spot, so I stuck with what I knew."

"Maybe you could try again?" Jenn hoped.

"Take a drive again with me, and I'll tell you a story that's one hundred percent made up."

"No. Today I have to rest and keep this pain down to a dull roar. Let's sit out front on the deck. You won't have to drive so you won't have the excuse of needing to pay attention to the other cars." She took in a long breath. Even those few sentences tired her. "Help me to the front."

They walked to the door, and a few steps later Jenn moaned as she sat on a gliding bench. Bennie sat next to her, facing her, with his right leg bent at the knee, resting on the bench between them.

"Ready?" He saw she had taken her time settling in, positioning pillows as she needed.

"It has to be brand new and completely fabricated. Make it interesting, too."

Bennie let Jenn set the pace of the glide of the bench. He carefully didn't jerk the glider or make any sudden movements, fearing it might hurt her.

"A story about very old times. Would that be OK?"

"Sure."

He paused for a long time. She closed her eyes briefly and felt the sun on her face. She put on her new sunglasses. He started. "Well, there I was walking. I had traveled extensively through the known lands and had come to the crossroads of our times." Bennie looked off in the distance. "We had all heard tales of other lands and the different types of peoples at the village tells, seated around the campfires. Each night in the summer, an elder would speak of his travels or show his satchel full of things brought back to the village. We kept the history that way."

"So far, so good."

Bennie's flashing eyes warned her not to interrupt again. She got the message.

"I traveled, walking. I saw the sights of different peoples from different lands. Some rode large unknown beasts. Many walked, like me. I saw different styles of dress, colors, skin tones, and sizes of people. There were young and old travelers. These sights tantalized me as I walked. I kept my small dagger carefully hidden under my tunic, like always. I carried it, my satchel and my sleeping roll. Nothing else."

Jenn stared at him. She closed her eyes as she imagined the scenes he described.

"Then I heard the sounds that different tribes make, their beasts roaring or screeching or mewing. The people played their instruments. The artisans used their tools to fashion clothes or bend steel, and they sang as they walked or worked. The sounds carried me along as I walked. Many of the sounds I will never hear again."

Jenn smiled only a half-smile, being unaccustomed to using those muscles.

"The odors of cooking from camps of peoples along the road shocked me at times and lulled me into complacency at others. Incense, spices and tobaccos all blended their aromas with dung, latrines and sweat. I followed my nose, like a good bloodhound. I started to think that I could taste the odors as I walked." Bennie looked at Jenn and saw her soften into the seat.

"Then, I began to run my hand along the stones in the wall bordering the road. Their textures varied, I thought, like the lives and ways of being of the many peoples traveling along with the masses of beasts, carts and wagons. I thought I could *feel* the textures of their lives, as I felt the stones' grooves and bumps." Bennie waited a while and let Jenn push the glider under them.

"Suddenly…."

Jenn opened her eyes as if to imply *this better be good*….

"Suddenly, I saw an ordinary man standing on the corner—someone who would be overlooked in any crowd—certainly in this entourage. At the very crossroads of our times, he was nearly unnoticeable, nearly *invisible*. He quickly gave me a small, round, white stone, about the size and shape of a small egg. I was so surprised at receiving the gift, I simply bowed. The man told me to take the stone with me on my journey. I slipped it in my bag and walked on, bowing again. How he knew about my travels, I don't know."

"Yeah?"

"I'm getting to it." Bennie gave her a sidelong glance.

"Sorry," she quickly said, turning her eyes to the ground.

"I walked on and strangely, my satchel seemed to get both heavier and lighter. This was subtle and hard to notice at first. I tried to ignore it because I was so distracted by the other sights, sounds, odors and textures. Eventually, I could no longer pass this off as just fantasy or fatigue. I finally dug out the stone and held it in my hand as I walked. I couldn't be sure, but it seemed that the stone itself also got both lighter and heavier. And as it got lighter, it became more transparent. As it got heavier, it became more densely white. I became certain. I had never seen or heard of such magic. I had to see the man who had given me the stone and ask him about this."

"Wow."

"I ran back to the corner of the crossroads of our time. I found the ordinary man standing as he had been. Holding the stone in front of me, walking towards the man, the stone got lighter. At the same time, it became more translucent. *And the man on the corner seemed to fade.*"

"Wow."

"When I got to him, I watched him become denser while the stone I held became heavier and whiter. He said to me, 'Come. Stand with me. Learn the art of falling and the meditations of time.' I'm sure I looked confused."

"I would have, too," Jenn agreed.

"The man took another stone like the one he had given me and held it in one hand. He pulled a feather from his pocket and held it in the other. He dropped them at the same time. The stone fell quickly and crashed loudly on the gravel. The feather floated and eventually landed without a sound. He said, 'They fall at different speeds and they land in different times.' He repeated that a few times, and it began to sound like a chant. I started to hear that chant in my head. I was almost under his spell."

"Uh-huh?" Jenn's anticipation showed on her face.

"I felt a little light-headed as if I was a cobra charmed by a snake charmer. I knew I could not stay with my fellow traveler. I bowed deeply and left him, knowing I had to do my traveling through distance. While I walked away, I felt my satchel getting heavier and, at times, lighter."

"No way! You didn't make that up on the spot. You couldn't have. It's too good a story."

"Well, I have to admit…."

"I knew you were a liar!"

"I have to admit that I thought of it last night because I was intrigued with the challenge of it all. Could I make up a story good enough to distract you? I really wanted to so that I could help you with your pain."

"You never read or heard that story before?"

"Honestly, no."

"Unbelievable. That's even a better short story than yesterday."

"I made it up last night and refined it this morning as I was doing my morning calisthenics and meditations."

"So you get half credit…but you did distract me. And your story is really good. What did you mean by travel through distance?"

"Oh, I just tell the stories. I don't explain them." He laughed until he saw the stern look on her face. "Honestly. What it means to you is the important thing. Not what I tried to say. Your interpretation is the creative part."

"So now *I* have to be creative*?*" *Yeah, like I can think of anything but this pain, all the time,* she thought.

"Turn-about is fair play, don't you think?" he cajoled.

"I'll have to think about that. And I'll have to think about the story, too."

"Take your time with it. How about tomorrow? Same time and place?" He got up and extended his hand. She shook her head and closed her eyes. He walked off and left her to sit in the sun and glide on the porch.

"I'll have to hear more stories before I believe you made that one up," she called after him.

He laughed.

4

"Come in. The door's open," Jenn called from the small bedroom in the back of her apartment.

"Hi, Jenn."

She slowly walked to the sitting room in the front. She walked a little less stiffly but moaned softly, nonetheless.

"Hi, Bennie." She stopped as if she thought of something new. "You know, I don't know if I've ever heard your last name."

"My full name is Bennie R. Grimm. With two m's. Like the fairy tales."

"Shit. That's where you get it from."

"Get what?" he asked.

"The storytelling," Jenn answered.

"No. I prefer to think that I come by it honestly. I worked hard on the story for you. I took my time with it, to make it good for you." He looked offended, then smiled broadly.

"Could we take a ride today, too?" Jenn asked.

"Sure. Where to?"

"You're driving. Is it warm and sunny again? If not, I don't want to get a chill. That would make me even more miserable." It was obvious she meant it.

"It's fine. On the warmer side, and sunny." Bennie was glad she wanted to ride.

"Okay, then. Help me to your car, but I want to walk a few more steps, too."

He pulled up to the driveway across from her front door, making her walk an extra ten steps. After they settled into the car, Bennie asked where she would like to go and if she wanted any kind of distractions. She thought about it for a few minutes as he pulled onto the highway; he moved slowly so she wouldn't be jostled by the bumps. Jenn noticed that he had spread a comforter over the seat to act as a cushion.

"You could tell me a story, but I want to know that you're making it up on the spot. I think a challenge would do you good. And I like watching you squirm under the pressure."

"A challenge? Like what? What would be more of a challenge?" He was intrigued.

"I don't know…like let's drive on, and when we see an interesting person, that person has to be a part of the story. So, you have to make up a story that I know you haven't heard before." She looked confident that he would rise to the challenge.

"Okay. Then we should drive through the village slowly so that we can see someone who you think looks interesting. You pick. I'll slow down, and we'll pick up as many details as we can. I'll weave that into a story. Okay?"

"It's a deal."

They drove to the small town's square. The village gazebo in the square housed a bandstand. On the large mowed lawn, several of the locals who played in the village band practiced passages from John Phillip Souza's marches and other well-known pieces. The musicians played only common music that the people instantly recognized. The conductor intentionally kept to music that didn't stretch his performers' repertoires or challenge their listeners.

As they drove, they saw children playing. "No children in the story," Jenn warned. Her voice was sharp.

"Okay." Bennie wondered why she would have made that stipulation but didn't ask. He quickly checked to see if anyone was obviously following and saw nothing.

A man stacked pumpkins along a white picket fence. There was a sign reading, "Small twenty-five cents, large fifty cents." The man wore old jeans, a faded blue plaid flannel shirt, and a railroad conductor's hat. He carried a satchel.

"How about him? He is ordinary, and yet he might tell interesting stories," Jenn suggested.

"This is your game, after all. But let me drive around the square and have another look at him. I won't spook him, though."

On their second pass, they also noticed his thick glasses, deeply lined face, grey hair and stubbly beard. The satchel he carried on a strap strung over his shoulder looked old and softened by its long use. Bennie drove out of town, to the highway, the same way they had gone on the trip a few days before.

"I'm waiting." What had been intended as imperious and imposing came across as comical to Bennie and he burst out laughing. He had had life-threatening challenges in the past and found her impatience over something so inconsequential churlish.

Bennie started his story. "So it was at the end of my student days. I had learned a lot—all the math, engineering, physics and sciences. But also, the philosophy, languages, logic and art. I had had enough of the learning from books and classes. I wanted to travel. My mentor, an elderly gentleman, invited me to stay at his small house to enjoy his gardens, to be in nature and get away from the school for the summer or as long I wanted. He had also come to the age where he needed help managing himself and living independently."

"Not good enough yet," Jenn warned.

"I'm getting to it." He sneered and laughed. "I know a challenge when I see it. Give me a chance."

He drove on for a minute. "*As I was saying*, after I had had enough of the didactics of school, I gladly joined my mentor at his small house. He asked me to assist him with the lands, the house upkeep, the garden tending and so forth."

After another minute, he continued. "I spent the summer staining the small house a deep grey, with the windows and fence a bright white. I replaced the broken stones in the walkways, smoothing out the uneven areas. This built up my muscles to the extent that I had not felt before. I was surprised at their supple strength. As a student, I hadn't had the opportunity to exercise consistently.

"I studied a small stream that I drew water from to tend the garden. The same stream flowed all year long, but the water was always different. I walked through the stream trying to experience the water and knew it was only an instant that I could know—the next instant, the water had moved on. Throughout the summer, the water quieted, became clearer under the sun's bright illumination and became softer to the touch." Bennie pulled onto the Northway, slowly.

"I tended the garden and kept the plants watered and weeded so they could grow. I was particularly excited about a pumpkin in the back of the plot. It grew large and green, its vines thick and nourishing. I was amazed at the hard, woody texture of the vine that had grown so quickly over only that summer, starting as a single seed.

"The sun in the sky was the same sun, but as the season progressed, it moved from lower in the sky to directly overhead and then lower in the sky again, as the fall came. The days became shorter. I kept watch over the stream, gardens, pumpkins, sun, sky and stars."

"Nice."

"As I was saying…." Bennie rolled his eyes at Jenn. "I carefully watched that larger pumpkin, in particular. It grew very large, then turned from green to green with orange spots, to a bright orange. Other fruits were harvested as they became ripe. Crops were sold or canned and preserved. I decided to be in nature and watch and be a part of the process of the change of seasons. I deferred further travels."

They drove along on to the Northway. The road seemed smoother to Jenn.

"Other smaller pumpkins were picked and stacked along the road and sold. The white picket fence fringed the solid orange of the pumpkins, and the contrast made the pumpkins' color seem even more vibrant. They sold quickly and my mentor was proud of his harvest. I resisted selling the largest pumpkin, asking him to let it grow to its fullest.

"Finally, all the other crops had been harvested. My mentor had resumed his teaching of the younger students, and I became restless. I discussed leaving his house and walking on. He entreated me to stay for a few more days. And I did so, mostly out of respect for him.

"The days became shorter and the winds became cooler. I had experienced the fullness of the seasons and the garden. Awakening the next morning, I found the first snow of the winter season had lightly covered the grounds. I ran to the garden. I could see that the pumpkin was the same pumpkin, but the top and edges were now fringed with white. The creases in the face of the pumpkin looked deeper and more defined in the duller light of the fall. The pumpkin had aged." Bennie paused. Jenn was not sure if this was only for dramatic effect.

"And so had I. I had become older and had experienced the seasons. I began my wanderings. I left my mentor to travel with a new satchel—a gift from him to collect memories and mementos."

"Not bad," Jenn reported. "Not bad, at all."

By this time, they had stopped at the same overlook and rested on the same bench. Bennie had brought along some breads, cheeses and wine. Jenn refused the wine, saying even the wine made her muscles ache all the more. She accepted only the fresh cider from the local orchards.

5

Sheriff Wilkins got back in his patrol car, starting to drive slowly down Main Street in Lake Placid. He enjoyed this part of town—active with tourists, shop owners keeping up with business, bicyclists, cars and tour buses—all overlooking Mirror Lake.

After the electromagnetic pulse caused by Gary Canig and his unsuspecting hip replacement patient turned the water in the lake to a filthy, brown foamy mess, the shore had gradually returned to its glistening clear sand shallows. He appreciated how nature cleaned up men's disasters. The beautiful populations of trout, salmon, perch, bass and panfish couldn't tolerate such a shock to their ecosystems, washing up on the shorelines, dead. The villagers filled up three dumpsters with their carcasses, coming out in crews to restore the lake they loved. The fish were restocked immediately after water testing assured the biologists that they would survive. Thankfully, the ducks, geese, loons and gulls resumed their migratory patterns with only a small percentage of their flocks affected.

The work of healing the town's people would take longer. It might take years to allow confidence to replace fear and compassion to replace hatred for the man who knowingly perpetrated this assault on their homes, businesses and possessions. This is where the generosity of Demian Listing was so helpful. The trauma of being unable to go to their homes, work in their businesses, go to school or carry on a normal life was interrupted only briefly. Demian supported all the businesses, paying back bills and payrolls and paying to restock the shelves of stores and convenience gas stations so that they could resume employing the villagers. There was a gap of a few days to a few weeks that the businesses needed to clean out unusable stock and start anew. Without being asked to do so, those people who were out of work, but still receiving a paycheck through Demian, volunteered to clean the shores of the lake, help their neighbors and deliver food and sundries to those who were less mobile. It filled Todd with pride that this outpouring of effort proceeded to get the town back on an even commercial footing. It also restored the villagers' confidence in each other, their elected town officials and police.

An online donation site had been arranged by Bennie's friends. The hospital, school and churches were refurbished with numerous generous small donations anonymously. The visitors to Lake Placid's attractions read through flyers suggesting that they pay a surcharge to their bills to help fund all of this effort. Tourists gladly paid more than the sums suggested.

In his heart, Todd knew the village would get back to normal. He had just completed his interview of Suzette, Jim Tower's assistant. She seemed to be a reasonable person, with good people skills—able to assess a client's needs, know when she was understood and offer appropriate help. So, it became important to Todd to look into these three men. They had unnerved her. She could not describe why, but she was worried.

Todd drove carefully, slowly, knowing people with bad intentions might be lurking nearby or in their midst. He disliked acting as if the people he passed might wish further harm and injury to the villagers or environs, but how could he think that getting surveys of the old Listing lands and then reviewing the newspapers for the last twenty years could be anything other than nefarious? He knew he should keep an open mind, that each person should be looked upon as innocent until proven otherwise, but the recent devastation of the town gnawed at his conscience. It didn't do any good for his digestion, either. He needed to discuss this with his old friend, Demian Listing. He needed to bounce this off another reasonable person to know if he had become overly worried—paranoid, even.

He decided to walk on the Main Street, passing all the curiosity shops, tourist traps, bars and restaurants, the busiest traffic in Lake Placid. What Todd truly liked was how the small district fringed Mirror Lake. The shops along the road backed up to the lake with the intervening swaths of green grassy parks, gazebo, or walkways between. As he walked, the lake blinked on and off, he thought, as he could see between the buildings only when not in front of them.

Bud, the owner and head bartender of Bud's Bar and Grill, stopped the sheriff. His friendly manner suited his profession. "Todd, how are you? Everything back to normal?"

"I sure hope so. I've been seeing a lot of progress along the street. You back to full business?"

"Yup. Thanks to Demian." Bud continued to sweep his sidewalk in front of his establishment. "Demian even mentioned to my doorman that he thought that phones, pads, computers or what have you should be turned off before entering. Didn't take him or me a second to agree. Now, our bar is even better. It's a technology-free zone. People *talk* to each other. Get some real conversations going. And I've turned off the blaring televisions. Don't need Fox or CNN to ruin our days here with all the bad news they can find or manufacture."

"So the changes are all good?" Todd asked.

"As far as I can see—and my patrons love the new feel of the quiet and easy talking. Maybe the old term 'speak easy' really meant something."

"I guess so." His look turned serious. "By the way, you haven't seen three men with German accents in here, have you?"

"No. But I can call you if I do?" Bud looked concerned.

"That would be good. I'd just like a word with them. All in a day's work."

The two men parted, leaving Todd to continue his walk and conversations.

6

"So why don't you tell me something that's completely true about yourself?" Jenn and Bennie rode along going south on the Northway as they left their small town near Albany. Bennie, on a whim that day, had decided to go to the south, not to the north.

"All right. You may have hit upon something that's harder than making up stories, you know," Bennie replied.

"I should have guessed that about you. You do play your cards close to your vest. Like, tell me if you've ever held down a job? You don't seem to work now," she queried.

"Held down a job? Shit, Damn!"

"Sorry if I hit a touchy spot…." She genuinely looked concerned that she might have hurt his feelings, seeing his muscles ripple under his shirt.

"You did, but you didn't know it." Bennie's lips continued to move, cursing under his breath.

"Sorry. You've been good to me these last few weeks, and I would never want to repay you with meanness." She looked sorry as well.

"My reaction harkens back to being very sensitive about military service. Most civilians don't have a clue about the sacrifices that active duty entails. I worked my way up to the rank of captain in the Army. I ordered my men into battle and tried to keep them from getting shot, killed or otherwise injured. We routinely found and defused multiple IED's on every mission. That's a responsibility civilians can never even dream about. That's several full-time jobs all at once." He shifted quicker, with more jerking.

"Could you slow down, just a bit?"

"Sure. Sorry." Bennie noticed she said that without wincing this time.

"So you went to the academy. What did you study?"

"Computers. Engineering. And a few other minors. But we all had to study warfare, prior battles, military planning and strategies. We all had to undergo strenuous physical training, discipline training and hazing from the upper-classmen and instructors. It was four years of hell and the best time of my life, all in one."

"So then you went to Iraq?" she continued.

"No."

Frustrated, she said, "Why don't I just let you tell me the story at your own speed?" She gave in to his halting retelling of whatever he thought was appropriate, and as slowly and aggravatingly as he wished to.

"Why not?" He drove down to the campus of West Point. He continued, "I should say that all I ever wanted was to be in the Army and go to West Point. I worked my nuts off to get the necessary appointment from my congressman. I spoke to everyone who might have some pull for the appointment, did well in school, got my parents to get some of my speeding tickets fixed by a lawyer they knew. In short, I did everything that anyone could think of to get ahead of the others on the list for the appointment and to remove any blemishes from the application that might show up in the extensive background checks."

"Wow." Jenn was all ears.

"Each U.S. congressman and senator gets to make one appointment to each Academy—Army, Air Force, Navy, and Coast Guard. They can also trade appointments if they don't have someone for an Academy and another con-gressman does. That's a real political favor that they would owe in the future, but that's how Washington gets things done, for sure." Bennie knew he dragged out his story but enjoyed teasing Jenn with anticipation.

"I went to the academy, met my best friend—the one I recently saw and helped through a difficult time. I became an officer, did two tours in Iraq, got a master's in philosophy funded by the military, went to Special Forces training and eventually ended up here."

"You know? Your fictional stories sound more plausible than your sup-posed real ones."

"Yeah. I was driven, in those days, I guess," Bennie replied.

"Where are we?" Jenn saw the armed guards at the entrance to the Military Academy. None of the guards looked friendly in the least. Their rifles had that ominous look—black, angular, with tactical attachments. The enlisted Army personnel took being on guard seriously. None of them smiled.

"I thought I would show you West Point. General George Washington, himself, chose this campus site." Bennie presented his military ID to the guard at the gate, got a very sharp salute in return and drove on to the grounds of the academy. As they drove away, one guard pointed to their car and spoke to the other in hushed tones.

"Wow. What kind of ID did you use to get that response?" she asked.

"My Special Forces ID. They don't see many of them, after all." Bennie let that linger, then asked, "What do you know about this place?"

"Only that it's the Army Military Academy."

"Do you know why Washington chose this particular area to build the campus?"

"Not really." Jenn felt embarrassed not to know more about her nation's only Army Military Academy. She worried that she might seem unpatriotic, or worse, uncaring.

They saw a lot of parking spaces in the visitor's lot, but Bennie kept driving onto the wide swath of land overlooking the Hudson River. "With this ID, I get to drive anywhere I want to," he laughed. "Our first president chose this location because in the Revolutionary War, this is precisely the spot where he thwarted the advance of the British up the Hudson River. They were set to attack Albany and the northern New York areas. The British had to suffer through until the next spring, waiting to attack on foot, bypassing the Hudson River. Do you know how he did it?"

"No."

"He surveyed the area and found there was a very narrow bend in the Hudson overlooked by a high bluff. He had his men fashion a huge linked iron chain and string it across the Hudson at precisely that spot. *This spot.* The British ships were stopped by the chain and fired on by cannons atop the bluff. It took two hundred horses to string the chain and pull it across the river. They still have a few of the links from that chain as a monument to the episode right over there." Bennie pointed to large circular links about a yard in diameter now preserved with a commemorative plaque describing everything Bennie had related. They looked old, painted in dark, thick black nautical paint—like huge, interlacing, dark-chocolate donuts.

"Wow."

They sat on the grass in the same place General Washington had looked out from two hundred and forty plus years previously. He offered Jenn a lunch of sandwiches and juice. He hadn't brought wine this time.

"You said you did Special Forces training?" she asked.

"Yeah. After my two tours in Iraq, I had real difficulty coming home. I mean *really coming home*. I had post-traumatic stress disorder, at least to a degree. I went to Special Forces and passed that training. The day I graduated from it, I retired from the Army."

"Why?"

"Why what? Why did I retire? Or why did I retire after completing the training?"

"Both, I guess." She looked mildly vexed at his reticence.

"I'm no quitter. In anything. I'll complete a project even if I discover it's not for me." He gazed over the Hudson. "I went through the training as a way to regain my confidence. I needed to prove to myself that I could do the hardest thing in the world. I did that and immediately knew that I needed to do something else."

"That must have been at least ten years ago?"

"More or less," he answered between swallows of cider.

"What have you done over the last ten years, then?" she asked.

"Well, there's another story or two. Maybe for another day."

7

"Hi, Will. This is Bennie." He called his friend while driving his little BMW.

"How could I forget or ever mistake your whining voice?" Will answered. "What's up?"

"I just wanted to call and make sure you're all right. I hear the trial was short and sweet for that slimeball Canig," Bennie chuckled.

"Yeah. Not even his high-priced lawyer thought he had a chance. They bargained for life in prison, repayment of all money stolen, and complete restitution to the town of Lake Placid. Sarah—that is Elisabeth, now—got reinstatement, back pay, benefits and retirement. She'll never work for the CIA again, but she'll have her respect back."

Will sat in his office in the high school physics department. They had replaced all the computer equipment after the electromagnetic pulse had essentially fused all the electronics in the village. Gary Canig, the rogue CIA agent who had caused the pulse, had gotten his due, but he had also ruined a lot of people's lives. He had set up Elisabeth to take the fall for the theft of millions of dollars of an international cartel's drug and human-trafficking money. Subsequently, she had to hide out in the New York City underground, supporting herself with prostitution. Will wondered if she would ever think she had any equitable restitution for all of that.

Canig had forced surgeons to use a new design of hip replacement with carbon-fiber mesh and nanoelectronics inserted into both hips of an unsuspecting man at the same operation on the same day. This man then traveled to Lake Placid, and the strong vibrations of the earth's energy in that location interacted with the hip implants and the thousands of computers, causing the

EMP. Canig used this unsuspecting man as a bomb dropped on the whole village of Lake Placid. He had successfully weaponized an unsuspecting human being. Bennie had subsequently captured Canig at knifepoint. With reluctance, after extensive pleading from Demian Listing, he didn't kill him on the spot.

"Quite a good end to what could have been a continuing shit storm. I hope Canig settles into a long and uncomfortable sentence. Where else but jail could you get a hundred girlfriends all named Bubba?" Bennie asked. They laughed. He knew a thousand bad jokes covering almost any topic.

Will had called Bennie to help his friends solve the disaster at Lake Placid and capture Canig. Demian Listing, Will and Sheriff Todd Wilkins helped with the capture.

"How are Madison, Gunner, Demian and all the others?" Bennie asked.

"They're busier than ever. Doing well."

"Mention to Demian that I need to talk to him sometime." Bennie hoped he didn't sound concerned.

"Anything I need to do or could do for you in the meantime?" Will asked.

"No. But I do have a friend here that could really use some healing. I can't seem to get her to go anywhere to get help for her severe chronic pain and all."

"The door is always open. You *know* that. Tell me her name and where she lives and I'll get Gunner to do his distance healing for her if she will allow it."

"I don't know, he may have to shoot in the dark until her attitude improves and she'll accept it. But thank you for the offer of asking for his help." Bennie had hoped that would be his response.

"I'll tell Demian to expect your call," Will offered.

"I may decide to speak to you both about something delicate; I just haven't come to a conclusion in my own head yet," Bennie softly said.

"Just let me know. And call Demian. He's as smart a man as I have ever known. And he's made all the mistakes before, so we don't have to. We can just learn from him and his example." They both laughed, then disconnected.

Will looked around his office and thought, *What was that all about?* He had become tenured as a science teacher, concentrating on physics, and had had many students win the science Olympiads of Northern New York State. After meeting his lifelong friend, Bennie, at the Military Academy and serving two tours in Iraq, they had both dealt with their demons of PTSD. Will had settled in the Adirondacks, teaching. Bennie had never really settled at all, but roamed around, finishing the yearlong Army Special Ops training and then abruptly quitting. He lived more in the underworld and online than in the real world. How he had supported himself, Will could only guess and didn't want to ask.

At 11:00 AM, Bennie knocked. Jenn answered and ushered him into her apartment.

"I've never said thank you for coming here and visiting. I don't know why you do, though."

"You don't have to thank me." His offhand manner made her believe it.

"Well, *Thank you* nonetheless."

"How're you feeling today?" Bennie asked.

"I answered the door, didn't I?"

"Yeah. That's one step forward. Keep that in mind. Don't dwell on all the past."

"It's hard. Like the old Blood, Sweat and Tears song said: 'I've been down so long, the bottom looks like up!' It's hard," Jenn restated.

"Good. Admitting something is hard is the first thing you have to do. Then you've got to commit to getting it done. Or even getting it changed. Or even looking at the same old thing in a different manner." Bennie hoped that all these options would sink in—that she did have alternatives.

"How'm I supposed to get done what all the most expensive doctors and therapists couldn't?" This didn't sound whiny but was rather an honest question.

Bennie took hope in this. "How do you eat a whole elephant? One fork full at a time. How do you walk a journey of a thousand miles? One step at a time. Just keep plugging along."

"Yeah, well, so for today, what shall we do?" Jenn's depressed mood reasserted itself.

"Why don't *you* tell *me* a story?" Bennie asked.

"No. I don't do that well. I don't have the energy to even stand here for long. So, if we're going for a ride, let's get to it. If not, let's sit down."

"How about a short ride. Ever been to Saratoga Springs? It's so pretty. The shops and the little town square are so picturesque. We might even go to a little restaurant or brewpub."

"You're driving. Just watch the bumps." She didn't need to remind him and realized she was being rude. "Sorry. You know that."

"It's okay."

They drove up the Northway and got off when the signs announced the Saratoga Performing Arts Center. The drive went quickly on a weekday morning. Bennie mentioned that during a concert of some famous group or performer at the Performing Arts Center, the drive took hours to get the short distance from the main highway to the center.

Driving through town, parking was abundant. The village had maintained its small-town feeling by promoting only small businesses in the main square. Barbershops, hat shops, dress shops and haberdasheries of the old style mixed in with repair shops of all types. Now the newer businesses of computer and phone repair and tutoring for national college entrance exams also popped up and blended right in, occupying old buildings. The local zoning laws had done their job of excluding newer, drab building styles. Bennie and Jenn did not see the larger box stores—these were limited to locations outside the village proper, where they couldn't ruin the demeanor of the town.

They chose to stop in front of a 'shop of curiosities' and several brew pubs. They browsed the shop and picked out an old, worn, leather satchel for Bennie. As it had aged, it had become soft, brown and warm looking, with little crinkles around all the seams.

"Maybe I need one of these for my journeys? Like in the story I made up?"

"I think so," Jenn replied as affirmatively as she could.

"How about this for you?" Bennie pointed to a dark green piece of what he thought looked like sea glass.

"It's Cleveland glass from the 1830s. Made at the Cleveland, New York Glass Works," the sales clerk said, being overly friendly. Bennie turned his back on her and handed the glass to Jenn. It was about the size of a tennis ball, smooth and roughly round in shape.

"How do you think they got it to be so perfectly round and so smooth?" Jenn said, being momentarily mesmerized by the silvery green spray of light bouncing off the ball.

"I think they did it like they made musket balls. At that time, they dropped the molten lead off the second stories of buildings onto strained sand. The motion of the lead falling through the air rounded off the edges, and it cooled enough to keep its shape in the sand. The glass might have been dropped into water, though." Bennie turned to the officious sales woman and asked, "You know how they made this so round?"

"Probably just like you said." She looked flustered and walked away.

Bennie handed the glass ball to her. "It suits you. And now you have something that you can gaze at that will truly look different in changing shades of brightness. Maybe it'll even get lighter, too."

Jenn liked the idea of having the glass to see if it might appear to fade or glow, like the stone in the story Bennie had told her. "Thanks. I'll buy it. I can't remember the last time I bought something on a whim. Feels good to be just a bit frivolous."

"It's hardly frivolous, I think it represents new possibilities, new ways of seeing and looking at things. Maybe new ways of feeling?" Bennie hoped he hadn't just pushed his luck a little too far.

"Yeah. We'll see."

They bought their glass and satchel and left the store to look down the streets of the village. They went next door to an outdoor café. While Bennie drank a local beer, Jenn had a clear beef broth and said it was just enough for her. The vast expanses of the southern Adirondacks sloped upward as they extended to the north.

"While we're sitting here, tell me something and I'll guess which parts might be true." Jenn said.

"About what?"

"Anything you like—real, fanciful, present or past. Doesn't matter."

Bennie thought about it while looking towards the foothills. They sat in the sun. "Look at the mountains. I wonder what it would have been like to be the first man to see these mountains. I don't mean just the European settlers, either. I mean the Native Americans. I wonder if walking through this valley, I would have avoided the mountains altogether?"

"Hum?"

"I wonder if I would have been walking or traveling by raft on Lake Champlain or the Hudson River? I would likely have found game to be abundant. There would have been many fish in the waters. I wonder if I would have been alone or traveling with a hunting party, or with a family unit? So much we don't know."

"Wow."

"But I can guess—no I feel very sure that I would have been in awe of the mountains. The oldest stories of the Native Americans spoke of the mountains as being the keepers of the memories. They said that men belonged to the mountains, not the other way around. That the mountains' blood flowed through your veins."

"Hum." Jenn enjoyed the images of freedom to travel, the outdoors and the feeling that the land around us owns us and maybe moved through us.

"The oldest Incas used to imagine an etheric cord reaching from the mountains to the chest of a man. This cord helped a man remember where he came from, and, in broad brush strokes, reminded him of his beliefs. Native Americans were never kicked out of the garden, like the Europeans and their descendants, but continued to draw their strength from the mountains and their wisdom and memories from their collective stories. They never betrayed their gods, never had the feeling they had anything to atone for hanging over their heads."

They paused and enjoyed the view.

"You know, that wasn't really a story, but it was good. I think all of it is true. As I sit here and take in this panorama, I believe all of it. The mountains are like the collective knowing, aren't they?" She smiled and let her eyes wander.

"Yeah," Bennie replied.

"While I was sitting, I didn't once think that my back ached or my feet hurt because I have shoes on. I am tired, though. Could we go back?"

"Sure. Just wait at the sidewalk in front of the café, and I'll drive the car over to pick you up."

8

"Hi, Demian. Got a minute to talk?" the sheriff asked. After sitting in his office brooding, he had finally convinced himself to call his old friend.

"Sure, Todd. Always. For you. What's up?"

"I don't know that anything is up. But I want to talk over a situation with you."

"Shoot." Demian sat at his large desk, in his office. His scalp tingled. He didn't enjoy that sensation—it usually meant he, or someone around him, was in trouble. "I'll put you on speaker." He did so and reached for his large coffee mug, blew on the steaming black liquid and took a loud slurp.

"Jim Tower called me yesterday and told me that his secretary, Suzette, was worried that three men with German accents were looking up deeds and survey maps to your family's old land holdings on Jay Mountain. Then they went to the library and read through newspapers dating back quite a few years."

"Huh? Any ideas?" Demian put down his mug and stared intently at the phone.

"No. They didn't do anything else. But they spoke to no one. It unnerved Suzette. My read on her is that she's a good judge of character so I tried to find out more about them, but they seem to have vanished. They didn't check into any local hotels and signed in to the library as only Hans, Fritz and Pieter. Only scribbles for last names."

"No idea where they are now?" Demian asked.

"No."

"Any idea about which papers they concentrated on? Why go through the papers, anyway?"

"Don't know. That stuff is all on microfilm, from way back or digitized in the computer data banks more recently. So, someone could fish through and the librarians don't know which they focused on. But they did spend three days doing it." The sheriff sounded concerned.

"Can you think of any reasonable explanations for anyone to do all that?" Demian asked.

"Yes, of course. Maybe they represent real estate developers. Maybe they're history buffs. Maybe you're famous enough to have biographers."

"Now *there's* a really scary thought!" Demian laughed.

"Yeah, well it unnerved a reasonable person, so I thought I would pass it on. I'll keep a close eye on anything in the future. I'll let you know." The sheriff was starting to think the phone call showed weakness.

"Thanks for calling me." Demian sensed his friend needed affirmation. "Always good to have you out and about looking out for us."

"I'll call you if I have anything further." The sheriff hung up and turned to look out his large windows. He drummed his fingers on his desk and whistled. He stood and went to walk on his favorite streets. *Just to be sure*, he told himself.

The next morning, Will stopped in at Demian's office in Lake Placid. "Bennie called and said he wanted to talk with you. He wouldn't say about what, though."

"I wonder what about? I owe—we both owe—that man a lot," Demian replied.

"Don't know."

"If he calls again, you tell him my door is always open," Demian said as if he were giving an order to an underling. As the wealthiest person in Lake Placid and possibly in upper New York State, he had given a lot of orders in his sixty plus years. He was the only heir to the Listing estate and had done very well for himself in his own business ventures. He kept himself in good shape with daily swimming, walking through the village and mountains and hiking, so his imposing physical stature added to his voice's commanding authority.

"I already did."

"How are you, Will?" Demian asked in a softer manner that still demanded an answer.

"I'm really good. After all the dust settled and things got back to normal, I feel really good." He quickly looked to his coffee. "I'm so glad that we're no longer slaves to our computers, like we used to be. Now, computers, phones, instruments and gadgets are just our aids. Not our masters. After the electro-magnetic pulse ruined all the electronics, we started to live again without need-ing to check our emails and all that other distracting stuff."

"Amen," Demian said, momentarily closing his eyes.

"I hear that at Bud's Bar and Grill the doorman makes you turn off all your stuff at the door. And he's as firm about it as if he were making sure you didn't carry weapons. If you can't turn off your devices, you can't come in." They laughed.

"And that's the way I like it. I suggested it to Bud, and it didn't take a nano-second for him to agree." Demian laughed hard enough that he had to put down his coffee. "He only makes an exception for the sheriff. Todd really stepped up to the plate for us, didn't he? He stood in front of a known killer and saboteur and faced him down, knowing he wouldn't come quietly."

"Yeah. And I hear you floated loans for Bud and a lot of the other business people to keep in business while the town gets back on its feet. Thank you for that." Will's tone was heartfelt. He visibly swallowed.

"I was going to give him an outright grant, but he wouldn't have it. So, what I've set up with John is that the repayment of all those loans will fund a new initiative and foundation. And we're not aggressively collecting on the no interest loans—what comes in is great, that which doesn't come in we won't be calling for. Next year, in Lake Placid, the new foundation, which we have yet to name, will convene a worldwide convention of healers. Anyone who can justifiably call himself a healer can come and participate. We want to start to understand what healing is all about and want the best minds to help guide us with a full out effort to bring healing to the world."

"Demian, I thought you gave up being so grandiose. It's not good for your blood pressure, is it?" Now Will had to put down his coffee cup or risk coffee stains on his shirt from laughing.

"I've got our best people focusing on it. Marion, Madison and Gunner are over the top joyous about the concept," Demian answered.

"Has anyone even come up with an inclusive definition of what healing encompasses?" Will asked. His scientific background asserted itself.

"No. And that's a big part of the problem. All the healers I know think of healing from their own vantage point. There is no inclusive, definitive definition. And you know any definition could also limit the scope of our endeavor. So, we have to be careful that we don't discount or discourage any legitimate practitioners." Demian had thought about the problem of the expansive nature of such a grand endeavor causing a dilution of the real healing methods. If he included every charlatan, how could he or the convention proceed and make headway? The first problem was that they couldn't even agree on a definition of healing or what constituted a real, workable practice of healing.

"Yeah, but people are all different—their energies are different, their talents are different. And I guess having such an array of possibilities works well to heal a spectrum of patients who are anything but the same. The patients seem to know how to seek out healers that will help them," Will offered, trying to be enthusiastic.

"I agree. But without a definition, we flounder around and wonder if a new or strange sounding therapy might be real. We also need a hierarchy of healing modalities in order to know what might be a better treatment for an individual patient, or the specific condition a treatment might be most useful for."

"You have your work cut out for you." Will looked thoughtful. "And how is the Western medical care system going to look upon all of this?" Will worried that they would be chastised for anti-establishment practices.

"At least Dr. Ardane is one hundred percent behind us. He lived through the crisis with Hal Foss—the poor, unsuspecting patient who had both hips replaced with what turned out to be a bomb that caused the electromagnetic pulse—and knows that Marion helped Hal the most. Not the fancy machines, x-rays, labs, or medications. It was Marion who acted as a healer, through and through. In fact, the computers and computerized machines almost killed Hal. He only improved after all the electronics were shut off."

"Well, that says a lot, when a neurosurgeon is behind a healing conference. Where do you propose to hold the conference?" Will wondered if there was a venue large enough to hold such a meeting in Lake Placid.

"I've had talks with the managers of the Olympic stadium and most of the hotels in the village. They're all so overjoyed at the prospect that their rooms and restaurants will be full for an extra two weeks that I haven't been able to buy my own bourbon in any bar in town. I also recommended that the stadium and ice rink and athletic center should get a makeover at my family's foundation's expense," Demian continued.

"That's just terrific! They couldn't refuse that, could they?"

"Not with their boards of directors needing to watch the bottom line like they do. I've also invited the governor to come and deliver a keynote speech. I even recommended a title: 'The evolving process of healing in healthcare settings.' We might have to adjust the title, but I want to focus on exactly that—healing in healthcare settings—hospitals, nursing homes, private doctor's offices and clinics."

"Demian. Slow down. Now you've got to worry about your blood sugar, too, if you keep up this frenetic pace." The two men roared with laughter.

"Did the governor accept?" Will asked.

"You could say that I twisted his arm, or you could say that he owed me a huge favor after we let him take the credit for finding and capturing the criminal behind the Lake Placid crisis. Who cares? He's in. And big time." Demian said in his booming, authoritative voice.

"Wow." Will was speechless at the audacious power Demian wielded with reckless abandon—this power extended to the governor's office. After being with Demian all this time, it shouldn't have surprised Will, but it still did.

"Yeah. I guess I should leave the heavy lifting to the younger generation. But at my stage of life, I have nothing to lose. And I have to consider my legacy…"

"The town already owes you so much, your legacy is in the bag," Will asserted.

Demian hesitated. "I do have something serious to ask of you."

"Anything." He let that linger. "Except posing nude for Playgirl, marrying a supermodel, running for the presidency of the United States or something of that magnitude."

"Don't worry about all that. I've *done* all that and it's not what it's cracked up to be." Demian looked around his office. The placards, trophies, letters from presidents, and other memorabilia adorning the walls substantiated his claims. Will had seen pictures of Demian's first wife—a former Miss New York State beauty contest winner.

"I can see you *have* done all that. And, I can also see that the first hyperbole doesn't stand a chance around here…" Will momentarily got lost in looking at the walls and the awards from presidents of the United States. "Neither does the first lie!"

"Not likely. But seriously, I wanted to ask you to be on the foundation board of this new initiative. We need people of integrity and hard science to vet all the claims we're likely to hear. We need credentials behind the foundation to give it real credibility. Will you do it?"

"I've never been on a board, except the tequila board down at Bud's—man, ten of us lined up to drink our shots as the board was tipped, hands tied behind our backs. We had to guzzle so as not to smell like booze spilled all over us." They laughed again, knowing Demian had lived through many a challenge like that as a youth. "I've slept on a board, surfed on a board, built with a board but never served on one. If you think I'm the right person, I will gladly do so."

Will smiled, but he felt a little insecure. "I do, and you are. Thank you. I've also tapped Gunner, Marion and John. John may seem like an odd choice, but if anyone can see through a scam, it's him."

"I agree with that. His background is certainly checkered, but he has shown himself to be a dear friend to Lake Placid and all of us here. He and Elisabeth are settling into small-town life quite well, don't you think?"

"Yes. So, that's the deal. I'm putting you on the board," Demian declared.

The men finished their coffee. They had, happily, not spilled any on their clothes.

9

Jenn brought out a patterned red tablecloth—one of her mother's. She had hired a taxi, paid the man to wait while she shopped and suffered the indignity of needing to use a motorized cart to purchase the few extra things she needed. Her portion of the lunch consisted of beef and mushroom broth, coconut milk, multigrain bread and mild, soft cheddar cheese. She hoped Bennie would like the local microbrewery's best porter, beef on wick roll, mustard, pickle, onions and sharp cheddar cheese.

She set all of this out on the porch overlooking a grassy meadow. A gentle breeze blew only enough to keep the mosquitoes away. The sun climbed high in the sky. As he roared up the drive and got out of his car, she poured the porter. Its firm white head covered the deep brown liquid. Gorgeous to see, let alone drink, she hoped.

"Jenn, this is beautiful. I hope you didn't overdo it shopping and setting all of this out for us." He smiled and gave her the flowers he had picked up on the way. He didn't have a clue what types of flowers were included in the bouquet; he selected them only on the basis of their colors. He thought that the reds, golds and yellows made a beautiful presentation for Jenn. He recalled his vague awareness of his mother teaching him to match colors. This gave him some cause for concern that he overcame with including a lot of different colors.

"No. I'm fine. But no rides for today. We'll just have to make the best of visiting here and sitting in the sun. OK?" She looked at the flowers. "Those are beautiful. They match my apartment colors."

"Sure." He set the bouquet on the small table, sat and drank a sip of the porter. "Man, that's just right. Some of the stouts that so many people like are too bitter. This is complex and not overpowering. Just right, as I said." Bennie licked the foam off his upper lip and smiled.

"I'm glad you like it. Dig in. I bought beef on wick. I hope that's OK for you too?"

"Shit, damn straight, it is. Where did you get all this?"

"Oh, I have my ways," she said.

As they ate, Bennie noticed the bread and mild cheddar cheese were the first solid things she had eaten in front of him. "This is truly beautiful here. Thank you for this nice surprise. I wouldn't have asked you to go to this effort just for me." Jenn's rented apartment was in a small cul-de-sac. The road saw only a few cars that passed on the way to and from their owner's work. Her apartment occupied the first floor and opened on to a cement patio overlooking a pond as well as the grassy field.

"It's for you *and* for me. I'm trying to do more things, even though I know I'll pay for it later. Maybe I've decided to stop missing life. Maybe I'll try new things more often…."

"That's it. One step forward. And enjoy the day to its fullest." He finished the porter and held up his empty glass. "You've hit upon one of my weaknesses—good porter or ale. Can I get myself another? If it's in the fridge, I'll get it myself."

"Go ahead. And bring me another cup of the beef and mushroom broth?"

"Sure."

When they'd finished, Bennie insisted on doing the dishes and clearing the table. He made Jenn sit in the sun. After those chores, he joined her with another porter, sitting on the porch swing.

"So, tell me something more about you—something I don't know," Bennie said.

"Why?"

"I would like to know, that's all."

"OK. But, I don't want to bore a world traveler like you, though." She truly didn't want to and feared she might. Her life experiences had been severely limited after the age of fourteen—and those were mostly horrible disappointments.

"Nothing bores me. How could I not like to spend the time here with you? The sun, breeze, lunch, and porters—they're all beautiful. And don't think travel is all it's cracked up to be. Third-world countries make you want to turn around and run home as fast as possible. Sharing something like this is the best."

"What do you want to know?" She steeled herself. She really didn't know what to tell Bennie.

"Anything. And you can make it up, if you like," Bennie offered.

"Do you ever have any physical pain?"

"Only if I really deserve it—like I bang something, or overdo training, or beat myself up doing something."

"I can't even *imagine* a day without pain. It weighs me down. Stops me from doing everything. It takes away my future…. That's why I have to tell you thank you for coming. It's given me something to look forward to. I really stretched to get this meager lunch together, but I wanted to do it. That's the other thing—I don't ordinarily allow myself to do or even think about doing things—too much aggravation and trouble, and I'll spend days recovering back to a baseline of only constant pain. Such a life." Jenn looked despondent.

"Nobody has any idea why this has happened to you?"

"Not the best doctors in the world. And believe me, they were the most expensive, too." She started to rub a small scar on the back of her right wrist. "And after they were done with their tests, biopsies and failed treatments, I had new areas that hurt all the more, like this little scar on my wrist. It was a biopsy of something or other that showed nothing at all."

"So, could I tell you something about me?" Bennie could see Jenn was uncomfortable talking about herself. He also worried that the retelling of her story could re-traumatize her. Just the act of telling about past injuries or traumas makes the brain re-experience all the turmoil, and the subconscious has no idea about time—talking about the past brings it to the now and can reinjure all over again. He had read extensively for his own information and recovery from his PTSD. This is one of the things in modern psychiatry that most therapists just don't get—retelling the story for the one hundred and eleventh time is no more helpful than the one hundred and tenth time. It only re-traumatizes the patient and brings the injury to life again.

"Sure." Jenn was happy that the spotlight had shifted from her, at least at this moment.

"Well, there I was, just minding my own business." This reminded them both of a comedian's opening line. This made Jenn groan; she thought this might be the start of a bad old joke.

"I tried to blend in the best that I could. Like I was a plain vanilla wrapper. I had just arrived at the Military Academy. The upperclassmen were roaming around the parade formation, picking out cadets at random to do another twenty-five pushups in front of the parade of cadets. They hoped to embarrass us in front of all of our peers." He wiped the back of his hand across his lips to smudge off the porter.

"Uh, oh," Jenn said. She could see this would end badly.

"That's where I met my best lifelong friend, named Will. He's the one I went to help a few weeks ago. Anyway, we had been selected and did our pushups and then got ordered to do twenty-five more, and we did those too."

"You could do that many?"

"We did, without complaint. The upperclassmen were either mean or fascinated we could do them and then ordered us to run in place. The sun was hot and directly overhead. We were in parade dress, shoes, and hats. Hotter than hell."

"That does sound more cruel than instructive, I would say," Jenn moaned.

"That's the thing. We looked in each other's eyes and knew neither of us would ever give up. I hadn't formally met Will yet, but that look in his eyes, and in mine, meant we could feed off each other and get strength and endurance. Neither of us was going to let the other down. Then or ever. It was one of those moments."

"Neat. And you hadn't even met him before?" she asked.

"There were twelve hundred new cadets each year, and with all the physical training and all the coursework for engineering and the minor I took, I couldn't possibly meet everyone. I kept my head down, pretty much constantly. We all tried to be completely average, so as not to be noticed or singled out for more abuse."

"What happened then?"

"The rest of all the cadets started to run in place as a show of solidarity and defiance to the upperclassmen. It was our collective way of saying, 'Sir!

Bullshit! Sir!'" Bennie had unintentionally shouted the phrase and was embarrassed when he realized it. He quickly looked around and saw no one else in the area. He continued in a softer voice. "We were dismissed without any further abuse. So, we learned to look a problem in the face and take it on. It would either kill us or make us stronger."

"Wow. Where is your friend now? Do you see him much?"

"He lives with those healers I want you to visit in the Lake Placid area. I hadn't seen him in about twelve years before a few weeks ago, but it was just like we had never been apart. We took up where we left off. I helped him and his friends capture a rogue CIA agent that killed people, poisoned Mirror Lake, caused an electromagnetic pulse and essentially ruined the life of a young lady. That prick!"

"All that in a week?" Jenn looked overwhelmed, then quickly a little dubious.

"Yup. You've got to put your mind to a project, get ready and get it done."

"I really want to hear about it all in detail, but for now, I need a rest. This was lovely. Can we do it again? Even see you tomorrow?" she asked.

"On the condition that tomorrow's meal is on me. I'm planning and presenting."

"Oh, *presenting* is it now?" she enunciated the word slowly to aggravate him.

"Yup, like you presented today. You don't expect me to let you outdo me, do you?" Bennie asked.

"Wouldn't think of challenging your ego." They laughed until Jenn winced with the motion.

"Tomorrow…."

10

Madison tucked a curl of her strawberry blonde hair behind her ear. She fidgeted while she sat in her friend's office. "Gunner, I'm not all right. I don't sleep well. I'm worried about the kids and it's a real struggle to let them go to school." She looked desperate.

Madison and Gunner were the co-founders of the Jay Mountain Healing Center, in Jay, New York. A beautiful, residential healing oasis, the center offered many modalities, including Reiki, acupuncture, psychotherapy, massage, manual therapy, herbal therapy, medicinal foods, physical therapy and training. Madison had had a healing practice in Reiki and acupuncture for two decades. Gunner had been a psychologist, now reformed to practice a variety of healing modalities.

"Oh, no." Gunner could see how deeply affected she was. He sat across from her. "What's going on?"

"Mason doesn't know a thing about this. I haven't wanted to worry him. And I haven't told you, before this, but it keeps getting worse all the time."

"Just settle in and tell me. I'm here for you; you know that." Their long history as friends, associates and partners at the center flashed through Gunner's mind. All that Madison had done to help him and lead him to a new profession made him admire and adore her. He would try to move mountains for her, if it came to that.

"I don't feel safe. I'm even locking the doors of our house when we're home. I wake up—if I sleep at all—and I have to check the doors and even the windows, again and again."

"Shit!" He put down his coffee and leaned towards her on his elbows. "When did this all start?" He knew he could guess that it would be after the capture of Gary Canig and all the devastation that he had wrought, but he had learned after years of practicing psychology and healing that initial assumptions usually turned out to be incorrect. There was also healing in allowing a patient to tell the story. Admitting that one is bothered is the first step towards a resolution of an issue. Placing the problems in the fields allows their healing like unwrapping a wound to expose it so it could be evaluated and treated. This was both painful and necessary.

"I'm sure you can guess. Right after the electromagnetic pulse poisoned Mirror Lake and Hal Foss had his horrible hospital stay. Right after Will, Demian, Bennie and Todd captured the CIA agent in our front yard. Demian *shot* him in our driveway," she sobbed. "I know he had to do it to keep everyone safe, but it was in *our* driveway, right where the kids play *every day*. Right where we *live*."

"Oh, no." Gunner waited.

"So every time I see someone in a uniform or someone who even sort of looks official, I get frantic. I can't easily go to the store. I can't let the kids out to play. And, you know and I know that we live in the safest place on earth." She paused to wipe her nose and wring her hands. "I'm losing it."

"No. You're not."

"Don't patronize me!" she shouted in a shrill voice.

The suddenness of the outburst surprised Gunner. "I wouldn't think of doing that. You know I have way too much respect for you to do that. You saved my life, even if you can't acknowledge it at this moment," Gunner surprised himself with his own response.

"That whole incident was so *random*. I keep thinking that we're not safe in the world anymore. I've had so many patients say that to me over the years, and I used to fluff it off. But it's the worst kind of fear. I can't trust myself or the world."

Gunner knew that because she came to him, at least she had reached out. At least she had the strength to work with her problem, even if she didn't recognize that truth in herself at this moment. He settled in for a long day and possibly many, many sessions of therapy.

"And don't tell Mason. He would think that I had no faith in him or our relationship if he knew how I feel." Mason and she had been married for fifteen years; their relationship was otherwise rock solid.

"You know we share a sacred trust, here. I won't consult anyone without your permission. Can I consult anyone else—Marion, Demian, whoever?"

"Didn't you hear? Not *nobody*. At all."

Now he knew how deeply she had been affected. Marion had been her mentor and guide to her practice of healing and had taught her everything she now uses. Then Marion had taught Gunner how to integrate Western psychology and healing practices into what Gunner now based his therapeutic framework upon. If she didn't want Marion's help or couldn't bear to have him know she was having a problem, this affected her hugely.

He handed Madison a box of Kleenex, sat next to her and let her cry it all out. It took two full hours on that first day. It didn't solve the problem, but it allowed her to vent out all the excess emotion. Now she was left with the fear and distrust of everyone and everything.

11

The next morning, Madison opened the door to her office at the healing center, after looking around the drapes in the smaller side windows. She saw Gunner, carrying a vase of flowers, waiting impatiently. "Well, I can't refuse flowers from the gardens here, can I?"

"No. I had two of my patients today pick them as part of their therapy. Getting ones' hands dirty is good for the soul, don't you think?" Gunner tried to make light of Madison's turmoil and saw immediately that this approach wouldn't be helpful, to put it mildly. He only had to see the hollow look in her eyes.

"You might as well come in."

"Thank you for *inviting* me. I checked your schedule and saw you canceled all your patients for the foreseeable future. It's getting even harder for you, isn't it?" he probed.

"Yeah. Not sleeping, paranoid, anxious, drinking way too much coffee just to stay awake, then I can't sleep. But I don't trust everything is OK to sleep, so I drink more coffee."

"Shit."

"You don't use that language with all your patients, do you?"

Gunner heard acid in her voice. "I do, when I mean it," he answered. He waited for them both to sit and take a breather. The room was light and airy, unlike Madison's mood. She displayed finger paintings from her patients and the local kindergarten students who visited the healing center each fall as part of a health-week teaching program. These paintings were strung on a wire from one corner of a wall to the other in a drooping pattern, like Buddhist prayer flags. Gunner had often thought of them as just that—prayers to the earth and each other, from the earth's children. Madison used to cherish them.

"What can I do for you, Madison. I want to help you so much. You're such a dear friend and mentor." He waited.

She stewed inside. "I can't do my practice. I can't meditate. I can't do my self-reiki. I'm a mess." She didn't respond to his offer of help.

"How much coffee have you had today?" Gunner asked.

"Don't start your shit about coffee, too! I don't want to hear it!"

"You need to stop your excessive intake. It's hyping you up until you can't settle and do your work. That, in itself, is not a complete answer. But start there. Make one step at a time." He paused. "Steady progress will let your subconscious accept the fact that change is possible."

"Mumbo-fucking-jumbo. I expect better from you." Her eyes bored holes into his chest.

"OK, then. Why don't we just sit and rest a moment?" Gunner said tentatively.

"We're already sitting. Can't you see?" She openly mocked his efforts.

"Madison, I'm trying to find common grounds to work from. You tell me, then."

"You are a pathetic little man, aren't you? I don't know what I need any better than you do. Why don't you have me put away and medicated? I think I need that. I can't relax at all. I can't sleep at all. I'm burning myself up. I'm paranoid, even though I know no one is out to get me." Her words flew out so fast, Gunner could hardly keep up with them.

"Let all that anger out. Call me anything you wish. Say anything you wish. Get it all out." Gunner used his best 'understanding' voice, and it irritated her all the more.

"I don't feel safe here. I want to run away and get away from these mountains. I need something different. My husband doesn't understand me, I hate my kids, and the staff members take one look at me and step back. I haven't helped anyone with anything since all this happened. *So, I quit. I resign.* I can't stand the human race." Madison's tears started like gushers—the sobs like the wailing of elephants.

Gunner's emotions ran the gamut from anger at being sworn at to depressed that he couldn't find a way to help his friend. He sat, motionless, waiting for the next torrent and wondering if all of this would be helpful to her. Cathartic at least, he hoped.

"Look, just go away. I know you're trying to help, but I think I'm beyond help," she sobbed.

"Do I have to worry about you hurting yourself?" Gunner quietly asked.

Madison rolled her eyes at him and wouldn't answer.

"Look, give me a straight yes or no to my last question. I need to know you're safe," Gunner demanded.

"I'm safe. I'm not fit to be around, though."

"I'm here to help you in whatever way you need or want. Just call. As your friend, can you call me when you figure out how to let me or anyone else help you?" Gunner tried with several other similar pleas to let him help her. None were effective. She wouldn't let him even hand her a Kleenex. He instinctively knew that sitting beside her, putting his arm around her shoulder, or any gesture of comfort would be soundly rebuffed. Inwardly, he sobbed too.

Gunner hadn't intended to study Madison, but it started to happen. He began to look at her closely. She started to have a Parkinson's-like tremor. It started in her fingers. He had studied the 'pill roller's tremor' and had seen it in many of his patients. Her thumb and first two fingers made the typical movements of rolling small amounts of medicines into pill shaped tablets, like the old-time pharmacists used to do after decades of rolling thousands of pills a day. He stopped being amused that he remembered this from his studies when he recalled that his friend was suffering.

Then the earth stopped.

Madison began having right-sided weakness. She tried to lift her right arm and leg and couldn't do so. She grasped her right wrist with her left hand to move it and looked at Gunner in a horrified manner. Her left face drooped. She couldn't smile, speak, or even give her name—in contrast to the verbal barrage she had just inflicted on Gunner.

He sprang into action. Gunner flipped out his phone and dialed 911. He stated his location, he gave particulars about Madison's condition—likely a stroke—and demanded they come immediately. The next number he called was Dr. Ardane. The chief of neurosurgery and the head of the neurosurgical ICU promised to meet them in the ER to evaluate and treat Madison.

The ambulance arrived and took them to the hospital in record time. Gunner was glad of that. He knew that if this was a stroke, time was clearly of the essence. Dr. Ardane ordered labs, x-rays, a CT of the head and an EEG. All of these came back perfectly normal. Madison slowly regained her ability to speak, move her right side, and smile, although she remained a little weak. Her slurred speech improved to the point that Gunner was afraid she would start to verbally abuse him and the other staff.

"Look, I know all the tests are normal so far, but can you explain all this?" Gunner demanded. He had intercepted the doctor as he passed from room to room. Dr. Ardane was the attending physician on call for the neurosurgical ICU. All of the patients on the unit were under his care. After years of hard work there, he had become accustomed to walking quickly and not being interrupted.

He snorted. "No. Sometimes all we can do is tell people that nothing horrible is going on and watch and wait to see what happens next," Dr. Ardane responded.

"That's just not good enough." Gunner was clearly exasperated. "I know her. *We* know her. She's the most kind, levelheaded, compassionate person we'll ever meet. She's been paranoid, depressed, over caffeinated, stressed out and suffering from PTSD since Demian shot Canig in her driveway. She made me promise not to tell, but when I thought she was having a stroke and you're taking care of her, you've got to know."

"Yeah. I saw her a couple of times for a tremor I was developing, and she really helped me. That could have been a career-ending thing for a neurosurgeon. I owe her a lot. Tell me more about how she's been acting and when?" the neurosurgeon asked.

Gunner filled him in.

Dr. Ardane looked deep in thought. He went to the nurses' station, flipped through a toxicology handbook and said, "I need to look into a toxicology screen. I'll call Dr. Evans over at poison control and order the right tests. In the meantime, we'll keep her in the neuro ICU and observe her. You remember Julie? She's on call here as the head nurse and nurse clinician specialist. I'll make sure she'll take special care of her."

"Make sure you detox her from caffeine. She has been drinking coffee by the gallon." Gunner looked sheepish at that admission. "I know. I told her to cut down, but in her state, she needed to stay awake, keep vigilant, and be on guard. I don't know from what, but she needed to stand her ground."

"On it." Dr. Ardane had already started to type his orders into a computer. He didn't look up to acknowledge Gunner or the nurses from that point onward. He ordered Haldol in decreasing doses to calm her down and to help her withdraw from caffeine. He checked her blood level of caffeine, a drug screen for illicit drugs, a toxicology screen recommended by the poison control center and all the other tests he could think of. "We can't overdo the testing for her. She's not your average stroke or TIA. I need to think way outside the box for her," he muttered to himself. The doctor kept typing in orders without looking up at anyone, muttering to himself.

Gunner visited Madison in her room in the neuro ICU. In comparison to other hospital settings, it could be called pretty. All the machines were beeping, making squiggles or doing what they do. None of the monitors acted up as they had with Hal Foss. He felt glad for that small favor. Hal Foss had been the patient who had had the implants with nanotechnological wiring that caused the disastrous electromagnetic pulse in Lake Placid. When he was admitted to the same ICU, his monitors read only gibberish. He continued to become sicker until his monitors were turned off, unplugged and moved away from him, at the urging of Julie, the ICU nurse specialist.

"Why don't you go home?" Madison asked him.

"I called Mason and told him I would stay with you until he came. I'm so glad you didn't have a stroke. It sure looked like that was happening to you. I had to get it all taken care of. I had to call the ambulance and all. Dr. Ardane is taking care of you and ordering all the testing. He remembers when he consulted you and you helped him. So, he's returning the favor."

"Who's looking after the kids?" Madison momentarily looked horrified as she asked about Ali and Deborah.

"Mason said they're over at a friend's. He'll be here shortly. The kids are fine."

"Don't tell him anything. You promised." Her look could melt glaciers.

"Yeah, OK. I'll tell him I was worried that you might be having a stroke, is all." His hands were raised in front of him like she had a gun to his head.

It had been three hours since she had been admitted to the ICU. Madison had been given two doses of Haldol, and now looked a lot calmer. The nurses had also refused multiple requests to bring in caffeine, in any form. Her blood caffeine level was twice the normal toxic level. The lab had repeated the test twice and run their control specimens to confirm the results.

Dr. Ardane came by to see her and looked at her curiously. "I have to ask how much coffee you've been drinking. We've never seen blood levels like yours. That could have killed you." He looked in her eyes, tapped a few reflexes, gave a harrumph and left without further questioning.

After he arrived at the hospital, Mason drew Gunner out into the hall. "What happened? I knew she was stressed out, but a stroke?"

"It looked like a stroke. She couldn't speak, raise her right arm, her right leg was flaccid and her left face drooped. I called an ambulance and asked Dr. Ardane to see her. If it turned out to be a stroke, time clearly would have been of the essence. We couldn't waste any of it," Gunner answered. "We had to get her to evaluation and treatment as soon as possible."

"So, she was caffeine toxic, is *that* all?"

"So far, that's all the results we have back. Dr. Ardane called the toxicology experts and they recommended tests to follow up on." Gunner paused. "I know how worried you must be. I've been worried too. She's been way out of sorts lately."

"Yeah. And I don't know what that's about either. Nothing's going on at home. It must be something with work." Mason looked questioningly at Gunner.

"Nothing new at all, at work."

"So my healthy, forty-year-old wife almost has a stroke? No way," Mason said disbelievingly.

"Let the doctors complete all their testing and we'll see," Gunner pleaded.

"Yeah. What choice do I have?"

Julie Stills, head nurse of the Neuro ICU, wrote out her notes in longhand in a tri-fold paper chart. She looked at Madison closely. "You look like you're feeling better?"

"I don't know. I don't know what's been happening to me. They told me that my blood levels of caffeine were high enough to kill me. I had no idea. I didn't think I was drinking that much."

"I have to ask if you had any intention of harming yourself?" Julie hoped she phrased that gently enough.

"No. I'm miserable, though...."

"How do you mean?" She put down her pen and sat next to Madison on the bed. She looked right into her eyes. Julie made note of Madison's left facial weakness—it had slowly improved, along with her diction. She waited for Madison to answer, knowing that the Haldol she had been administered may slow down the answering of questions.

"Don't tell anyone about this." Madison seemed distracted then refocused. "After the CIA agent was shot in my driveway, I haven't felt safe. I'm maybe paranoid. I don't feel good in my skin."

"I should tell Dr. Ardane so he can figure out if this is from the caffeine or something else, though," Julie answered.

"Yeah. Whatever. You people are all working together."

"Working for *you*. We want you to feel better. We want you back at your position at the healing center. Your kids and husband want you back. Gunner has been miserable because he's been so worried."

"Yeah, well I've said enough." Madison closed her eyes and turned her head away from Julie.

"When you're ready, I'll be here to listen," Julie offered.

"I've heard enough of that shit. Leave me alone."

12

"How are you this morning, Madison?" Dr. Ardane looked at her expectantly. His voice was soft and smooth.

"What do you think?" she responded.

Dr. Ardane couldn't be sure if there was an edge to her voice or not. "I don't have anything to tell you, yet. All the toxicology reports take at least a couple of days. All the other tests when we admitted you were normal except the caffeine. I can see your facial muscles are pretty much equal, and your speech is good. Any sensation changes? Any trouble finding words? Anything else that seems different or changed?"

"Yeah. That damn Haldol is making my thoughts slower. *You* know it makes it hard to find the right words."

"Yes, but you're withdrawing from shocking levels of caffeine intoxication. That's keeping you from having another episode like last night. I only want you on it a couple of days; we're already tapering down the doses to wean you off it." His authoritative voice was back.

"When can I get out of here, then?" she demanded.

"Today, if you're up to it. And if your caffeine levels have gotten down to a dull roar. We'll check them shortly." He wrote away on the order sheets. "I do want to ask you how you're doing otherwise. Anything I can do for you? Are you feeling calmer?"

"I told Gunner not to tell anyone about my anxiety. That bastard." She felt betrayed.

"He had to give me the full information to try to do the right thing for you. You didn't have a stroke, but you're lucky to have had him there to make sure everything went right until you got to the hospital." He paused. "A lot of people go through a lot in life. I'm old enough to know that stress and anxiety can do any number of bad things to good people. Do you want to talk about it?"

"No way. And now I can't even trust Gunner not to tell, even when I made him swear to it."

"Madison, you're wrong about Gunner. He had to help you. He thought you were in dire distress. He might have been right about the stroke by the way you looked when you came in. You might have been having a severe stroke." He sat in the chair in the room and looked at his patient. He had a quizzical look on his face. "You know? Medicine is easy. It's everything else that's hard. I know more ways from Tuesday how to fix tumors, aneurysms, or whatever. But I really wish I could help you as a friend. There's no 'one size fits all' here. I used to think that I could help my patients with all their problems—medical, physical, psychological. Then I grew up."

Julie Stills walked in. "Julie, I wish you better luck than I've had here, today." Dr. Ardane left the chart on the nurse's podium and walked on to the next room.

"How are you, Madison?" she started.

"Jesus, get me my blood sample so I can get out of here. You people are all ganging up on me."

"The only way we're ganging up on you is by caring for and about you. That's my truth," Julie replied. "I only come to work to do that."

"Maybe I was rough on you, but can you help me get out of here? I have to go. I need to go. Something about being here, I can't trust." Madison craned her neck to see in the hall. She couldn't see much around the curtains. That added to her paranoia.

"Yes. I'll get that blood sample going for you." She left the room to find Dr. Ardane.

When she could pull him to the side of the hall, she whispered, "Dr., I think Madison is floridly psychotic. Paranoid. Anxious. Do you think that was all caused by the caffeine toxicity?"

"No. I don't know what else it could have been, but she is otherwise an elegant, kind, very together woman. I don't know how to explain it all. Her labs showed no other drugs, alcohol or anything else yet. Medically, she's fine. The tox screen might be the answer."

"Do you think we can safely let her go home?" Julie had her doubts.

"I'll call Gunner. Get that follow up caffeine level but don't tell her we have it until we can watch her some more. Gunner should give us an opinion about her discharge, you think?"

Julie admired the neurosurgeon, but she loved how he respected her and valued her opinion. "Sure. And I'll go and be with her to try to calm her down, as best I can."

"Julie, there's no one who's better at that than you. Please stick by her and do what you do best."

Gunner showed up at the hospital at about 11:00 AM. He had spoken to Dr. Ardane about Julie's concerns that Madison had become psychotic before he arrived. He walked to the nurse's station and had Julie paged out of Madison's room.

"Hi, Julie. What bothered you this morning about Madison?"

"She said we all ganged up on her. She was pissed that you divulged something to Dr. Ardane that she asked you not to." She booted up the computer and got the caffeine level—well below the toxic level it had been the night before. "See that? That's really good."

"Let's hold off on telling her that until after I evaluate her?" he asked.

"Sure." Her crisp white uniform whisked with every step as they walked down the hall.

They walked into her room. Madison looked tired, washed out and angry.

"I really need to get out of here. I need to take care of my kids. I need to go. Doesn't anyone hear me here?" She looked frantically at one and then the other and slammed her head and upper back into her pillow. "Fine. You're all in this together."

"Madison, we all care that you'll be OK. That's all," Gunner quickly said.

"We're working for you. We want to do the right thing for you," Julie added.

"Madison, I can see from your frown, your balled-up fists and moving legs that you haven't had a stroke, that whatever happened yesterday is resolving, thank God," Gunner started.

"Yeah. But I want *out of here.*"

"If you can, answer the last question I asked you last night." Gunner tested her memory and tried to protect her privacy in front of the nurse.

"I'm fine. I won't hurt myself," Madison grunted.

"I'll find Dr. Ardane and tell him I think you're fine to go home." He turned and left, hoping Julie could make more progress in reassuring and comforting Madison than he had.

13

"Hi, Bennie," Catherine said. "This is such a nice surprise visit. You surely drove a long way to come up here. What's up?" Catherine, although elderly, kept in very good shape caring for her employer and long-time friend, Marion. He was an even more elderly gentleman who needed meals made, housework done and most importantly, company. They also had large gardens, orchards, a hothouse and beehives.

"You told me to come back to see you after you did a healing for me. That was really great, and I feel so different, I can't explain it. And I have questions about what's right in a situation that's developing." By this time, they had entered the small house, sat down at the kitchen table and shared some afternoon tea.

"Marion is in a long meeting with Demian about the conference they'll put on next year. I haven't seen him so happy in a long time, planning for the conference, making sure the details all work right together, writing—he hasn't done that in a long time either, at least after his last book—and being with Demian. They do *manly* things together. Which turns out to be sharing a few beers at Bud's. Then Demian drops him off here when they're done." She looked at the clock on the wall and said, "They should be there for a few more hours, if his recent patterns hold true."

"It's good to hear that a man of his age is still productive, happy and anticipating completing projects and all," Bennie opined.

"Yes. I think Demian includes Marion to get him out of the house and continue to be active as much as he does for his help," she responded.

"But it's more than that. Marion is brilliant. A magnificent healer. The pinnacle of both historical and current knowledge. I've read the reviews of his last book. They were blown over with Marion's knowledge and what he's contributed. I tried to read his book itself, but it was way above my abilities."

"I know," Catherine smiled as she replied. "But what's up with you?"

"I did drive a long way. I wanted to see you again, maybe get my hands dirty helping with whatever you need? After we first met here, I feel more grounded with my hands in the earth. I also wanted to ask you to continue your exquisite healings for me. I need them. I feel differently after the first session. Now I want to become whatever it is that I will be."

"Why do you say that? What is it that you're afraid you haven't achieved so far?"

"Man, you are good, aren't you?" Bennie looked appreciatively at her. "That's what I don't know."

"Let's dress up in the gloves, hoods and overalls to move some beehives. We can also harvest some honey for you to take home if you like?" Catherine didn't wait for an answer; she walked to the hothouse, showed him the equipment and helped him into his protective gear.

"I've never done this before, but if you need help, I'm all in. And I'll never refuse fresh honey."

"Follow my lead. We've needed to move the hives for some time, but I haven't told Marion. I haven't wanted to stress him or make him do the work himself."

They dressed in white over clothes, hats with netting covering their faces, long gloves and pant legs tucked into high boots. When they covered themselves completely, they looked identical. They worked methodically to move six white wooden containers to the far end of the orchard. The paint on the beehives glistened in the bright sun. They also harvested honey in large jars that shimmered with a deep golden-brown color in the noonday light. The work progressed slowly in the heat, and they both breathed sighs of relief when they could shrug off the protective gear. Neither of them got stung. Catherine explained that they did their work slowly, and this didn't challenge or frighten the bees. It also allowed the honey to be sweeter in that the bees remained calm during the collection and depositing of the honey in the hives.

"See, life is like this. Sometimes we need to protect ourselves. It's natural. Then, it feels so good to remove the outer protection and breathe. Doesn't it?" Catherine's gentle voice reassured Bennie. "But when we are first shown how to shed our protections, it seems unfamiliar at best, or frightening, if we're not able to understand it all."

"I had no idea you could turn beekeeping into a lesson. You are amazing...."

"When the student is ready...." Catherine turned and walked into the house.

They went to the treatment room. Bennie had removed his shoes and sat on the massage table. "I remember our verbal sparring the last time I was here."

"Why did you choose to say sparring? I merely used your words to help you understand yourself. We didn't fight." Catherine had a gleam in her eyes.

"I know we didn't fight, it's just a phrase I chose," he shrugged.

"Not all in life involves combat or bumping up against obstructions. Sometimes, life is about compromise, integration, and becoming more. Compassion and forgiveness, even." Catherine had washed her hands and had put on some lotion.

Violets and lavender, Bennie thought.

Catherine smiled. "The last time you came, we had to get your feet planted firmly on the ground and let your roots establish a firm base for you to branch off from."

"Wow."

"You're doing it again. Using words that I can't dissect." Her wagging finger warned him to be more expressive. At her age, she didn't like to have to dig the story out of her clients. She waited until he continued.

"I couldn't out wait you any more than I can outstare Marion or Demian."

"What's up?" Catherine waited again. "This is hard for you, isn't it?"

"Yes. And I don't understand why, either. You're the easiest person to talk to."

"I'm not the only one who has to listen. Your subconscious needs to formulate ideas to be able to listen to them. When you talk, *you're* the intended audience as well." She moved to him, touched his shoulders to indicate he should lie down and went to stand in front of his feet. "As I work, let your voice be silent and give voice to expressing your subconscious."

"*What?*" That really didn't make any sense to Bennie at all. So, he closed his eyes to help him think about how to do that. The next thing he knew, he was being gently awakened.

"How was your experience?" Catherine rested her hands on his shoulders and looked in his eyes.

"I must have slept or something." Bennie really didn't know.

"Yes, you started to try to understand how your voice could be silent *and* let your subconscious speak. I deliberately gave you contradictory messages. You responded by tuning out. So, I just did my work." She smiled.

"Did I do OK?"

"Sure. This work doesn't even need you to be awake or aware. You had a great time," she laughed.

"I'm glad I enjoyed myself, then." He returned the chuckle.

"Let it all process. I'm sure that new possibilities will open up for you…"

Bennie got up, put on his shoes and gave Catherine a big hug.

"But you're not done, yet. What was the situation you mentioned when you first came in?"

"Uh, well…." Bennie wished she didn't have as good a memory as she did.

"So is it a well, like with water? Or is it a health situation?" She looked discursively at him.

"OK. Verbal sparring it is." Bennie raised an eyebrow. "The situation is that there is a young lady I know. Her life is essentially ruined by chronic pain that none of the doctors can figure out. Even walking is a problem. I've been looking in on her and want her to come here to see you and Madison and Marion. I *know* you could all help her."

Catherine jumped to the wrong conclusion. "I don't have any advice at all about love lives. I've never been married. I always thought that it wasn't for me." Catherine spoke in an uncharacteristically halting, clipped manner.

"It's not about that. I don't know if I'm helping her or not. And I don't want to be the cause of another in a long line of failures in her life," Bennie responded.

"There is something that I do think is important. Marion once told me about the victim's triangle. You want to avoid it at all costs. You should never be the victim, victimizer or rescuer in any relationship. All parties must be equal or the triangle entangles and strangles everyone in it. And I'm old enough to think that there should never be more than two people in a relationship."

"Maybe that's what I needed to hear." *And maybe not*, he thought.

"Only you know that."

"Are all healing sessions so different from each other, like my first two?" Bennie asked.

"If they are to be valuable, all sessions have to take what is brought to the experience and work with that. Unless current questions are dealt with, the healings are not individualized. One size never fits all. And the same size doesn't work time after time."

Bennie took a long time to think on his drive home. He passed through Jay, Upper Jay, Keene, and Elizabethtown then down Route 87, called the Northway by the locals. He had to drive about 120 miles. He changed his mind and decided to slow down to enjoy the scenery, hopping off the interstate and onto Route 9 to pass through beautiful little towns, mountains overlooking lakes, and forests lining both sides of the roads. He had told Jenn he would likely be away for a few days and enjoyed the thought that he didn't have to see her, if he felt a little bit lazy. He needed to think about the advice Catherine had given him. He was still not sure that it held any relevance for him and his situation.

Catherine was a remarkable woman and healer. She had been with and looked after Marion for over forty years, being his caretaker but also his protector. She did all the small things that allowed him time to write, meditate and become a sage. She had very likely prolonged his life and writing career while managing his daily household chores.

Bennie had also been present when Catherine, Madison, Marion, Gunner and the others had done a healing for Will. At that time, Bennie sat quietly to the side and knew he was surrounded with healing energy and compassion as they all worked. Some of the healers sat; some stood and placed their hands lightly on Will. Everyone proceeded reverently. The air in the room lightened and had a sweet smell at the conclusion of the session. Remarkably, after the session, Will stood, looked calmer and walked home unaided, visibly strengthened.

Prior to this healing, Will had had two recurrences of PTSD from his Iraq War experiences. He essentially had melted down to become a mass of nervous, paranoid, uncontrolled fear and anger. He had to ask for assistance going down his front steps. Will looked completely different after the healing session. This is why Bennie had asked Catherine to do a subsequent healing for him. That first session was glorious. *That is exactly the right word*, he thought. Today, he had driven to the westerly slope of Whiteface Mountain, starting out from his room very early to catch Catherine in the late morning. She had told him that her healing sessions proceeded more easily at that time of day.

He reviewed the first treatment she had done for him. He secretly needed to steel himself to protect his friends at all costs and with all methods as they captured a rogue CIA agent. They had rightly been warned about this agent's potential for subterfuge and violence. His friend Demian had shot the agent in the ear while Bennie physically restrained and then slashed him deeply with his combat knife. The captured man's wounds would eventually heal, but the strength in his right arm and hand would never be the same.

After his first healing, Bennie started to look back upon this episode differently. He now felt regret that the agent had been injured. Before this time, he would have only been concerned with himself and his fellow soldiers. What needed to be done had been done, he knew, but now he looked upon this capture with the feeling of a loss. *What a change.* And, he was sure all this was a result of the healing that Catherine had performed for him.

Bennie finally arrived at his small dark motel room. He didn't bother with the lights. He undressed and went to sit and then lie down on his small cot. He sweated in the heat; the air conditioning hadn't worked well in years. Because it was also smelly and loud, he left it turned off. He tried to sleep, but thoughts interrupted him. He remembered his best friend and himself graduating from the Military Academy, their chests distended with pride, walking gracefully in their new dress uniforms. They even had some medals won at the academy—expert marksman and others that didn't amount to anything important, but they did draw the attention of the ladies. At that time, they could envision a future full of great things. Killing opposing soldiers could still be looked upon abstractly. It wasn't in their immediate futures. They could feel their pride and invincibility grow. The real world of combat had not intruded on this idyllic bubble yet.

Immediately after graduation, Will had chosen a master's degree program in physics while he had chosen philosophy for himself. They separated for the year that the degrees required. Somehow, they reunited in Iraq for two tours. Will and Bennie suffered the loss of many friends and the wounding of others. They, themselves, suffered both survivor's guilt and PTSD, along with minor physical injuries that completely healed. The very worst of the guilt came from "moral injury." This term, coined after the Viet Nam War, described the injury that comes from direct superiors giving orders that are contrary to the moral codes each soldier carries with him. Both the men had done things under orders that they would never have contemplated otherwise.

All of this flashed through his mind and, surprisingly, he let it go easily. This had never happened before. In the past, he pored over every detail, wondering if he had made the right command decisions, whether he could have avoided the losses, and if he was still man enough to lead a troop of soldiers. Now, all of this stayed in his mind only long enough to make note of it. Now, these were only a collection of historical facts.

He finally slept.

14

Gunner sat in his office thinking about Madison's predicament. She couldn't tell anyone else around her that she suffered from PTSD because they would all blame themselves or possibly lose faith in her ability to heal others. She forbade Gunner from consulting anyone, especially Marion. He was perhaps the best healer and certainly the wisest person in the eastern United States in terms of ancient and modern healing practices, but Madison felt too ashamed to let Marion know.

Preparing for the days' patients, he decided to close his eyes and sit. He intentionally let his thoughts wander. His mind drifted to the peak of Death Mountain, outside the small village of Jay. Will and Madison both had their homes down the mountain from that peak. In numerous meditations, he had practiced a ritual called destiny retrieval where he would journey among the stars and find a more appropriate destiny for a client and bring this alternative back to the client in the form of a strong prayer. This could be acted on or not, according to the internal wishes of the client.

He sat and prayed, continuing to let his thoughts wander in a non-directed way. He waited for impressions to come to him, like they had in his prior meditations. This time he could see clearly and hear clearly, but he got no messages or intuitions. He suddenly knew that a change in direction would help. He let his attention drift to the Beaver Dams area, where he had first learned to meditate. His intuition told him that he needed to plant his feet firmly on the ground, out of the heavens.

He could visualize the dams, trees, two stone pyramidal stacks, and animals of the area. It felt glorious to him to be able to know all that happened at the ponds. He rapidly had multiple images come to him. A kaleidoscopic vision jumbled the stone stacks, Madison, Marion, Will, Demian and himself, inside—like in a tornado. He reached out to grab the stones to steady himself and felt a particular stone give way. Gunner knew this was a significant clue to the mystery of the stone pyramids. He quickly roused himself and made plans to see Madison at her home and hike up to the Beaver Dams to investigate. He remembered all the trips to the area he had made in the prior years. He believed it had more to tell him, and he hoped it would involve helping Madison to overcome the severe case of PTSD she had recently developed.

He looked up from his meditation. In the Jay Mountain Healing Center, he had two beautiful consult rooms, adjoining small area for him to write his notes, a bathroom and large windows overlooking the gardens that Marion had designed incorporating Zen and Feng-Shui principles. Many of the paths through the gardens formed a labyrinth-like pattern, easily seen through his windows. He allowed his eyes to follow the paths.

The best aspect of looking out over the gardens involved the expanse to the west that allowed viewing all the way to Wilmington and the Whiteface Mountain Ski Center. This was where two Olympics had been held. These slopes were both admired and feared. Only expert skiers should have challenged the steepest slopes. They often became sheets of ice, the snow blown off by winds that seemingly never stopped. On those rare calmer days, after recent snowfalls, the courses were simply delightful, however.

Gunner had sat and looked out or meditated in front of these windows for the last dozen years. He had become accustomed to rely on the strengths of his meditations and stored memories. Now, he asked them to come to the help of his dearest friend, Madison. He secretly feared he might not be able to help her while relying only on his own talents.

He also had thoughts of a different nature. He really didn't want to go there but was drawn into a spiral of thoughts about Madison. She was beautiful in a healthy, clean way—never needing makeup or expensive clothing to embellish her looks. Was he feeling love for her? Was that proper? How should he proceed and still be her friend and co-worker? Could he be her therapist with personal feelings for her? Heretofore, he had successfully resisted acknowledging all her charms and remained a friend. Now, time would tell if he could continue this balancing act.

15

"Hi, Jane." Demian answered the door of his condominium to let her in. It opened into a large space with an unused top-of-the-line designer kitchen and an unobstructed view of the Olympic ski jumps through a number of picture windows. These panes of glass occupied a whole wall, at least thirty feet in length and ten feet high. The largest ski jump was closest to the row of condominiums and had an elevator to the top so as not to tire out the athletes before they jumped and flew down the course. Otherwise, carrying their skis, poles, helmets and assorted equipment up seven double flights of stairs would have limited even the best-conditioned ski jumpers.

"That is breath-taking! Can you imagine anyone going down as fast as they could to fly out over the course as far as they could? Were you here to see it at the last games?" she questioned. Then she frowned. "Oh, no. Don't tell me you were a ski jumper yourself?" She stood before him with both hands on her hips.

"Sure. Nothing like it," he smiled broadly.

She didn't know whether to believe him or not. She remembered his boastful, robust sense of humor. "Well, if you did, I hope you'll keep your feet firmly planted on the ground from now on."

"Yup. The take-offs are easy. The landings keep getting harder." He had opened a very good bottle of Californian red wine and handed her a glass. "I hope you can relax and share some of this. It's really good," he chuckled.

"A little. I'm covered for the night. The vice presidents now do their share of call for the hospital, too. They're taking over more of that so that I can ease off and get some much-deserved rest."

"That's great. We should all slow down more. I've been delegating more to John to deal with. He has a knack for knowing a good deal when he sees one, and now, he's all about deals that help everyone concerned." They sampled the wine and toasted.

"Damn, this *is* good," Jane exclaimed. "I always wondered if a bottle of wine could possibly be worth hundreds of dollars. Occasionally, I think it might be if it's this good." She savored the bouquet. "Roses. That's what I smell in here."

"Yup, and a lot of other more delicate fragrances. Also, probably something heavy, like honey? Then the taste isn't anything like the aromas." He smiled, "How do they do that?"

"Don't have a clue," she truthfully answered.

"Well, I've been thinking. About a lot of things." He let that linger.

Jane looked at him through narrowed eyes and a half-smile. She walked into his embrace. "*I* think this is really nice." She moved a little as if they were doing a slow waltz.

"You know? For most of my life, I've been *consistently* wrong about everything. I think I've made all the mistakes that a person can make." He paused. "I want you to help me with something." They both suddenly stopped moving.

She looked at him with surprise. "With what?"

"Help me make sure I don't make any more mistakes. With you. Please. I don't have that many years to get try-overs if I make an ass of myself again."

"Demian, it takes two to play ball, and I was a big part of our prior mistakes. I share that blame, too." She held her wine glass in front of her and ran her finger around the rim. It made an irritating whining sound. She stopped after she saw him cringe.

"Well, there. I've said it, and I want to say that I'm sorry for all our prior heartache. I want a part of my growing older to include you to the degree that you'll want that too. Let me into your life at the rate you think you want me."

"I did come over, didn't I?" she asked demurely. The couple had shared a few dinners after the electromagnetic pulse had paralyzed Lake Placid. Demian had promised to help the shop and other business owners to rebuild with grants or loans to manage payroll, replacement of equipment—essentially everything with electronics in it. Jane noted with admiration that he had done exactly that. Lake Placid was re-emerging with gusto.

Jane had accepted his offer for dinner at his condominium with only minimal hesitation. Was she ready to start again with him? She would see.

"Yup. And let's see what the chef at Bud's Bar and Grill made for us." Demian started to rifle through a large brown bag with 'Bud's Take-Out' in bold red letters on the sides. "He likes you," Demian said nodding to her. "The chef credits me with saving his job, so, every once in a while, he makes me a gourmet, off the menu meal. I told him it was for two tonight. You know what he said? 'Don't mess it up with Jane. She's special.' I told him I certainly would try not to mess anything up. I swore to try to treat you like a princess. He laughed. I didn't."

"A princess, huh?" Her smile was even wider, if that was possible.

"And I mean to do it. Why don't you sit by the windows and savor the wine while I get out all the table fixings? Don't worry about all the noise; that stuff hasn't been opened or unpacked in this condo yet. I've only been here twelve years. It was all boxed up from the original hunting camp up on Jay Mountain. You remember?"

"How could I forget?" her voice either showed playfulness, regret or anticipation. Demian could not be sure.

"I'm glad you remember way back then. In the meantime, enjoy yourself. It'll take a little time to get out all the proper settings."

"Don't rush it, then. It's been twelve years, after all." Jane sat down, smiled, drank the wine and let the glow of the evening come to her. She gazed out through the huge bank of windows and thought back to the time as a young woman when she had been thoroughly captivated by Demian. She clearly remembered spending many afternoons at the old camp and that she left it all behind to pursue her career in hospital administration. She regretted that she had intentionally let Demian feel that he had wronged her and driven her away. It had been her choice to leave all along. Over the years, the stories of his three failed marriages filled the local papers. So maybe she wasn't so disappointed with her decision, after all.

"Demian? Why don't you refill my glass? And if you're taking the trouble to walk all the way over here, why don't you give me a kiss too?"

16

Jenn opened the door to her apartment. "Hi, Bennie." She wore a sweatshirt and very loose-fitting jeans. She moved slowly. "Everything all right?"

"Yeah. Everything is fine." He put the bouquet of flowers in a vase and placed them on the table.

"Can I ask where you've been? I know you told me you might be away, but I'd like to know where you went if that's all right." She didn't know if she pushed her luck or not.

"Sure. I went to see a marvelous healer named Catherine. She's in her late eighties, but you wouldn't know it. She can out-think anyone. And I needed her advice."

"Tell me about her while I get a light lunch for us?" Jenn moved to the kitchen to stir some soup, open a porter and slice cheeses. She worked methodically, every step and motion intended to save effort, so that she would hurt less and hopefully be less exhausted at the end of the day.

"I helped her with some chores; then she did a healing for me. Then I asked her about you."

"I'm not going to any healers. *Ever* again." The quickness and sharpness of the reply surprised Bennie.

"I know she and the others could help you, but I respect your decision." Bennie looked disappointed.

"I told you I've been through enough—and too much—that hasn't changed a thing except to make me worse." Jenn knew she had been badly treated by the "experts" that her parents had consulted. Every test they had performed only brought pain without any useful answers or plans to change her situation.

"Yeah. That's not what I wanted to ask her about you, anyway."

She stopped and turned to face him. "Sometimes getting the real story out of you is frustrating. Getting fantasy is easy as pie."

"I don't even remember what I did manage to ask her, or how I phrased it, exactly. She gave a rambling and oblique answer. But after all that, I did come to the conclusion that I should tell you about me."

Jenn haltingly walked over to her small table and sat in a chair. She rested her chin in her palms, her elbows on the table. She sat and didn't speak until finally Bennie sat across from her.

"I knew your father at the academy. I was his senior cadet when he was brand new."

"I never knew my father went to the academy! You didn't tell me all this." Now she started to boil.

"No. I didn't. It didn't seem germane."

"Out with it! All of it! What have you been withholding?" Jenn's face reddened and showed more color than he had ever seen.

"I was your father's senior cadet. We were charged with the younger cadets' discipline, training and introduction to the military way of thought and life. I did my job well. He was an excellent student and would have been terrific as an officer and gentleman. I know it," Bennie started.

"What happened?"

"He fell on a training course, broke a leg and left school because he couldn't do the physical readiness tests. They told him it would take years to regain his physical strength and stamina. He had two surgeries on his tibia and fibula. He would have flunked out, and he hated to fail at anything. They allowed him to transfer to MIT after that, and the rest you know. He became a software designer, did very well for himself and here you are."

"So you knew him as a first-year cadet? He had to leave because he was injured and couldn't complete his training?" she tried to absorb all of this correctly.

"Yes. He only had one semester finished."

"How does this relate to me? Why are you telling me this now? Does this relate to you coming here and seeing me all these weeks?" She acknowledged a growing anger and fear.

"Part of the training and introduction into the army way of life is the pledge to take care of each other and each other's families' needs. We all swore to it. We all pledged. It's a solemn oath. We live by it."

"Where were you for all these years after my parents died?" Her expression showed either anger or frustration.

"I only learned of your parents' deaths recently when I was texting my online crew of misfit friends and computer hackers. They looked him up for me. I had never met your mother, though. I learned your story and wanted to see if I could help."

"Shit. The only reason you've been coming around is to repay a debt to my father?" This anger was the first unfiltered emotion Jenn had ever exhibited to Bennie.

"No."

"Out with it, you reticent bastard." She was boiling over now.

"Originally, I did come to see if I could help you, but then I really got to liking being with you. I think I'm learning to relax and let life be what it is just being with you. I'm getting as much as I give."

"Bullshit. I wondered if you came around to take advantage of me. Now I hear that you're helping yourself while you're spending time with me?"

"It's not that. I don't take advantage of anyone. I defend my friends and family, sometimes to the death, but I don't use people."

"Whatever."

"What Catherine implied to me was that a relationship has to be between equals. I shouldn't be the savior. You shouldn't be the victim. So, I want to enter into a relationship, if you want that as well, of equals."

Jenn's eyes started to tear up.

"Did I say something wrong? Did I hurt your feelings? Are you so angry that you can't stand me?"

"No. But how can I possibly be your *equal* in any way?" She started sobbing.

"When you just try. Even after all the years of pain and torture you've been through, if you can muster up the energy to try, you're more than anyone's equal. You've won, outright."

The tears started flowing freely. Bennie went to get Kleenex for her, and she buried her face in his chest.

"All these years. I've been limiting myself to the drudgery of just pain. I'll try and we'll see where this all goes."

"I think that sounds fine. And I'll continue to tell you all about me." Bennie continued to hand her Kleenex when needed, as she cried. "I have to admit that I don't like thinking about some parts of my past, but that's for me to get off my chest as well—if you think you would be strong enough to hear it."

"Let's eat and we can talk all day long if you want to." She picked up a glass of cider, drank a bit, wiped her eyes and motioned for him to sit.

17

"Demian, tell me about everything, will you?" Jane looked dreamy. They awoke in Demian's condo. He approached the bed with a tray of coffee, cream and sugar.

"How much of *everything* do you want to know?" He laughed, but he had expected such a talk would be coming. "What do you want to know?"

"I want to know how we got here."

"Oh, that. That's easy. I could say that not even you are immune to the Listing charms. That what you mean?" He laughed again and slid into his bed next to her.

"No. I mean tell me about the old hunting camp and when you tore it down and everything after that."

"That's a lot harder."

"Looks like we have a lot of time to recover. Just tell me what you did with all the memorabilia at the old camp?" Jane knew she had to narrow down her questions or she would never get anywhere.

"Well, that was maybe the hardest part. Everything there was donated by old hunters that my father and grandfather knew—they're mostly dead now. They would bring things to be helpful, or practical or as a complete joke. For example, one of those guys brought a phone—you know, the old kind, black, you could use it for third base and never kill it—knowing it would be impossible to bring phone lines up those mountains. It'd never happen. They all knew that. He attached it to the wall, with a hand crank for a ringer and all. Every time he thought it would be funny, he'd pick up the phone to call for a pizza or a maid service, or for whatever seemed hilarious at the time. The group would roar with laughter. My father once picked up the phone and pretended he was talking to the governor."

"Hmm…." *That really doesn't sound that far-fetched*, she thought.

"Each of the artifacts had a similar tale to tell. It was hard to let *any* of it go. I called all the old hunters and travelers still alive at that time who might have visited there and asked them to come and take anything they might like. No questions asked. The surprising thing was that they all came and took something that they had made notice of or that had been important to them. And I could never have predicted who would have taken what. After that, it was a lot easier to finally move out of the camp."

"It must have been hard to let it all go," she said.

"Yes. The best thing I did was to convince Jim Tower—you know the local historian and curator of the Central Adirondack Museum—to take the camp, dismantle it, restore it and display it as an example of life in the outback. He really did it justice by cleaning it up and restoring it, and now it's the centerpiece of his exhibits at the museum. I left the biggest racks of antlers and bearskins to go with it. Once in a while, I meet with Jim and we visit the exhibit to watch people gawk at the camp and wonder out loud how people could live in the hills like that. They all think that the camp was so primitive, whereas we all thought it was modern and homey when we spent the falls hunting there."

"It's two perspectives of the same thing. Both quite opposite, and both quite correct, as well," Jane opined.

"You must have dealt with multiple disputes with two warring sides at the hospital, just like that?"

"No. Usually there were three or four completely different factions looking at an issue from their own viewpoint, demanding completely different things and all thinking they were right and should be kowtowed to. I couldn't win. As soon as I agreed with one faction, the others joined together and ganged up on me. I learned to look completely disagreeable to everyone. Such a life." She pantomimed old comedians like George Burns by rolling her eyes and putting her hand on the side of her face, her chin resting in her palm.

Demian laughed. "Let's promise to compromise and not demand anything from each other."

"Agreed. What made you give up the whole mountain, Beaver Dams, a thousand acres and all?"

"You remember the Beaver Dams?" he asked tentatively.

"Sure. Don't you remember I took pictures of you naked on the ice at the dams?"

They both laughed. Demian continued. "Looks like I would have done anything for your attention. Even risk frostbite of certain parts." He was secretly hoping that those pictures would never see the light of day. He didn't ask where they might be now.

"But why? Why did you give up those lands? They were in your family for generations," she persisted.

"I had several healings with Marion. He never really told me to *do* anything, but after the sessions, I knew that I had to change my ways and do things that would help people. I had Mason build the huge mansion that I gave to Will—I should say sold to him, but it was a ridiculously small amount. The only proviso was that he would allow any of the original hunters to come to the thousand acres and enjoy the area. Will had the idea to have Mason build a house for Madison and himself right there as well."

"You must love Will like a son."

"So you noticed?" Demian said slyly.

"How could I not?"

"Will, Marion and Will's friend Bennie all figured out the clues to the disaster of Mirror Lake. They all helped solve the problem and capture the villain—Gary Canig—who, I hope, now is spending a completely unenjoyable time in perpetuity in prison."

"I know. And then you helped the hospital, village and local merchants get back on their feet again. You don't know how thankful everyone is for all that you did and continue to do." She looked with wide eyes at Demian.

"Remind me that there are two other things that are equally important to tell you about those mountains. But for now, either let's be completely lazy and snooze, or be creative…." Demian caressed her naked breast.

"You'll never change."

18

Gunner drove his black 1973 Porsche 911 up the mountain roads to Madison's house. He loved its powerful engine, tight handling and steering. It was the best car ever built, as far as he was concerned. Unfortunately, it backfired when his shifting lacked finesse. This happened at the top of the hill, before the down slope to Madison and Will's house. This violently shook the car, stalling it. Gunner restarted the car and it backfired again. He swore in two languages.

Madison froze in her tracks. She had been in her house taking down dishes from the higher cupboard shelves to wash. This ritual of spring-cleaning was handed down through the generations and didn't skip her, as so many more obvious traits did. She moved only her eyes until she could see Gunner's sports car. She willed herself to move and hand her pile of dishes to Deborah, her twelve-year-old daughter. She hoped she didn't display the torrents of fear and helplessness she felt. This mixed with the growing anger at Gunner to make a vicious lashing out in her mind that she could not share with anyone else.

"Geez, Mom, it was only back firing from Gunner's car. What's got you so jumpy about everything?" Deborah asked.

"Nothing. Just nothing. Don't worry about it." She secretly worried that her unseen malady might inadvertently be revealed. She feared what Gunner might say; he wasn't all that deceptive—he wore his emotions on his sleeves. Recently, he had even betrayed her to Dr. Ardane.

Gunner got out of his car, walked up to the front door and was disappointed to find it locked in the middle of the day.

"Hi, Madison." He startled when the front door jerked open. "I wanted to see how everyone is and possibly go up to the Beaver Dams."

"Everything is fine except that damn car of yours backfiring. Scared me to death. Almost dropped an armful of dishes on Deborah." She looked at him scornfully, and then quickly turned her head to make sure her daughter didn't overhear her.

"Sorry about that. Otherwise that car is perfection." He hoped to defuse the situation.

"Yeah. Right." She had always favored American designs and certainly found the older engineering in the 1970s cars lacking in refinement.

"Listen, I want to go to the Beaver Dams and see if my last meditation shows us an important clue or not. Are Mason or Will around to go with me?"

"No. But I wish you would take Deborah. She's always underfoot. She can't seem to leave me alone."

"Probably senses that something is bothering you and wants to help," Gunner replied.

"Well, don't say a word to her. Or anyone else. You swore to me to keep that promise!" She made a fist and waved it at Gunner. He had never seen her do such a thing.

"I will." Gunner wished she had been more receptive. After the backfires, she looked as if she could kill him. "I wouldn't mind company going up to the dams, would you ask her for me?"

"Deborah? Get your stuff on and walk up to the dams with Gunner!" she yelled towards the kitchen.

"Do you always ask so politely?" Gunner muttered under his breath.

"Yeah, wait just a minute while I change and get my gear?" Deborah called as she excitedly ran up the stairs to her bedroom.

"While she's up there, how are you?" Gunner asked, hoping for miracles.

"No fucking good at all." She stared through Gunner. He could feel the heat it caused in the pit of his stomach.

"Well, that about covers it then, huh?"

"I'm awful. I only know how low I am because I've been so good the rest of my life." Madison almost sobbed but choked back the tears because she heard Deborah running down the stairs.

"I'm working on it." Gunner stared Madison in the eyes.

Deborah came downstairs with long jeans, a jean jacket and work boots on. *She looks very attractive for an adolescent,* Gunner thought.

"'Sgo." She walked down the steps to Gunner's car.

Gunner followed and put on his hiking boots, got his pack and sleeping bag and cooler out of the nearly non-existent back seat of his Porsche and slung the pack over his shoulder. "'Sgo."

While starting up the trail leading to the Beaver Dams, Gunner gave Madison a long look. She closed the front door and slammed the lock closed with a loud click. This slap in the face hit him in the middle of his chest. He had always hoped he could be her confidant—if not something more.

"Why are we hiking all the way up to the dams?" Deborah asked, after they had gone a quarter mile.

"Why not? And it's a beautiful day." Gunner started to feel the weight of the packs and food.

"Look, I don't know what's going on, but my mom is nastier than a black snake and won't let me out of her sights. Poor Ali has to get notes from all his friend's parents if he wants to go over and play. I don't get it."

"I don't know…." He hoped that would convince her.

"Yeah, you do. She never talks to you like that. She likes you the best of all her colleagues."

"No. I *don't* know. The reason I wanted to make this hike was to clear my own head. I also had a meditation that I want to check on. Something important, maybe."

"So, you meditate? My mom taught my brother and me when we were younger. I guess I never really got into it."

"I meditate daily for myself and for my clients to aid them in their recoveries. It really helps, and sometimes it's the *only* thing that helps them heal."

"Wow. So, tell me about this meditation?" Deborah asked.

"Just let me catch my breath and shift this weight around." He slowed and tugged on the straps of his backpack. He moved the weight higher on his shoulders. They had gotten to the middle of the slope up to the rim around the Beaver Dams. From there, the incline increased. They had to lean into the mountain to make progress and not lose their footing.

Gunner looked at Deborah. "So you're a good climber. Have you come here often?"

"What? A pick-up line from you?" Deborah was clearly disgusted.

"Huh?" His Austrian accent showed through.

"You know. Come here often? Don't I know you? Haven't I seen you on the cover of a magazine? On and on. The boys at school are full of lines. I can't get away from them fast enough." She stomped as she walked up the slope.

"That was a simple question. You seem to know the way so well. And your hiking stamina is great compared to mine. I only wanted to know what you know about the dams so that I wouldn't bore you to tears before I answer your question," he added.

"Sorry. Maybe being around Mom has put me on edge a little."

"Yeah, well I'll tell you about a time before you and your brother were even born. OK?" Gunner stopped to ask her.

"Yeah, if you can speak and walk too." She laughed inwardly at the ease in which she ascended the slope. Gunner sweated profusely now. His slowness irritated her.

"Well, about fourteen years ago, I climbed over Death Mountain from the other side. We climbed starting up the slopes on the shores of Lake Champlain and went through the historical site of the home of John Brown. I came with a client of mine who was older, a retired obstetrician." He pulled out his bandanna to wipe his forehead and neck. He knocked the dust off his hat.

"Now *there's* a hike all right!" She caught herself looking at him admiringly, then abruptly stopped when she realized she might look goofy.

"It was late in the day. We were exhausted and lost, and we had to make camp at the Beaver Dams area for the night. We were so bug bitten by the time we got to the old hunting camp the next morning that we didn't stop itching for days. That was the older camp that your father helped remove. After that, he built the lodge Will lives in now." Gunner stopped to breathe deeply. "That original camp went back over 100 years and was in Demian's family for generations."

"You must have swatted flies all night long. It couldn't have been very restful," Deborah added.

"Sure wasn't. But we got here. Then the hunt for the gold began, and I came up here to these dams time and time again. This is where I learned to meditate. I sat at the base of the larger stack of stones, and the energy of the area came to me—like in pictures or motifs with grand themes. I could know things. While your father made progress on the new house for Will, the rest of us solved the riddle of the stone stacks. We solved the puzzles of the maps and found where the gold was buried. My client found out why, too, after reading about the woman who died in childbirth."

"Huh? Gold? And someone died in *labor?*"

Now I've got your attention, Gunner thought. "Well, in those days, medical care, and especially obstetric care, was not very sophisticated. Either the baby could be delivered naturally, or the mother could die in labor. No such thing as a caesarian section."

"Really? I thought labor would be painful, but to die from being in labor and trying to deliver? I can't believe it." Deborah looked like she had been offended just with the thought of it. Her whole body shuddered.

"Until about a hundred years ago, the mortality rate of normal pregnancy and delivery was about ten percent. Unbelievable. One in ten women would die from being pregnant and all its possible complications." Gunner leaned up against the trunk of a large first-growth tree. "Give me a breather, will you?"

"Sure. I don't want you dying on me from just *walking*, after all." She hadn't even broken a sweat.

"Who would be left to tell you stories?" Gunner gasped, having overdone the forced march uphill to keep up with the youngster.

They rested and marveled at the magnificent trees as they looked down the slope to the dams. "You can see the larger stack of stones there. You can't see the smaller stack unless you get beyond the natural berm that hides it."

"My mom told me you found the smaller stack. None of the other hunters for over a hundred years had ever seen it."

"I was led to wander over that way by a meditation. Otherwise, I wouldn't have ever found it. The puzzle of the buried gold could only have been solved with taking the two stacks as landmarks, so unless I did the meditations, I and everyone else would never have found the other stack and would never have completed the puzzle."

"You mean that?" she asked, still uncertain.

"Clearly the truth. All the others will confirm it."

"But what about gold? I never heard about any gold," she questioned.

"I'm telling you to convince you that there is more grandeur in the world than you can imagine. That there's more than can be learned by study alone. That the world of inner being is just as important and powerful as the outer world." Gunner stared at the dams.

"You sound convinced."

"As convinced as anyone could ever be."

"So, tell me about the gold?" Deborah asked. Having reached the dams, Gunner had regained his composure, rested and drank some water he pulled out of his backpack. Deborah didn't even appear winded.

"Not much to tell. None of us knows how much there was. Demian made us swear an oath to avoid the area and not dig for it ourselves." Gunner looked at the larger, then the smaller stack, then wandered around the base of the larger pyramidal shape.

"So, why would I or anyone else believe you about this gold?' Deborah asked. "You guys are pranksters at best and outright liars at worst. No one dug it up, as far as you can prove."

"We have proof," he said, pointing to the flat stone at the base of the formation.

"What?"

"Come here and look. You can't see all this on Facebook, or whatever sites you're always on."

"Very funny," Deborah grimaced. "As if I haven't heard that a lot lately."

"Look," he said, pointing down to the largest stone at the base of a corner of the pyramidal-shaped stack of stones.

Deborah walked over while Gunner wiped off a thin layer of dirt and new growth of fungus with a soft cloth he had carried up the mountain. She began to see the outlines of a map of the area. She quickly took out her water bottle to help clean the rock and said, "Jesus, you guys might be on to something."

"Believe me now?"

"Look, there're the stone stacks. The Beaver Dams have changed over time, but the stream doesn't seem quite right, though."

"Did Sherlock Holmes have a sister? If so, that could be you, with your amazing powers of observation."

"Don't mock me," she replied angrily.

"I'm not. You got all that immediately. We didn't. It took us a lot longer. I had to do a meditation and find the other map before we saw all that you saw immediately."

"Where's the other map?" she demanded.

"I wonder if you'll figure it out without a meditation—now that would be even more impressive. Think of this as a puzzle. Created in the 1850s. Try to think as a new graduate of the Military Academy at West Point might think. You can do it," Gunner encouraged.

Deborah looked at the Beaver Dams, mountains, sun overhead, and then directly at Gunner. She walked to the smaller stack of stones, standing on the berm that blocked it from view, and looked over the scene from there. "I don't get it. Where's the other clue you talked about?"

"Shall you find it yourself or shall I just show you?" Gunner smiled broadly.

"I take it that it's perfectly obvious. Otherwise you would be more helpful?"

"Yup."

"OK, then let me think and scout around a little. I'm not giving up that easily." She stomped off and circled the dams, two stone stacks and the rest of the depression around the dams. She poked around for about a half an hour and shrugged.

"Come over here." Gunner pointed to a similar large flat stone on the opposite side of the larger stack. They both hurriedly dusted off the map and compared them.

"Jesus. You were right. I couldn't have believed all this was true if I didn't see it all myself. You have to admit that you guys are such jokers, why would I believe you on face value about anything?" she showed a semi-disgusted look on her face.

"Yeah, I know. But you see why this area is special—I mean outside the beauty of the area, the terrain, the mountains and the stacks?"

"I can sure see all that and the beauty of the engravings. They must have taken a long time to do. They must have been very important to carve. How do they solve the puzzle, though?"

"That, I won't tell you. Demian asked us not to."

"You bastard!" Deborah's fists balled up.

"Now, now. What would your parents say about such language?"

"Then you'll have to explain how a twelve-year-old girl gave you two black eyes."

"Not even a threat like that can pry this information out of my mouth." He turned his head away from her direction in an act of mock defiance.

Deborah pantomimed boxing in the style of eighteenth-century England. "Marquis rules? Put 'em up, Pilgrim."

Gunner burst out laughing so hard at the juxtaposition of John Wayne's famous line and intonation with the old English boxing style that he couldn't defend himself, or even stand up straight. He continued to laugh, grabbed his chest and sat on the flat stone map. "When I can breathe again, we'll enter into mortal combat. OK?"

"Yeah, you say. I could take you any time." Then she burst out laughing.

"Truce?" Gunner pleaded in jest.

"Yeah, old man. But don't forget, I could take you any time."

19

"So tell me about 'just trying.' How do I do that?" Jenn asked, after Bennie and she had settled into his BMW. They had started to drive, this time to the east. After passing through Albany, they traveled to the gorgeous town of Bennington, Vermont. Majestic churches, the beautiful campus of Bennington College with its ivy-covered stone buildings, brewpubs and small shops greeted visitors.

"I don't know. I guess that answer is different for everyone." Bennie knew this to be true after all his years in the military and observations of everyone around him.

"I do want to think I might be equal to anyone. All these years, I've pitied myself so much that I couldn't consider myself anything other than less than everyone else."

"Well, the first order of business is to stop that." He shifted as they glided down the sharp twisting turns on Route 7 into the small village. "You must remember something that you're proud of, before all this happened?"

"Yeah." Her eyes teared.

"I didn't mean to offend or embarrass you. But I want to hear about your life before all this pain took over."

"I guess my life was pretty good, now that I think back on it. I haven't thought about all that in a long time." Jenn didn't seem to mind the bumps as much as before. She didn't whine each time a curve pushed her against the armrest. "My parents were alive, I had friends that I could do things with and I had gymnastics."

"You were a gymnast?" he asked, shocked.

"My specialty was the balance beam. I had just perfected a standing back flip on the balance beam and made it look graceful. Took years of extra work. My coach told me that very few gymnasts could ever do it, at that time. Now the Olympics are full of kids who can do it even better. I guess each age brings new challenges and thinks that what we once struggled with is easy."

"Hard to believe. They used to think a four-minute mile was impossible. Now it won't even qualify you for the games," he added.

"I never used to hurt or have pain unless I fell or overstretched," she grimaced.

Bennie knew he should change the tenor of the conversation. "So, I want you to do some things for me. First tell me about how the gym would smell, or did the balance beams have an odor—the mats, the chalk or any other odors you can remember from those days?"

"Yeah. Now that you remind me, the chalk was dusty smelling, but it always excited me, because I always got to do the beam after I chalked up. I could feel my muscles ripple under my uniform when I rubbed the chalk into my palms, and I liked the strength in my arms and legs. I had the shoulders of a weightlifter, 'cause of course, I was in those days."

Bennie continued. "Were there any colors that stuck out for you, like did you have colorful uniforms? Were the mats a special grey? How about the hair colors of your teammates, or their eye colors? How about your gym bag?" He hoped to pick things that would have made sense to Jenn.

"I don't know. I did notice that the other teams had patterned, bright colors in their uniforms, but they could only wear them at the local-level tournaments. At the advanced-league meets, they had to use white so the judges wouldn't be swayed with the colors, to make everything equal. So, we over bleached everything to be as bright a white as possible. That was the brightest white I ever saw. Or have seen since then, too."

"How about tastes? Was there any taste associated with the gym that you miss or haven't tasted again?"

"The coach would give us sour lozenges to wake us up before competing. I don't know what they were, but they were the sourest I have ever tasted. And I usually liked sour flavors. I don't eat much anymore, but I used to like pickles, citrus fruits and so forth."

Bennie seethed inside but was sure he didn't show it. He knew what the sour lozenges were made of—amphetamines. The English Army gave it to their men in World War I to rouse their energies for battle. He and many of the cadets at the academy had used them to complete projects and pull all-nighters studying before exams. "Would white be your favorite color now, and would sour be your favorite flavor?" He quickly tried to change the subject.

"No. Anything green would be my favorite. Let's try sour today for lunch, though. I still think it would be my favorite," she answered.

Bennie thought that it was amazing that she hadn't even eaten her favorite flavors in such a long time that she didn't know if they were still her favorites. "What was your favorite feeling or emotion, in those days?"

"I *loved* the feeling of nailing the backflip on the beam. Everything had to be right—my foot position, my mental rehearsal, the take-off, the grip of my feet as they felt the beam on the landing. *All of it*. But when it was right, it felt so good. Like I could fly. And the silkiness of my muscles moving all felt so good. I can't compare it to anything else." She smiled as she relived the memories. "I was the best of all my teammates at that. Everyone could do the standing routines, horse, rings and so on. *I* was the best on the beam."

"Wow. I can't even think of attempting anything like that. And I went through Ranger Special Operations schools," Bennie's eyes widened. "I was trained to think that I could do anything I could imagine. If I could think of it, I should be able to get it done."

"That took extra years of my life. Yeah, and now what do I have to show for all the work?" She started to tear.

"The memories." He waited for a traffic light on the main street to turn green. He shifted and continued. "So, I want you to think of those colors, smells, sensations, and tastes. Close your eyes and imagine them the best as you can. Right now. Do it." Bennie knew he sounded demanding but wanted her to re-experience her best days. While she did so, he pulled into a brewpub parking lot on the main street and parked in the rear, shutting off the motor.

She opened her eyes, smiled, and asked if they could try something sour.

"Sure, now that you've remembered yourself at your best."

They eventually got a table in the busy brewpub, ordered a porter, lemonade and a cheese, crackers and pickles plate and were sitting quietly. Bennie noticed a young man about Jenn's age staring at her. "Don't look now, but you have an admirer sitting at the bar. Looks like a nice kid about your age."

Jenn gave Bennie a sidelong glance. "Why did you say it like that? Why is age always such an important thing?"

"Because I'm old enough to be your father, and I knew your father. Go get his phone number, or email address or whatever it is you do nowadays."

"No." She looked down and avoided his eye contact.

"I can. I'll just go over and introduce us right now," Bennie threatened.

Jenn clamped her hand around his wrist and hissed, "No!"

"OK, then. Why don't we finish our porter and lemonades and we can saunter out after that?"

The young man came over to the table before they could do so and said, "Jenn? It's you. I went to high school with you. I'm Billy Farnsworth." He was tall and very large, not fat, but muscular. "I was on the football team. We all thought you were great on the gymnastics team."

Bennie pulled out a chair for him to sit. Billy couldn't take his eyes off Jenn. Bennie had to thrust his hand out for Billy to shake to get his attention. "I'm Bennie, a friend of her father's."

"I'm sorry I don't remember you in school," she apologized, looking as if she was searching all her memory banks.

"Well, it's nice to see you again, after all," he tentatively continued.

Bennie stood up and muttered about the men's room. He left the two at the table. When he got back, they were laughing. Billy had a way with words, it seemed.

20

"Sometimes I just need to get out and walk around," Demian said. He had walked from his Lake Placid condominium to the hospital. He went straight to Jane's suite atop the tower of offices and five stories of patient rooms, operating rooms, labor and delivery rooms, and shipping and receiving. Demian thought it was appropriate that she had her office on top of the rest of the hubbub of all the hospital business. She could see and hopefully better manage everything from there. She could also feel the normal pulsations of the workings of the large hospital and hopefully intervene before things could get too far out of hand. It seemed there was always some crisis or another.

"Your secretary let me right in. No waiting. I must pull some weight around here, huh?" And, he hoped, he wasn't *pushing* his luck.

"Demian, it's always good to see you. What's up?" She walked around her desk and gave him a pleasant peck on the cheek. He had wondered how demonstrative she would be at work. She usually maintained a very professional demeanor in public.

"I needed to take a walk and I've been thinking about you." He smiled broadly.

She tried to deflect that comment. "This is where I work. You haven't been here before, have you?"

"No. But I love this view. Up so high we can see both Mirror Lake and Lake Placid. We could see Whiteface Mountain if we had a vantage in that direction."

"Yes. It is gorgeous. Keeps me focused on work to know such a beautiful landscape is right outside." They both enjoyed the views. "Then, I think we're merely human. How can we rival nature's beauty and grandeur? I get the idea that a good number of the doctors here believe they can. When I need to keep their feet on the ground, I invite them to this office as my secret weapon. They feel small as compared to this grandeur." She smiled at Demian. "What really brought you here?"

"You did."

"You don't have better things to do?" She walked closer to him, but they didn't touch.

"Not really. I missed you."

"You saw me yesterday. Are you that needy?" She was joking, but he didn't laugh.

"I guess I am." Demian thought to himself that she might be right. He had been alone for many years after his three failed marriages; could it be that she had so totally captivated him?

"Well, sit and have some coffee as I get ready for this meeting I have up-coming." She sat at her large desk, shuffled some papers and arranged her notes that she still kept on paper. She finally looked up at him. "Tell me why you're here?"

"I wanted you to know how special I think you are. And how much I want to be with you." He said it in a calm voice that covered his nervousness.

"Thank you. I really appreciate your walking all the way over here. Did you want to wait here until this meeting is over, or can we meet later?" she asked, as she stood to leave the office.

"Meeting later would be fine. I'll leave you to your work. I know how important it is."

"Good. I'll call you. I'll let this be a surprise on what I'm planning." She smiled. "Got you with that one, didn't I?"

"*Now*, I'm intrigued," he agreed.

"I knew you would be. Listen, this is not a great place for intimate discussions. We both have important work to do. Let's leave it for later, when we meet. But I'm getting to feel the same about you. No mistakes this time. We shouldn't rush a thing."

They both smiled.

"I'll walk you out. Or my secretary can show you around the hospital—anywhere you want if you haven't seen it all. Which would you like?"

"I'll tour the hospital. I haven't seen much of it except the neurosurgical ICU, Dr. Ardane's lair." Demian chuckled.

"He is a formidable force of nature, isn't he?" she asked.

"Yes. Thank you for seeing me and letting me feel wanted. I'll talk to you later."

She had known Demian since high school. She had gone from girlfriend to lover, to pushing him away to pursue a career, to admirer. She had to admit she did admire a lot about him in his later years—not so much his younger years, though. He was self-made, generous to a fault when it came to Lake Placid and his friends and larger than life. She wondered where all this would go. Continuing on as hospital president took a lot of time. She was at the pinnacle of her career at the time when many of her friends were slowing down or retiring. They were devoting themselves to enjoying their time and their partners. How could being so busy with her career fit into a new relationship? And, could she ever refuse Demian again?

She put all this out of her mind as she mentally prepared for the upcoming meeting with Dr. Cramer. She needed to listen to him with a clear mind and objectivity. The doctor always managed to bring a little chaos with him for her to deal with.

At about eight o'clock that night, she knocked on the door to Demian's condominium. She brought strawberries, ice cream, and chocolate to melt. She knew he already had a selection of the best champagne, wines and bourbons.

"Well, it is good to see you." Demian held the door open with a flare, doing his best Liberace imitation.

"I felt bad that I was busy today at the office. I would have given you a tour of the hospital myself," she answered. "Let me know when you're coming and I'll clear my schedule for you, any time."

"What did you bring, you naughty girl?" He leered at her.

"Maybe I was presumptuous, but I thought we should start with dessert. You know, I wouldn't want to shock our stomachs with solid food until we warmed them up with dessert."

They went to the kitchen, cleaned the berries, mixed the ice cream with honey and port—a special vintage from Portugal—and stirred them all together. Demian insisted on freezing the mixture for a few minutes in his subzero freezer.

"So, which of the jazz greats do you like best?" Demian asked while getting out old vinyl records, CD's, cassette tapes, and turning on his Harman-Kardon amplifier with Klipsch speakers.

"If you crank up those speakers, even the people three doors down will call the police. You don't want to put our friend Todd Wilkins on the spot, do you? He would have to come and reprimand you. You would have to look contrite. You'd have to bribe him with the dessert we just put together. Then he'd never leave," she chuckled.

"I'll be careful. What do you want to hear?" he repeated.

"If you're talking smooth and mellow, Tony Bennett is my man. But if you're talking classic jazz, how about anything Miles Davis from the sixties and before?"

"My thoughts exactly. Let's start with the Tony Bennett."

"Shouldn't we be having some champagne or something while we wait?"

"Hmm. We sure could." He went to the wine closet. He had converted a butler's pantry into a room with as many wine racks as he could squeeze in. It held at least 300 bottles. His contractor had even created a rolling rack system like the medical records racks at the hospital used to be, before the computerized medical records systems reduced paper to electrons. Now, he could slide the racks by pushing them on a rail to expose whichever he wanted. "You know? I've got to electrify this. It would be easier for you to get your favorite bottles out."

"Presumptuous, aren't you?" she said with both eyebrows raised.

"No. Practical. I want it to be easy for you to come here and be with me. I don't want you to have any silly excuse like, 'It's too hard for me to get my favorite wine out of the closet,' or some such thing." He looked her in the eyes. "You know I would do anything for you, to make you comfortable to be here." His tone changed to deathly serious.

"I get it. Put on anything Tony Bennett and we'll talk. But fill my champagne glass first."

Demian did so, put on a charming album of Tony doing Italian heritage songs and sat next to her on the sofa. He adjusted pillows for their heads. They toasted with very good champagne. "So is it reasonable to ask if you feel for me like I'm feeling for you?"

"Reasonable to ask, but presumptuous. How do you feel? I can only agree with how you feel if I'm sure what that is, don't you think?" she giggled.

"Think of the best of anything. That's how I feel about you."

"Oh, so the best bank, or church or school. Like that?" She wasn't making it easy for him. But she did continue to giggle.

"No, silly. I really like you and want you to be around. I need you, and hope you feel the same."

"Oh, that. Why didn't you say so?" She kissed him until she spilled a little champagne on her blouse.

"It'll come out. Don't worry. But you have to take it off right now, and I'll soak it."

"Man, you're desperate." He heard more giggling as she shucked it off, leaving only a camisole.

"I'll get you a sweatshirt, or something." He left and came right back with a navy-blue thick sweatshirt. She put it on over her head. "You even look great in that. I can't believe it."

"Why don't you get the dessert and I'll lay out the ground rules since you don't seem to be able to do so?"

He brought the strawberries, ice cream, honey, and port in two martini glasses. He put them on the coffee table with spoons and said, "Before we indulge, shoot. I've always known that women were better with affairs of the heart than men. You say."

"Demian. I've been told, and agree, that before a relationship gets firmly established, a couple should spend four seasons together. That would be a whole year if you didn't follow?" She looked expectantly.

He nodded obediently.

"I would like this to work. But we need to move slowly and be sure of all the steps. We need to let time pass, spend time with each other, experience new things with each other and we'll see."

"So, it's more of a long-term evaluation of our relationship that we need to do?"

"Exactly. And an honesty we need to share. There should never be any doubts between us. If we say we'll be here or there, that's where we'll be. If we promise something, that's what we'll do."

Demian leaned back, thanked his lucky stars, opened his eyes and saw how lucky he was to have her in his life. He handed her the desserts, followed by more champagne, Miles Davis, and a night full of creative fun.

21

"So, exactly why did you drag us both up here again?" Deborah asked. "You're not talking about the gold, so I might as well listen to whatever else you have."

"I needed to get up here to spend as long as it may take to get my head straight and help myself and my patients." Gunner hoped that Deborah didn't infer that included her mother, Madison.

"How is it that you do that?" she seemed genuinely interested.

"I've told you. I clear my head and meditate. I trust that the themes or visions I have when I meditate are helpful and healing." His voice adopted the tone he used when he wanted to emphasize a point with his clients.

"You sound like my mother. She's always saying things like that with her work." She paused. "I don't know what's bugging her—or should I say everything is bugging her like I've never seen before. She acts paranoid. She locks everything, rechecks the locks and still looks out the window to be sure no one's coming or lurking around ready to break in. When your stupid car backfired, she about jumped out of her skin. I've never seen her like that."

"I don't know what's bothering her either." Gunner responded with no conviction whatsoever.

"I know you do, but you won't say," she angrily fired back.

"Then don't push it."

He stared out over the water and saw fish rising, making note of how the blues and blacks of the pond contrasted with the greens of the trees and plants. Deborah made a show of standing up to leave.

"Before you go, let me tell you about my last meditation? Please?" Gunner worried that he had angered Deborah.

"Well, we are here. And remember, if you bore me, I can knock your block off," she pantomimed the British boxing style again.

Gunner wasn't sure how much of that threat was in jest. He quickly continued. "Well, I saw in my meditation, that a stone was loose in this taller stack." He walked over to the pyramid, at about eye-level and grabbed a stone about the size of a football. "Right here." He pulled it, and it easily swung out of its place. The rest of the stones remained in place without as much as a quiver. "That couldn't have happened by accident, for sure. The whole top of the structure should have imploded after I pulled out the lower supporting stone." He put it on the ground to reveal a small cavity behind the space previously occupied by the stone. Gunner started to reach inside.

"Watch it! Don't just reach in there. There may be snakes, or a trap or something!" She grabbed his elbow and pulled it down before he could come close to the cavity.

"What? You've been watching too many Indiana Jones movies. Don't worry." He turned to face the gap in the facade again.

This time she grabbed his arm with both hands and pulled him away. "Please!"

"Okay, let me go. I'll get my light and we can look in first." He opened his pack and found his flashlight. They slowly turned to the stones.

"No. Let's look at the stone you removed first," she demanded. "Let's not overlook the obvious."

"Now that's a great idea." *Perhaps the girl might be right about snakes or traps or whatever,* he thought. They turned the stone over. It had a thick growth of moss on the underside where it was flatter. The builders of the stack obviously considered the shapes of the stones to make the total structure stable. Gunner took the stone to the water, dunked it in, rinsed it and then brushed off the area.

"Man. I love it when I'm right!" Deborah almost shouted. Another map was slowly unearthed under the moss. It appeared to be an accurate rendering of the area around Death Mountain. It extended to Bitch Mountain and Arnold Mountain. The area around the dams was only a small representation on the map.

"Shit! Damn!" Gunner looked embarrassed after he swore in front of Deborah. "Don't tell your parents I swore," he pleaded.

"Don't worry. I've heard worse. And said worse myself."

"You're growing up too quickly, I think."

"Says who, old man?" She raised one fist threateningly.

"Me." He paused. "Well, forget I've been a bad influence on you. But what do you think about the map?"

"It sure looks like it was engraved by the same person who did the other two…"

"I think so too."

Deborah compared the stone etching to the surrounding mountains and made small clucking sounds for each landmark when it appeared that each was an accurate representation of the geographical oddities that could be confirmed by the naked eye. "See this stone and map are accurate. I don't get it. The other engravings were like clues and not accurate representations of the real areas."

"Yeah. That's what I think too," Gunner repeated.

"So you had a meditation and saw this stone was loose?"

"Something like that. Meditations aren't always that clear. This meditation had a hurricane. I grabbed onto this stone so I wouldn't just blow away, and it came off in my hands, so I knew I should see what was special about it. I didn't really know until we looked at it, and I found it was loose."

"Wow."

They spent the rest of the afternoon comparing the three maps, surrounding mountains and thoughts about what this might mean. Deborah used her cell phone to photograph the map from various angles, then the two maps on the lower stones. She walked down the path to her house in the afternoon leaving Gunner to rest, set up camp and begin his daily meditations. She had finally let him look into the cavity with a flashlight, and then feel inside. They found nothing.

22

"It's really nice to see you again, Bennie," Catherine said as she opened the door. She led him through the entryway and motioned him to be quiet with her finger to her lips. "Marion is meditating in his rooms this morning."

"I'm sorry to barge in. Is it OK that I'm here today?"

"Yes. Marion lets me see whomever I want to, as long as I don't disturb him and I manage to get the meals on the table on time. Why don't you help me? I've got some chopping, cleaning and cooking to do before I make the soup for our evening meal. I'll invite you to join us. Marion should be done by then. He'd love to have your company."

"Only if you don't think I'm intruding." Bennie had already come in, removed his boots and hat and paused in the entry into the kitchen.

"Don't be silly. I can use the help." Catherine pointed to a large simmering pot and motioned it should be removed from the top shelf of a walk-in pantry. In short order, she directed Bennie to retrieve, pull out of cupboards, disassemble, and disinfect mason jars. Then she started the thick berry mash to be stirred and made into berry jams. These preserves required constant stirring and the precisely timed addition of sugar, then pouring into the prepared jars. Covers were screwed on tightly. The jars were wiped clean of any jams that might have leaked out and neatly lined up in rows to cool, upside down. Finally, after they cooled, they could be labeled and stored right side up in large cupboards.

"Wow. That's hot work, for sure," Bennie finally said.

"Yup. You've almost earned your keep. Chop these cucumbers into spears, clean and chop the garlic, make the brine, and we'll pickle some nice dill pickles, as well." He had already retrieved and prepared the larger mason jars to do so. He set up the boiling pot to use to preserve the slices.

He did exactly what Catherine directed, wiped his brow several times, sharpened his long knife more than once and kept moving, although it was very tiring work. "Were you going to do all this alone, before I came?"

"I may be old, but I'm not crazy. I know when I can easily coerce free help if I need it. Now, keep at it—we're almost done. No need to complain."

"I'm not complaining; I'm just saying—"

"Quit your bitching." Her back was turned to him so he wasn't sure if she was really angry, or not. Her sense of humor usually wasn't like that, though.

"Yes, ma'am," he responded in an embarrassed whimper. By this time, he had become too exhausted to argue.

"You might tell me why you came all the way up here, Bennie," she commanded.

"Yup. I need to figure that out for myself as well. The last time I was here, you told me that when I speak, I also hear myself talking and that that's the way I figure things out."

"Yes. Mostly. Sometimes someone has to guide you and ask the right question, though," Catherine answered.

"Good point." He reached for another large dish of cucumbers to slice. He nipped off each end and sliced them into spears. He also made some slices to fill in the spaces around the spears in the jars. He occasionally stirred the brine, flavored with long strands of organic dill, garlic, lemon, vinegar and pickling spices. The odor filled the kitchen even more so than the berry jams. It hung in the air, thickly.

"So either I can find more and more projects to last all night long, or you can start talking. Which will it be?" Catherine looked exasperated.

"I'll finish with all of this; then we'll sit down and talk."

Finally, there were three dozen jars of various jams, two dozen large-mouth mason jars full of pickles, and the salad for dinner had been chopped and seasoned. It rested in the refrigerator, letting the seasonings seep into the lettuce and kale picked from the gardens this morning. They sat down outside in the shade of an awning, sipping unsweetened iced tea.

"So tell me." Catherine waited for his response.

"Where do I start?" His honest question sounded flippant to Catherine.

"Bennie, you've earned my full attention. Without you, all of that would have taken me weeks to finish up. The berries would have gone by. The cucumbers wouldn't be small and sweet, and the spices wouldn't have lasted in this damn heat."

"I'm pleased to have been of help. Please call me if I can ever help again?"

"Sure, but listen, I'm not getting any younger. Tell me why you drove all the way up here." Catherine now demonstrated that her sense of humor could be tested.

"Honestly, where do I start?" Bennie asked earnestly.

"Maybe you can't tell because you've never told anyone the whole story before? Start as early as you can remember."

"What? You mean at a very young age and go from there?"

"Yeah. Right. You had to make a joke of it all. There is something important lurking there that you've had to avoid or would like to deflect attention from." Catherine noticed Bennie's head pull back reflexively. It was one of the very rare 'tells' Bennie gave off. His long years of training, and especially the Special Ops, allowed him to control most of his unconscious reactions.

"OK. Let me think back and verbalize it as I go?" he asked.

"Fine." She rolled her eyes and then raised one eyebrow.

"The first memory I can clearly recall is maybe when I was two or three. We went to a family reunion of sorts of only my parents, uncles, aunts and cousins. Maybe a party? I don't know what the occasion might have been."

"Good. Go on," she encouraged.

"Well, I can't remember exactly what I did, but I was the laughing stock of the party. Everybody including my parents, uncles and aunts were laughing at me. Not *with* me. I remember the hurt and feeling that I would never be good enough. I've done a lot of things that I'm sure any average person would be amazed at, but I've carried that feeling of inadequacy with me my whole life. This is the first time I've admitted it, though. And the first time I've clearly brought it to my mind."

"Take your time and think about it all. What might they have been laughing at you *or with you* about?" Catherine deliberately introduced and emphasized the alternative explanation.

"I don't know. I just remember the feeling that I would never be good enough."

"Drink a little of your iced tea, then put it down. Settle in the chair. Feel the armrests. Feel your feet on the ground. Breathe evenly and slowly." Catherine deliberately began to speak more slowly. "You might put your glass down to rest your hand, *now*," she had to remind him, but Bennie did so. He closed his eyes while his breathing slowed. He felt tired enough after the drive and kitchen work that it didn't take any effort at all. "You can think back to that or any other time in your life. Let your mind drift."

Bennie did so, not knowing what he might remember. His body felt heavy. Sifting through memories became like swimming through syrup. Time slowed as he felt warmer—especially his hands, feet and face. Catherine also radiated a feeling of safety to him. He knew this came from her, like with the healings he had had from her. He knew this warmed him and protected him.

Then the episode he had recalled before came into focus. He could see all of his relatives laughing after his father had made him make a face that he had taught him. The whole episode was only that. No emotional overlay, no unworthiness on his part, no belittling occurred. "I remember it now. I wasn't being made fun of. It was just the laughter of adults over how cute an infant or toddler can be." He looked dreamy—eyes closed, half-smiling, almost not breathing. "I don't know why I remembered it all differently than it really was."

"Kids perceive differently and then attach to those memories. The earliest impressions become written in stone. Subsequent events are handled on the basis of those understandings—or *mis*understandings. They don't have the adult equipment to interpret events properly with. Let your new realization sink in. It will start to filter and let the rest of your foundation memories mature, as well."

Bennie didn't know how long he might have been resting. He didn't know if he had been sleeping or dreaming. He drifted until Catherine gently touched his arm.

"Tell me how to deal with all this?" he asked her.

"Your subconscious already is doing so. No need to do anything further except to acknowledge that you'll start to feel differently now that your base ideas have been reinterpreted with adult understandings."

"Wow."

"Shall I tell you a short story?"

"Sure," he looked excited.

"Well, once upon a time, there was a little boy. He lived in a large house with big front steps leading to a large front door. It was difficult for the boy to go up and down the steps—they were so large. He played in the front yard where a boulder leaned up against a large tree. He would try to climb the boulder to be able to climb the tree and had to struggle to do so." She paused and continued, "Then the boy grew, moved away, established himself and had his own family."

Bennie nodded and closed his eyes, visualizing it all.

"One day, the young man wanted to see where his beginnings had gone. He drove to the area where he had grown up. He was surprised that the village was very small. This was not his recollection. The house was also very small, the front door average size, with two short cement steps leading to it. In the front yard was a landscaping accent stone leaning against an old apple tree. He realized these were the same tree and stone." Catherine waited.

Bennie began to smile.

"The thing is that both viewpoints are true and factually accurate, but sometimes we outgrow our old stories; they don't serve us well any longer. We move on."

Bennie trusted that he would start to feel differently as his subconscious re-oriented to the understanding that the feeling that he was not worthy was a misinterpretation. He even felt sure that his memories of his father would be gentler.

23

The next morning, Bennie knocked on Jenn's door at 11:00 AM. She yelled for him to enter and he did so.

"So, you know that guy named Billy? The one we met at the brewpub?" she asked.

"Sure." Bennie waited for whatever might come next. He hoped it wouldn't be a horror story. They went out the front to sit on the porch in the swinging love seat.

"So, he's been calling almost every day. He wants to take me here or there. I just said no." Jenn related this in a matter-of-fact way.

"Why? He's good-looking, and I thought he was well mannered. Did he offend you in some way?" Bennie poured iced tea for himself and lemonade for Jenn.

"No. But he's too persistent. And I don't want to be forced," she responded.

Bennie thought this sounded a little lame. "That all?"

"Look, what am I going to do with all the chronic pain and all? I can't go long distances, ride for a long time or go for walks. What could he do with me that he would like?"

"Oh."

"Yeah. Why would anyone be interested in me?" she whined.

"Because you're courageous and have been making strides to help yourself with this pain. Look at what you've done with me in just the last few weeks." Bennie could see her tremble. "You want me to tell you what I think?"

"Yes." She responded with an emphatic tone in her voice.

"There are really two issues here. One is do you like Billy and do you want to get to know him better?" He waited.

"Yes?"

"Well, that wasn't a rousing endorsement, for sure. So why don't you go very slowly? Only go to public places. Only local and get back very early in the evening. Take it really easy until the answer might be more positive." His voice became gentle.

"That sounds right." She started to push the swing.

"Yeah, it is. Whenever a new relationship starts, go slow. No use rushing over anything."

"OK."

They sat and glided slowly.

"What was the other thing?" she asked, almost afraid.

"Well, you haven't wanted to hear that I know some fantastic healers. I just saw Catherine again. She really helped me to feel differently about myself." Bennie could see Jenn recoil. Her expression was either fear or anger. "Calm down. I wouldn't force you to do anything you don't feel you can do."

Jenn's expression turned to stone, with an ashen color. She didn't respond.

"I think I can more reasonably assess how you've been doing than you can. I've had a more objective viewpoint because I haven't lived with the pain. But I have seen you do different things, go different places, eat different foods, and, in general think of more possibilities than you would have in the past. You've been able to dream and hope. You haven't done that in years, in all likelihood."

By now, Jenn's tears flowed in a steady stream, and she had stopped pushing the glider.

"Sometimes, the worst things are what we do to ourselves—how we limit ourselves to our own self-imposed miseries. I did that to myself for my whole life. I thought I was unworthy in all regards. That limited what I thought might be possibilities in my future. You get it? We know you have pain, but you've allowed the thought of the pain to limit you. The last few weeks, you've broken out of that mold. Take that and run with it," Bennie encouraged.

Jenn sat straighter, pulled her chin in, stopped her tears and looked like she had come to an internal resolution. She still didn't speak.

"So I'll leave it in your hands. Catherine helped me to see and understand my own self-limiting thoughts. She helped me. She didn't do any testing, biopsies or anything other than make me feel that I could understand myself." He waited. Jenn's expression didn't change. "You tell me when you're ready to make that ride and see my friends in Lake Placid, when you feel strong enough to make the trip."

Jenn remained silent. Bennie finished his drink, gave her a kiss on the forehead and left.

24

"Demian, we've both been working really hard lately. Why don't we take the day off and just do something together?" Jane asked. She had never done such a thing since she had been inaugurated as the hospital administrator over twenty years ago. She had had many planned vacations, taken many working trips to large conventions in exotic locales and made sure that her staff members had all had sufficient time off. But she had never called in to say she needed time off on the day that she did so. She had never been too ill to work and never shirked her responsibilities.

"I'd love to spend time with you. Where do you want to go?" Demian asked.

"How about if I make you breakfast in bed? Then we negotiate it all?" Jane replied.

"How hard are the terms of negotiation likely to be? Do I need to call my assistant for back up?" he chuckled.

"If John shows up in the middle of our negotiation, I'm out of here. This is going to be a quiet, non-verbal session." Jane smiled and raised one eyebrow.

"Man. I'm all in." He had to stop himself from licking his lips.

"I thought so. I'll get busy with breakfast. I hope I can find everything I need in that cavernous kitchen."

"While you do that, I'll make my famous Mimosas. I know which champagne will nicely complement the orange juice and such. Special secret ingredients, you know?" He looked excited to mix the drinks and spend more time with Jane.

"I thought it wouldn't take much to convince you. But first, show me where everything is?"

"Where shall we go, then?" Jane asked. They had just climbed into his Range Rover. Jane had had to use the large running board and hand grasp above the passenger's door to step up into the front seat. "Jesus, Demian, couldn't you find a *larger* SUV?"

"Nope. They don't make them any larger. I checked." Demian adopted his John Wayne smile.

"We can go anywhere." Jane looked excited to think about the day off. She hadn't had much experience with taking the opportunity just to be restful or take a drive.

"Montreal for the day and evening? Vermont and Burlington? Take a cruise on Lake Champlain? Why don't you say? I want to make this special for you," Demian continued.

"We don't have to go far. But this is my first day ever of playing hooky. I would like it to be different. Maybe somewhere from our past?"

"You did mention the Beaver Dams. Why not there? They are certainly pretty and there are two other things that I wanted to share with you about them. You really have to be there to understand it all."

"Then I need to drop by my place to get on my hiking boots and jeans to walk up there."

"Done."

"Demian, why me and why now?"

"Why not you and why not now?" He paused and thought his first answer bordered on trite. He slowly continued. "I think back on you and us as the one thing in my life that I didn't get right and wished that I had. And I think when our paths crossed, back then, we were both younger and unable to connect like we are right now." He looked directly at her. "I made a serious request of you—that was to make sure that you help me not to make any mistakes this time. I seriously want you in my life." Demian looked a little unsettled and uncertain about what Jane might say.

"That's a two-way street. I want to ask the same thing of you. And I'll be in your life as long as it's working for both of us." She read the concern in his face and reached over to give him a kiss. She had to unlatch her seat belt to do so. "Damn this car is huge. Necking in the front seat is not going to be easy, not like it was with your father's Lincolns." They laughed.

"Yeah, but it does have cup holders. I'll get you coffee and a Danish to go from the gas station down the street. I haven't been able to buy anything there since the owner's and all the other businesses in town were bailed out through my foundation. Chip won't have it. He's told his whole staff that anyone who charges me for anything from a Danish to a tank full of gas will be fired."

They laughed as Jane settled in for a nice ride. "Demian, why don't you tell me about something fun you've done recently?"

"Like what? I mean other than being with you, I've been working most days and weekends. Seems like there's always something going on in town. Some business or other has an event and invites me. I really can't just say no and not go, can I?"

"Yes. You could. They are only saying thank you for all you've done for them to keep them in business."

"I don't know, then." He looked as if he questioned his last few months.

"See, that's what I meant about we don't know how to make the last few decades of our lives as full as they can be. There isn't any writing about that era that's good enough to rely on. I want to direct my staff to study, write, and come up with the definitive work on that. Or at least get the ball rolling. If we only manage to start an argument among other researchers, all the better." Jane looked resolute.

"I can't wait to hear about it all. How about Julie, the ICU nurse who convinced Dr. Ardane to turn off all the computers in the ICU to save Hal Foss? She has a way about her. I would believe almost anything she might propose. And she can motivate the rest of the staff you choose."

"Great choice. I'll call her the next time I'm in the office."

25

Gunner sat at the base of the larger stack of stones. He had already tried to see if any other stones might have been designed to swing free or had further maps. He had checked the smaller stack and also found none. He reviewed the new stone's map. As far as he could tell, it showed an accurate rendering of the area surrounding the dams extending all the way to Lake Placid and north to Plattsburgh. It also extended to the east on the shores of Lake Champlain and to the west and the center of the Adirondacks.

As he sat and relaxed, he thought about Madison, his best friend, mentor and co-director of the healing center. He had to help her. He could only imagine how deeply she must be affected with the PTSD. Even with Madison's best efforts to hide it, her daughter Deborah had noticed its awful effects on her moods and actions.

Gunner reviewed all the healing techniques he had encountered or devised in his long career. Nothing seemed quite right to help Madison. He took in a deep breath and let his back muscles relax as he exhaled. His eyes closed slowly. He felt the sun was shining directly on his forehead although he knew he was in the shade of the stones.

Gunner knew the territories of his Destiny Retrievals well. He had done the mental rituals regularly for over twelve years. What he did not expect, however, was that the sun was clearly in the same sky and in the same galaxies that he explored. He had never seen this before. This gave him some comfort with its warmth but also over-illuminated and obscured many of the areas he found himself drawn to. He turned his back to the sun and used his shadow to allow the structures to be seen. He reflexively looked away as he saw scene after scene of horror. He steeled himself for a longer search and knew he must not attach to anything except the healing outcomes he hoped for. He feared the years of his past practice might not be enough to help shepherd the process safely.

He noticed a gentle shake of his shoulder. Demian and Jane appeared at the dams looking down on him, chipper and refreshed after the long climb. "Gunner. Are you OK?" Demian asked. "We hope we didn't disturb your reverie."

"I'm Jane Parker, you remember? We've met several times at the hospital galas and fundraisers," she added. She offered her hand to shake, and Gunner stood to take it.

"Of course I remember. I've always been in awe of your administrative abilities, keeping the staff and all the other hospital personnel in line in times of severe monetary crises." By this time, he had been fully aroused and focused on his friends. "What are you two doing here?"

"I know what you're doing here. You're trying to regain your composure to do your spiritual practices," Demian said as if that was completely obvious.

"Hum?" Jane said.

"Remember, I told you that there were two other very special character-istics of the Beaver Dams area?" Demian reminded Jane.

"Yes. You sounded mysterious," she answered.

"Nothing too exotic, really, just the way the earth's energies line up," Demian started.

"They're called lay lines. The energy patterns of the earth are average in most areas, but right here, around the Beaver Dams, and extending to Lake Placid, the energy is the strongest that I've ever felt. I traveled extensively in Europe and the U.S. and I've found nothing like it anywhere else. It's like the electromagnetic waves are concentrated—maybe by the mountains, streams, or whatnot in the earth itself." Gunner shrugged. "The opposite is also true. For example, Death Valley, in California is particularly low in the earth's vibra-tions. Nothing grows there because of that, also the heat, dryness and so on. But other researchers and I feel it is the severely diminished earth's vibrations that make the area so desolate."

"It's the earth's pulsing energy. That's what Gunner comes here to experi-ence and align himself with so that he can be effective in his healing practices.

Marion stayed here in the Lake Placid region during the latter half of his life to feel that. He said it helped him with his meditations," Demian said.

"So that's also what drew Hal Foss to the area, and then the nanoelectronics and hip implants caused the electromagnetic pulse that almost wiped out Mirror Lake?" Jane asked.

"Yes, and the interaction with so many computers that all fed-back on each other and amplified each other in a harmonic frequency. Then the pulse happened," Demian concluded.

"What I had to do was to come up here and get my head on straight. I could finally help Hal after that. I had meditations, just like Marion had, which led us to think that the earth's vibrations had been thrown off and caused the EMP to happen. Marion figured out it was the nanoelectronics. Dr. Ardane removed the meshes that held the electronics and dissolved them in acid. He had to do so to cure Hal. Then Demian, Will, Bennie and Todd captured the rogue CIA agent who caused all the turmoil in the first place. That prick was eager to let an innocent, unknowing man be the source of the EMP. He wanted to weaponize the implants and spring it all on an unsuspecting population. It happened here because the earth's fields are so strong and the computers amplified it to disastrous proportions." Gunner finally took a breath.

"So that's one thing about the area being special. Dare I ask the other?" Jane questioned.

"That may be a whole topic for another day," Demian quickly said. He continued before he could get any contrary arguments. "Gunner, are you overly busy right now?"

"I was just sitting here." He looked around quizzically.

"Jane and I are going through some changes." He paused, as Jane looked befuddled. "This is the first day that Jane has ever played hooky from work. We're relaxing and trying to relive some of our pasts. But, more importantly, maybe we both need to reorient ourselves to our priorities for the rest of our lives. After we put Canig away, Jane mentioned to me that this segment of our lives, the last decade of work or after we retire, is not well studied or understood. I agree. No one has a manual for us to read and plan with. Now, we're both starting to think about what comes next."

"I get that. And you're right. No one has done the definitive treatise on aging—how to do it gracefully, fully, fruitfully, and maintain your zest. But you two seem to be doing just that. How can I help?" Gunner finally asked.

"Maybe you could search through our destinies for us?"

Now Jane looked completely lost.

Demian chuckled. "I do surround myself with the most extraordinary friends. Let me explain. Gunner has studied and performed what he calls 'destiny retrieval' for his clients. He meditates, goes to the stars and future and brings back more appropriate destinies for those he 'travels' for. That right so far, Gunner?"

"Yes. And then the person has the option of acting on the new destiny, which was there all the time anyway, or not. I bring back the destiny in the form of a prayer."

"Every time I think I've heard everything…." She laughed. "You wouldn't believe all the instruments, diagnostic machines, potions, lotions, pills and therapies I've been pitched. All flashes in the pan. And very expensive at that. My rule of thumb was to give every one of them to a committee. Death by committee. I could count on it after I appointed Dr. Cramer to be the chairman that all the committees reported to." She paused. "At least I can rely on you and Demian to be honest, hard-working people who wouldn't be taken to extreme beliefs if they proved to be unfounded."

"Gee, I think that sounds like it might almost be kind of a compliment." Demian laughed.

"I realize this must sound a little far-fetched," Gunner offered.

"But here we are," Demian suggested.

"I walked all the way up here to reconnect with a segment of my past, maybe I can connect with something of my future?" She didn't say, *This better not be a waste of time!*

"Demian, set up your camp chairs right here, and you can both settle in and get comfortable. I'll do a guided imagery for you, let you rest for a few minutes and then wake you up. OK?"

"Yes," Jane responded unequivocally. She surprised herself.

"Sure," Demian said.

They arranged their chairs near the base of the larger stack. After they had taken a few moments to relax, Gunner started. "Let yourselves relax. Feel the gentle breezes on your faces." He spoke more slowly with each phrase. "Hear the rustling of the leaves, birds sing, creaking of old tree limbs and murmur of the water flowing. Smell the air—the dankness from the water, the sweetness of the honeysuckle, and all the other aromas of the woods. On each out-breath, let a little more tension go. Just rest."

Gunner had already been sitting on the large flat stone at the base of the stack. He closed his eyes and let himself drift. He went to the top of Death Mountain, which Madison had renamed Life Mountain because he used it to bring new life alternatives to his clients. He drifted and chose Jane as his first client. She had many options to select from. Surprisingly, all of the scenarios were positive and pleasant. He chose an intertwining future, knowing she had been single all these years. He directed that prayer to her. Next, he drifted among Demian's possible alternative futures. He chose a similar future and let that be a prayer for him, as well.

Madison still weighed heavily on his spirit. Again, he could find no possible alternative future for her that looked promising. He carefully disengaged from the process and decided to try to clear his own mind and align himself with the good in the cosmos before he tried to help her further.

He also brought the new map to the future to see where it might lead him, Will and Demian.

Gunner was jolted awake from the process. "Demian! I just got a vision that something is terribly wrong with Todd Wilkins. It's not part of the destiny retrieval. It's separate. Please. Get to him as soon as you can. Call him from Madison's house. Have his men look for him. I don't know what it is, but you need to find him and help him now!"

"Can you run with me?" Demian asked Jane urgently. He had only taken a second to try to understand what Gunner had just told him.

"I'm in at least as good shape as you, for sure. And it's mostly downhill," she answered.

"Just go, and I'll clean up camp and haul all your stuff down for you and drop it off at your condo," Gunner demanded.

Demian stood, offered Jane a hand up and turned to trot down the mountain. He felt reassured that Jane was at his back. He heard her breathing and knew she followed only two steps behind. He became worried about his long-time friend, Todd, but felt comforted that Jane was with him. He remembered his father's rather vulgar admonition to him, after he had asked about dating, to find a partner that he could "fight, fuck and footrace with." He now knew in his heart that she had become that person.

Jane easily kept up, maintaining an even speed. Turning an ankle out here could be disastrous, but she felt she needed to hurry to help Todd Wilkins. She remembered how he had been very helpful to her nursing staff after a stalker terrorized them walking to their cars late at night when getting off their shifts. Todd had arranged for all of his deputies to stake out the garage and parking lots at the hospital. Even off duty, they had been ordered to put the area under tight surveillance. Finally, the culprit had been apprehended, placed in jail and sentenced to a long prison term on the basis of a testimony given by the sheriff and his deputies. The staff calmed. Jane had had to beg several long-time nurses to continue working during the crisis, but she knew that the sheriff and his staff had their backs during the long siege. It boiled down to knowing they were safe due to his vigilance.

Demian remembered the conversation that Todd and he had shared, and he started to breathe more heavily. He stole a glance behind him to see a very determined look on Jane's face.

Jane considered passing Demian but felt that might be dangerous—one or the other of them might slip and fall. In ten short minutes, they knocked loudly on Madison's door. They waited and pounded again. Then shouted. She finally opened the door.

26

"Hold on. I'll try his cell and radio. He's out on patrol," the deputy dutifully said.

Demian, confident that he had impressed upon the man that his boss could have been in serious danger, waited a full five minutes.

"I'm not getting any response. The last radio check-in was due east of town, along the AuSable River. No one was with him. This is not like him. *At all.*"

"Look, this is Demian Listing. I insist that you get your men and put out an APB on him. Right now. I'm driving to the AuSable. I can be there in just a matter of minutes. Where exactly did he call in from?"

"Right where he saved those people from drowning way back," he quickly answered. "We'll roll from this end as well."

Demian and Jane heard over the speakerphone in his Range Rover muffled but loud voices in staccato then a siren. "Meet you there." Demian jammed on his seatbelt and motioned to Jane to do the same.

They had left Madison's house after they quickly understood how much stress she was under. They chose not to involve her or worry her all the more. Demian had never seen the anxiety etched into her face like it was today. They mentioned that Gunner would be coming down the mountain and that they wanted him to call as soon as he did so.

"Yeah, whatever," was her only response.

"Man, I've never seen her like that. She's usually as solid as a rock—kind, giving, supporting and comforting. I don't know what's gotten into her." Demian was shouting now over the roar of his SUV in low gear, winding down the serpentine corners.

"Maybe you should slow down? We don't have any proof that anything's become of the sheriff, do we?" She held on to the front grab bar with both hands and still felt jerked around by the large car lurching over boulders and around turns.

"He's never not answered his phone, the deputy said. He's also at a very dangerous area on the AuSable River. I was there when he saved the woman and her children. That water runs deep and strong. It drains the whole of Whiteface Mountain, and more."

"Yeah, well, make sure we get there, will you, please?" Jane shouted back.

"OK." He slowed the car, but still hit a bump really hard. Without their seatbelts on, they would have at least hit their heads on the ceiling.

"Jesus. Don't kill us!"

"OK, I heard you. I'm just terrified that something might have really happened to the sheriff." He took the next sharp turn and barely missed an exposed rock. "He's become a really good friend. He stood up for us like a man when we had to capture that Canig fellow. That dirtball might have been able to hurt or kill one or all of us if he hadn't."

"Yeah. I heard you shot him. Did you have to?"

"I sure as shit did. I had to punctuate the fact that he was clearly captured. Bennie was still wrestling him. He resisted arrest with gusto and was about to reach for his gun." He finally turned onto the paved lower section of the road and took his truck out of lower range gears and sped off. "I only shot him in the ear. He'll need a new specialty earring, for sure."

"You shot him while Bennie was in the middle of wrestling him? You could have missed and hurt Bennie. After what I learned about how bad Canig was, I wouldn't have shed any tears if you killed him, but what if you hurt Bennie?" Jane started to cry.

"With all the confidence in the world, I took that shot, and I would take it again. I know I could make it all day long. I would never have endangered one of our friends or anyone else. I wouldn't have hurt Bennie under any circumstances."

"Well, just keep your mind on driving." Jane wasn't sure about Demian's over-confidence. *Maybe getting involved with him again wasn't such a good idea?*

"It's right around this bend." They had quickly passed through the town of Jay while his emergency flashers blinked and he beeped his horn. They took a back road to the AuSable River as a shortcut to the place where Demian and Todd had rescued a motorist and her children from drowning some twenty years ago.

They saw Todd's car, the driver's door open. It sat empty otherwise, on the bank of the river. Scanning up and down the water, they couldn't see him. Demian and Jane ran towards the car until Jane grabbed his arm and pulled him back. "Look at the footprints. Some really scuffed in. Maybe three sets. There was a struggle. We can't disturb the area before the deputies get here. He's not in his car, at any rate." They walked about ten feet to the side of the other tracks and saw them disappear into the water.

"What? Did they have a boat or something?" Demian asked.

"Oh, no. There's blood. Stay clear of it. It'll have to be tested," Jane warned.

"You're right again, Jane. I'm glad you didn't let me blunder in on this and ruin any evidence or the footprints."

Jane was surprised at his acceptance of her advice. She had remembered him to be headstrong, *at least*. "Call it in to the deputies?"

"Yeah, right now." He found he had cell phone tower access and did so. After speaking for a few minutes, he slammed the phone closed. "If they did abduct him, the only reasonable way to go would be downstream. There are a whole lot of places to get lost in that direction but not up-stream. I've got to go follow down the stream. Will you come with me, or do you want to stay here, protect the scene and handle the deputies? I have to say they're not the brightest bunch, but their hearts are in the right place."

"I'll stay. I would only slow you down, and you can cover more territory if you don't have to worry about me. Call me with anything, will you?" She briefly kissed him and gave his hand a squeeze.

"Jane, how did I ever let you get away, before? I'll call. I'm going to move quickly. I won't approach anyone suspicious. I'll call it in." He turned and left her waiting for the deputies.

"I've got this end. Just be careful. If they've abducted an officer, they don't care about social niceties. They wouldn't hesitate to shoot anyone else."

He just looked back at her and nodded.

27

"Jesus, Demian. Some first day playing hooky, huh?" Jane sighed as she slunk into a chair.

"I'm glad you were there to block the sheriff's deputies from destroying evidence. You really had to remind them to take impressions of the prints, photograph the whole area and get a sample of the blood?" Demian asked.

"Yup. They would have trampled the scene like a herd of buffalo if I hadn't been there. They were so afraid for their boss; they weren't thinking until I set them straight. They were going to jump in the car and see if he was hiding in the trunk or glove compartment."

The counter clock in the large kitchen chimed midnight. They had returned to Demian's condo, opened a bottle of great red wine and were staring at the ski jumps. "If anything, those jumps look even bigger in the dark. They loom over the valley. Ominously," Jane said.

"Yeah. I've looked at those jumps in all the seasons, at all times of the day, and in all types of weather. You're right. They look ominous, especially in the dark. But in the spring, they look like a giant gardening tool that just might have moved all the dirt of the valley to create the mountains. They have a more positive feeling to them at that time of year." Demian puzzled at his own description.

"The deputies have already established that the blood type doesn't match Todd's. At least that's true. That's at least hopeful," Jane continued.

"Yeah, and they'll run it through all the usual databases for known criminals for possible matches. But that'll take at least a few days."

"You didn't find a thing going down the river?" she asked. "You were gone for four hours."

"Not a thing. Like they vanished. And I'm a pretty good tracker after all these years of hunting. I got all the way to AuSable Forks. Must have been twenty miles on foot and none of it level. Walking on uneven ground means that you leave more sign as you duck under branches or climb over rocks and so forth. I would have thought that two or three men dragging a prisoner would have left a lot of easily visible signs. The police dispatched their chopper and nothing either."

"Demian, how worried are you?" Jane asked, pulling close to him.

"Very. He hasn't called home, called into the station, filed a report for the day or anything that I would expect a responsible officer to do."

"Shit. What other resources do you have that might help? You have friends in high places, don't you?" Jane asked.

"It's my friends in all the low places that might be more helpful. I'm going to call Will and ask him to call Bennie." He pulled out his cell phone, dialed and waited. "Yeah, Will, it's me. I'm here with Jane. Listen, I'm afraid that something awful has happened to Sheriff Todd. Possibly abducted. We found his car empty with signs of a struggle and blood at the scene, but nothing else." He waited as Will responded. Jane was sure with a string of profanities. "I think we all need to meet, and could you call Bennie to come? We might need him and his hoard of hackers to help put all this together." They spoke a few more minutes, and then he clicked off and turned to Jane. "That's started."

"What else can we do now?" She had already moved to him, slipped her arm around his waist and handed him back his glass of wine. They started to move to the imaginary music again.

"Jane, please stay with me. I'm a little rattled. You calm me. I need you."

"Such an admission from his highness?" She laughed. "Of course. It feels right to be here. I'll do anything you need me to do."

"Just stay here. I would be worried if you were out of my sight," Demian replied.

"Worried for me or for you?"

"Both, I guess. I felt a whole lot safer when I knew the sheriff was doing his work even when he didn't show his face. I always knew he was there, in the background, protecting us."

"From what?" Jane asked but was afraid of the answer.

"Maybe Canig has friends who are exacting their revenge? That even sounds stupid when I say it, but I have a feeling something bigger is afoot." Demian looked out the window and closed the floor to ceiling drapes. *Was someone out there?* he thought.

"Who knows?" Jane started. "Then if you think this is Canig's crew, we better warn John and Elisabeth, right?"

"Shit. Right you are again." He looked perplexed. "Now or in the morning?"

"Now, dammit! Tell them all now. We can't sleep anyway." She let go of him. "I'll find some old shirt or something of yours I can slip into, make coffee and be right back to help you."

While Jane left the room, Demian called Albert, an acquaintance from the distant past. He had called Albert when needing to find out the true status of Elisabeth and Gary Canig. True to his word, Albert found out the information needed, spent a lot of money doing so and lorded over him the fact that Demian had needed his help again. With some reluctance, he started, "Yeah, it's Demian Listing again."

"What silly shit have you gotten yourself into this time?" Albert could be crude and cruel.

"Remember the Gary Canig thing?"

"Yeah, dumbass. I clearly overcharged you to find out the info you needed and you still paid me. I wonder why you're such a pansy in your old age?" Albert laid it on thick.

"I need to know more about him."

"That prick? He's right where he should be. In jail. Thanks to you and me." Albert coughed. "Why are you asking? What happened?" His concern was audible.

"Apparently, three as yet unidentified men showed up, looked at deeds, researched maps and very likely kidnapped the sheriff who took down Canig with us. Sheriff Todd is still missing, but they found blood at the scene. Now, the rest of us are possible targets too. I need to know, through channels that aren't traceable, what his finances show. Has he hired a hit squad? Who has called or visited him in prison? What the fuck is up?" Demian finished and waited.

"Shit. You don't get in much trouble anymore, but when you do, it's big, isn't it?"

"Yeah, tell me something I don't know." Jane returned to the room wearing Demian's oversized flannel shirt—and not much else, except a smile. She picked up her wine glass and motioned to the bedroom.

"Any ground rules like last time?" Albert asked.

"No. The sky's the limit. Fast. And get at least one group of new age hackers on it too. They seem to have different ways of thinking and getting things done on the net, off the court, way in the outfield—and any other poor sports metaphor you might like. Get it done."

Albert laughed. "Kid, this's got you rattled. I'll get on this right now and be very liberal spending your money. I'll call you back."

Demian heard the phone disconnect. He turned to Jane. "One of my prior contacts who should know the underworld; he owns most of it and rules the rest. I've called him and hired him to investigate for us."

Jane waited patiently as Demian called Will to also ask him to make sure to have Bennie get his gang of hackers on Canig's finances. He called John and filled him in and asked them to come to breakfast at eight the next morning. Finally, they headed off to the bedroom.

28

"So, when will everyone be here?" Jane asked, trying to clear the cobwebs after awakening.

"Eight AM. Likely sharp, if I know the bunch of them," Demian answered.

They rolled out of bed and showered. Jane dressed in yesterday's climbing clothes, having not been home to collect others, while Demian put on his best jeans, white shirt, boots, and a wide belt.

"You *do* look good." Jane smiled. "I wish I had a chance to run home and change. Or I wish we had a chance to be creative right now, without being interrupted." They kissed.

"You could just move all your things over here. Then you wouldn't have to worry about having a clean change of clothing." Demian tested the waters.

"No. Not yet. We have a lot of living to do and need to get to know each other better—in more ways than in the bedroom," she answered.

Demian hoped his disappointment didn't show. "OK, just sayin'...." Demian reverted back to John Wayne.

"You wish," she put on her best valley girl inflection.

"I'll start the breakfast, could you help?" he asked. They had coffee in a tall coffee maker bubbling in no time and moved on to eggs, toast, meats and freshly squeezed juices, getting the table set before the first guest arrived.

Will arrived at five minutes before the hour. He had visited the condo many times and found himself right at home, not even knocking to enter. "I'm the first?"

"Yeah, but not for long with this group," Demian answered.

"Here's your coffee." Jane handed him a large mug. "Demian said black with a little honey."

"Perfect." Will did not miss the fact that Jane had been at the condo for longer than a few minutes this morning.

"I checked in with the deputies. Nothing new, but I'll fill in everyone else when we're all here," Demian called from the kitchen.

"Great. I'm hopeful you're unnecessarily over-cautious, but you're not taken to excess in that regard, are you?" Will asked. "Bloodstains do rile you up, don't they?"

"I would be delighted to have this be a reunion breakfast of sorts. And I'll be glad to take the abuse from all of you if I'm wrong. I just don't think I'm wrong, though."

"I called Bennie. He had things to do this morning and will be here as soon as he can. He's already called in his gang of hackers. They love an opportunity like this to show off for each other. They try to scoop each other and beat each other to the punch."

"That's fine, as long as he's watching his back when he travels up here," Demian warned.

"He's always watching his back. He went through Special Forces training and couldn't stop checking his surroundings if he tried," Will responded.

"I know."

John and Elisabeth arrived and were introduced to Jane. Gunner arrived last and had private words with Demian. They all had breakfast and settled in to hear Demian speak. "I know I've upset you with the news and my feeling that Todd has been abducted by Canig's cronies. I really have no proof of it. But I sense it's true. I'd feel so much better if all of us were careful and this turns out to be nonsense."

"How did you know that something had happened to Sheriff Todd in the first place?" John asked.

"Jane and I were at the Beaver Dams and Gunner was doing a meditation for us. He finished that and then told us to run, that the sheriff was in danger. I guess an impression or something?" Demian looked to Gunner.

"It was in a meditation. But I knew it was serious, just not what exactly," he responded.

"We phoned the police station and went looking for him at the location his deputies said he last called in from." Demian poured himself more coffee. "I searched down the AuSable River for twenty miles walking along the bank. No signs of him or his abductors. All we found was his deserted squad car with the doors left wide open, scuff marks on the sand, bloodstains that weren't Todd's and nothing more. His weapons were missing including a shotgun, flare gun, Taser, his sidearm and ammo. Even the flares for the flare gun. They've received no demands for ransom."

"He's a strong man. He can take care of himself," Elisabeth added.

"We know that. He's been a very good friend to us all." Demian scanned the group. "So we have to proceed along the lines that he's still alive and in captivity. Otherwise he would have let us know he's fine."

"That's the other thing," Gunner interrupted. "I can't say why, but Madison is dealing with her own issues and has to be looked out for. She can't help us or know we're dealing with all this. She can't know that we suspect Canig's men might be involved. And it has to be very secretive. If she found out we were looking after her, she'd be offended." He looked at Will and Demian. "If we're all possibly at risk because we were part of Canig's arrest, then she and Mason are at risk too. We can't tell her, so we have to protect her."

"We get it," Demian and Will said at the same time. They both looked at each other in amazement, then smiled with the recognition that their thought processes were so similar.

"Bennie's coming today. He's already got his cronies and hacker friends on the case. He'll know if anything is obvious and can tell us when he gets here. They're looking into Canig's finances, everyone who might have visited him in prison, any communiqués to him in prison and so forth. We'll know. And having him stay at my place, he can watch the mountain and Madison and Mason," Will offered.

"That's great," John said.

"I can't believe it. Now, you think I might be hunted again? After all this?" Elisabeth broke out in tears. "I've been thinking that this was all going so well. My nightmare of a decade is over. Well, it's not. Shit!" She slammed the table with both fists and stood up so fast that her chair hit the floor, tipping over backwards.

"Let us deal with it, will you?" Demian said in his commanding voice.

"How are you going to deal with possible abductors who were so bold as to kidnap an officer in broad daylight? How did they know the AuSable River well enough to know how to do it?" John demanded. He had grabbed Elisabeth's arm and helped her back into her chair after righting it.

"That's a great point. They nabbed him at precisely the point in the river that the sheriff and I saved a woman and her two small children from drowning. How would they have known about that? That was about twenty or so years ago," Demian continued.

Will interjected. "So it seems that, tactically speaking, the best place for us all is at my house. Elisabeth, maybe you could be of help to your cousin? I'll have Bennie get there ASAP and set up a perimeter on the road to the houses."

"Demian, you're pretty exposed here, don't you think?" Gunner asked.

"Yes, and now I can see that this breakfast meeting might have been very ill-conceived." Demian was surprised that Gunner came up with that conclusion. "We need to move. And I mean right now. We all need to go directly to Will's. Don't go home, to the healing center or wherever. Go directly to Will's."

"What about me?" Jane asked.

"I don't want you out of my sight. I need you to be with me so that I'm sure you're OK. OK?"

Jane sighed. "I can't imagine that they might know anything about me, or would have connected me to the Canig affair. I need to go about my business." She looked pleadingly at Demian.

"I need to keep you and everyone else safe. For the time being, just let's get everyone to Will's."

Will turned away from the table to dial his phone. "I've got Bennie on the phone. He's outside Jay right now. He'll set up a perimeter on the mountain road. I've also warned him to steer clear of Madison and Mason." Will listened for a few moments. "Shit. You're right." He turned to speak to the crowd. "What about Catherine and Marion? Do they need our protection too?"

"I'll call them and pick them up on my way up the mountain," Demian concluded. He realized he had made another mistake not including Marion and Catherine to protect them.

The group all went to their cars, drove to Will's house and dug in for what they feared might be a long siege.

29

Bennie had pulled off the old logging trail leading up to the Beaver Dams area. Below the dams, Will and Madison had built their homes on a beautiful flat knoll, about three hundred yards apart. He carefully surveyed the area. He hid his small car behind a rise, and walked down the trail, about halfway to the paved section where he could overlook the road. He knew that 99% of all the people who would approach the houses would be going up that road. Only real fools or devils would dare go over Death Mountain, through the Beaver Dams and down to the clearing. Still, he had checked the area and found no evidence of approach from that direction.

Bennie had called Will and Demian and was filled in on Demian's fears that the whole group might be at risk from associates of Canig exacting their revenge. Bennie considered the CIA agent captured by himself, Demian, Todd and Will. This rogue agent had embezzled millions of dollars from the agency and organized crime and fellow agents, subsequently setting them up to be accused of his crimes. Elisabeth Billow had fallen prey to this and had spent over a decade of her life avoiding capture by Canig. She could never establish herself in an acceptable, full-time job, fearing she might be discovered and killed. She fell into a life of prostitution, avoided social contacts or any friends at all and managed to avoid being killed by him or the Italian mafia that Canig ripped off implicating her for the crime.

What a story, Bennie thought to himself. This scoundrel had used an unsuspecting man, having nanoelectronics embedded in hip implants with a carbon fiber mesh to cause the electromagnetic pulse to test its utility as a weapon.

He had used the whole town as guinea pigs! He frankly could not believe the audacity. "Maybe I should have just killed him when I had him in my grasp. That would have been quicker and safer by far," he said aloud to no one.

Now, he watched as the cars Demian had listed for him found their way up the mountain, bringing anyone who had had anything to do with the capture of Canig to the safety of the mountainous compound. He could see no one else in the area or any other disturbances to the plants, no tracks in the sandy trail or signs of any menace. For the moment, he could feel reassured.

Madison watched from behind the drapes in her living room. She had checked the locks on the doors and windows again and again. She felt drained from her inability to sleep but could not resist watching and guarding. She startled with each new car's arrival but recognized each as belonging to Demian, John and Elisabeth, Gunner and Will. Unable to relax, she continued to drink her third pot of black coffee and kept her vigil.

Demian and Will went to the gun safe and armed themselves, noting Bennie had been there and already selected an M1A1, multiple clips, a SigSauer 45, tactical knife, flashlight and camo.

"Well, we'll only see Bennie if and when he wants us to," Demian said, chuckling. "He knows his weapons and what he needs."

"For sure, his Army Ranger Special Forces training included a big dose of evasion and survival tactics. He could be lying twenty yards away and we'd never know." Will paused. "How bad is all this? Do you know anything that you didn't want to tell everyone else at breakfast?"

"Yeah." Demian said nothing further while he loaded several clips for his favorite Kimber 45. He put it in a holster at the small of his back.

"Well?"

"Lake Placid is a famous tourist destination with thousands of people enjoying the outdoors, sports, local cafes, nightlife and so on. We expect a lot of traffic of that sort. But, last week Todd called me about unusual visitors to the town offices, looking up deeds, old maps and then wanting to go through recent newspapers. Jim Tower, you remember him?" He looked at the offended scowl on Will's face. "Of course you do, sorry. He called the sheriff, who then called me. Todd was going to snoop around and get back to me. I didn't hear any more of it."

"How many of them were there?"

"Don't know. Probably three from the descriptions given by Jim," Demian replied.

"Shit. So, this is an organized group, willing to do their homework and stage an organized attack after planning it all out. How did Jim hear about their visit to the town offices?"

"The new deeds clerk, the one who took over from Madison, called him to help clarify questions regarding the local history. Jim Tower is nobody's fool, for sure. He put two and two together."

"Did Jim tell you about which areas they were most interested in?" Will asked.

"Yeah. The AuSable River, this property and the surrounding mountains."

"Could they have been just innocent real estate investors?" Will probed.

"Could have been, but now Todd's missing, having been abducted in the area they researched." By now Demian had loaded several Ruger Mini 30s with extra clips, and his Anschutz, a super accurate 22—the same gun he'd used to shoot Canig in the ear.

"How do you plan to do this?" Will's question obviously concerned the protection of the group.

"It's you, Bennie and me in shifts. We can't alarm the others, so we'll sneak the weapons out the back. I think one of us on the road, one of us in the house and one walking outside. That should probably be me outside to start so as not to worry the others. I'll have rifles staged in the house and outside. We'll spell Bennie. I called him on the way up and he agrees to all of this."

"Do you think any of them are crazy enough to come over Death Mountain and down from the Beaver Dams?" Will remembered the story of Gunner's and Dr. Crandall's entrance to the camp from that direction.

"No way. But, we'll watch the whole perimeter," Demian said. "You remember Dr. Crandall—who is very familiar with the area—and Gunner got lost and couldn't find their way out of the Beaver Dams? Anyone not really familiar with getting out of there would just *stay* lost, too."

"Yeah. But you know, Gunner is no outdoorsman." They both laughed. "Did Bennie's hackers have any other info?"

"Not yet, and I've called my sources, as well. We'll have to wait for them to do their searches. The deputies are questioning the clerks who assisted the visitors at the town offices. They'll come up with sketches. Nothing yet on the blood found at the scene, either. But in the meantime, we need to be on our guard."

"Got it."

Bennie sat and waited. He had taken protective overlook positions countless times in his two tours in Iraq. *That was different.* In those days, his friends and comrades were in harm's way. He could be vigilant and guard for days on end if needed. He could detect the telltale sign of a rifle under an outer coat or burka. He knew when a bulky load of explosives or a suicide vest made unlikely bulges under clothing. All this he remembered. And he remembered taking the shots when he needed to, to save his men. He didn't miss.

This was also different. He knew he could protect his friends. He knew he would protect his friends. But this was his country. Something profoundly bothered him, here and now. This should not be happening in his homeland.

He remembered telling Jenn that he would likely be away for the foreseeable future. He had wondered how she might have taken the idea that he would not visit her as frequently. She reacted coldly to the news. Then she reminded him she had given her phone number to the high school acquaintance they had met. Maybe he could move on from her now. She had just as much pain as before but had learned to tolerate it better. Maybe she had succeeded in writing a new story about herself and the pain? At any rate, he was at least her father's age. Even if Jenn might have desired more, it would never have happened.

Then it struck Bennie. He had seen Catherine twice recently. She had done healings for him. He knew he should feel differently afterwards but hadn't yet discovered how or in what way. He simply did feel like a different man, now. He still had all the old skills, but now they could be framed in a new story of *his* own. He suddenly relaxed. His muscles became supple. His shirt seemed to fit better if that was possible. He sat on a log and felt he rested lower on it. It suddenly struck him that he wasn't the man who had returned from Iraq—shattered, incomplete, unable to make new friendships, unable to rest fully, always tense and looking for the next fight. Now all of that had changed, lessened, and maybe even left? He felt like melting ice cream on a hot August day—no hard edges, softening, sinking.

"Yeah, Will. I'm OK. Nothing on the horizon. But I'm not OK, either. I'm overcome with the need to sleep. I can't explain it, but I'm not solid on watch." He listened to the response. "Yeah. I'm overlooking the first turn after the bridge. Yeah. I'll wait for you here. I don't get this. I've never been unable to take a watch."

"Bennie! What the fuck?" Will had walked up on Bennie and found him asleep. He gave him a kick to the bottom of his right boot. This jolted him awake.

"I saw you coming. I checked the area and couldn't keep awake. I don't know what the fuck either."

"The area is clear?" They both looked out over the road going up to the houses—clear. "Yeah. Well, we have a couple of things we could do. One is to let you sleep it off right now. The other is to talk about what the fuck is going on. What'll it be?" Will demanded.

"I don't know. I feel deflated. Like all my muscles have been drained of energy. I tried to stand and walk a few minutes ago, and I was like jelly. Couldn't do a push up right now if my life depended on it. Like someone flipped a switch and turned my muscles off."

"What happened?"

"Shit if I know. Except I've had two sessions with Catherine in the last few weeks. I knew I'd feel differently, but this is like I'm a popped balloon." Bennie struggled to finish his sentences.

"Well, then sleep. Lie down here and I'll wake you in a couple of hours. I'll take your watch."

Bennie lay down. Will noticed that his muscles went limp and showed none of the tension that they usually had. His face softened, looking at least ten years younger. Instead of a curled snake ready to strike, he saw a Labrador Retriever stretched out in front of the fire after a long day of swimming. Bennie's breaths became even, softer and more fluid. Will could no longer see the jerky quality of a man's breathing while on patrol.

What the fuck? Will thought. He took up the position overlooking the road and concentrated on lines of sight with shooting lanes if they became necessary and put his friend's changes out of his mind for the next four hours. He had informed Demian that he had to take over the watch from Bennie. Demian didn't ask, but Will knew he wondered why.

30

John approached Demian outside the house. Demian held a rake with gloved hands and appeared to be absorbed in beautifying the area leading up to Will's house. He had raked the undergrowth from the lawn into large piles of furry detritus. He sweated in the sun and needed to wipe his brow frequently. He used those opportunities to take stock of his surroundings. "I've been thinking about us all being here. Aren't we better off if we all go to different places where it's unusual for us to be?" John asked. "Somewhere we wouldn't be expected? Out of character?"

"Maybe. But we don't know the whole story yet. Bennie, you and I have all sent out inquiries to our friends in low places. We have to give them time to get on with it and reply," Demian answered.

"Yeah, but we're all here, just waiting. I feel like a fish in a small fish bowl, with the cat ready to stick his paw in." John's face got redder as he spoke.

"I know. But, we're safer here than anywhere else because the road is covered and there's only one way in except over Death Mountain. I've only gone that way once in my whole life—nearly killed me." Demian smirked over his choice of words.

John wasn't amused. "Listen, I need to take care of Elisabeth and myself, now that we're married. I'm responsible."

"Yeah, and the best way to do that is to stay here until we've heard more." Demian's curt reply stung John.

"We'll see." John muttered something else Demian didn't catch. "And why shouldn't Elisabeth see Madison? What the hell is going on here?"

"I don't know. Gunner just told me that Madison needed our protection and couldn't get caught up in the whole thing."

"I can't go on that alone. She's asking to go to see her cousin. Madison can see our car here in the driveway, and it would seem way out of the ordinary if she didn't at least visit."

"John, please stay the course here. We'll figure this all out. We're still not *sure* anything is seriously wrong or even that the sheriff has been abducted."

"Business partners shouldn't hold out on each other. Neither should friends. I'm being upfront with you; why can't you come clean with me? There must be more than what you've told me already. And where are Will and Bennie? What are they up to?" John looked visibly upset.

Demian put his hand on John's shoulder. "I am. I am as open as I can be. We don't know yet." He paused. "There is something more, though. There were probably three men researching deeds to this property, looking over maps to the AuSable River where the sheriff's car was left. The sheriff was likely abducted there. The unknown men were also looking up local newspapers of the last few years. The deputies and now the FBI and state police are all over it. They're combing the area, using dogs and helicopters again. They're covering it. We're covering the road going up here. Will and Bennie are doing that. It's all we can do."

"No, it's not. We can get in our cars, drive somewhere unknown to us all and hide. I've done that. Elisabeth has hidden out for a decade." John balled his fists involuntarily.

"You could, but do you know if you're safe even getting out of here to the main road in Jay?"

"Where are the police? Shouldn't they be guarding the road too?" John persisted.

"They're doing all the investigative work in Jay and on the AuSable River."

John spit on the ground between Demian's feet. He turned and walked into the house. After a minute, he and his wife Elisabeth got in their car and started to drive off.

Demian stepped in front of the car, then walked around and leaned down to speak through the driver's window. "I wish you would be smarter about this." John shook his head. Elisabeth had been crying and would not meet his eyes. "At least don't continue to be targets. Make sure to use cash only, don't go home, call in only with burner phones, don't reveal your location and go at least as far as Vermont. Call me as soon as you get out of Jay, so I know you're both safe. Don't say anything that can give your location away."

"Look, Demian. It's not like we've never done this before. We'll be fine. I've got no choice," John answered.

Demian understood that very likely Elisabeth had become so rattled and fearful that she could not stay. "Your most dangerous zone is where the logging road gets to Jay. From there take random streets. Let me at least scout out that area for you?"

"No. We're going right now. Every second, the three men could be closer," John fired back. He didn't let Demian say another word. They sped off.

Demian called Will for a status report. As Will filled him in, Bennie walked up the road.

"Shit, damn. Bennie, what the fuck?" Demian was clearly in Bennie's face.

The strange thing is, though, that I don't feel threatened, Bennie thought to himself. In the past, he had meticulously guarded his personal space as a matter of survival.

"What the fuck, Bennie?" Demian grabbed his forearm and dragged him to the side of the house, placing the small lean-to woodshed between them and Madison's views out her windows.

A few minutes later, Demian received a call from John. He and Elisabeth had decided to "get ice cream" and would be taking the afternoon to sight-see.

31

Bennie sat in Will's office on the second floor of the large house. He entered an online chat room that was accessible only on the dark side of the net. He started with a bland-looking site that advertised, among other things, baby diapers, formula, feeding nipples and bottles, and, of all things, garden implements like shovels and rakes. Not a racy website, for sure. He looked for the hidden icon in the formula section, clicked on it and found himself in a password-protected area. He entered the correct codes and started to chat with the group.

"Yeah, since you started the team builder, I called a few friends," Scatman 16 typed.

"Have you got anything for us on this Canig character?" Bennie asked.

"Man, oh man. You seem to be able to pick the worst enemies, for sure," he typed back.

"So spill it all for me." Bennie showed uncharacteristic impatience.

"Don't get your panties all tied up in knots, huh. But maybe you should. This character should be offed by the guards just because he's such a slime ball," Scatman 16 opined.

At this point, Bennie was all eyes reading through the text messaging. "Just fucking tell me or I'll come down from this mountain and ring your neck!" he demanded.

"OK. Let me tell you. I'll list all the shit he's gotten into even from his jail cell."

"Get on with it."

"First, this is one first-class shit head. He don't care about nothing. Not you, not his mother. Get that straight."

"OK," Bennie feared this might take all night.

"Next, he was supposed to turn over all his assets to the feds when he went to jail as part of his plea bargain to avoid the death penalty. He didn't—by a long shot. The guys figure he has another two billion in hidden assets that they've found, *so far*. Shit, this guy is still loaded. Even the interest on that is enough to fight over."

"What? That was a condition of his imprisonment. He had to turn over all the assets he outright stole or embezzled." Bennie was pissed, now. *I should have killed him when I had him in my grasp. I had to clean my knife, anyway.*

"About a quarter of his wealth was recently diverted to a new account in the Cayman Islands. That's good and that's bad. The Cayman authorities are, on the surface, not allowed to pass along any financial information. But after all these years of looking at other people's money accumulate; greed gets the better of these guys. They can accept a seemingly insignificant amount to be liberal with their oversights. They can be bribed." Scatman 16 took a long time to continue.

"So what did you find out?" Bennie couldn't stand the wait.

"It's worse than you think. This prick seems to have hired at least two teams of three assassins each to 'deal with' all the people who put him in jail. He also wanted to bonus the first team to complete the mission. This includes the governor, sheriff, all of you and two people named Marion and Catherine." Scatman 16 paused.

"Jesus. The governor of New York State?" Bennie groaned as he typed. His fingers hammered the keyboard to the point the others in Will's house could have heard it in the next room.

"Yup. And the bonus is bigger than the original payments of a million dollars to each team. Shit man, you're fucked."

"How did he get out the information to arrange all this? He isn't allowed computer access, or a cell phone or even phone calls."

"Get this. His lawyer is arranging it all. And he's siphoning his one-third fee off the top."

"Do we know who the assassins are?" Bennie asked.

"No, just that one team is from South Africa, the other is from Germany. Top of the line in all ways."

"Send me everything you've got. The usual way. Encrypted." Bennie urged.

"Watch your back. We hear they've already got the sheriff. They think you're all country bumpkins, easy pickings. They might let their guard down, but not for long."

"We could call in reinforcements, if you think you need them," Biggie 23 chimed in.

"No way. We need quiet and seclusion, Biggie," Bennie answered. "By the way, have any of you guys figured out where we're holed up? I need to know how dark we need to be. If you guys are on to my location, maybe we need to move?"

"We can only narrow it down to the Lake Placid area," Biggie 23 wrote.

"If anyone figures out our location, call me at once. We'll evacuate. We can't protect against two teams of assassins. We'll also be looking for the sheriff. We might be more visible than I like."

"Will do. Watch your ass. I hear these guys attack from the rear." Scatman 16 signed off.

"This is Biggie 23. I'll call you immediately if it looks like you need to move. For now, just stay put. You can trace a person by his smoke when he moves, you know?" Bennie understood that all too well, having trailed multiple persons on multiple continents.

Bennie got offline and went to find Demian and call Will. He still didn't feel strong or able. He knew he would rally, but he hadn't felt that yet.

Demian paced around Will's office after Bennie filled him in on what his contacts had found out. From the windows, he looked out the side of the house, down the expanse towards the very small town of Jay. He had just connected with Albert, and they had listened on speakerphone as he detailed what he, his hackers and hired new age computer geeks had been able to find out. "Shit, man. There is a storm about to come down on you," Albert croaked and coughed.

"How is he doing it from jail?" Demian insisted.

"His fucking lawyer, we think. There's a real slimeball. It wouldn't be a waste of a nickel if someone put a round through his brain. For sure."

"Bennie just told me his hackers found two teams of assassins—one from Germany, the other from South Africa—gunning for us all including the governor of New York, too."

"That's what I mean. A real shit storm," he rattled again.

"Can you give us any more details? We have to know enough to protect ourselves."

"Yeah, well, I don't know. Even the federal witness protection people wouldn't want this detail." Albert filled him in on the rest of the information his people had gleaned. Essentially the same chatter that Bennie's hackers had heard. "I hear they have the sheriff and are holding him to be used later as a possible bargaining chip if needs be. So, for now, he's alive, at least."

"Thanks, Albert."

"Listen, send me the payment today. You're not likely to make another week."

"I will, you fuck." Demian slammed down the phone.

"Nothing good?" Jane asked.

"No."

"Anything that my group of hackers didn't find out?" Bennie asked.

"No."

"Demian, how did you make the acquaintance of Albert? Or maybe I don't want to know?" Jane asked.

"Jane, I wasn't always completely on the up and up. Albert goes way back to my father and, I think, my grandfather. They were 'in business' together, and I can detail all that, so he treats me with kid gloves. I never used any of his muscle, but I can call in favors regarding hard to get information from time to time."

"I guess I don't want to know. You're right." She sighed and looked downward.

"I only can promise you that, in the future, everything will be for the greater good. I want to run my life like that now. I know that's what you want me to do, as well."

"How do we get out of this mess?" Jane's words were pinched and quick.

"I don't know. I have to make a phone call, then we'll decide." Demian took out a leather address book and flipped through it. Jane wondered what other information might be in that book. Bennie left to get a long drink of water, hoping he'd feel better after that.

"No! He can't return my call sometime later!" Demian shouted into the phone. Jane shivered with the demanding, acid tone of his voice. "This is Demian Listing. The man who'll get you fired if you don't tell the governor who's on the line. Yeah, I'll be *pleased* to hold." He looked at Jane.

Jane just said, "Jesus, Demian, be nicer." She began to intuit the enormous power Demian wielded.

"Nicer doesn't get it done." He held on to the phone but took her hand with his other. "I know, I need to get through to the governor, and then I can revert to nicer. I want that, too."

"I know."

"Yes. Thank you for taking my call, Governor," he said into the phone.

"Demian, what are you up to now?" the governor asked.

"I have some bad news. You probably heard that Sheriff Todd has been abducted?" He paused. "Yes, well, we have information that two hit teams are gunning for all of us here who had a part in Canig's capture, and for you."

"What?"

"Alert your private security details to smother you. We hear these are top-of-the-line three-man teams. One from Germany, the other from South Africa. Both teams are offered a bonus to be the team to get it all done first. The bonus is over a million dollars. The original payment, you don't want to know."

"What the fuck? Who's behind all this? No, don't tell me—Gary Canig?"

"That's what my sources tell me. So, you need to cocoon up somewhere safe with all the security you can muster." Demian knew that wouldn't go over well. He knew the governor never shied away from controversy or a threat.

"Shit. This is an election year. I've got all kinds of events and fundraisers."

"All I know is that we have to be careful. Can you do anything about Canig in jail? Can you do anything about his lawyer who we think is the moneyman and arranging all this for him? And, we hear, so far, that Canig has another two *billion* dollars and counting that he hasn't turned over to the government—that was a condition of his imprisonment and lesser sentence, as I know you recall."

"Yeah. That's something I *can* do a lot about. I'll call my top people at the jail, haul in that lawyer and we'll have our investigators see if they can confirm that amount you just mentioned. We could use that money to plug some big holes in our budget. We will certainly get right on it."

"Good."

"How are you guys protecting yourself, and where are you?"

"Rather not say."

"Right. You shouldn't. You never know…."

"Right. I wanted to warn an old friend. Otherwise, we're going very dark here. And let your secretary know to put me right through if I need to call back. I'll let you know through other channels if there is anything else you need to know. And I'll let you know about how to collect the rest of Canig's loot—numbers of accounts and so forth."

"Jesus, Demian. Watch your back." Before the governor clicked off, Demian could hear him shout to his secretary to get his security team together.

"I can't believe you just called up the governor and spoke to him like that," Jane said, astonished.

"My father and grandfather go way back with the governor and his father, a prior governor. My family helped his family get elected, after all."

She rolled her eyes in amazement. *"After all."* Then she got a cold feeling in her back and neck. It seemed that there was a lot about Demian's past that didn't sit well with her. "Then, could you tell me what we're going to do?"

"I'll pull all of us together and we'll plan this out."

32

Bennie didn't know what to say or think. He felt better after the few hours he had needed to sleep on watch—more centered, resolute, more able to make a decision, and, he thought, back to his old self. He knew that some kind of change had come over him, but couldn't describe it to himself, much less the others.

Catherine came into the large living room with Marion. "How are you, Bennie?"

"I don't know. I was down the road watching out for us and I needed to sleep. I couldn't keep the watch or protect all of us. I needed to sleep so bad I couldn't stay awake. I called Will to take over for me. Now Will is out there and I'm here."

"Demian told us all about the two teams of assassins aiming for us," Marion said. "I hope we can protect ourselves. I don't know how such an evil thing could happen. And they've already kidnapped the sheriff." The old man shook his head. "The best thing I can do is to keep calm, let all of you do what you need to do, and stay here with Catherine and meditate. It stresses me that I need to do my practice under such extreme circumstances, though."

"Do you know what happened to me?" Bennie asked, almost whining. Immediately, he recoiled inwardly, having shown weakness to the others. Then he softened, knowing this had changed in him as well. Now he could show his vulnerabilities.

"Yes. I've seen it. It's a healing process. Catherine told me about the two healings she did for you. You were ready to move on to a more centered and accepting life. You let go of your need for the high stress and confrontation of a combatant's life. It was like letting the air out of a balloon—or should I say, popping the balloon. Your drive faltered. You needed rest. You're recovering now, though. You've made some pretty big changes and they'll take some time to integrate."

"*That's* what all that was?" Bennie was surprised that he could have been so strongly affected by what Catherine had done for him—it seemed so gentle. After so many years of being a warrior with unquestioned resolve to do what he was ordered to do, he felt changed.

"Yes."

"Am I safe to do things, like take a watch and protect us?"

"Yes. You just got rattled around. This adjustment would have been smoother for you if this crisis hadn't popped up at precisely this time," Catherine replied.

Bennie jumped up, thanked them both, and went to find Demian.

"I don't know what will happen," Catherine said to Marion, concerned that they had all become targets.

"We never know. But I do know that we'll continue to meditate, try to heal the situation and continue to be the quiet people that we are," Marion answered.

Gunner entered the room and shook both of their hands. "I know this is disruptive to you, to be taken from your home and then be threatened by the assassins. You only tried to do the right thing helping Elisabeth. And look what it got you."

"Don't be worried about it," Marion said.

"I think of it as being on vacation, only an exciting one." Catherine smiled.

Gunner thought to himself that they must have been through much worse situations.

Demian and Bennie walked in.

"Well, we all know what's happening, here. We all need to protect ourselves. Gary Canig continues to be an evil force in the world. We have our sources looking out for us and Will, Bennie and I are taking shifts guarding the road up the mountain," Demian announced.

"What should we all do in the meantime?" Jane asked from behind them.

"Just keep calm and wait. I have the governor and his people on it too," he answered.

"Marion and I will do that and cook and keep the place up," Catherine added.

"I want to show everyone here a special addition to the house. I planned it for the time when survivalists were popular. Come with me, everyone. The only one who knows about this is Will, and Mason, of course. He built it." Demian led everyone to the basement. He went over to a plain-looking cement wall, reached to a beam overhead, pulled a lever and the wall moved. Inside was a shelter, with chairs, cots, water filtration system, generator, computers with satellite phones, blankets, clothes and many closets lining a whole wall.

"Jesus, Demian!" Jane sighed.

"I never expected this would be necessary. It's self-contained for a month for ten people. I hope we all get along, here. Otherwise, it's likely to be stuffy," Demian said in a put-on British accent, raising his nose haughtily.

"This is perfectly hidden. Amazing, really," Catherine said. "I couldn't see any seams, hinges or other giveaways. And there's no structure above it. It must be all underground?"

"Yes. And it's not on any builder's plans, either. Perfectly invisible and no one has any information that it's here." Demian smiled. "We don't think they're on to us yet, but if we give the word, get right down here. Will and I are also going to hide the cars so it looks like everyone sneaked off or hiked out of here." Demian motioned to Will to show the others the cooking supplies, toiletries, small shower and toilet and survival foods.

Later in the day, Gunner pulled Demian to the side. They were upstairs in Will's office. "I had another meditation. I saw a stone was loose in the large stack of stones, at the Beaver Dams. When I went there to investigate, a stone at eye-level easily swung out from the rest. It was the stone I saw in the meditation. The pyramid was built to accommodate removing only the one without the stones above it falling down. Guess what? It had another map engraved of the whole region. I took a few pictures of it with my phone."

They looked over the pictures, and Demian said, "No distortion, here. This is a really good map of the region. Mountains, streams and proportions are all really good. Were there any other loose stones?"

"Not that I could find."

"What do you think this could mean?" Demian clearly remembered the prior stone engravings. This was created, at great pains, by the same engraver and must have been done for some important reason.

"I don't know. It's not like the other maps on the stones. And before we took the stone out, the engraving was not visible," Gunner replied.

"Well, another mystery on this mountain. If we survive long enough, maybe we can figure it out."

Gunner got a phone call. He saw the caller was Dr. Ardane. "Yeah?"

"Gunner?" Dr. Ardane started.

"Yeah."

"I've got news that's not good. Madison was likely poisoned with a new combination of amphetamines and street drugs. The toxicology center docs and the police have not seen anything like it. Where is she?" Dr. Ardane answered.

"At home, close to where we are now."

"Well, she's likely all right, and the drugs will work their way out of her system, but we don't know how she could have gotten those drugs into her system in the first place. The police want to question her. I want to see her and make sure she's OK."

"You can't. We're in the middle of a real shit storm up here. I'll go talk to her. I hope that accounts for her florid psychosis. And that it'll resolve?"

"As far as the toxicology guys know, it should. I really would like to see her, though. I'm concerned and want to know that she's all right." Dr. Ardane had an uncharacteristic, pleading tone in his voice. He was not used to asking for anything. Gunner thought that he had ruled his small part of the world in the same authoritarian manner that Demian had ruled his.

"Can't. We don't want you tied up in all this. I have to get off the phone. I'll see her and keep in touch." Gunner abruptly hit the disconnect button, muttering under his breath.

Demian had heard the two talk on speakerphone. "Shit—was that the work of the assassins?"

"I don't know, but it started with the PTSD about a week ago. Then she got floridly paranoid, didn't trust anyone and had to be admitted to the neurosurgical ICU after what I thought could have been a stroke. She had double the toxic dose of caffeine in her bloodstream. That, alone, could have killed her. We didn't know about the other drugs in her system until now."

Demian swore an impressive stream of expletives.

"Yeah. And now I've got to go tell a paranoid woman that she *was* drugged or had an attempted poisoning? Life is good, at times, I guess." Sarcasm dripped from Gunner's voice.

"At least you have an answer. Maybe you could phrase it like that. She was not crazy, but she was reasonable to feel people were out to get her." His expression clouded. "But listen, maybe Mason and the kids are at risk too? We don't know anything about how the drugs were introduced. And was Canig a part of all of this? Is that the work of his assassins? Would they dare to try to poison a whole family?"

"Shit. We'll get right over there."

"Wait." Demian flipped open his phone and dialed the police. The deputy answered, said he didn't have anything new and finally stopped talking long enough to have Demian break in. "Call Dr. Ardane. There's a new poison combination that he found used on Madison Gregg. He'll tell you all about it. Just tell him I told you to call. See if Interpol has any information about it being used in Germany or South Africa. Just do it. Get back to me only online now. We're going dark here. Very dark." He listened for a few seconds. "Just call Dr. Ardane and do it now. If you need help, call the state police. The governor knows all about it. Mention my name." He turned off his phone and took out the battery.

"Let's go."

"Yeah. Can't wait."

33

Gunner and Demian walked the short distance to Madison and Mason's house. The intervening lawn measured 300 yards by 100 yards. While Will meticulously mowed this area with his large John Deere tractor, he admitted that he liked driving the tractor more than having perfectly manicured lawns. On many occasions, when Ali helped to drive the large tractor, he left tufts of grass unmowed, going to seed, and gouged-out grooves when the corners were taken too quickly. The two men needed to dodge these scoured-out channels or risk twisting an ankle.

They finally creaked up the front steps of Madison's farm-style house and knocked on the front door. Curtains parted in the front windows, and the door slowly opened. "Come in."

The two men entered the front door to the odor of cookies baking. Gunner relaxed, realizing that baking meant she was, at least, somewhat less agitated. "We have very important news," Demian blurted out.

"What?" Madison questioned. Her mood was uninterpretable.

"Actually, a lot of things. Can we sit? And is anyone else around?" Gunner asked.

"No one else is here, right now. I expect them all back shortly." She raised her eyebrows questioningly.

"Well, we'll start at the beginning. Demian already knows about all of this because it affects us all."

Now she was pissed. She made a shushing sound with her lips, like she was about to swear, but didn't.

"We got the lab reports back. They think you were drugged or poisoned," Demian blurted out.

Now she did swear, in several unrelated languages. "What? How? Who would have done such a thing?"

"All we know is that the poison control center in Albany found amphetamines and blood levels of a new designer street drug in your bloodstream. It could have combined with the huge levels of caffeine to make you have that stroke-like temporary paralysis." Gunner waited a minute to judge how Madison was taking the news.

"What the fuck?" she said reflexively.

"That's what we want to know," Demian interjected.

"Madison, how do you feel now?" Gunner asked with his most concerned expression and body language.

"I did feel a lot better until you told me that, but I was *poisoned?*" She couldn't believe it.

"Yeah, and we need to know how and by whom," Demian answered quickly. "We have other news. Sheriff Todd Wilkins was apparently abducted. And the question is whether the same group has poisoned you? We don't know. But we need to make sure you're safe. And the thing is that the poison could have affected your family. Are they all alright?" Demian let that news settle in.

"What the *fuck*?" she repeated.

"Think back. Is there anything different about your diet? Anything new? Any gifts that involved eating or drinking? Anything?" Demian scowled. Gunner looked expectantly.

"There's nothing that isn't completely normal and everyday." Her eyes darted around her house. She scanned the rooms, went into the kitchen and entryway to look further and came back to sit down. "I don't see anything different here that's edible or drinkable."

"How about at the healing center?" Gunner asked. "Gifts, or even candies, or anything? Did you drink anything with anyone you don't know around?"

"Is the rest of your family all right?" Demian asked again.

"As far as I know…."

"How are you feeling now?" Gunner repeated.

"I was all right, I thought, until all this. I did slow down the caffeine and I was glad I had the painkillers Dr. Ardane prescribed for the withdrawal headaches. They helped. Now, I'm not paranoid, but *I fucking should be!*" Madison started to pace, looked out her windows from behind the drapes and continued to swear under her breath.

"I have even more disturbing news. Gary Canig has hired two teams of hit men to attack the governor, all of us and Marion and Catherine. We've heard it from two sources of online hackers—friends of mine and friends of Bennie. We're sure it's true," Demian said.

At this point, Gunner could see Madison might explode. Her eyes opened widely and got red and bloodshot. Her fists clenched and her chest tightened. Gunner was afraid the top of her head would blow off. "Madison, please breathe. Calm down. We're here to help and keep you safe," Gunner was pleading, now.

"We'll take you and your family to Will's, to the shelter no one knows about in the basement. We can hide there as the police do their jobs." Demian offered. "Marion and Catherine are there now. Bennie and Will and I are covering the road up the mountain. We'll protect you and your family."

"That's bullshit! How is Canig doing all of this? He ruined Elisabeth's life. He'll kill us all, I know it!"

"The governor has already had the state police arrest Canig's lawyer. We're giving over the numbers to accounts that Canig hasn't surrendered to the state like he was supposed to, as a part of his plea agreement. They'll seize those accounts. The commissioner of prisons is on Canig in jail. We're getting it done. We just need to keep you safe for the near future until it's all handled." Demian offered his hand to her.

Madison totally surprised both of them when she accepted it and said, "I've got to get things together for everyone to stay over there. I'll call Mason and get them back here right now. It's time I started to trust and let you take care of this bastard for good."

Within the hour, Madison, Mason and the kids had packed and moved over to Will's house. They investigated the safe room and settled into a large upstairs bedroom, ready in case they needed to evacuate to the cellar.

32

John and Elisabeth drove through northern Vermont. They had had time to explore the region when they had evaded capture by Gary Canig. Demian, Will, Bennie and Sheriff Todd Wilkins had lured the rogue CIA agent to the driveway in front of Will's house and arrested him. Demian had shot him to emphasize the point that he was, indeed, overwhelmed and should surrender. Having been shot in the ear did convince him. Sheriff Todd had then locked him up in the Lake Placid jail. Demian had arranged with the governor himself that the Lake Placid sheriff should maintain control of the prisoner until the courts could complete their findings. This prevented the CIA from taking Canig into their custody to protect him from prosecution.

The couple drove north to the town of Stowe. They stopped at the Trapp Family Lodge and rented the largest available suite. Well-schooled in the art of leaving no traces, they paid cash, used a new computer, bought burner phones and did not use credit cards or ATMs. They spoke to the desk captain about needing absolute privacy to avoid any of their staff finding them—they "needed their rest after a busy sales season. This short respite would allow them to reorient themselves and design new projects." A fresh hundred-dollar bill ensured they would not be disturbed.

With the confidence that the front desk staff would keep their anonymity, they rested in their suite. "You know? I think we can use this time to help the others. We shouldn't just be hiding, we should be finding Todd's kidnappers, or the people after the rest of us," John said to Elisabeth.

"Yeah? Like what? How do we help and not get kidnapped or killed ourselves?"

"Why don't we go on the offensive? Why don't we take the game to them? They would never expect it from people in hiding." John looked like he might enjoy the idea of a game of cat and mouse, with the mouse holding a bazooka.

"No way. Keep us out of it. You know how Canig ruined ten years of my life?" she demanded.

John was well aware that Canig had set Elisabeth up to take the fall for the theft of millions of dollars from an international cartel. From that point on, she had been hunted, could not get a regular job, slipped into a life of prostitution to sustain herself and avoided all meaningful contact with anyone. She stopped living except to protect herself. But this was also the way that John and she had become acquainted—she had propositioned him, he'd accepted and they'd developed an ongoing Tuesday morning and late Thursday evening "engagement." These meetings had not varied over two years. Then, when John sensed that he was being targeted, he'd asked Elisabeth to help him evade his pursuers. They'd traveled as they did now—very low on the radar, managing to evade capture.

"Yeah, but we owe Demian, Madison and the others. Maybe we could find out what the kidnappers are up to? I have my sources as well, you know," John pleaded.

"I just can't be hunted like I was before. We have to stay very dark. The only things we can do will be to get online with the new computers, use our burner phones and pay cash. We also need to move every two days at least. Your contacts can get back together with you online." She took a deep breath. "I can't be hunted again. I can't go back to that very dark place. You know that. I'll die." She started to sob.

"You know how much I love you. I'll do anything for you. You know that. I gave up my practice in the city for you. I'll do it all for you," he pleaded. He thought, to himself, before his relationship with her, he would never have pleaded for anything. Ever. He would never have given up anything for anyone else.

"Just make sure we'll be safe. I can't put myself or you in the line of fire." She made a fist with one hand and struck the center of her other palm.

"OK. Let me start with my old employees?"

She only nodded in response. Then she got up, undressed and went to lie down.

"Listen, Eddie. I'm on a burner phone. I'll get in touch the old way. Wait for it." He closed the burner phone, got out his new computer, signed on with a new email account and sent an email. In it, he listed everything he wanted Eddie to do and what Eddie could expect for payment. He detailed everything Demian had found out and further instructions. Shortly thereafter, John got the ping of an incoming email. He scanned it, approved it and the ball was rolling. He had regained some of the old feeling of being in control, being in power and paying for his underlings to do some very heavy lifting.

He crawled into the large bed and held Elisabeth until she stopped shivering.

Several hours after that, they were awakened by another ping. John opened his computer and received a lengthy response detailing Eddie's email titled, "BAD NEWS!"

"Jesus, boss. You've got two top-notch teams after everyone there who had anything to do with this Canig's capture. Go deep and stay there. Keep going. We do have some ideas, though," he wrote. "First: leave no paper trail. These guys are good, and they could find you. Both of your pictures were all over the newspapers getting married and all. Avoid anything to do with facial recognition—public safety cameras, ATM cameras, traffic cameras or anything else."

John and Elisabeth read the long message together. "Guess I'll go to a blonde, frumpy ex-hippie, flower child. The woods are full of them up here. I'll blend right in."

"Yeah. I'll slump, grow a beard, beat up some jeans and sweatshirts 'n go bohemian," John added. "I happen to have brought that New York Yankees baseball hat with the sweat stains around the brim. I'll wear it low on my face anywhere there might be street cameras."

"That's what's lucky about being way up north—very few cameras and very few eyes on them. But you're right. We both have to change our appearance."

They continued reading. "Second: carry any piece you can get your hands on." John sighed, regretting his refusal of Demian's offer of a pistol.

"Third: I'll spend whatever we need to get more information. We'll figure this out and put a plan in place to intercept the teams. We've got your back. We all owe you that much." The email concluded without signing off.

"OK. It's you and me. I'll take good care of you," he said as he held Elisabeth in his arms.

"Yeah. I know. We'll be smart. We have to leave tonight, though." She went to shower and get ready to drive on. "We'll stop at the Wal-Mart to get the disguise materials and anything else we need. How about camping at national parks?"

"What? I've never slept outdoors in my life and wouldn't know where to plug in the coffee maker and whatnot." He laughed, but Elisabeth got the message.

"That's *exactly* why we'll go camping. Trust *me* this time. No one would ever expect *you* to go camping or have anything else to do with the great outdoors."

"I have to let Demian know that we're on it too. I'll email him on a secure account that he uses for his more delicate work. He told me about it the other day at the office."

35

"Uncle Demian? Did Gunner tell you about the new map we found at the Beaver Dams? Did you figure out what it means?" Deborah asked as the group gathered for dinner.

"Uh, no. We have been busy with a lot of other important things," Demian answered as he passed a large bowl of salad to his left. He had asked if anyone had a preference as to the direction. None had, so he declared to the left. This prevented a free-for-all passing back and forth across the wide table.

"We took pictures of the new map and the two other maps. Ali and I have been looking at them and trying to figure them out."

"That's great. Everyone loves a puzzle," Jane said.

Deborah moaned at the implication that this was just a childish game. "I mean we've been studying them and think we know something important about the new map." She let the adults know she had caught the innuendo that she was childish.

"What did you find?" Gunner showed genuine enthusiasm. "In the first place, I should say that Deborah is the one who found the map. I wasn't looking carefully enough at the stone and would have missed the fact that there was a map completely."

"So you found it?" Demian asked her.

"Well, I had the idea to wash the bottom of the rock that Gunner saw was loose in his meditation and look if there was something there or not."

"Well, then you do have a connection with the stacks and maps. Go ahead. Tell us what you're thinking," Demian urged.

"Ali and I went over all the pictures. We think the same person engraved all of the stones. They're beautiful in their own right. They have the same style of using small dots to make a picture—like on a dollar bill." She ate a bite of potato salad, swallowed as the adults waited and continued. "We saw the first two maps were part of a puzzle and needed to be superimposed on each other to solve the riddle. That was *really* obvious." More food was consumed. "We found the new map on the underside of a large stone about six feet off the ground. It was positioned higher in the stack, so we think it's more important than the other two maps."

"Makes sense," Jane added, hoping to sound agreeable to the younger girl she had just offended.

"It was hard to see, at first. Then we compared it to Google maps, paper maps that my Dad still has around and Uncle Demian's large New York State map of the Adirondack Park. The park was designated in the early 1900s—about a hundred years ago. Since then, no new large roads have been constructed, especially way up at the Beaver Dams."

Gunner anxiously butted in. "Tell us what you found?"

"We think that map has a trail on it. It's not a road. It's not a river. It's a trail that would make sense to someone on foot or on horseback or with wagons. It's not on any other map or satellite image we've seen. And we don't think this trail is something you could know was there from studying another map. You'd have to walk the land; then it would make sense." She finally stopped talking long enough to eat again.

"Yeah. Like when we go hiking, Uncle Gunner. We don't go in a straight line. We follow a stream or go around trees, like that," Ali added.

"Why don't you kids go upstairs and copy out the pictures on my enlarging copier and we can look at those after dinner, after the table is cleared?" Will smiled broadly at the two kids. "I want to see where this trail goes and where it passes through. It might just be very handy to know."

The kids ran upstairs and shuffled around.

"Jeesh, out of the mouth of babes," Gunner joked.

36

Bennie and Demian met after dinner in the large study. "Bennie, how are you?"

"I'm good, now. I saw Catherine and Marion, and they did their magic for me again."

"Yeah?"

"They did acupuncture and reiki. They also explained that after the two treatments I recently had from Catherine, I might have had a reaction like that, adjusting to the treatments." Bennie didn't feel he made himself clear. He could see Demian's questioning look. "They both said that I'm fine. I asked them specifically about the tiredness—it's completely gone now. They told me it wouldn't come back—that I am good to do anything I need to do. I want to go back on watch and relieve Will. He's been out there for the whole day. I'd feel safer if he were here with everyone else, too."

"Do you really feel strong? Can you defend us with all means?" Demian's eyes pierced Bennie's.

"Yes. I do. And yes, I can." Bennie looked resolute.

Demian heard no equivocation. "What is it about Marion and Catherine? I've never met anyone like them," he asked. "I saw Marion only three times, and he changed my life. I completely gave up making money for money's sake and now only look at deals that are beneficial to all parties involved and the earth itself. I won't use anyone or anything just to make a buck." Demian looked off in the distance. "Yeah. If they say you're OK now, go and relieve Will. Call in every two or three hours. I've got to check emails and the deputies and see what's new. I'll also call the governor and his people."

Bennie put on his camo and left to pick up the rifle, pistol and other gear, stored outside in a locked locker hidden by wood in the woodshed. He disappeared almost immediately walking down the long driveway, his clothing blending in so well. But it was also his style of walking—almost so slow he didn't move at all. Demian watched and was surprised and reassured to see him vanish so quickly while he would have been plainly visible dressed in usual clothes or being reckless with his movements. Bennie had become cat-like— a predator. He turned on his computer, signed on to his secret accounts and read through John's message. He knew John and Elisabeth would be safe and welcomed any help John might be able to arrange.

Madison, Mason and the kids played a game of Scrabble in the upstairs bedroom they had occupied. The father-daughter duo had clearly dominated the board, making Madison frustrated. Ali walked away from the rest of his family and covered his head with a pillow, lying on the bed. He had had enough.

Catherine knocked and entered. "How is everyone?"

"We're all good. Except Ali and I have been slaughtered at Scrabble," Madison answered.

"Marion and I wanted to talk with you if we could. If you're not too busy?" Catherine looked straight into Madison's eyes leaving no room for discussion.

"I guess we can't let them continue to demolish us, can we?" she asked Ali. He only groaned in response.

They walked downstairs to a small room sequestered off the living room with French doors. Marion waited for them, having finished setting up a massage table. While Madison sat on the table, Marion and Catherine waited for her to start.

"I didn't mean to offend you by not telling you how bad I felt. I was too embarrassed to tell you that I got worse each day. I couldn't meditate, concentrate or even do my work. I was so stressed out." She looked bewildered.

"We know. We could feel the stress. Demian filled us in on everything, too," Marion replied.

"Jesus, does everybody know?" Her eyes teared. She couldn't meet their gaze.

"You can always come to us with anything. Do you want to talk about all this, or do you want us just to do our work? We won't pry if you don't want us to," Catherine said.

"God. If you could only help me feel like I did before Demian shot that awful man in our driveway. That would be good."

"Do you or the police know anything more about you being poisoned?" Marion asked.

"Not that Demian has told me. He's being very protective of me and won't tell me because he doesn't want me to worry all the more. Mason and the kids can't figure out how it was done. Nobody accepted any strange food or drinks. We didn't get anything edible in the mail. Nothing new or different at the healing center. We can't figure it out."

"Tell us what you want to, or just lie down and we'll work." Marion motioned to the massage table.

Madison looked quickly over her shoulder, to make sure they were alone. "I just don't know how I could have gotten so out of control. I was paranoid, worried about the kids, angrier than I've ever been, unable to work. I was a real wreck." She sobbed. "Now I'm not quite so bad, but I'm not good, either. I'm still angry and overprotective. I don't trust anyone but you two and Mason."

"You were poisoned," Marion said matter-of-factly as if he said the sky was blue.

"I wasn't good even before that. It started right after Demian shot that creep. Now, even in jail, that devil's been able to contract two teams of hit men to kill us all—you included."

"We have to trust Demian, the police and all the others. They're good men." Catherine was trying to soothe Madison.

"Please lie down. We'll start right here. From this moment forward, let yourself trust people around you. You don't have any responsibilities anywhere else, right now. Remember back to a time when things were easy for you— when you trusted yourself, the land, the mountains, Mason, the kids and everyone and everything else." He started to speak more slowly and emphasized the words "easy" and "trusted."

"Yes. Just float. If your eyes are tired, they might close on their own."

Catherine covered her with a sheet and put a pillow under her head and knees. "Are you warm enough?"

"Yes. Thanks," Madison answered slowly. Her eyes closed. The wrinkles around her eyes softened. Her forehead smoothed out.

Marion grasped her left hand as if he wanted to shake it. He checked those pulses, then moved to her right hand. He stared at her skin and sniffed the air around her. "Madison, may I do a healing for you?"

He saw a faint flicker of a smile at the corners of her mouth.

Catherine sat on a chair at the side of the table and placed her right hand on her heart and her left hand on Madison's shoulder. "We're never alone. We have the spirits and each other to watch over us. I envision a glowing ball of universal energy that shines on us. There are also the discarnate beings who make all the little things happen to enrich our lives as we muddle along." Her voice had become softer.

Marion used his smallest needles' and put one needle just above her chin, one on each side of her jaw, near her ears and one in each palm. He left the needles in, occasionally turning them slightly, back and forth.

Catherine could see a cloudy, brown fog rise off Madison's body and float above her blanket. She opened the window to let the fog clear.

Then, Marion took those needles out and placed a single needle on the inside of her left instep and one on the inside of her right forearm, near the wrist.

Catherine moved her chair to the head of the table, slipped her hands under Madison's head and waited. In about a minute, she felt a shift, then a circular motion. This made the shape of a spiral and Madison's head flexed and turned in wider and wider motions until this, too, quieted. Catherine allowed Madison's head to rest on the table again. The room smelled sweeter and felt a little cooler. Marion closed the window.

Marion removed the needles, knowing Madison would arouse herself in her own time. In a few minutes, her eyes opened.

"I feel lighter, like a heavy weight was lifted off me." She looked directly in Marion's eyes for the first time that evening. He smiled, knowing the demons that had plagued her had left.

"Yes," he replied.

"What was all that?" Madison asked.

"Do you want to know the technicalities? Or should I tell you a story to help you understand?" he asked.

"Please. Tell me a story. You've told me so many over the years. They've always helped, even if I didn't get the whole meaning behind them," she answered. Her voice sounded calmer and stronger.

There was a long pause. "Well," Marion started. "About a hundred and fifty years ago, there was a very good physician. He was a researcher, too. He lived and worked in Germany, where the best microscopes had been invented and then continually improved over the centuries. He was brilliant and started looking at everything he could imagine microscopically. To make a very long story short, he discovered that bacteria caused skin infections. This was way before any notion of viruses."

Catherine wondered where this was going. She had developed trust in Marion's methods and studied with him for years. She listened; Marion never stopped amazing her.

"After that time, many other doctors concluded that other diseases were the result of infections, as well. Prior to this, rogue demons or spirits were thought to attack and be the cause of all illnesses. These could also have been unhappy ancestor spirits who attempted to coerce a person to do what the spirits wanted. But before this physician made his discoveries, it all boiled down to the fact that you deserved your fate based on what you did or did not do."

Madison's eyes closed again.

"Yes, that's right." Marion waited.

Catherine wondered what he meant until she noticed that Madison was hypnotized.

"So, our modern interpretation of why we feel ill is that a bacteria or virus has infected us. It's not our fault that we might become ill. But, before the time of this physician, all illnesses were thought to originate from spirit attacks." He paused to let Madison take a couple of breaths. "Sometimes we do still suffer from collective cultural Karma. We need to atone for all of our societies' misdeeds. It's nothing personal. I just freed you from that Karmic debt. Now you can rest, feel freed from worry, anxiety and stress. Just understand that you were under attack, like they thought in the old days."

Madison took in a deep breath and let it out. Her muscles relaxed into the massage table cushions. Her hands, balled up only moments earlier, opened and relaxed. Marion and Catherine let her rest until she awakened fully.

37

Deborah finally got the copier and enlarger to work in Will's office. She laughed that Demian had repeatedly told her he could never manage that feat. She carefully inspected the maps she printed out from her cell phone's camera. It showed what she had suspected and talked about with Ali. While she ran to find Demian, she remembered him joking that he couldn't figure out how the pictures got out of the camera, all the way to the printer, either.

"You've got to see this. It's really, *really* important, we think. The maps clearly show a new trail. I had to look at the photos again and make sure that the thing we saw wasn't just an imperfection or crack in the stone—it wasn't."

"OK. Slow down. Let me look it all over." Demian came from the kitchen carrying two mugs of coffee. "Bring them all into the fireplace room. Jane and I are resting in there."

"'Sgo!"

Demian chuckled at her youthful enthusiasm, walked into the small room and gave the coffee to Jane. He apologized as he switched on the larger overhead light. Jane blinked until her eyes adjusted.

"Hi, Deborah," she said.

"We wanted to show you the pictures of the map I found. Well, I was with Gunner at the time, and I wouldn't have been there at all if I hadn't gone up there with him. But still, I told him to look at the stone he removed. He wouldn't have thought of it, I'm sure."

"So this really is your find. You should take the credit." Demian looked resolute.

"You *should*," Jane echoed.

"After Ali and I enlarged the maps, it's even more apparent." They unfolded the large paper over the coffee table. Jane wisely moved the mugs out of the way of the excited pre-teen. "See. The map is actually perfect. All the mountains are there and right where they should be. See. There's the Beaver Dams area. It even has the two stone stacks." They went silent as they compared what they knew of the position of the geographic details of the mountains and Beaver Dams to the map and ticked off the features of the map.

"As far as I can see, you're right." Demian gave a very approving smile.

"Good job," Jane added.

"Yeah. But look at this black line here. It's not just a crack in the stone. That's what Ali thought, at first."

The adults followed it with their fingers.

"We compared the line to an old topographical map my father had. This runs along a clear line of elevation, like a trail would."

"Yup. It does," Demian said, approvingly.

"It also dodges bends in the stream and around the beaver pond," Deborah continued.

"Yup." Demian's voice got higher.

"It also looks out over gullies. It keeps clear lines of vantage on all the surroundings."

"Yes! It does!" His excitement mounted.

"So it's a trail." Deborah had baited the hook for Demian. "So why is it on the map, do you think? Why was it so important to engrave this? No one travels up that high, to the Beaver Dams. It's way too remote and difficult to get there. And, no one stacks two stone pyramids for no apparent reason without bulldozers."

"It might have been their escape route," he concluded.

"Where does it end up?" Jane asked as her eyes followed the line.

Taking out another enlargement, Deborah answered, "On the other side of Death Mountain."

"I never knew about such a trail. I've climbed parts of the far side of Death—the long, hard, unbelievable side—too many times. No one knew about the easier trail. Gunner and Dr. Crandall came over that mountain, straight up the top, the first time they came to the old camp—before you were born. I'm sure they would have liked to have known about this trail."

"Could the trail be more important than that? I mean an alternate route, that's all?" Jane thought out loud.

Demian had to conclude that made sense. "What do you think, Deborah?"

"Well, we don't know. But it must have been important to them. That's for sure. And Ali and I have really been thinking about it, too." She caught a glance shared by the adults and knew they wanted to share some alone time. "We'll keep working on it. It's a real puzzle, all right. Not your obvious Scrabble game, for sure." She got up, turned off the overhead light and left the room.

Demian could see the glow of the fire reflecting in Jane's eyes. "She's a great kid, don't you think?" he asked.

"Yup. I hope she's forgiven me for speaking to her as a child," she answered.

"I'm sure she has. Why don't we enjoy our coffee? I've mixed in a few special flavorings—a hint of this and that. No alcohol. We need to be sharp."

They rested until Jane fell asleep. Demian got up, covered her with a blanket, left the room to go get on the secure computer and get filled in on where the police were in their investigations. He touched in with Albert, Will and Bennie. After that, he allowed himself only three hours of sleep—full of dreams of maps, chases, horses and police.

38

Passing through Berlin, New Hampshire, John and Elisabeth saw an old, weathered sign with an arrow pointing to a hunting camp with cabins. "What do you think? That's a compromise that we can live with? It's not camping with a tent, but it is rustic enough looking." John hoped to do anything to avoid sleeping on the ground.

"OK. We can break you into camping with staying in a cabin." She yawned the tired sigh of someone wanting to get off the road and rest for the night.

"Good. Let's drive up there and have a look."

The road quickly turned into rough gravel and then dirt. It sloped up sharply and climbed to the top of a mountain. John remarked that this might be just like the Jay Mountain hunting camp—if it were more rustic and higher up, farther away from the town.

"Will this do?" he asked Elisabeth.

"Yeah, at least for the night."

They paid cash, found their cabin in the sparse light of a single street lamp overlooking the single lane of parking spaces and settled in. John had asked for the furthest of the one story, log, single-room brown structures. They reminded him of Monopoly houses. But it did serve them well to be on the end of the row. They could hear anyone driving up to the camps and would have time to retreat out the back if the need arose.

"Yeah. A real Ritz, don't you think?" he asked her.

"Why don't you quit bitching? I couldn't drive much longer. This is perfect at least for the night," she chided.

They settled in and went to sleep quickly.

In the morning, they walked to the "office" to see about breakfast. The larger room opening off the business desk led to a dining room where a simple breakfast of pancakes, eggs, bacon, ham, juice and coffee had been prepared by the owner, chief cook and all-around maid and grounds keeper—there were no other employees. The few locals who came for the breakfast called him Brud. Elisabeth later found out that Brud was short for brother—a sign of affection used in northern New Hampshire.

"You folks got in late last night and you and I didn't have time to get acquainted. We all need more rest as we get on, don't you think?" The man looked to be in his eighties, at least.

"Well, we're glad we saw your sign in Berlin and found you," John replied in his most sociable voice.

"We, around here, pronounce that Berlin—rhymes with Merlyn the Magician. Not like the city in Germany."

"Sorry. See how new we are here?" Elisabeth joked.

"Will you folks be wanting the *special* breakfast? It's the only one on the menu." Brud laughed.

"Then I guess that's what we'll have. We'll both be glad to have it. The cool mountain air is invigorating and makes us hungry, too." John picked up a newspaper full of the local wedding announcements, police reports of drunk drivers, obituaries and advertisements—quaint, old-fashioned news—interesting to read, definitely not world-shaking.

Elisabeth had followed Brud to the coffee carafe and came back to the square table covered by a plastic red and white plaid tablecloth carrying two steaming mugs. She wondered if Norman Rockwell himself would wander in and sit down. "Here. This'll wake you up. Just like the real strong stuff I grew up on."

"Jesus." John took only a sip and found it very hot and very strong.

"How long'll you all be stayin'?" Brud asked. John got the idea it was more than passing curiosity.

"Well, we don't know. You aren't overly busy, are you? We don't have to vacate for other customers, do we?" John responded.

"Not until hunting season. Then I'll be full up for six weeks. I guide for the people who have to use wheelchairs and such. I can still get them close enough to deer—they love it. We hunters up here think that hunting is about eating the meat, sharing time in the woods *and* about charity. We give all we can to food banks. But we also care for our neighbors and less lucky friends who need extra special help to get to the great outdoors. They get to experience the woods and flora and fauna around here. They get to be treated like they're able to do things and are important." By this time, Brud had seated himself at their table and had their full attention.

"You know, that's great. I hear that a lot of organizations are doing things like that for the wounded warriors and disabled children and other groups. I haven't considered it myself because I'm a city slicker through and through. I haven't been in the woods much myself," John admitted.

"No time like the present, I figure." Brud took a long drink of his coffee. "I'll get your breakfast." He disappeared into the kitchen. The aromas coming from that direction enlivened their appetites.

"I like him." John smiled.

"People like him are what the north areas are full of. Honest, hard-working people who look out for their neighbors and those a little less fortunate. They live off the land, try to do right and get by. They don't ask for anything more."

The elderly gentleman returned to the table. "If you folks are up for it, I'll take you on a walking tour of the woods above here. I need to check trail cameras to figure out some hunts for my guests, and you two can come along." John and Elisabeth nodded quickly.

"We need to check in with our friends online, though. Is there any wi-fi around here?"

Brud laughed until he had to catch his breath. "I got me one of those things. It's still in the box. If you can hook her up, you can use her. I was waiting for a kid to come along and help me with it. I always have to have some neighbor kid help me get those new things working. I'd rather be in the woods or the kitchen than fiddling with wires and connecting computers—all that is just fussing with electrons, after all."

"Well, I would be glad to get it all together and working for you after breakfast. Just tell me where you want it set up," John offered. He felt he would like to do the small project for his new acquaintance.

"I'll get out the box, and you can set it up in the corner on the stand next to the jukebox. I'll give you a few quarters to spin some records to pass the time while you're doing it."

John looked at the ancient jukebox and saw that it, indeed, was full of old 45s, arranged in a circle. The mechanical arms that selected the correct record and played them in any order fascinated him. *The younger generation doesn't hold a candle to this engineering*, he thought to himself.

They spent an hour hearing Brud tell stories of the area and hunters who stayed at the camps, laughing the whole time. "We'll be right back to set up that wi-fi for you," Elisabeth promised.

"I like him. He's a genuinely kind man who does good work and tries to do something for his fellow Berliners. I like him," John restated.

"Me too." She paused for a minute. "You know, this is so far off the beaten path, I'm confident we're safe here. I can't imagine international hit men would stray this far from the targets to find us. Why don't we stay here for the foreseeable future, until the mess is sorted out?"

"I agree. It will be fun to hang here and help Brud, get online and organize our friends from the city to see what we can do. I can't help but think about how different Brud is than any other character that I've met in the city. It would be really nice to get to know him better. I can see why they call him brother," John said.

They changed and brought their new computer to the office and dining room. While John set up the wi-fi, Elisabeth set up their new computer with passwords, new emails, and security systems. They used the computer to test the wi-fi and found it slow, but functional. Brud thanked them and reminded them of the offer to guide them on a tour of the area. He promised to bring along a special bottle of his own blackberry wine, homemade multigrain bread and selection of local New Hampshire and Vermont cheddar cheeses.

John and Elisabeth went to their room to change and check in with the people in New York. "Took you long enough to email us back," Guido started off. John noticed he started the email without as much as a "How do you do?" Elisabeth read over John's shoulder. He liked her breath on his neck and how she nestled her breasts into his back. He sat as she read over his shoulder.

"Nice to be able to check in. We needed to set up secure wi-fi and a new computer," John snarled as he typed and wished the words on the computer screen could convey his facial expressions.

"Whatever. We've been busy, too. We alerted the New York State police to three men staying in Saratoga. Don't ask how. They were planning to 'meet and greet' the governor. Now, they have a lot of explaining to do. We planted enough evidence in their electronic trail that they'll give it all up in short order."

"No shit? Great. How about the other team? And are there any more than just the two teams we know about?"

"Not that we've detected," Guido responded. "So far, we haven't picked up on any other teams. We can't help on that yet."

"At least that's good. We're holed up way out yonder. We've found a nice place to call home for a while." Elisabeth smiled and gave John a "reverse hug" pressing into his back.

"We don't have any leads on the other team yet. None. Beats us how they can get in the country and leave no traces. No purchases of firepower, no credit cards, no computer traffic. These guys are *good*. And that means that you all have to be very careful. *Very* careful."

He signed off after telling Guido to pass along some more instructions to the others.

"Well, I'm glad we're here. I can't imagine a safer place, or one more out of the way." She moved into him again. She felt good, pressing into him. "We do need to make ourselves presentable and go on a hike, don't we?" she teased.

"Yeah. But hold that thought until we get back. Every step I take, I'll be thinking about what I would rather be doing, though. Won't you?" He laughed.

"Yes. So, let's change and get going."

39

Albert made Demian's computer repeatedly chime until Demian opened his secure emails section. He typed, "How do you make it ring until I had to answer like that? No one else's messages do that."

"Shut up for a minute. We have news. A group of three men was captured in Saratoga. I should say they were set up by anonymous information that led the state police to capture them. No shots fired. No one hurt."

"Who were they?" Demian asked.

"Who do you think, genius? Assassins gunning for the governor. I've got no love for your usual politician, but foreigners coming to this country to gun down our leaders—that's not acceptable on any grounds."

Demian could almost hear Albert snort as he typed. "What about the other group? And did your guys find any more than that one other group of three?"

"No. No information at all about the others. So, watch your back. If they're that good that we can't find them, they're slippery. And underhanded."

"Yeah."

"Do you guys want some more protection up there, wherever that might be?" Albert typed.

"No." Demian fired back. "We think we can limit our footprint by not having too big a presence."

"Yeah, maybe. Don't forget all the press you've gotten since you turned to the good side. Everyone knows your name and face. Hard to hide like that."

Demian laughed as he thought about the famous Star Wars movies and the talk about the *dark* side. "Well, fame has its downsides too, I guess."

"Remember that the other group has had access to the town's maps and such through the land offices. They've had access to prior newspapers. That's likely how they knew where to kidnap the sheriff. We haven't heard any more about him either. We still think he's being held for ransom or trade if the need arises," Albert continued. "Listen, kid. We go way back to your grandfather, and while I sometimes didn't get along or get my way, I generally liked both him and your father. I don't want anything to happen to you. You get the good headlines and while everyone is paying attention to you, I get to do pretty much as I please. Get it?"

"So I've become a distraction for you to do as you please? That's why all the nice guy act with me?" Demian asked.

"Yeah. That and I owed your father big time. What I'm telling you is watch your back. I can't seem to find anything that'll help. Watch yourself and all your friends."

"Any word on the poisoning of Madison? Any info on that particular combination of amphetamines and designer street drugs?"

"Oh, yeah. Just a word, though. Seems there is a chemist that works mostly in Germany. He specializes in that new brand of street drug and combining it with all manner of prescription medications to get the effects his pushers want. He tries to stay one step ahead of what's illegal. He designs a drug; his sellers sell it until the locals outlaw it and he designs a new one. The sales are legal until the new drugs are specifically outlawed. Takes about a year to go through all that. Get it? It's a real law enforcement merry-go-round."

"How does that help us?" Demian felt frustrated.

"We're looking into his stable of hired hands. The ones who would do anything for a price. You know the type."

"If you can identify them, that might give us someone to look for, you're right."

"Don't rely on that. They'll sneak up on you before you know it, and I think sooner rather than later. Watch your back. I'll crack the whip down here and push for the information. I like spending your money and adding on a commission for me."

Demian could hear the laughter even over the typed words. "Got it." He signed off.

Demian returned John's text regarding the capture of the three villains who were staging an attack on the governor. He congratulated John's group.

Jane awoke the next morning. "Listen, Demian, I need to go to work. I can't stay here and ignore the hospital. There's always some disaster that I have to manage—some fire to put out, some personnel issue that they threaten to strike over or some shortage of medication or even the latex exam gloves that they all use. Think of it. A shortage of exam gloves almost crippled us in the eighties. We couldn't examine, so we couldn't treat. That was during the whole latex-allergy thing. We had to invent new gloves to wear. If I wasn't there to beg, borrow or steal enough exam gloves, we would have been out of business."

"It's been less than forty-eight hours since they kidnapped the sheriff. I'm sure they'll make their move in short order. They know we're looking for them. John's friends found and anonymously turned in three assassins in Saratoga who were gunning for the governor. They forged a huge electronic trail leading straight to them and the state police, FBI, CIA and others have them in custody. They might just flip on their other team. That would end this quickly. But if I wanted to commission two groups of assassins, I wouldn't tell them anything about the other group precisely so that they couldn't turn the others in for leniency." Demian held his arms around Jane and kissed her. "Just hold on a while longer. We're protected here. *I* want to protect you. Going to the hospital and driving or going to your house leaves you out in the open."

"At least let me call my staff and tell them to man the fort for me while I'm gone?"

"OK. I have the satellite phone. Don't give any information that could imply where we are. Just say you're visiting friends," Demian instructed.

"Yeah. I know. I just feel I've abandoned my staff. I know they can manage for themselves and I'll get off the phone as soon as I can." Jane smiled at Demian.

Demian and Will had taken turns moving all their cars to Will's house. They secreted them away at various locations—old barns, lean-tos, and behind the town garages at the Jay Mountain reservoir about halfway down the mountain. Bennie carefully watched to make sure the men were safe during the moves by guarding the road to Will's. Demian's plan was to make the place look deserted, as if everyone drove away in the night. If the assassins attacked, they would hide in the secret safe room, call in the police and wait for them to do their job. The plan had been discussed and accepted by everyone. Demian's closed-circuit video monitors would feed real-time information with night-vision technology, ground sensors and radio contact with the posted guard down the road leading to the house.

Demian did not divulge the flash-bang explosives in the cellar, set to detonate by remote from inside the safe room if it looked like the secret room might be breached. He would stop at nothing to protect his friends—his family. Although none of them were blood relatives, they had become his family.

40

Brud led the way up the steep slope behind the hunting camps. Multiple signs in dark green lettering over a beige camouflage patterned background pointed the way to different trails. They had been given a trail map and held it in front of them as they walked. They tried to piece together where they went in order to be able to retrace their steps and find their way back to the camps. Brud kept up a banter about the season, the deer they had seen on their trail-camera monitors, prior years' harvests and food plots and apple trees the deer frequented and at what times of the day. He also told an unending line of jokes having to do with different animals going into a bar. "So, a horse walks into a bar. The bartender says to him, 'Why such a long face?'" Brud laughed the most at his own jokes. John and Elisabeth politely groaned.

"How much farther is it that we're going?" John panted. Brud looked at him and chuckled. He wasn't tired or stressed by the climb.

"I can slow down if you need me to?" Brud smiled. "I do get carried away up here. I just love thinking about the hunting season. I love the charity we do. For me, this is the best part of the year."

"I can see that," Elisabeth answered. "You know? I went hunting with my father a few times. We didn't see anything because he said my perfume scared them off. I thought they might like the floral fragrance. I thought it would fit right in with an orchard or a meadow."

After Brud stopped laughing, he related the story that a man might walk into his mother's kitchen. He might say, "You're baking cookies." A deer might walk into the same kitchen at the same time and say, 'You're cooking with eggs, milk, cinnamon, flour, chocolate and water. And that stove is really hot.' Actually, it's been proven that a deer can discriminate at least a dozen aromas at a time. No wonder they can smell us and avoid human contact so easily," Brud continued.

"So wearing Elizabeth Arden perfume wasn't a good idea while hunting?" She giggled.

"No, not really." The old man continued to laugh. "Turn around and look out over the valley. The slope is gentle, the woods are green, only a hint of the wild color changes to come. All is good with the earth."

"You're the only one who thinks so. The earth is being polluted, the political and economic systems are busted and people are distracted with computers and cell phones. How is it you keep your positive outlook?" Elisabeth asked.

"I'm not as young as I used to be and I don't take everything as seriously or as personally." He paused and looked like he tried to choose his words well. "There is a famous book by Don Miguel Ruiz titled *The Four Agreements*. Now, I haven't read that many complete books these last few years, but that's one I took to heart. I try to do the four things he mentioned every day. It keeps me young. Start with 'take nothing personally.'"

"I'll look that up and give it a good read," John said.

"You about ready for the wine, cheeses and snacks I brought?" Brud asked. "You want to sample the best of New Hampshire?"

"We'd love to." Elisabeth helped spread a red plaid plastic tablecloth, like those in the dining room. They sat and enjoyed the day.

After the lunch and the wine, the old man continued. "You know? It is important to do what you love, with people you love, for the people you love. I think that's the secret of life. Also, don't smoke too much, drink too much, exercise too much, or do anything else to excess. Just keep rolling along between the ditches. Try to avoid the really high highs and the very low lows." He gazed down the mountain again. The others followed his gaze, feeling no need to speak further.

41

"Will, are you hearing this as well?" Demian asked as he talked to Bennie and used the earbud radios he had issued to the two men. "I'm here with Bennie. John's friends tracked one group of assassins online. They turned them into the state police and left enough damning evidence that they will likely just give it up. Appears they were after the governor."

"Great news," Will crackled in the other two men's earbuds. "What about the other group of three men? Anything further?"

"Not a word," Demian answered.

"My sources can't locate them either," Bennie added.

"How are you, Bennie?" Will asked his old friend. He feared he had been a little too tough on his friend.

"Really good. I'm really good. I'll be able to talk to you both about it at length, after this is all over." Bennie spoke with a strong and grounded voice. Demian smiled at him.

"What's the plan since we hid all the cars? Anything new?" Will asked.

"No new plans. We'll keep a lookout. If anyone we don't know approaches, we hide in the secret room. But, I'll tell you two only. I have the outer basement wired with flash/bang explosives to blow by remote control if it looks like they figure out the safe room. I've got secret video surveillance inside and outside the house, as you know, night vision included," Demian added.

"So we let the assassins get to the houses, let them think we all snuck away, call the police and have them intervene unless they try to breach the hidden cellar panel?" Bennie asked with an incredulous tone in his voice.

"Yes. We do. We don't want any innocent bystanders hurt." Demian knew this didn't sit well with Bennie. He hoped that Will understood. "We keep in radio contact, and we wait. I don't think it'll be long. The assassins know time isn't on their side. If they lurk around long enough, they expose themselves and leave a trail."

"Why don't you ask the governor to put out broadcasts about the other team being captured? It'll rile up the team after us. Call him and get him on it. He'll do it if you ask him." Will spoke emphatically.

"I agree," added Bennie. "If the governor doesn't want his people to do it, mine will, gladly."

"I'll call him and ask. I know he's making life *very* unpleasant for Canig and his lawyer. Bennie and John's groups are finding more and more undisclosed money that Canig tried to hide. The state is confiscating it all. The governor doesn't take kindly to someone arranging assassins to attack him and his people. And he doesn't cotton to being lied to, or anyone hiding funds that were supposed to have been turned over to the state as part of a plea agreement," Demian said.

"If the plan is to let them infiltrate the mountain, then when do we defend ourselves?" Bennie asked. "This seems like we're trusting that our safe room is unknown and will remain hidden from the assassins. That's a very large assumption, isn't it?"

"I'm confident the room is secure. If we're in it, we can always blow the cellar alone. I want the three of us to defend ourselves only if we're approached directly but let the state troopers deal with the other team if they get to the mountain. Got it?" While Demian asked, the other two men grumbled.

"Yeah. Got it," Will affirmed.

"OK. But I won't let anyone threaten us. I should have killed that bastard when I had the chance. I knew it," Bennie said.

"Listen. I know how this will go down. The watcher tells the others when company is arriving. We all get to the safe room and hide. I switch on the closed-circuit video. We call the state police and governor and we wait. If anyone is personally confronted, they defend themselves and the rest of us. I blow the outer cellar if I need to." He waited. "Got it?"

They answered affirmatively.

John and Elisabeth rested for the afternoon after they climbed the mountain behind the Berlin hunting camps. Their room was warm, so they stripped off their clothes made sweaty from the climb, showered, slipped under the sheets and slept. That is until John awakened and felt refreshed. He let his intentions be known and they enjoyed themselves.

"I need to get online," he said.

Immediately, he called Elisabeth over to read the screens. John started wildly typing to Demian. "Jesus, I hope we can reach them. This is not what we expected. At all." He typed furiously.

"I'll call, too. I know Madison's phone number. I know she'll be up." Elisabeth frantically dialed and paced.

"Shit. I knew my guys were good, but they're *really* good. And creative, too. Guido hired a young hacker and told him to think way outside the box. Star Wars outside the box." John continued to mumble as he typed furiously to Demian. "I hope we can get to them. We know how the assassins will approach now."

"Madison, pick up!" Elisabeth shouted. There was no answer, and it went to voicemail. "That either means that she's turned off her cell phone, or is out of range, or—"

"Yeah. Why isn't Demian answering, either?"

"So someone named 'Little Anthony' figured it out and back-checked it all? We're sure he's right?" Elisabeth asked.

"The others confirmed it. They've figured it all out," John answered.

"I'll call the state police and the Lake Placid deputies. They'll know how to get in touch with them and get right up there. You keep trying to get Demian."

42

Marion sprung up from his sitting position. He had been meditating as he always did in the afternoon. Catherine and Gunner were with him. "We've got to go, and I mean right now. Gather everyone and let's go to the safe room. Alert everyone. Now!"

"What is it?" Gunner demanded.

"They're coming. I just had an intuition that the assassins will come right now. Tell everyone."

Catherine and Marion quickly walked to the cellar door and disappeared down the stairs.

Gunner yelled to everyone. They had discussed making a notification chain so that everyone would be sure to get to the cellar safe room. They all did as they had practiced. While Bennie sat overlooking the lower road, Demian and Will ushered the others to safety and closed the swinging wall access panel behind them. Demian spread a mixture of concrete dust on the floor to cover any footprints or markings on the floor that might have led the assassins to suspect a hidden safe room. Gunner did a head count and confirmed everyone except Bennie was there.

Demian turned on the closed-circuit videos and computers and kept in communication with Bennie via the earbuds. "Bennie? Come in."

"Yeah, Demian. All clear here," he quickly responded.

"Marion alerted us to get to the basement. We're all down here. Anything on the horizon?"

"No. All clear."

At that time, Demian's shelter room computers finally booted up. He had entered the passwords and saw the emergency message from John. "Wait a minute, Bennie. Just got an email from John." He paused and read. "Shit. I didn't even think of that. Shit. Bennie, get back here and take up a position overlooking the parking lot outside the houses. One of John's guys figured it out. They're going to attack by helicopter—not by car or over the mountains. I'll call the state police. You double-time it up here. Hide if you hear any prop wash. Don't engage unless you're defending yourself. Got it?"

"Yeah. Running now. I'll watch out overhead, too. I'll call in when I'm in position." Bennie jogged with his rifles slung over his back. His best time for an approximately two-mile run uphill had been at the academy, about twelve minutes, fully weighted down with a rifle, helmet, additional ammo and gear. He knew he could make the distance in less than that today. This would be the day to do so.

Demian answered John back. "When did they steal the chopper?"

"This morning just outside Montreal from a sightseeing helicopter company."

"That's about a hundred and twenty miles from here." Demian thought that would be a leisurely ride for a helicopter if it didn't need refueling or need to make other adjustments. He switched to the earbud communication system and heard Bennie's fast breath. "Yes, so any time now they'll be in range. Watch it. Elisabeth already called the state police and the Lake Placid deputies. They're on their way. I hope in time."

"That's the group that has the sheriff hostage. Anything on him?" Demian typed in furiously.

"Not that my men found out. But that's actually good news," John reported. "They would have found him if the kidnappers wanted him dead and had already killed him."

John and Elisabeth held each other knowing this could be a tragic end to the lives of their friends and family. "What if the assassins have a machine gun or grenade launcher? Could they fire it from a sightseeing chopper? Would one of those demolish a whole house? Will they all be OK?" Elisabeth rattled on. She blurted out all the questions they feared and didn't know the answers to. "Listen, what else can we do?"

"A good question for the boys, especially 'Little Anthony,' I would think." John began furiously typing again. He asked and then begged for more information and a solution to the imminent attack on Will and Mason's houses. They waited only a few minutes for any possible answers, but time dragged for the couple.

In under ten minutes, Bennie had run up the mountain road to the area overlooking the lawn between Will and Madison's houses. He breathlessly keyed his microphone. "Demian. I'm in position overlooking the two houses." He panted. "What else do you know? Cavalry on the way?"

"Yeah. Get to the overlook position that Will used when we took down Canig."

"Yeah, there already." He was still panting.

"They hijacked a sightseeing helicopter. Don't know what they intend, though. John's guys found it out. Whether they intend to come right now or later, I don't know. A helicopter could sneak along under the radar and never be detected by air traffic control or the police, so our best protection is you as our lookout. The state police are also coming."

"I'm here," he panted.

"Shit! Shit!" Bennie could see a bright orange helicopter approaching from the Whiteface Mountain area, flying very low to the ground. It looked strange. Instead of the usual slats making up both side's landing gear, there were two tubes on each side. He immediately recognized them as missile tubes like he had seen in Iraq. All of the American helicopters had frames to hold the weapons. The enemy forces jury-rigged the missile tubes with straps, bars or whatever happened to be available. That is exactly what he now saw.

"Bennie! What's up?" Demian yelled.

"I'm going hot. They've got four missile tubes."

Demian could not hear anything else inside the cellar safe room. The closed-circuit video monitors only showed the grounds in and around his house. They didn't capture the sky.

Bennie unloaded two magazines of 30-06 into the pilot's side of the chopper. He didn't know if he hit or not and saw no smoke, but the pilot abruptly turned and swung away, flying down the slope in a jerking manner. Either the pilot had been injured or the aircraft had been disabled, at least to a degree. Bennie kept shooting but knew it made little difference after about 500 yards. He reloaded.

"Demian. I unloaded as many rounds as I could into the pilot's side. They turned and flew down the slope. I either wounded the pilot or dinged the mechanicals because the chopper flew erratically. I don't see them returning."

"Shit. Damn son!" Demian looked to all the faces staring at him. "Hold right there. When you see the state police, retreat to the Beaver Dams. We don't want to explain all that."

"Roger that." Bennie could not see or hear the chopper. It could have landed or crashed below his line of sight and beyond hearing. The next thing he saw was a long line of state police cars coming up the road, driving slowly, careful not to miss a turn over unfamiliar roads.

"Demian, I'm backing out now. The state police are here. Get everyone out of the safe room so they don't find it. You don't want anyone finding out about that safe room. I'm gone to the stacks." He moved away from the houses in a modified run, crouching over so as not to be seen by the police. When he had cleared the line of sight to the area where the police had parked, he ran fully upright again. He stopped halfway down the slope to the stone stacks and the Beaver Dams. He finally rested and waited by the smaller stack, knowing it was out of sight of the area around the dams.

Demian ushered the group out of the safe room. Madison carefully told the kids not to talk about the safe room. They all went out to meet the police in the driveway.

43

John couldn't stand the waiting. He took Elisabeth's usual phone and called Demian's number. He did this so that Demian would see who was calling and could either decide to answer or not. He knew Demian did not know the numbers of their burner phones.

"Yeah, John. We're fine. Surrounded by state police. Don't know what they want yet. I'll call you when we get a better grip on what's happening." He signed off without waiting for an answer or further questions.

Elisabeth had overheard and looked at John with a quizzical expression. "Does that mean the chopper didn't come to attack?" She thought for a moment. "No. He must not want the police to know he knows about the chopper for some reason."

John said, "I'll get online and see what the guys might know." He got to the password-protected screen and typed quickly and waited. "Jesus, I wish we could have been there, but then again, I know we helped them the most by passing on our computer genius' information. We very likely saved them all."

"I just couldn't be a target again. Not again," Elisabeth choked on a sob.

"I know. I know."

John split the screens when he saw many messages coming in all at once. They read on both sides and quickly learned that the police radar had caught a helicopter zipping away from Jay, heading towards Canada. They could not follow the aircraft when it ducked below the radar's sensors. John didn't ask how they might have had access to police communiqués. He asked for further info as soon as possible.

John called Demian again and let him know the company from the north returned. Demian again hung up with no response.

"The governor seems to like you, a lot," Captain Nicholas Green said. He was a big man who moved his large frame deliberately. He looked like he hadn't recently worn out any exercise equipment. "He told us to get on up here, help you with whatever you need and to follow your orders explicitly." He turned and spat on the ground. "Every day, it's a new experience taking orders from superiors—the governor, even the civilian secretaries, and now you. I used to like to go to work."

"I do know the governor. I like him and he likes me. This isn't about any of that. It's about foreign mercenaries coming to this country to attack us. It's about three of them that you've already captured in Saratoga. They would have tried to assassinate the governor. The other team was going to attack here. Do you have any info on them?"

"There are a lot of things I don't like in the least. Your common thief, down on his luck, trying to feed himself and his family, I can almost understand. Your common tax evader—I think we both could spend our money better than the government does, at times. But it'll piss me off to find out that foreign mercenaries tried to attack our sovereign citizens. The only thing I despise worse is child molesting. Just hold right there." He kicked at an imaginary stone, walked back to his car and got on his car radio.

Demian couldn't hear the whole conversation but saw the captain get red in the face. This progressed to crimson, and his forehead broke out in a line of sweat. He finally saw the officer throw the radio hand unit on the front seat. He straightened up, took a deep breath, put on his hat and marched back to stand in front of Demian.

"So, it seems you're right. There was a team of assassins captured in Saratoga that was going to try to assassinate our governor. They all hold South African diplomatic passports. Imagine that. Now we can't do anything to them except escort them to their airplane to get to their homeland. Bullshit is what *that* is." The captain was only beginning to warm up. "You know what else? When a rogue CIA agent uses an unsuspecting civilian as a trial terrorist bomb and attacks Lake Placid. That about *ruins* my day. Raises my blood pressure even higher. My doctor is about to have a coronary himself, trying to deal with me. I've got a small house on Mirror Lake and with any luck, my wife and I will retire there in less than two weeks. Now what is it that we can do for you to help put that bastard's other crew of hired assassins away?"

"Any leads on finding Sheriff Wilkins?" Demian asked.

"That's another thing that frosts me worse than these long winters around here. Kidnapping a good man like the sheriff really gets me. The only reasonable explanation is that they used a helicopter to fly him away from the scene of the abduction. Possibly to Canada. My teams went up and down that river with bloodhounds and we couldn't find a thing."

Demian flipped open his phone and asked John to have his crew look into the possibility that the sheriff might be being held in Canada. He flipped off before John could squeeze another word in.

"My boys are going to have a look around the houses and grounds, that OK? We don't need any excess paperwork like warrants. We need to be sure you folks are not under duress from someone held hostage." The captain made only a small head gesture towards each house and two squads dispersed to check the outbuildings, houses, grounds and nearby woods. "I think a perimeter down the road with a roadblock should be in order, too." He made several quick hand gestures, and three cars with troopers sped off down the road.

A younger-looking trooper approached his captain, saluted and said, "Sir. When we drove up here, I was in the lead car. I could see the chopper. It had four missile tubes fastened to the landing struts. Saw a lot of that in Iraq. Mavericks, I'm sure. They would have demolished all the houses and hundreds of feet around would have been pelted with shrapnel. Maybe the helo backed off because we were approaching?"

"You're sure about all that?"

"Yes, sir!"

"Dismissed."

"Your troops seem very well trained," Demian said admiringly.

"That's what we do. We're the toughest section of the state trooper forces. We go from the Canadian border to Albany and from Watertown to the shores of Lake Champlain. We've got it all covered." The captain smiled.

An officer ran up and gave the captain a plastic baggie with spent 30-06 shells. The corporal gestured to the spot where Bennie had been positioned to shoot at the helicopter.

Demian quickly grabbed the bag and said he had done some target practice that morning. "You can keep them if you guys reload." He handed the bullets to the patrolman.

"Tell me about what's uphill from here?" the captain asked in as polite a manner as he could muster.

"First-growth forests, hills, mountains that would like to kill you if you climbed over them. Many good woodsmen and hunters have gotten lost for days back there. That all leads up to Death Mountain. And believe me, you would rather die than climb over that. But if you did make your way up there, the slope is almost impossible for about a third of the way down to Lake Champlain on the other side. It's just bare granite showing. Nothing to hold on to or slow your descent." Demian hoped this description would deter any interest in having a look around in Bennie's direction.

"Any marked trails up there and back?" the captain asked.

"Nope. No one wants to go there, so we've never marked a trail there."

"Humpf." The captain walked to his car, got on the radio again, spoke for a long while and got out. After checking in with his men, he came back to Demian and the others. "We've got a perimeter down the road, near the reservoir. We've got air surveillance of the area, in case an attack by plane or helicopter happens." He looked at Demian squarely in the eyes. "What I don't have is a feeling that you're telling me the whole story. I've heard about this character Canig, his lawyer, his hit squads and all his money. My men and I will do our best for you and everyone here, but we could use the whole story."

"It really reassures us that you're here. I don't know any more to tell you. I wish we could find the sheriff, though. He and I have been through a lot," Demian added.

"Yeah. Well, we'll do our job. If anything comes to your mind that we need to know about, call me pronto." The captain gave Demian his card.

The rest of the troopers got in their cars and drove off. Will made a careful count of the number of officers who came and made sure they all left. "That was close, huh?"

"Yes, it was." Demian tapped his earpiece. "Bennie, can you read me?" He was not surprised when he got no answer, knowing that Bennie was in the depression of the Beaver Dams. The terrain up there effectively cut off communications. The radio waves couldn't follow the decline of the slope down the other side of the ridge.

"Will, would you mind taking a walk in a few minutes and bring a satellite phone, a few beers and supplies to Bennie. I can manage here, especially after the state police are forming our perimeter. Make sure to make that trip unseen, though. Slip away when everyone else is otherwise occupied. Can you? And remind Bennie to watch out for air surveillance."

"I'll need to stretch my legs in a few minutes. I'll get a pack together." He walked away like he was bored.

44

John put down Elisabeth's phone between them after contacting Demian. He had activated the speakerphone function so that Elisabeth could listen in. Neither of the men had anything new to divulge. Demian had told John about Bennie's shooting at the helicopter. John had heard follow up on the stolen helicopter and the burning of a specialty shop known for metal fabrications of all sorts, just south of Montreal. He wondered if the shop had fastened the missile tubes to the landing gear struts. *After the work was completed, were the workers killed and the large hangar and garage torched to cover any evidence?* It would likely be days before the authorities knew what started the fire, and if there were any bodies hidden among the wreckage. Apparently, the acetylene tanks used for welding torches could burn for extended periods, at extremely hot temperatures.

Demian admired, and at the same time despised, the audacity of this group of assassins. They had thoroughly planned their attacks and covered their tracks. "John, do we know what happened to the group after Bennie shot at them? He thought he either hit the pilot or the chopper. Have your guys concentrate on anyone arriving at an ER with gunshot wounds or another repair shop fire or holdup. Anything that happened today, possibly connected to the attack here." He paused. "Your guys are good, even being able to know what happened in a foreign country."

"Already did so. My thoughts exactly. They must have had backup plans. No one is this thorough without one or two alternatives, or plans for escape," John said. He noticed that Elisabeth was glued to his conversation with Demian. "My best guys are on it, and I've given Little Anthony a *big* bonus.

I'm sure that'll wet his whistle for more—the rest of the guys, too. All of them will get on what's happening as soon as possible. We'll know and you can plan anything you need to do after we hear."

"Thanks, John. Say hi to Elisabeth. I'm glad you're both safe and away from here. I know she would have been frantic with the close shave here. Bennie saved the day."

"Yeah. We've got your backs, even from afar." John signed off and kissed Elisabeth. "You heard Demian. He cares about you and is glad we're safe."

"I know it. You know, I just couldn't wait there and become a target again. But now we can be his eyes and ears and your friends can find out what else is happening. Can't they?"

"Sure. Just like today. They'll scan the net and all the social media and get these guys," he said.

"Wonder what the supper special is today? Is it always the same? Doesn't matter, I'll have it. And it was a really good breakfast. And his coffee was just like home to me." Elisabeth had finished putting on her makeup. She and John had abandoned trying to be the frumpy ex-hippie and the poor man down on his luck. They dressed in nice clothes and made their way to the office-restaurant-meeting area after resting for most of the afternoon.

"Afternoon, Brud. We were wondering what might be on the menu for dinner and when you serve it?" Elisabeth said.

"Yankee pot roast. That is with potatoes, carrots, onions, organic beef in a gravy of my own concoction and all of it cooked slowly in an oven bag." He looked at them slyly and added, "Might have some more of that raspberry wine to go with it, if you two are interested?"

"Wow. That sounds just right. When will you serve?" Elisabeth asked. John could see the excitement in her eyes over having a real homecooked meal. The wine was just the right blend of dry and sweet when they had sampled it in the afternoon, and it looked like a nice rose in the glass. Elisabeth had had her first drink of alcohol in her mid-teens with friends at a party. It was something called Boon's Farm Apple Wine—cheap, available, sold by the quart or gallon and potent. She remembered how sweet it was and now understood how awful it tasted—the sweetness overpowering all the natural flavors of the apples.

"Coming out of the oven now. Could you give a hand?"

"Sure," they both said at the same time. Elisabeth followed Brud into the kitchen and helped him remove the large pan from the industrial-sized oven. She opened the oven bag and sliced the roast to put it on serving trays with the vegetables on the side while he thickened the gravy. John had set up the table for five after asking how many for dinner.

"My good friends who own a large riding stable about a half mile from here are coming," Brud said. "They offer lessons—have broodstock and a boarding stable where I'm sure the horses are very well cared for."

"It'll be nice to meet them," Elisabeth quickly said. She thought to herself that for the last decade, she would have been mortified to have uninvited guests attend supper—it was always possible to run into CIA or underworld operatives or someone who might know someone, and her cover might have been blown.

"Riding stables sound fun," John said. "I've never ridden myself, but life is long. There's always time to learn a new skill."

"Sounds like you haven't been out of the city much?" Brud probed.

"Nope. But now that I am, I love the country way of life, country people and getting away from the noise," he answered. "It is so very nice and quiet up here. I haven't heard a car horn, loud air brakes of a city bus or sirens from emergency responders in the city—seems like the emergencies never end there."

"I grew up near Lake Placid. Did a whole lot of riding when I was young and miss being around horses; their energy is so strong. They're so perceptive, knowing what their riders are feeling. I'd love to ride again," Elisabeth smiled broadly.

"That's what I thought until about five years ago; then it became too tiring for me to ride for a decent distance. I would come home exhausted. Tom and Ellen and I go way back to a time when we were all starting out in business together. We would steer business to each other and would come and work as assistants for each other as the need arose. We came to trust and rely on each other. Now, they help organize and run the hunts we offer for the disabled. They have inside contacts because Tom was a ranger in the Army. They put out the word through the VA system. He goes way back to Kosovo and the Balkan wars. Ellen was a surgical nurse over there, and they both saw more than they wanted to, I'm sure." Brud waited. "They told me they randomly ended up here, tending horses, and found being around the horses eventually helped them let go of their past and memories."

"All of our military men, their caregivers if they were injured, and also their families saw way too much. Then they came home to find it difficult to settle in. Or they had to adjust to new ways of being if they were disabled," John said. "One of my new friends is a ranger-special-ops guy who did time in Iraq. Another friend was with him in Iraq but didn't go to Special Forces training. They both came home with problems adjusting. I know they're fine now, but—"

"I know. I came back from the Korean 'conflict' not knowing myself anymore. I got lost in drifting around, doing nothing important until I found Berlin and this place. It was completely ignored because the man who owned it lost his sons—both of them—in World War II. World War I was supposed to be the end to all wars, right? Frank political bullshit is what that concept was," Brud exclaimed.

"I'm so sorry when I think of what men do to men," Elisabeth added.

"So, I guess my healing was to buy this place—I guess I didn't buy it, either. I homesteaded it until the bank foreclosed on it and gave it to me so that I could start a business, pay taxes, and whenever I might have need for a loan, I might know the right place to go. Anyway, I rebuilt this place and always included some of that giving back to the causes I feel are right, get it?"

"Yes. We do." John held Elisabeth around the waist. "We are lucky to find ourselves in a similar position now. We're ex-CIA and ex-law practice. But now we work with a man who devotes himself to trying to restore Lake Placid. Maybe you heard of the disaster there?" John asked.

"Sure did. I can't imagine a bastard like that rogue CIA agent using an unsuspecting man, who just wanted to have hip replacements, as a weapon to cause an electromagnetic pulse. They threw away the key on him, I hope." Brud's expression showed disbelief and righteous indignation. He finished the last of the garnish for the pot roast.

"Yeah, they did. But he's still raising havoc," Elisabeth said. They were interrupted by the sound of two people entering the dining area.

Tom and Ellen McCarthy entered the restaurant, introduced themselves and shared a glass of wine with Brud, John and Elisabeth. They had brought a bottle of their own, made from a harvest of their own grapes, pressed and bottled by themselves—all grown organically. This sauterne quickly disappeared, and they sat down to a sumptuous dinner of the pot roast, with liberal amounts of Brud's raspberry wine and local berries for dessert. Tom was tall and thin with the look of an outdoorsman, someone who worked physically and didn't have to watch his weight because of his active lifestyle. Ellen had the same look, and of the sun and wind, making her complexion a deep brown—a radiantly healthy glow highlighting her red hair.

"Well, Tom, Elisabeth here, says she loves to ride. Any chance you might be saddling up in the next day or so? And do you think that old mare of yours is up to taking a real city slicker along as well?" Brud asked. He poked his thumb in John's direction.

"Sure. I'm always ready to drop what I'm doing and go for a ride." Tom's smile welcomed the couple.

"I would love it, and we'll pay your usual rates for your time. And I think a gentle old mare would be perfect for my husband. He needs all the help he can get when it comes to getting him out in the great outdoors." She elbowed John who feigned severe injury from the poke and laughed.

"Yes. I do need all the help I can get, but the more I'm in the country, the more I love it," John declared.

"Tomorrow at nine. AM, that is. If that doesn't offend your sense of sleeping in," Tom offered.

"Great. We'll be there and ready to ride. We have warm clothes; can we rent helmets?" Elisabeth always thought safety around horses. She and many friends had been thrown when they were younger and were glad to have been afforded the protection of hard helmets hitting the ground instead of soft skulls. They had only suffered bruises to extremities and not the more serious head injuries.

"We've got all the stuff you need, no problem," Ellen answered.

The group broke up for the night. John and Elisabeth went back to their cabin and turned in after checking for any new developments. The guys were on the trail, but nothing new yet.

45

Madison looked at her two sleeping kids. She adored them—and the people they were blossoming into. She let the feelings of love for her family fill her chest until it pushed out the anger of the recent days' events. Then she could sleep. She could *finally* sleep.

Mason watched her as she made small breathy sounds and moved around a little. He knew she was sleeping deeply. He got up and went to find Will and Demian. He found them talking in hushed tones in the kitchen over mugs of coffee.

"Couldn't sleep?" Demian asked him.

"No. But now Madison is sleeping better than I've seen her sleep in weeks. So, I got up to see you and ask what the plan is," Mason responded.

"We were just talking about that. We're sure we haven't seen the last of those assassins. They want their payday and bonuses. And they want revenge. They want us and the world to know that they are not to be screwed with. They want everyone to know that they don't fail. That's for sure," Demian replied.

Will broke in. "That's why I've been talking to Bennie, and we feel we all need to leave here. We think they'll just set up their missiles within a five-mile radius—that's their effective firing range—input the coordinates and fire them off. If Bennie's right that those were Mavericks, you only have to get close, punch in the coordinates, fire them and leave. We can't know where they might come from, and the state police can't protect us by only cordoning off the lower road. There's just too much uninhabited, secluded territory around here to set up and fire from. They can't cover all that."

"We plan to leave as soon as we can tomorrow. Getting everyone going will be a real project. Bennie's out roving around protecting us from the very off chance that the assassins will climb over Death Mountain. I can't believe they will, but he's out there. He can't get any productive sleep anyway—he's wired after shooting to protect us this morning," Demian said.

"How do you propose that we get Marion and Catherine out of here? They can't walk a great distance at their ages." Mason looked concerned that Demian might not have considered them.

"Of course they can't. I'm working on it. We don't have a definitive plan in that regard yet."

"Bennie said the chopper carried four Mavericks. We saw a lot of them in Iraq. Usually the rebels would strap them to cars, trucks or troop carriers. That's what it looked like to Bennie, just strapped on and ready to fire. They must have been a sight to see coming at you. I marvel at Bennie—after a two-mile run uphill, weighted down, panting—he hit the chopper moving fast, at three hundred yards. Jesus." Will raised both eyebrows.

Demian nodded. "Looks like Bennie's back."

"I've got an idea that may sound very far-fetched." John started the conversation with Demian. He couldn't sleep, continuing to worry about his friends. He had let Elisabeth drift off, tried to close his eyes, and, when he drifted in the place between sleep and wakefulness, an idea arose. "We've run into some real trustworthy people over here in…where we're at now. I haven't told them about your predicament, but I wonder if a truckload of horses could be of help? Could horses get over Death Mountain from the Lake Champlain side and back again, so you could all make your escape?"

"What?" Demian didn't think he heard all that correctly. "You mean ride the horses over Death Mountain, pick us up, and take us away?"

"Well, I was thinking, is all. And we've met completely trustworthy friends here. Two of them have riding horses for hire. I'm sure they would be up for the intrigue, but I haven't asked them yet." John felt foolish for an instant until Demian started again.

"Listen, I've got to hang up. I'll check that out, and I'll call you right back." He closed the phone before John could reply. He nudged Jane, waking her from a sound sleep. "Jane. Wake up."

"Demian, I'm trying to sleep. Do I have to tell you I have a headache, or what?" She blinked to try to keep her eyes open. "Do I have to threaten your manhood so you'll let me get some more sleep? You know I have access to sharp things and you can't stay awake forever." Demian wasn't one hundred percent sure she wasn't joking.

"John just called. He's run into some new friends who are trustworthy and have horses. He wonders if we can ride the horses over Death and get to the Lake Champlain side and escape out of here from there."

"What?"

"You're not quite awake. John called. He has new friends who have horses. He wonders if we can ride them over Death to escape." Demian spoke very slowly, separating his words into phrases.

"Oh, wait. I get it. The new map that Deborah and Gunner found. I'll go get it. We left it in the fireplace room." She got up and slipped on one of Demian's robes. She shortly reentered the bedroom, turned on the lights and spread it out over the bed.

"Look. Deborah was right. This is an escape route. Maybe *our* escape route?" she asked.

"Yeah. I'm checking it. I would guess that I know the area the best of anyone here. I think the route could easily be traversed with horses." He traced the route with his finger, organizing it into segments that could be traveled. He got out the satellite phone and called Bennie.

"Bennie. Here's a wild idea. Could we possibly get over the mountain with horses, and sneak away as close to dawn as possible? We'd end up on the Lake Champlain side of the larger mountain and we could rendezvous at the famous place there?" Demian still didn't give any identifying names to key in his pursuers if they happened to be listening in.

"Yeah. It would take some doing. And horses, too." His mind was swimming with the details and planning logistics. "If so, we need to get on this right now. Wake up, Will. We shouldn't be the only ones to share the fun of planning it all out."

"Any commotion up there?" Demian asked.

"Nothing at all," he responded.

"Come back to the ridge overlooking where you are now. I think I need you closer. Then use the burner. It's safer than the satellite phone."

"I can almost guarantee that they're licking their wounds, not listening to us," Bennie replied.

"Yeah, but what if they have their own hoard of hackers too?" Demian asked.

"Good point. I just don't think so. They didn't need hackers to find you, John, Elisabeth and the others. They wouldn't have involved any more people than they needed to, too many possible leaks or snitches." Bennie thought that made sense.

"Right. But come back to the position I just mentioned," Demian urged.

"On it."

"Also, watch carefully to make sure the state police don't have any patrols out looking around, sweeping the area. Those troopers looked very well trained and could do military-style recognizance, I'm sure."

"Haven't seen any evidence of that." This time Bennie ended the conversation first by clicking off.

46

"Jesus, Demian. I'm going to throw this phone away and get a new unlisted number so that a Listing can't call me and wake me up at all hours of the night. Get it?" Albert was none too pleased to be awakened at 2:30 AM. "Old men like me don't sleep well most of the time, but when we do, we want to enjoy it. Got it?"

"Yeah, Albert. I'm sorry to have ruined your beauty sleep, but I need to know if your men have come up with anything new. I'm planning our escape and I need everything you have." Demian was almost polite, although the edge in his voice still commanded attention, even from Albert.

"I'm looking it up right now, you prick."

"Did your guys hear that we were almost fired upon with missiles from a helicopter? They already failed in their first attack attempt."

"*No!*" Albert gulped.

"*Yes!* One of our guys almost shot the chopper out of the sky with an old hunting rifle." Demian replied in a matter-of-fact tone.

"No shit. You guys are good. But maybe you're right about moving if those assassins are that resourceful?" Albert sounded genuinely impressed.

"Yeah. We figure they'll just launch their rockets from land somewhere within their five-mile radius limit and drive away. We can't protect against that. We need to know if you have any more info?" Demian repeated.

"No. I've booted up the programs and gotten on the dark side of the net. I don't see anything from any of my guys. I'm even more worried the attackers are good because they don't leave traces. How did they get a chopper, missiles, information as to where you are and almost pull this off?" Albert asked in amazement.

"We hear from other sources that they stole a sightseeing helicopter, went to a fabricating shop to mount the missile tubes and flew here from Montreal. All that was done in Canada. We're about a hundred and twenty miles from there. Then before they got here, they likely killed the fabricators, torched their shop and covered up all the evidence of being there in the first place," Demian concluded.

"Shit. Then my guys are looking in the wrong place. I'll get online and give them an earful and reorient them to the real world. Bastards. All of them."

"Don't be too hard on them. We got a new kid on it through other channels. We told him to think way outside the box. Star Wars way outside the box, and so he did. That's the only reason we knew in advance. He saved our lives, for sure."

"Well, I just finished checking in with my guys. Nothing new here. At all." Albert coughed and spat.

"Albert, do you smoke all your waking hours?" He adopted his best imitation of a kindergarten teacher's prosodic speech.

"Bastard. Pay attention to your own health, not mine." Albert coughed again.

"So, in hypothetical terms, do you think that this crew of assassins will reappear as soon as possible?" Demian queried.

"No doubt about it. Your guy shot at the helicopter—maybe he hit one of them. That's the only wild card. If they need to deal with that wounded guy, it may take longer. Outside of that, they would want to complete their mission as soon as possible before you sneak away, which is what you're asking about anyway, right?" As he spoke, he typed in new orders to his guys to look for any gunshot wounds needing care and any new fabricating shop fires in northern New York State and lower Quebec.

"Yes. I wanted to run by a plan we've been hatching. That's why I woke you up at an ungodly hour. We need to be solid before dawn if we're going to pull this off," Demian said.

"Let me have it. I wouldn't want to die before you have the benefit of my wisdom." The last syllable of wisdom came out as a cough. He continued to give directives via emails and caused the chime that would not stop until the emails were opened by his operatives. There would be a lot of sleepless hours for his men, but he felt they had failed him, so he really didn't care if they liked it or not.

Demian outlined the plan involving having horses take them over one of the highest and most difficult mountains in the Adirondacks. He included the fears that they had only a few hours until the assassins would find another way to fire on their position. The safe room would not protect them from an aerial missile assault like that.

"That just might be stupid and quaint enough to work, you know?" Albert said. "How about my men leak several other scenarios to social media and through emails supposedly from you to mislead the other team? Like you're showing off that you held off the attackers. How about you're going to wait a few days, rent armored vehicles and drive out of there? How about you feel that you've driven them off and now you feel perfectly safe—we know that's not true, but they don't? I'll have my guys throw in other subterfuge as they see fit. I like it. The escape is rustic enough to never have crossed their minds. I wouldn't have thought of it, for sure." As Albert finished, Demian could hear him light up another cigarette with the distinctive sound of an old-fashioned lighter cap being opened, then the flint wheel being turned and the cap closed.

"Good. That's what I wanted to hear. We're going black here, for the foreseeable future. I'll contact you only the old way. Watch our backs for us. I look forward to seeing you again, my old friend," Demian concluded.

"You didn't have to say *old*. I know I'm ancient. But I do want to see you again. Maybe you and your friends 'the healers' can help me stop smoking?" He laughed until he coughed and wheezed. "If we get you through this, you owe me that much."

Demian was sure that was true. But, now he had children and elderly people to sneak over a mountain to safety. Even if he succeeded, he'd be leaving two houses with all of his friend's personal possessions at risk of attack by missiles. Jesus.

47

John and Elisabeth knocked on Brud's door. Even though the old man had become accustomed to answering the door at all hours for customers, he looked irritated and then concerned when he saw them at his door.

"Come on in. The automatic coffee maker is in the back. Go find it and make three cups," he muttered. "I'll get dressed. Who needs to sleep, anyway?"

"Sorry to barge over and wake you up," Elisabeth said.

"No problem. I was already awake. Someone was pounding on the door." He laughed in an old man's stifled manner.

They eventually told Brud about themselves, their friends Will, Demian, and the others and asked him for help. He readily agreed after hearing about the situation. He offered to call Tom and Ellen. He sputtered at the audacity of Canig—his original assault on Lake Placid and now, even from jail, orchestrating an attack on the people who put him there.

"Yes, Tom. I know it's late, but it's important," Brud started.

"What? It's too early to be late." Now concern for Brud showed in Tom's voice. They could all hear on the speakerphone.

"Well, it's a long story, but one I think you and Ellen will want to help in bringing about a happy resolution to." Brud related the whole story, supplemented by John and Elisabeth where needed.

"So the guy who caused the electromagnetic pulse in Lake Placid is still behind all this and has hired teams of hit men to attack your friends and even the governor of New York? Unbelievable! These men were going to launch rockets at the house your friends are staying at? This was foiled by a ranger with an old-fashioned hunting rifle shooting at a moving helicopter? In America?" Tom exclaimed. "Shit Damn! I've got to meet this operator. No doubt about it."

"Yes. My friends were the ones who originally captured the rogue CIA agent. Mostly, it was the same ranger named Bennie. I don't know his last name," John added.

"Bennie? I haven't heard about anyone called Bennie. Must have gone through the training after my time. He did two tours in Iraq and then the Special Ops?" He paused. "That would be after my time." Tom thought out loud after doing the math in his head. "But we sure couldn't just let him dangle, could we?" he asked Ellen.

"No way." Her response was quick and firm.

"Could you help us then? Could we get enough horses to the eastern slope of Death Mountain before dawn, get them out of there and sneak away?"

"Brud? You available to help?" Tom asked, knowing the answer.

"Damn straight. You know I can and I will."

They hammered out the details. John called Demian again, confirming everything. John and Elisabeth looked their new friend in the eyes and knew he would not fail them. Brud smiled back.

No one on Jay Mountain was happy. In the least. Will and Demian woke up all the rest of the people at the house. Each griped about something—not sleeping, not eating, leaving the house in the middle of the night or having to climb and pass over Death Mountain. At least they all agreed about the nastiness of having to get up at that hour. They all complained about that.

Demian wished he had been a fly on the wall, hearing John and Elisabeth ask for help and explain their situation and themselves to their new friends. John could be very persuasive and Elisabeth had that down-home look about her—like the girl next door, or your first girlfriend. Whatever it was, she charmed everyone she met.

"Listen, could you be sure to help us?" Madison asked Jane.

"Sure. We're in this together. I'll help. What is it?" she responded.

"Marion and Catherine look excited, but the most exercise they've gotten in years is very light yard work on tractors. I'm not sure how far they've walked at one time recently," she responded.

"Got it. Any suggestions?"

"I think they can and still would like to ride horses, but getting up the slope to the Beaver Dams will likely be impossible on their own."

"Have you asked them?" Jane questioned.

"No. But I don't want them to start out, embarrass themselves, fail, slow us down and need to change the whole plan," Madison answered.

"I'll make it happen. I'll talk to Demian. He very likely already has a plan, anyway. He's usually two steps ahead of us." She paused. "How are you, Madison? I heard you've been through some tough times recently. I hope you're coming around to seeing life is more positive than not?"

"Yeah. Well, I was floridly paranoid. Enough so, I even thought the weather was against me. I seemed to get better; then I was told I was poisoned. Now I know I had good reason to be paranoid. I don't know. I just don't know," she spoke with balled-up fists, but her words did not have the staccato of the days before. Her voice remained smooth.

"That's at least one step better. Now you question how you should feel instead of being overrun with emotions, not in control, and untrusting of everything. What brought about the change?"

"Marion and Catherine did a healing for me last night. I feel like a huge weight has been lifted off my shoulders. Like I feel good in my own skin, now. I didn't feel that before, for sure. I don't know about trusting the world, yet. I think it'll take time."

"I hear they are amazing healers. I've never been treated by them myself, though," Jane answered.

"I hope your turn will come. Though I hope you don't have to go through what I did."

"Don't worry about Marion and Catherine. I'll make sure no one is forgotten. Even if I have to carry them up the mountain myself."

48

John called his favorite former employee on a new burner. "Listen, I have an idea. I want you and at least three of the other guys to lay down false tracks for us. Be careful, though. Use the old corporate credit card, my personal credit cards, as many ATM's as you need and take off to the west. Go fast enough that you aren't caught, but lay down enough receipts that someone might think it's a legitimate trail. Don't go anywhere that you have friends or family because you might be followed and that would put them in danger. But live it up. At least a week. Start tomorrow morning, renting cars in Lake Placid. Go from there. I'll tell you when to come back. Pick at least three trails going to different tourist destinations and have the time of your lives."

Lefty liked what he had just heard. He needed a vacation. In the few weeks that John had been gone from the firm, he had done most of the heavy lifting in terms of keeping up with lawsuits, private investigations and, most tiring, corralling the rest of the other men to keep them in line. "Yeah. Fine. I think we should travel in pairs, though. We'll shop, eat, drink, be merry and then duck out of town and pay cash for the night in the next city. We'll happily keep that up until you say to stop. I'll get Alfonse and Billie, and then maybe Nicky and String. Any limit to our fun?"

"No. But keep a good look out on your surroundings and don't get caught up. These are bad characters. They were going to fire missiles at us to kill us. That's badass for sure." John hoped he made himself clear. He really didn't care about the debt these guys might run up. The more they would spend, the more visible they would become.

"Got you, boss." Lefty paused and silently scowled. "I'm sorry, that just slipped out. I always used to call you boss. I guess I miss you around here;

being the boss isn't all it's cracked up to be." Lefty sighed. "I guess what I want to say is that I want to hear that you're safe and sound—and the Mrs. is too. We'll all do our best for you both."

"So round up the guys and get to Lake Placid by tomorrow morning. Go to the Avis car rental and live it up on my nickel." John hung up.

Demian had told John that Albert's guys had begun to spread Internet rumors that would dovetail nicely with his former employees leaving false trails to follow. John knew Bennie had not interacted with his group of hackers, he had been on watch, but he thought those angles were covered. Bennie's friends had had a lot of opportunities to operate autonomously. They preferred it. On the net, it was every man for himself, with the goal of protecting one of his own. They knew when to act immediately and would do so.

"Demian, what about getting Marion and Catherine up the mountain. How do we do that?" Jane asked. They changed into their hiking clothes—heavy boots, jean jackets, jeans and layers to keep them warm. They had each chosen a backpack to carry water, apples, an MRE each, and anything else they might have thought essential.

"Yeah. I've been thinking about that. We all have to be out of the house way before daybreak. Then we have to get over the ridge and at least on the Beaver Dams side of the slope. Deborah has taken charge of copying the new map of our escape route and giving each of us a copy. We'll each take a slightly different path to the larger stone stack so we don't leave a clearly visible trail going up the mountain by not stomping in a single file formation." Demian finished filling his pack.

"But, what about Marion and Catherine?"

"I was getting to it. Will and Bennie will use the one-wheeled deer haulers to carry them up the mountain. I've talked to them and they feel they can easily do it."

"What?" Jane had never seen one of these.

"They're a rack, with two handles like a wheelbarrow, with one wheel in front. My father and grandfather used to use them to transport the deer they shot off the mountain that way," Demian explained. "It takes some effort to go uphill, but Will and Bennie are taking it as a solemn duty to do so. They'll leave first. That leaves you and Gunner to shepherd the others up the slope and to the larger stone stack."

"What about you? Where will you be?" Now Jane's voice showed a very unusual quality for her—fear.

"I'll be here, making sure the assassins don't show up. And if they do, I'll make sure they don't follow us. I'll give everyone else a head start and enough time to get to the dams; then I'll come." Demian drew Jane to him and smothered her lips with a kiss before she could complain or refuse. She tried to break away, but as she did so, he held tighter until she understood he wasn't going to let her win this argument. She finally relaxed.

"So, I can't persuade you to be right with me all the way? I need you, too." Jane's eyes moistened.

"I'll be looking at our rear and flanks, to be sure we're OK. I'll join up with you at the larger stack after everyone is there." He took a long time to gaze in her eyes. "I promise I won't mess this up. I won't lose you again."

"Fine. I'll hold you to that," she said, slamming her backpack closed. She walked out of the room, leaving him alone.

He shouted from the upstairs hall, "Five minutes, everyone. Five minutes and we're out the door. See Jane if you need anything else before we go." Demian went to a safe he kept hidden in the guest bedroom. He took out $20,000 in hundred-dollar bills, his favorite Kimber 45 automatic pistol, a tactical light, a fully charged satellite phone and ammo. He added all of these to his backpack.

Demian had called Bennie to come to the house. He came in the back door to a round of cheers and slaps on the back. He looked sweaty but confident. He got the supplies he needed including extra full magazines for his rifle, food, water and extra batteries. He brought in two rakes and leaned them against the counter in the kitchen.

Bennie met up with Will, standing face to face, eye to eye. "I knew you had our backs. I knew you wouldn't let us down. You had the balls to shoot at a missile-armed helicopter with a rifle?" Will asked Bennie.

"Yeah. It's not the size of the tool; it's the way you use it." Bennie embraced Will. "My good friend. I could never let you down."

"All of the shit yesterday is gone?" Will probed.

"Yes. I feel great. And I can hold off a chopper with my rifle again if I need to," Bennie answered. "I may use a lot of bullets, but…."

"Good, my man. That's good, my man." Will smiled broadly. "I have to applaud you for your balls. A peashooter against modern weaponry mounted on a helicopter, and you held them off. They'll talk about this at the academy for decades."

"I don't think so. They should use that as an example of having the proper equipment going into battle. That's what this lesson should be about," Bennie said dismissively.

"Are you nuts? They'll be talking about using the tools at hand. And winning."

Marion and Catherine came into the kitchen. "We are told that there is a means of conveyance that you two have available to use to transport us up the mountain?" Marion asked.

"If, by that, you mean we'll use haulers to help you up, then yes," Will responded.

"We remember being in Beijing—the rickshaws hauled everyone from the emperors to common people everywhere. We realize that we're not quick enough on our feet to keep up with the rest of you. We don't want to slow the whole group down, so we'll take you up on your offer to chauffeur us up the mountain. But, on the down slopes, we'll walk. OK?" Catherine asked.

"Fine by us. Bennie and I will take you up the tough slopes and let you walk down the easier slopes, as you want," Will answered. "Then there'll be horses."

"We've both ridden a lot. We should be okay from there," Marion said.

Deborah went to each person handing him or her a new, highlighted map of the trail leading around the peak of Death Mountain. "We all talked about it. Will and Bennie will be using the haulers to take Marion and Catherine up the slope to the ridge. They'll pick different routes so as not to leave a trail that's obvious to anyone if they try to chase us. We all have to be careful not to leave any obvious markings. We'll meet at the larger stone stack. That's where Gunner and I found this map."

Deborah had numbered the maps and given each person a copy. "I destroyed all the other maps, deleted our photos of the map and eliminated anything that could give away our route out of here. It's Ali and my jobs to get us out of here safely and to leave no trace."

"We have two rakes. I'll start with one and switch off with Deborah. Demian will use the other. We'll wipe out any tire tracks from the haulers or any tracks from the rest of us as we get up the trail," Ali said, determination in his youthful eyes.

Demian had photographed and emailed a map to John. Brud, Tom, Ellen and Elisabeth had loaded their horses in large horse trailers at about one. The drive from northern New Hampshire around the southern end of Lake Champlain took four hours. Driving to the eastern slope of Death Mountain took another two. They didn't use the ferries on the large lake, avoiding the inevitable waiting time for the scheduled departures. The earliest ferry left Burlington at 7:00 AM—way too late.

It was still dark when the two horse trailers, with vans doing the towing and an additional car, pulled into the parking lot of the designated New York State historical site of John Brown's cottage. The very small, single-room log house had burned in the late 1800s, but the site was maintained by the state in homage to Brown and his part in the Underground Railroad prior to and during the Civil War. A large blue placard with white lettering gave the details of the site and the historical relevance of both the man and the area.

The group looked over the maps Demian had emailed and saddled up the horses, with each rider holding the reins of a second horse. After coaching John, he settled in to ride the old mare he had been promised. She dutifully plodded along, wisely ignoring all of John's miscues. Ellen assured him. "Just hold on. She knows what to do and will take care of you."

"I don't have to drive, or steer, or anything? Where are the brakes?" he asked.

"No. A good horse knows what you're thinking and will help you, even if you don't know anything about her. Watch out for your emotions, though. They can sense fear and uncertainty. Just be calm and let the horse take care of you. It's their job—their way of being with their tribe, or fitting in."

"You talk about them as if they can think." John looked incredulous.

"Better than most of the humans I know. There's no pretense or ulterior motives, just work to be done." Ellen looked a little annoyed as she rode off to speak with her husband.

"Horse owners love their animals more than they love most people. Don't be offended. You probably touched a sore spot is all," Elisabeth said.

"We have to move. The others are maintaining radio silence. I want to get to the part of the climb that's steepest just at daybreak," Tom directed. He took the lead with Brud, John, Elisabeth and Ellen in single file, leading their spare horses. Brud had taken the time to put together small packs and lash them to the empty saddles. These held water, food and small first-aid kits.

49

"Look. Go slow. You can't see all the rocks and other branches on the ground or hanging low. Tripping or gouging yourself with unseen obstacles is a real risk. You all have lights, but use them only when you need, at least until you get over the ridge," Demian advised. He had designated that the group split up. Gunner, Jane and Madison would walk with and watch out for the children. Mason went first and would get as far as possible to meet up with the horses and riders coming from the other side of the mountain. He smiled at Madison, gave the kids a kiss and stood fully erect as he walked away into the darkness.

Demian stared at the two houses as the group left. He and his family had had a long history in these mountains. Now he and the others prepared to completely abandon all their possessions. Mason's house had become a real *home* with children. Demian had lived in the grand lodge for a year, before selling it to Will. For about a hundred years, a hunting cabin with a fireplace for heat and a wood stove for cooking had served as a place to come to hunt and be with friends in the fall. Mason completed the demolition of that camp after building the new lodge, but the memories still lived on.

Demian could not detect any signs of an invasion from the assassins coming up the only road to the compound, but he stood watch to make sure the group's rear was protected. He knew the trek up the mountain to the Beaver Dams would take them roughly two hours in the darkness. He planned to stand guard until the others would have cleared the ridge between the houses and the depression making up the dams' area. While he waited, he felt he was leaving his past but letting his future walk away from him in the opposite direction. At first, he didn't know which force was stronger. Then he looked at Jane and knew.

"Like we talked, Will. I'll hold back," Demian said in a subdued voice. Will nodded. Bennie gave the smallest of gestures consisting of a half-wink of his left eye. The group slowly started the climb up the slope to the Beaver Dams. In the dark, it took considerably longer than the trek would have taken in daylight.

Will and Bennie each pulled a hauler behind them, Catherine seated in one and Marion in the other. They had lined the carriers with comforters folded many times to cushion the metal bars. This made for a very smooth ride, except for occasional roots or stones that the wheels bounced over. The two men separated in order to avoid leaving a distinct trail. In the darkness, Demian, Deborah and Ali used the rakes to smooth out any obvious footprints or tire tracks.

"This is going to be harder than I thought," Deborah told Ali.

"Yeah, let's trade off more often, and when we're not raking over the trail, we can make sure the others are good," he answered.

"Yeah, they're not the climbers we are. Uncle Gunner took forever getting up to the Beaver Dams with me the other day. He was out of breath and sweating and had to stop three times on the way," she told her brother quietly enough that Gunner couldn't hear.

"Give me the rake—my turn," he urged.

"In a minute. I'm getting this patch and then it's your turn," Deborah directed.

Gunner held back and let the kids catch up with him. "You two OK?"

"Yeah."

"You need any help with the raking?" he asked.

"No, uncle Gunner. You know I could whip you with one hand tied behind my back. My brother could dribble a basketball all the way up the slope and still beat you." Deborah wondered if she had been too tough on him. "Really, thanks, but this is our job. We'll do it." She turned to Ali and said, "Here. 'Sgo."

They couldn't see Gunner's smile in the darkness.

Will was "chauffeuring" Marion. He had decided to go about a hundred yards to the east of the usual path up to the Beaver Dams, while Bennie pulled Catherine up the slope about two hundred yards to the west. The easterly path proved to be more unpredictable with branches and larger rocks to pull the hauler over. He went slowly to protect his friend and limit any severe jostling. "You've had quite a life. Ever had any adventures like this? You might as well regale me with tall tales as we inch our way up there."

"There was a time, in China, after World War II. All the Caucasians had to evacuate because of growing anti-western sentiments. It was really bad—so many of my friends were rounded up and jailed for no more reason than their origins. Most of them were never heard from again." They came to several trees that had fallen—some they went around, some under, and some over. This took time. Will switched on his headlamp when they were far enough away from the houses not to have any flashes of light visible from that area.

"Anyway, I traveled in the local Chinese uniforms—black pants and tunic, large woven straw hat, and mostly after dark. I hunched over to hide my height and blend in. I learned to see in the dark. I developed a sense of being able to know where things were—almost like seeing without my eyes and feeling without my hands. I had to go slowly, but then I got so good I was able to sense my surroundings. I haven't told anyone about all this. But this is where I started to be able to know about things outside of us."

"What things?" Will asked.

"You have a background in physics?" Marion started, knowing this would likely catch his friend's full attention.

"Sure. I love the elegant truth of that explanation of our world. It's simple, verifiable by anyone and has stood the test of time."

"I get it. I do too." The old man paused. "Have you considered relativity?"

"Sure. But, that's another large step removed from what's at our fingertips. Special relativity applies to things that happen at the speed of light."

"Exactly. So, what exists beyond our grasp, sight and other usual senses is the world of spirits."

The old man has just stepped over the line, Will thought. He kept quiet and pulled onward.

"Everything has spirit. The rocks, trees, water, air, animals and humans all have spirit," Marion continued. "Just follow this analogy for a second."

Will wondered how the old man could sense in the dark that Will doubted the worlds of spirits and gods.

Marion continued. "So, you know about the electromagnetic fields around an object? Anything in motion can arouse a change in the electromagnetic fields of anything else in the area surrounding it."

"So far, so good." At least this conversation was taking Will's mind off the dragging.

"What if we learned to feel and see with that field, or could sense our surroundings using the change in fields elicited by other objects?"

Shit. That almost makes sense, Will thought.

"What if the electromagnetic fields are only one small part of the spectrum of physical to energetic, to spiritual, to universal phenomena? Just like the energy spectrum includes visible light, radio waves, and other radiations."

"Yeah?" Will pulled the hauler over a large rock and had to immediately slow the descent over the other side. He groaned a little to do so.

"What if our usual senses were only a part of our sensory abilities? What if we could teach ourselves to see, or feel or know in different ways to include the rest of the energy spectrum?" the old man continued. "Try it. I can help you. Turn off your light and stand for a few seconds." Marion knew he asked for a lot.

Will turned off the headlamp he had been using. He stood still until his eyes adjusted to the darkness, although he still couldn't even see his own two feet.

"Now, close your eyes."

Will reluctantly did so. He continued to stand still and wondered how the old man knew his eyes were, in fact, open.

"Do you feel a large tree about ten feet to your right? It feels warm, for lack of a better description. It's like a soft, warm bump in that direction."

Will hesitated, then said, "I think so?"

"I can feel that you do. I'm sensing the field change as you start to open up to the sensibilities I've studied for years. I'm helping you do so now."

Will stood and turned slightly to the left and right. Then he had an inkling that there were separate trees with an opening between them. He started to move slowly and found his way along.

"Good. Start to feel confident. Start to have a confident awareness. You're doing well. Bear a little to the right, there," he warned.

Will consciously chose to suspend disbelief. He started to move a little more quickly. Then he slowed down and started to enjoy the fact that he could know there were things in the environment without having to see them. "How are you helping me do this? I know I'm not doing this alone."

"That's my trick," the old man quickly answered. "I've studied this for years. Now, I think I can help by increasing my own awareness. You feel that and can use that, too. It's like intersecting fields, with the stronger field influencing the weaker."

"Jesus, Marion." Will pulled onward and when he perceived a particularly crowded area, he turned on his headlamp. At intervals, he enjoyed the darkness as well, as they trudged on.

Catherine and Bennie were having an easier time ascending the ridge. The trees, roots, rocks and ruts that they traversed made Catherine feel only slight shudders. No blown down trees blocked their paths.

"Bennie, I can see and feel that you've regained your usual vitality. I'm sorry that you had a difficult time after my two treatments. They sapped your energy. I should have warned you that that could have happened. But, I can also feel that there is a new calmness that will grow inside of you. You will see and feel differently and be able to incorporate new things in your life. You can learn how to trust many people, now. Not only one or two people but also anyone who honestly and openly approaches you. I expect nice changes for you," Catherine concluded.

"How is it that you can be such a healer?" Bennie asked.

From his tone, Catherine knew this was a real question and that he wanted an answer. "Well, Marion and I have spent our lives learning about and doing healings. It's our honor to be available to you to help, in our small way. But, you know? The healing someone receives is not *from* us. We can only stir up the energies to do what they will do. We don't give anything to you, we just set up the conditions that will allow you to process what you need to process and leave behind those things that do not serve you well, anymore."

Bennie considered this and wondered if it sounded too self-effacing. How long would he have floundered if he had not had such interventions? About that time, they joined the others at the larger stone pyramid.

50

Demian assured himself that he had waited long enough to allow the others to climb at least to the high ridge before the Beaver Dams. He factored in the slow progress of the haulers and the poor nighttime visibility. He knew the others were in good physical condition and could make the climb, and he trusted Jane, Madison and Gunner would see to it the group stayed together and safe. He could see and hear no evidence of the assassins approaching up the road.

For a brief while, he considered calling the state police captain, but knew the lines were not secure. He couldn't risk having the conversation intercepted. He decided to rethink this and ask the others for their opinion about when to call the captain once they got to the other side of Death Mountain. Demian respected this unit of the state police and the captain and didn't want to have them waste their time protecting empty houses.

He turned to start to climb up the slope, using a rake to cover any tracks the children might have missed. Demian crossed the ridge leading down to the Beaver Dams, seeing the first wisps of light cross the horizon. He had seen this many times while hunting, getting into position to hunt deer, but it always gave him pause. He saw the same mountain, slopes, trees and rocks. But the way the light played on everything continually changed. The shadows disappeared slowly as he finally got to the Beaver Dams. The rest of the group came out of hiding as they could see Demian was not an unknown assassin.

"Anyone know how far Mason got? Where are John and Elisabeth and the horses?" Demian asked.

"We don't know, but we do know Mason came through here. He left me a mark that no one else would see. He's probably over the top of the mountain by now," Madison said.

"Here, Demian. Here's where we found the loose rock with the map," Deborah pointed up to an empty spot on the pyramid. "We found it right here." She had grabbed his hand and pulled him to the larger stone stack.

"Yup. I can see where the rock was," Demian said in an admiring manner. "How did you know to look at that particular rock? There are sure a lot of other rocks in the area and in the stack."

"Gunner said he had seen the loose stone in a meditation. He went to it and pulled it right out," Deborah replied.

Gunner, Jane and Madison had walked over to the stacks. Marion and Catherine followed. "There is more than can be dreamt of under these heavens and stars," Gunner added as he looked upwards wistfully.

Marion said, "So these are the stone stacks. I see why Gunner thought they must have been so important. They were built before any mechanized aids. And look at how that stone was designed so it could be removed singly without the rest of the stack falling down. Another sign of importance, I'm sure."

"Yup. You know in my life, I've had better guidance from meditations than most other things," Gunner added.

"Exactly!" Marion said.

"Well, if we're going to bet our lives on the map engraved on the stone, I would give it a world of importance too," Demian said. He walked to Jane, hugged her in front of the group and thanked her. The sun rose over the ridge and started to walk down the taller trees to finally touch the water, changing the dark colors to bright reds and yellows. They all stood and admired the scene.

Will left the group to walk back towards the ridge to be in a position to overlook the slope down to Jay, in case they'd been tailed. Bennie started to follow Mason's trail up and out of the Beaver Dams area to scout the trail and to make sure no assassins would overtake the party from that direction. Will and Bennie felt they needed to keep the perimeter. Demian did not try to dissuade them, although he believed this to be completely unnecessary.

"We have two options. One is to slowly make our way along the trail shown on the map Deborah found. The other is to wait here, regain our strength and make sure there is no way we could possibly miss the horses when they come." Demian looked at the group. "I vote we wait, not tire ourselves out and make sure we meet up with John and Elisabeth and their friends." He looked around and did not hear any arguments from any of the others.

"So, wait it is. We agree," Marion said.

"If we don't see the others in an hour, I'll climb Death and scope them out or try the satellite phone from there. It's no use here with the surrounding mountains. We can't get a clear shot to a satellite to call through."

The others broke out their canteens, treats and folding camp tripod stools and waited.

51

The assassins had been licking their wounds after being fired upon by a civilian hunting rifle. They all immediately knew that the shooter was no ordinary citizen, but a highly trained marksman to be able to hit a moving chopper at a distance of three hundred yards. They quickly landed their stolen helicopter on Grand Isle in Lake Champlain, unfastened the missiles and drove off in the van they had stashed previously. They wasted no time wiping down fingerprints as they knew they were in no databases. The blood was a different story. It could easily confirm that the pilot had flown the chopper. He had been shot in the forearm, causing difficulty controlling the stick, and had barely gotten the helicopter and other assassins to the alternate escape venue. None of the others could fly; they all felt lucky to have had a close alternate landing site planned.

The group set fire to the chopper by remote after they left the island. They drove their rented van with their missiles bouncing on the floor in the back. After they crossed over to upper New York State, they came to a rest stop on Route 87 to eat, rest and plan another attack. They did not discuss abandoning the contract. The pilot's wound was dressed and had stopped bleeding, but this would limit his close-range combat abilities. He would not be flying in the near future.

They noticed an independent trucker hauling a load of drainage pipes to a new construction site somewhere downstate on an eighteen-wheeler. The assassins overpowered him and kept him hostage. They positioned the missile tubes among the other pipes, nicely hiding them in plain sight, ready for launch. It looked like a collection of different sized pipes for sewer or water use. An unsophisticated eye would not discern the launchers.

Thereafter, they could drive down the road in daylight hours to search for a position to use to fire the missiles with impunity. They set up the Mavericks at the same area that they kidnapped the sheriff, having extensively scouted that location, knowing it was very remote, little used by the locals and presented an excellent stable platform. They programmed the coordinates and the remote computer controls and prepared to leave the area. However, the leader of the group, the pilot, refused to drive on in the rented van until he saw that the people who had wounded him were devastated, their lives and property destroyed. After arguing, they pulled back only to the AuSable River Road. From that vantage, they could see the missiles fly up Jay Mountain to their targets.

52

Captain Nicholas Green fumed at the insult of being told to set up a perimeter and wait. This was not what a self-respecting officer of the New York State Police should be doing, and he should never be *told* to do anything. He decided to drive and reconnoiter the area in his personal vehicle—a black Land Rover. He had installed a small gun rack behind the front seat, easily reached, if needed. His accessory service weapons—a pistol, shotgun, flare gun and ammunition for each—rode behind him as well. They were his backup and occasionally his moral support, even if he had never had to draw them. He roamed the small roads surrounding the Jay Mountain homes. He didn't believe for a minute that Demian had told him all he knew. But maybe that made sense. Even the governor himself had been targeted for assassination. Everyone should be on a need-to-know basis only.

"Get me the sergeant." The captain followed social norms and niceties only around his wife.

"Yes, sir!" the patrolman quickly answered and handed over the phone.

"Sir?" the sergeant inquired.

"Look, where would you go to launch the missiles, if you had to pick the best tactical position around here?" Captain Green ruminated.

"I was thinking about that, and I came to a couple of conclusions." He waited for the officer to tell him to go ahead.

"Yeah?"

"Well, I thought any level space within five miles would work out just fine to launch from. We can't cover all that." He waited.

"Yeah. And?" the captain demanded.

"I could launch the rockets anywhere, but, if I wanted to see them shriek through the air and hit and explode and burn everything down, I would have to be to the west because the ring of mountains would obscure my field of vision to the east and north. Get it?"

"Yeah. I grew up with maps, remember? I grew up before GPS, Google Maps, or any of that other nonsense." The captain gave a short snort.

The sergeant had hit a raw nerve. "I know that, sir. I'm only thinking out loud. Whereas the missiles can be launched from anywhere within a five-mile radius, the assassins could only see them fly and explode from the west. And I'll bet they'll be watching to confirm their kills. It makes sense for them to do so, I think. And they sure would want their revenge. They were foiled in their first attack attempt. Right?"

"Yeah. I agree. I'm out riding around to think this over from the ground level. I'll call you back if I think of anything else. Just keep the perimeter, for now. Over."

No one said "over" anymore, the sergeant thought. *Especially on a cell phone.*

Captain Green circled through Jay, Upper Jay, Keene and Elizabethtown. He noted nothing unusual. The traffic continued as it always had—local cars, school buses, large eighteen-wheelers, all intermixed with hikers, sightseers, and bikers. Motorcyclists couldn't resist pushing the limits around the gently sweeping curves of the mountain roads. The captain disliked them the most; they would easily surpass the speed limits by thirty miles an hour. On most days, he let them roar past him. On this day, he blipped his siren and flashed his overhead warning lights. The motorcyclists quickly slowed down and, for the few minutes they could be seen, paid attention to the prevailing signs and laws. One such Harley-Davidson touring bike slowed to the point it irritated the officer, making him go too slowly following on roads where passing was only possible in a few areas. He pulled the motorcyclist over. The man got off his bike and reached into his back pants pocket to produce his driver's license.

"Whoa, Bubba. Move slowly!" the captain barked.

"Hold on there. I'm getting out my license is all." The motorist raised his open right hand and slowly brought out his wallet with his left.

"Never can be too careful." He viewed the license, the bike's inspection sticker and the registration. "Been in the area long?" The captain noted his license gave an address of Long Island. He also made note of a decal from the United States Naval Academy.

"Nope, just riding through. Why was I stopped?" the motorist asked.

"Going too damned slow!" He took the time to spit on the ground. "I have to ask about the naval academy sticker," he said pointing to it. "I've got a nephew who graduated in 2004. He became a nuclear officer on a sub. Served a couple of tours in the Persian Gulf and one in Africa—on the horn. Djibouti. What the hell would they want a nuclear submarine officer in the desert for? No submarines there, for sure."

"The politically correct answer is, who knows?" He smiled and let time pass. "Graduated from the academy myself in 1980. Just retired from teaching warfare and tactics there," the man answered.

"Pleased to make your acquaintance." He paused, thoughtful. The captain continued. "I have a logistical problem for you if you can keep this to yourself, and want to scratch your head about it?"

"Still got my top-secret clearance."

"I'm thinking through a hypothetical scenario. If a pack of assassins had access to four Mavericks and wanted to launch them to strike about two miles uphill from here," he said while gesturing to the east, "where would they launch them from to see them fly and strike their targets?" The captain pointed uphill and then made a sweeping motion to cover the rest of the valley.

"Sounds a little more than hypothetical," he mused as he surveyed the landscape extending up the slope of Jay Mountain. "Hum, I'd say somewhere within five miles, but you know that." He paused again. "How about that flat area around the AuSable River in the saddle before the land rises up to White-face Mountain? It's secluded enough. It's got a good view up the slope, and it's next to the road going out of town for a quick exit." The biker had enjoyed the vantage from his lowered Harley-Davidson's seat. From there, the mountains and contours of the surrounding roads were more immediately apparent. He had felt and seen the mountains and valleys in a way a rider in a car could not, with the ceiling and windshields obscuring the landscapes.

"I drove the rest of this road this morning. You're probably right," the captain agreed.

The motorcyclist suddenly jerked to attention. "Shit. Did you say Mavericks?" he nervously questioned, as if recalling something.

"Yeah. What's up?"

"Well, I saw a truck carrying what looked like sewer pipes stopped at the bend in the road following the AuSable River. You could hide missile tubes among those pipes easily."

"Shit!" The captain jumped in his car, blared his siren, turned on his flashers and sped off. He stomped on the gas until he was going way too fast, then he let off only a little.

It took the cyclist only seconds to put on his helmet and gun his Harley to follow. He also keyed his helmet microphone to the rest of the crew of seven riders traveling with him. They had all scattered to local restaurants or bars for lunch. He told them that the state police needed them to establish a perimeter and watch for a truck with sewer pipes leaving anywhere close to the AuSable River. As he caught up to the captain, he filled in his fellow riders with the hypothetical question posed by the captain. Among the group were prior military, law enforcement and defense contracting engineers. They immediately got the picture. They immediately knew there was nothing hypothetical about the situation.

53

"It's actually a pretty good trail. Followed it in the dark easily," Mason told John. They had met up on the trail marked out on Deborah's map. Mason had made his way to the other side of Death Mountain, about halfway down the easterly slope.

"Can we make it easily with the horses?" Tom asked after introductions had been completed. He worried about the safety of his horses going over unknown terrain.

"For sure. There are no really big obstructions. And as the sun rises, we'll see a lot better."

"How far is it from here?" Tom asked. Ellen stood near him after checking all the horses. She found they all tolerated the climb well, so far, with no obvious injuries.

"On foot, it's about two hours in the dark." He thought for a moment, then continued. "I think it would be an easy one-hour ride from here on horseback. Got an extra horse for me?"

"Sure, here you are. Take the lead; you know the way." Ellen handed him the reigns. "This is Maggie. Treat her with respect, and she'll take care of you."

Brud had dismounted to go to talk with John and Elisabeth. "How are you two doing?"

"I'm loving it," Elisabeth answered. "John, here, looks a little tired, or is it the altitude? You do look a little washed out, John. Have some water and some jerky. That'll perk you up for sure."

"I'm OK except for my ass. I'm sore there, no doubt." He got off the horse and walked bowlegged, rubbing his buttocks. "Not a word about this to the others."

"Your pride and your secret are safe with us." Brud laughed. "If you're giving up on us, how about I offer to have you stay behind, watch our rear as the rest of the horses climb? You could call us and warn us if the bad guys approach from that direction?" Brud asked.

"No way. I'm sticking with Elisabeth. Where she goes, I go." John didn't look convinced as he said this. "I know I'll pay for this for days, though."

"I'll take care of you when we get home. You can rest all you want, then," Elisabeth said. This didn't help John in the least.

They all remounted and followed Mason up Death Mountain. The climb was easily accomplished in about an hour, ascending while avoiding the upper third of the peak, then descending to the Beaver Dams. The horses made enough noise to alert the others waiting that it was no surprise.

Once at the dams, and after introductions were completed all around, Bennie and Will returned to the large stone stack, having seen no intruders from either direction. "We're all here. Let's go. The trail should be easy to follow after you and the horses have trampled it down for us," Demian said.

"Sure. Let's all mount up after we let the horses drink their fill from the pond."

"It's good water. I've drunk it many times," Demian said. "But we humans should stick with our canteens to avoid the giardia."

They all mounted up and followed Mason on the trail to the other side of Death. The whole trip would likely take two hours, they calculated. Again, Demian held back to watch their rear and make sure no assassins followed. He rode back to the ridge and overlooked the area around the two houses.

As the group rode on, John asked Brud, "Can you accommodate everyone at your camps? You know you can't tell a soul about us being there. I know you're not busy for the moment. It's another huge favor that I'll owe you, Tom and Ellen—and the horses."

"My pleasure. Tom and Ellen know not to tell anyone about all this. And the horses wouldn't tell a soul. They're loving the ride for sure," Brud answered. His voice sounded younger up in the mountains.

"I thought that we could trust you, but thank you all the same. It does my heart good to know there are people like you who will go the extra distance to help," John said.

Jane had had a running conversation with Madison and her kids. Deborah and Ali understood this high adventure might be the most exciting thing they would ever do in their lives. They hung close to their mother, checking the maps, making sure that everyone except Demian followed quickly. It was their job, and they would perform it well.

Jane said to Madison, "They're so responsible, so serious."

Madison smiled with pride. "As we walk or ride along, I'm calmer. I'm thinking I and everyone else are OK. The mountains calm me."

"We are," Jane answered. "Trust Demian, Mason and all the others. I heard that Tom is ex-Special Forces, just like Bennie. That that's the reason he decided to come here to rescue us with the horses. He felt a solemn duty to one of his own."

"You're right. We couldn't be in better hands and couldn't make a safer exit out of the houses. I just hope they find the assassins before anyone else is hurt." Madison smiled again at her children as they did their job.

When the group reached the high point of the trail, they turned in their saddles. They looked out over the Beaver Dams, the ridge separating the dams and the slope down to the two houses, and the houses themselves. Beyond that lay Lake Placid, Whiteface Mountain, and the rest of the Adirondacks.

Tom said in a voice loud enough to be heard by them all, "At least you're safe. We'll get you all to the trucks and trailers, and eventually to New Hampshire. Berlin is a beautiful, sleepy little place that is so far out of the way, no one will ever find it. Let the police do their jobs and you'll all be fine. I'm sure."

The whole group believed him, but lingered, looking back on their homes and lives, looking back on all that they were leaving.

54

Captain Green had radioed in to his troopers to surround the road going to the AuSable River. He heard a very loud motorcycle follow him and several others' exhausts echoed from the surrounding mountains. He wondered if the motorcyclist might have called in friends. As they closed in to within a mile of the river, they heard three missiles blast off and shriek about two hundred yards off the ground. The missiles instantly converged on the houses on Jay Mountain, exploded and left flashes of light and then loud thundering echoes persisted for about ten seconds. Many smaller explosions followed at intervals of seconds to minutes.

The captain felt many things all at once. He feared that Demian, Mason, Madison and all the others had been killed. They couldn't have lived through those explosions. He worried the top of his head would start to blow off with anger. Civilians killed on his watch. He wanted to end this. He needed to end this. *Now.* He nearly broke the steering wheel off, pushing against it in frustration. Then he slammed the wheel with his fists and actually bent it slightly while saying every vile thing he could think of. This was *his* country. These were *his* people. He cherished their lives and freedom. Now they were dead. He slammed his forehead into the steering wheel, not feeling the deep ache in his skull.

The motorcyclist knew what he had seen—three Mavericks, their vapor trails leading to death and multiple explosions from each missile. He got off his bike, kneeled and prayed. Then he punched the seat on the bike hard enough to knock it over. His stomach burned as he spit out acid. He radioed his friends to report the missiles firing.

At the same time, Demian heard and then saw one missile home in on Will's house and another on Madison's. The third flew directly to the large attached garage at Will's. In milliseconds, the houses were flattened and burning. There was no way their safe room could have protected them, even if they could have gotten there in time. "Shit! Now, I'm angry!" he yelled to no one.

The rest of the group watched in horror. They could see the same thing in a more panoramic manner, from higher up the mountain. Even the horses stood at attention, staring down the mountain, their ears straight up, not seeming to breathe.

The adults and Deborah all had tears in their eyes. Ali refused to let anyone see him cry. The nine-year-old boy said, "We need to go. We need to get out of here, now." He rode on the back of Mason's saddle. He buried his face in his father's back and could no longer control the grief he felt. He wailed. He hung on for dear life, not believing he was safe. He worked his hands into Mason's large jacket pockets and gripped the cotton material lining until he thought he could feel it ripping.

The adults turned, and in a stunned silence rode on. They all immediately understood how lucky they were to have left the houses when they did. The explosions kept coming. These missiles had had additional charges designed to go off at intervals of seconds to minutes to complete the work of the original attacks. These had psychologically devastating effects on those poor souls who were bombed—they never knew when the explosions would stop. With each successive concussive boom, the group of riders fell further into despair, even knowing the explosions were far away didn't assuage their feelings of being violated.

Demian turned his horse to climb Death Mountain and rode quickly to catch up with the others. He couldn't watch the bombed-out shells of the houses burn. As soon as he received a satellite signal, he would call the captain and tell him they were all safe. He burned with anger, even if he felt extremely lucky to have made the prior night's decisions. He felt devastated to have lost all his family's history and to have seen the loss of his friends' homes and possessions.

Deborah cried. She thought about her clothes, computer, cell phone, and all her books. They all went up in flames. She knew they were gone. She sobbed after every subsequent explosion. Was it the missiles? What were the subsequent explosions? She rode along next to her mother, holding hands. "Oh, Mom, we lost everything."

Another explosion echoed around them. "No. We're all safe. That's what matters." Madison hoped she sounded confident but wasn't sure. "We'll be fine."

Deborah kept crying. Madison leaned over to kiss her on the forehead, feeling inadequate to comfort her daughter.

Jane had never been out of the United States for an extended period, had never been in a third-world country and never been anywhere near combat. Being the hospital administrator meant spending endless hours and years in her office or on call for emergencies. In that way, she had led a very sheltered life. She shuddered more violently after each explosion. She had ridden horses on vacations a dozen or more times but had not developed a deeper under-standing of how the horses care for their riders once the rider has won the horse over. With each explosion, her horse, named Star, got jumpier. After the final explosion, he startled, brayed and reared back on his hind legs. Jane barely held on. Star became jumpier as Jane became more frantic.

Tom rode over to grab the reins and quiet the horse. "I'm sorry, Jane. He's not usually this jumpy. It's the explosions and their echoes. If you could ride on like they were only fireworks, that would help."

"But, they're not. They're explosions. Why do they keep on and on?"

"The Mavericks. The missiles have timed after-impact explosives to de-moralize and decimate the enemy. They'll continue for at least ten minutes. You've got to fight the urge to be frightened best you can."

Jane sat up straighter, grabbed back the reigns and murmured to Star. "It'll be all right. I'm here for you." She patted the horse on its neck, and he settled down. When Star calmed, she felt more able to be in control.

Tom rode with her. "I can't imagine what you've all lost. I saw a lot of missiles in the Balkans. But I was military. It wasn't our concern to think about the civil-ians. We were trying to survive and kill the bad guys. Now, I see things differently. Now, I know how lucky and how devastated you must be—all at the same time."

"I don't live there. I'm the lucky one."

Demian finally reached the group. He rode up to Jane and hugged her. "Jesus, Jane. It's all gone." He wept silently.

"I'm right here. Everyone's here. I'll ride with you." Jane studied him carefully.

"I'm never letting you out of my sight again. Never happening." He cried, wiping away the tears and blowing his nose in a large red handkerchief.

Watching him cry made Jane admire him all the more. She wanted to soothe him, console him, hold him and try to lessen his pain. She held Star's reigns and whispered, "I will let you be with me every day of my life. We'll re-build everything. For everyone here."

"Damn straight."

Ellen and Elisabeth rode together. Silently. Ellen thought about her time as an OR nurse in a MASH unit treating wounded soldiers in the Balkans. Her two years in the country were punctuated with rocket, mortar, cannon and small arms fire. She had literally been on the front lines when the enemy troops had advanced more quickly than expected. She remembered how frightened she had been as a new nurse. Then the anger of seeing so many wounded, maimed or dying soldiers hardened her into a robot—metallic, so she couldn't be hurt. She had spent the last twenty or so years learning how to feel again. It wasn't easy. Tom had gently allowed her to take her time and heal. She thought she had fully recovered. Now, all of that war came crashing back. She remembered seeing the limbs of the soldiers undergoing amputations to save their lives. She remembered their screams as they awakened and learned they had lost limbs. She could not muster a single sound. She became mute. She held the saddle of Elisabeth's horse, calming the large animal and its rider wordlessly.

Elisabeth was simply stunned. Riding.

Brud stopped his horse and visually checked over each rider and horse. He called each of them by name, trying to bring them back to the present moment. His horrors from the Korean "conflict" replayed clearly, even after sixty or more years. After all of that time, he could mute the sounds of that war's violence but still feared for himself and all the others. Brud wanted to keep everyone grounded. He needed to play the role of the helper, assisting everyone else, tending to their needs to be here and now. After everyone passed him on the trail, he followed. He would make sure they all got off the mountain. He would do what he couldn't do in Korea—make sure to bring them all home.

Will and Bennie took the lead positions. They needed to be the point in the formation, leading their people away from devastation to safety. They had the most recent memories of the explosions, death, screams and losing good friends. They would not allow any of this group to die on this mountain. They both mentally inventoried their ammo, weapons and possible tactics to be used if confronted. This was their training. They reverted to completing these mental routines as the after-impact explosions finally stopped, their echoes eventually fading away. The silence became even more difficult to deal with as they rode on. They found themselves looking at each other, checking that the group followed safely, and searching the trail in front of them.

55

The assassins in their rented van reported via email that the mission had been accomplished. They did not notice a sole motorcycle following at a distance. That motorcyclist radioed the others, and they began to form a line behind the van. They all took orders from their leader via headsets without question, feeling they were in a military action. None would break rank and do anything stupid. But none would let this van escape. They would do anything they had to do. This was their country. There had been an attack on their countrymen. They all revved their engines in neutral, signaling each other, their motorcycles becoming snorting beasts waiting to pounce, their anger barely contained.

The captain pulled his car to a skidding stop when the motorcyclist he had stopped earlier in the day blocked the road in front of him, waving frantically to let him in.

"What?!" the state police officer demanded.

"Let me in. I think we've got the shits who launched the missiles." He got in the captain's large SUV and told him about the other seven cycles in his pack. The riders were happy to assist with surveillance. One of them had noticed a van pulling away from the eighteen-wheeled truck and followed without being noticed. He gave the location and direction of travel to the captain who radioed it to the other officers and swore an embarrassing string of obscenities emphasizing his orders.

"Let's move. You can handle yourself with a gun?" the captain asked.

"What? Are you fucking bullshitting me? I was born with a rifle in one hand and a pistol in the other. I can outshoot you any day."

"Listen, I forgot your name."

"Jed Edwards."

"I trust you can retrieve the firearms from the pouch in back of my seat and load them?" he asked as he drove like hell to the location given by the motorcyclist's gang.

"Damn straight." Jed rummaged for, retrieved, and loaded two Glock 17s and one Remington 870 while being violently jostled around from the captain driving way too fast around curves and over bumps. "Which do you want?"

"I feel like I want to be up close and personal. Back me up with the Remington. I'll take a Glock. Don't do anything stupid, and when my men get there, fade away. I don't want to explain why I gave a gun to a civilian."

"Got it. Fucking bastards. Firing off missiles in this country. I've got your back. And when your men get there, I'm gone."

"Jed, good to have you on board." The captain offered his hand to shake. They did so wordlessly.

Jed put on his motorcycle helmet to check in with the rest of the group. He got their current location and instructed them not to engage under any circumstances. He told all of them to pass the van and to ride far enough ahead of them to just be out of sight. The lone following bike should slow down to be out of sight. The surveillance therefore should be unnoticed by the van occupants.

A very quick roadblock was set up on Route 83 south of Keene. A long stretch of the road with no other access fronted a river on one side and the slope up Whiteface Mountain on the other. Three state police cars blocked the road while officers jumped out of their cars with weapons drawn. Several of the troopers flanked the area on each side widely. The motorcycle drew up close to the van to block it from turning around. The van's driver saw the roadblock and slammed on the brakes as the captain's SUV closed in from behind. The assassins immediately knew it wouldn't be pretty—they were trapped.

The captain jumped out of his car, weapon drawn. Jed jumped out of the passenger's side with the Remington aimed at the van. He stood behind the open door of the SUV, resting the barrel of the gun on the door frame. He wouldn't miss. Not today. The other state policemen stood their ground. A police chopper approached and began to hover overhead. It was all over in seconds. The assassins rolled down the windows, put their hands in full view, exited the van and lay flat on the ground.

The trucker who had been taken hostage lay bound up in the back. He was released and quickly confirmed the suspicions of the captain.

Jed leaned the shotgun on the front seat, radioed to be picked up by his group of fellow cyclists and vanished. Amid all the chaos, he simply walked away, unnoticed.

Captain Green said in a loud voice, "All you men. These are extraordinary times. These assholes have blasted off three missiles and killed our country's innocent civilians. You will wait, stand down and allow me to question the assassins. Understood?"

None of the other officers moved or spoke.

Captain Green went over to the assassin with a bandaged forearm. He stood over the man and said, "You can walk out of here if you give us information about Sheriff Wilkins. If not, it will be my pleasure to shoot you in the right foot, and then the left foot. If necessary, I will shoot every one of you in the right foot and then the left foot."

"We have diplomatic immunity." The assassin with the bandaged forearm laughed sarcastically in a thick German accent.

"Don't mean a damn thing to me. I'm no diplomat. And I'm retiring in two weeks. Don't give a shit anymore, now that you've launched missiles in my homeland and killed my fellow citizens." He cocked the Glock and pointed it at the assassin's right foot. "You'll never walk again unless you get a prosthetic foot."

"You don't have the nerve."

The captain fired. Screams filled the air. The other officers watched. None moved. "What'll it be? The other foot, too?"

"No, wait. I can tell you everything." The man held his hands up in front of him to try to ward off another shot. His screams continued.

"You better start talking. I'm a very impatient man. And you don't have that much time until you bleed out. What'll it be?"

"OK," he said between moans and outright screams. "So I'll give you his location in Canada. South of Montreal. He's still alive."

"I'm listening."

The wounded man readily gave up the sheriff's location.

Hundreds of police cars, ambulances, and onlookers quickly arrived. The civilians were all dispersed. Two teams of state troopers left to secure the missiles' launch site and the stolen truck on the AuSable River. The captain called the Royal Canadian Mounted Police and within minutes received word that Sheriff Wilkins was safe, alive and unharmed, having been imprisoned at the location indicated, south of Montreal. He had been helicoptered to that location from the AuSable River after being taken there by the assassins. The sheriff asked only that the state police hold the villains long enough to allow him to confront them personally.

The Canadian Mounties put Sheriff Wilkins on the phone with the captain. "I'm fine. How are the captives? You know they will assert diplomatic immunity?" Todd asked.

"Yeah, but, you know? The head of the group has to be treated for gunshot wounds to the forearm and to the foot. Apparently shot the first time by a sentry outside Demian's old house, and the next time while being interrogated by myself."

"Shit damn, man. I wish I could've been there," the sheriff said admiringly.

"Yeah. I may lose my pension over that, but time was of the essence. Before the whole world was a witness to it, I had to make my point to get your location. It was completely worth it. You get my drift?"

"You did that for me?" Sheriff Wilkins said in a resigned manner.

"I would do it for any of us. We're a team. We stand together. All of us."

"I know. The four assassins had four missiles. I saw them. I heard they bombed Demian's old houses. Have you been there to see if there are any survivors?" the sheriff asked, worried about his old friends.

"No, I haven't been there yet. Shit. Four missiles? Four assassins? That means there's still one more bad guy with a missile on the loose. Shit!"

"You shot a captive?"

"I couldn't delay effectively interrogating them because all too soon there would be too many eyes, ears and cameras rolling. All we could get was your location. I called it into the Mounties. I don't know any more about the other missile or any more assassins."

"Got it. I'm coming back down there as quick as I can."

56

"Captain, you've got a phone call. You better take it," his private said.

"Jesus. What now?" The captain grabbed the phone and looked stunned as he heard Demian's voice.

"Captain. This is Demian. We're all safe. I wanted you to know we left the houses last night."

"What? My officers didn't report that you left." Disbelief sounded clearly in his voice.

"Yeah, we left another way. I know you must be frantic thinking we were all killed, so I called as quickly as I could get satellite reception."

"Jesus," the captain said, profoundly relieved that no one had been killed on his watch. "I'm getting too old for this."

"The assassins don't know we're alive. I want to keep it that way, too." Demian worried that they were still targets.

"Well, you'll never believe how we happened to catch them. But I'm not certain that we have them all. And there's one missile unaccounted for and at least one more assassin. Wherever you are, keep going for the foreseeable future. I've got to button this up on this end. We've found Sheriff Wilkins safe and sound. He'll be coming back shortly." The captain waited.

"Captain, thank you and your men for all of that. We owe you a debt of gratitude," Demian concluded.

"Yeah. I don't know this is over yet. Don't contact me. I'll call you. Keep going and keep your head down, got it?"

"Yeah."

"I'll likely be put on administrative duties as they reconstruct the whole stream of events. I shot the leader of the trio in the foot to convince him to tell us the sheriff's location. I knew we had a very short window of opportunity before the whole world came to be onlookers, and I couldn't be as *persuasive*. So, I'll be behind the lines working, but I'll be your only contact. Don't let your guard down. I'll call you. I don't have to tell you how to hide. Keep going."

"I owe you an even bigger debt of gratitude. When I see you, I'll make this square." Demian clicked off.

The trail was easy for the horses to follow back the way they'd come earlier in the day. The flattened ferns, grasses and gouged-out hoof prints led the way silently. Demian felt a huge sigh of relief as well as a huge loss. He would sort out those feelings when he got his group to safety. His thoughts were jumbled; he couldn't immediately come to any conclusions.

The adults in the horse caravan rode on silently for a while. Will and Bennie had seen and heard explosions, like this morning, in Iraq. Brud had witnessed Korea. Tom and Ellen survived the Balkans. This brought back bad memories that had been lurking in the shadows of their subconscious for decades. They silently tried to deal with those demons—to try to stuff them back.

Mason, Madison, the kids, Gunner and Jane felt their world had been shattered. The ground no longer seemed firm enough to support them. With every sound the forest made, a new fear arose in them. Having no other choice, they bravely rode on.

What they did not know was that the horses—so large and solid, with their constant movement beneath them—soothed them. The horses did this by being calm, continuing along their path. Walking. Breathing. Steady. They accepted their riders graciously and moved on.

Brud rode his horse over to John. "You got them out before they would have all been killed. You're the heroes here. You and Elisabeth. No one would have survived that missile attack." The old man thought back to similar explosions he had witnessed in the Korean "conflict" and shuddered. He knew the more modern missiles would have had exponentially more devastating effects.

"Yeah. I guess you're right. I just don't feel that good right now. My friends lost everything," John answered.

"No. They only lost their *things*. Remember that. We'll be here to help rebuild. We have to keep going, to get to Berlin." Brud rode away slowly to get off to the side of the trail and again took up the rear.

"I'm here, and I'm not leaving you. I've got to get to Bennie. I'll be right back," Demian shouted, riding on, passing Madison, Jane and the kids.

The others rode on in various degrees of shock. Demian approached Will and Bennie. "Bennie. Are you sure there were four missiles? Could you be sure?"

"There were four tubes, just like in Iraq. Stuck on to the landing skids. I didn't see any more," he answered.

"The good news is that the captain has captured three of the assassins. He shot one of the assassins in the foot to get him to give up the location of the sheriff. The Mounties found the sheriff, released him and he's on his way home. But what we don't know is if there might be any more assassins and where the other rocket is." Demian looked both enthusiastic and worried at the same time.

"Shit, damn. The captain and his men captured three of the assassins. The sheriff is safe and well. It's a win-win except for the houses and belongings," Bennie shouted.

"So, the problem still is whether there are any other assassins and any more rockets. We should keep on going to New Hampshire and get out of here," Will said.

The others quickly heard about the capture of the trio. Empty consolation, at this point.

Demian rode ahead to Tom, Ellen and Brud. "I'd like to sincerely thank you for getting all this rescue together. It must have sounded a little crazy to start out in the middle of the night; we're sure glad you didn't put it off. We would have been killed in that missile attack—no question."

"John and Elisabeth made a strong case for moving quickly, and we're glad to have been in time to save you. What's your preference now? Do you want to go on from here to New Hampshire? Brud has room at his camps, and we have room to carry everyone in the vans hauling the horses and extra car to get us all there," Tom said.

"I like the sound of that. It's way out of the way, isn't it?" Demian asked.

"Well, you can't get there from here, that's for sure," Tom joked. They all laughed until the somber mood of the group reasserted itself.

"Well, I think that would be just fine. We need to go somewhere off the beaten path, rest, console ourselves and then consider what to do next," Demian said.

Marion and Catherine rode well on their respective horses, keeping astride their saddles with little effort. They spoke very little, concentrating on keeping themselves calm, to extend this equanimity to the others. The energies of the horses soothed them as they swayed on.

Jane saw Demian coming to her. "I'm glad you can finally be with me. I missed you. I needed you. We all had to push on without you; it wasn't easy." She gave him a kiss and a long hug. Then she leaned back in her saddle to stare at him.

Finally, the horse trailers appeared in the distance. Will and Bennie rode ahead to make sure the way was clear and safe. Finding no problems, they helped the others dismount, unsaddled the horses and loaded everything into the trucks and cars.

"Do you think it's safe to travel to New Hampshire?" Will asked Bennie and Demian.

"Yes. These people saved our lives. I can attest to their characters. John and Elisabeth both trust them. We have to go with that. We have to get somewhere to rest, plan and start to heal." Demian looked resolute.

"I can't imagine somewhere more out of the way. Seems OK to me," Bennie answered.

Tom walked over to the three men talking. "So it's good to know that once a Special Forces operative, always a Special Forces operative. Did you really shoot at a moving helicopter with a hunting rifle?" He slapped Bennie on the back.

"It was the tool I had at hand. Seems to have worked," Bennie answered.

"The captain said you got the pilot in the wrist and stopped the attack," Demian added.

"So that's what happened. How far away was it?" Will asked.

"Only three hundred or so yards, I think," Bennie answered.

"Well, there are a lot of congratulations to go around. I have to thank the little girl who found the map. And even more amazing, she recognized it for what it was—your escape route over Death Mountain," Tom continued.

"She is amazing, all right," Demian agreed.

"Well, we'll get in the trucks and get on with it," Tom said.

"Make sure no one breaks radio silence and phone silence. We have to have complete silence. We still don't know if there are more assassins or the whereabouts of one other missile," Demian urged.

"Got it. We don't want to be targets either. I'll pass the word to Brud and Ellen driving the other vehicles."

The group found the vans surprisingly smooth. The six-hour ride passed slowly through the mountains of Vermont and New Hampshire, with each rider thinking about what could have been and what they'd lost in the attack. They unloaded at Brud's camps before Tom and Ellen left to tend to their horses.

"I am very pleased to have had your help. I won't forget this. It's reassuring to know there are still people who will risk themselves to rescue complete strangers." Demian pressed an envelope with a thousand dollars in Tom's palm. "You wouldn't want to offend me by refusing this, would you? Gas and horse feed is expensive, after all."

Tom thought about it for a few seconds. "All right. But it isn't necessary. John has told us about how generous you've been to everyone who is rebuilding in Lake Placid. I'm pleased to have been helpful to keep that going. That would be our giving back—to keep you helping that community."

Demian pulled Tom and Ellen to the side. "I've heard about your pasts, as well. You might be able to help us if you can. Could you keep an eye on Will and Bennie? They're younger versions of you both, back from Iraq. I'm worried that this recent trouble might stir up their PTSD. Could you just keep your eyes open if you're around?"

Tom and Ellen looked at each other with knowing regret and agreed. "It took us years to come back from the Balkans. It took Brud decades to really come home from Korea. Yeah, we'll make ourselves available, keep our eyes open and gently talk them back if the need arises," Ellen said.

"We need to offload and tend to the horses. Then we'll be back. While all of you settle in, we'll arrange for dinner to be served here for Brud. He's excited by the day's rescue, but he needs to rest. We all need a little rest. Could we say we'll eat at seven? That way we can get everything squared away on our end?" Tom asked.

"Sounds fine to me. Make sure I get the bill, and don't skimp on the wine or beer or whatever Brud and you both like to drink," Demian insisted.

The group settled into their respective cabins for showers, rest and much-needed downtime. John also mentioned to Demian and Bennie that they could use their computers to let their contacts know about their flight and ask for further updates. Demian sternly ordered them to be as dark as possible, using new email addresses, giving away no information as to the group's whereabouts, and asking for updates on any new information. He told the two men about the captain shooting the head assassin to make him talk. They responded with stunned silence.

57

Bennie's online hackers all chimed in to tell him they were happy to hear about the group's escape. They had hacked into the police communiqués and had worried until they heard that Demian had informed the state police of their escape. The hackers warned Bennie not to let down their guards. If the police knew that they were uninjured, so did any other potential assassins. They found no new information of note to relay, otherwise.

Demian's good friend, Albert, had only one piece of new information. He had been rough on his group of "internet specialists" tasked with providing tactical assistance. Very rough, indeed. One of his hackers surveyed the German underworld. He could not uncover the identities of the assassins, but he came upon the idea of looking at all the German diplomatic immunity holders and their movements. He discovered a group of four men who had left that country in the time frame using those clearances. He passed on those names to the state police, German authorities and Canadian law enforcement officials.

"You're sure it was four assassins? Only four?" Demian asked.

"Yes." Albert seemed very pleased with those efforts. "Demian, watch your back. The other villain is very slippery. Of course, he's got other aliases. Of course, the authorities will never put him together with his credentials because he won't be using them in this country or Canada."

"I get that. But it's helpful to know there is only one more than the three already caught," Demian said.

"Already done. Anything else I can do?" Albert asked.

"No. I'll only call on this line. Keep your guys at it. And give the man who looked up the diplomatic immunity angle a bonus on me, will you?"

"Sure. I enjoy spending your money and tacking on my commission." He paused. "Why don't we get together when all this is over, sometime, old friend?" Albert asked.

"Now you're calling *me* old?" Demian winced.

"Yeah. This recent bullshit must have taken a few years off your life. You'll soon be as old as me if you don't watch it." Albert choked down a cough.

"I've recently reunited with a previous girlfriend. I'd like you to meet her. She's special. Very special. So, keep your guys on it to watch our backs. Please," Demian requested, reaching out his hand to Jane to come stand beside him.

"What? *Please* now? You're either really rattled or head over heels with this woman." Albert laughed until he coughed again.

"If you'll stop smoking long enough, we'll all get together." Demian hung up. He looked at Jane and said, "I love you more and more. I need you. I don't ever want to be apart from you. We all lost a lot today. But I still have you, and I don't ever want to lose you, again."

Jane hugged him and started to dance slowly. She said, "My cowboy. You rescued us all on horseback. It was a close call. Now we have to help our friends rebuild their lives. I'm afraid you're stuck with me as much as I'm stuck with you. Let's shower and get the grime of the trail off of us. It'll help us both. And then a little rest before dinner at seven?"

Gunner visited Marion and Catherine. They kept separate rooms. "I'm so glad that you two are all right. It was quite a trip. Are you both OK after the ride?"

"We're fine. The horses' energies buoyed us. And their swaying walk was like a really nice slow massage. We're fine."

"Would you both do me a favor? Could you keep us all in your prayers, especially Will, Bennie and Madison and the kids? Their worlds have been shaken. They were all vulnerable even before the attacks and now—well, we have to be sure they're OK." Gunner looked lost.

"Of course. We've been on it already," Marion said.

"I'll be bunking with Ali. He's a tough little kid, but I don't want to overlook him either," Gunner continued. "Deborah is in with Mason and Madison. Jesus, this is a bad situation all the way around. They all lost everything except the clothes on their backs."

"We know. We're here for everyone."

Demian went to find Brud in his office, after his shower and rest. "I don't know how to thank you for what you and your friends did. It must have been a huge leap of faith."

Brud started to arrange tables for supper. Demian jumped in to help the elderly gentleman. "I am honored to think I can be of help at my age. I wouldn't think of ignoring your plight. Just not right, is all."

"I find that refreshing," Demian responded. "Thanks. We all would have been killed. No two ways about it."

"I know. I saw those missiles, and it brought back Korea. So much destruction. For what? That stupid prick leading the North kills his own people at will. Just like his father before him. What did we achieve in that 'conflict' if we couldn't eliminate that ongoing carnage?"

Demian stared at Brud with no answer. He finally said, "Tom and Ellen are arranging dinner. That's all on me. We should take the night and sleep and hopefully recover a little. Then we'll plan what to do next. For the time being, we have to be very careful about our secret location. Tom and Ellen know not to let anything out. I know you do too, but we have to be scrupulous. No idle chatter, no Facebook and no tweets. No nothing until we're sure this is really over," Demian urged.

"I know. And I don't have a clue about all that computer stuff. So, you don't have to worry about me. And don't worry about Tom and Ellen." Brud nodded in the direction of the wi-fi John and Elisabeth had set up for him only the day before. The box and wrappers were still on the floor by the stand. "After months of having that stuff, John and Elisabeth put it all together just yesterday for me."

"I know." Demian looked a little embarrassed having been so demanding to a man who didn't deserve to be treated in that manner.

"So, I'll shower and get some rest. John and Elisabeth can set up everything for dinner. They know where it all is." Brud walked to his bedroom suite, closing the door behind him.

58

"Jesus, could you be any more obvious? What the fuck are you doing? The political candidates couldn't be any more obvious than you guys are." Bennie's hackers all chimed in the next morning, after Bennie signed on to the dark side of the net.

"What?" Bennie had just been told of John's men using credit cards and traveling west on an extended vacation.

Scatman 16 continued. "Yeah. It ain't no thing. We intercepted the police reports about you all sneaking away before the rocket attacks. Man, you should see the pictures of the smoldering remains of the two houses and I think that was a barn? The satellite pictures clearly show what the rockets did, and if anyone were still in those houses—well, they'd be gone."

"Yeah, that was a big pole barn. And we were lucky to be out of there. Should have heard the bitching about getting up early and all," Bennie typed.

"So tell me what the fuck? Why are you using credit cards to leave such obvious trails that anyone could follow?" Scatman 16 demanded.

Bennie just waited.

"Aw, fuck. That's part of your plan? Those are decoys?" Scatman 16 sounded disgusted that he had not figured that out.

"Yeah. And what we need to know is whether we're leaving any other evidence of being somewhere in the northeast. Get your best guys on seeing if there's any other cyber evidence of us doing anything else. Then continue to comb the web for another assassin who entered Canada and separated from the three that were captured here and the three that you guys had captured in Saratoga," Bennie typed. "He was traveling under a German passport with diplomatic immunity. That might help. But we're sure he has assumed another name right after that. Maybe have your guys cross check car rentals in the same time frame? I don't know."

"Hairy the Eye" broke in. "We don't have a clue where you are now, or how you got there. Good work. But I've been looking at the satellite images of the area around the missile attacks. Horses have been through there. Is it a popular riding destination? Looks pretty mountainous. Do horses like that kind of terrain?"

"Make sure to trace whether anyone else has downloaded the same images," Bennie fired back.

"Yeah. I'll be sure to do that. And I might just be able to alter what anyone else sees from here on if that's a priority to you?"

"Yeah. You guys are really good, aren't you?" Bennie said with pride as much as with astonishment. "Be sure to do that—alter what other onlookers might be able to see from now on, and what's in the old photos."

Scatman 16 typed in again. "If someone noticed the horse trails, they might have been able to research renting or using horses. Try to cover that on your end, and I'll make sure it's a dead end here."

"Make sure to go back to the day before the missile attack and alter all the pictures of Death Mountain as soon as you can. Shit. I've got to get off." Bennie slammed the computer closed and threw it on his bed. He raced to find Brud and Demian.

Demian, Jane and Brud were talking in the office. "Sorry to interrupt. I just got offline with my contacts. My guys tapped into the police communiqués and knew that we all managed to escape. We have to assume the other assassin knows that, too. Then they picked up trails of John's guys using his credit cards going west. They looked at satellite photos, from 'unusual sources' and could see a lot of recent horse trails around Death Mountain." Bennie finally finished.

"Well?" Demian demanded.

"I'm having my guys alter the satellite images from there, including the morning of the escape. That should already be done. That's easy enough."

"Yeah?" the others chimed in, almost in unison.

"What if there are also images from earlier in the morning, when the trailers were parked. Any way to distinguish those trailers—logos, phone numbers for advertisement, license plates, anything like that that could be traced?" Bennie asked.

"Shit. We'll have to assume so." Demian looked concerned.

"What about Tom and Ellen?" Jane asked.

"Bennie, round up Will and fill him in. We should drive to Tom and Ellen's right now and let them in on this. Your choice, Bennie. Stay here or come with us to talk with Tom and Ellen and leave Will here to protect the others?" Demian asked.

"We shouldn't split up; bad tactics to do so," Bennie warned.

"Yeah, but we shouldn't call Tom and Ellen using our phones. We don't know for certain they're secure. We've got to tell them in person," Demian fired back.

"How good are the satellite images? Could they *really* see logos or license plate numbers?" Jane asked.

"If you're holding a *New York Times*, they could read the headlines," Demian said.

"So we have to assume that someone could know we're here or suspect that Tom and Ellen might have some information about us?" Jane continued.

"Yeah. Let's go. Can you drive, Brud?" Demian asked. The old man nodded.

Demian's phone rang. He listened for a few seconds. "Todd, are you sure you're on a safe line?" Demian asked. He had only answered because he had an inkling that it might be Todd calling.

"Yeah, it's a new burner. I had to call to say thanks. I hear you walked the whole length of the AuSable River bank looking for me. Thank you," Sheriff Wilkins said.

"You're welcome. I was hoping you'd get out of that safely. We go way back. You didn't deserve to be kidnapped."

"At least I still have my house," Todd answered.

"Whose blood did we find, anyway? It wasn't yours—we know that from blood typing," Demian asked.

"One of the four men who grabbed me. I couldn't resist a quick head-butt to the nose when my only opportunity arose. Hit square on and heard the snap, crackle and pop. Guy was out cold. Didn't see him again, either. I've given Captain Green a drawing of him. He got out an APB after I completed the drawing with the sketch artist," Todd continued.

Demian spoke to Todd as Brud drove to Tom and Ellen's. As they drove in the driveway to the horse stables, Demian could see the horse trailers with huge blue lettering announcing "Watkin's Horse Stalls and Riding Stables," giving phone numbers and addresses. "Shit. Listen. We may have a little issue with our get-away. We're in a safe place, but there might have been a glitch having to do with satellite images when we left. I think we're OK, but we might need you." Demian got out of the car. "I'll call you right back. I need to talk to some new friends."

Bennie, Demian, Jane and Brud greeted Tom and Ellen. "Nice to see you. I thought you might lie low for a few more days, though," Tom said. They all shook hands.

"Yeah, well, there might be a problem. Bennie, would you like to tell us all about it?" Demian asked.

"I have online hackers and friends who've given us new information. Thanks to you, we left the houses before being attacked. My friends found that out through the police communiqués. The police systems aren't well protected. We have to assume that the remaining assassin must know, too. My hackers also looked at satellite photos after the missile attack and saw the houses were leveled. They also saw a lot of horse tracks on the mountain. We don't know if the bad guys have access to those photos or not. My friends have already altered that data so that from now on, no horse trails are seen. They have also erased the trucks and trailers that transported the horses and the rest of us. But, if the villains got to look at the photos, the lettering on the side of your trailers would lead them right here." He motioned to the horse trailers with the large lettering and numbers. It would have easily been distinguishable in satellite photos.

"Shit. So, *if* the assassins got satellite data before your guys erased it, in precisely *that* window of time, they'll know to come here looking?" Tom asked. "And, *if* they connect the horse hoof prints to our get-away?"

Brud asked, "What do you think the chances are all that is true?"

Bennie shrugged. "I don't like playing any odds."

Jane added, "Even if we *are* safe here, we still have to worry about that one assassin, don't we? We're not home free until he's dealt with definitively."

"We know," Demian said in a soft voice.

59

"Let me talk to the governor. Do I have to remind you who I am and that I can get you fired if you don't?" Demian once again demanded in his sharp voice.

"Yeah, no problem. Hold on." The governor's secretary put Demian on hold. He waited a full five minutes, then called through to the inner office.

"Took you long enough, or was it your secretary not liking being ordered around?" Demian asked in his friendly voice.

"Yes, there is that—Captain Green let me know immediately, after you called, that everyone was just fine, and that you all got away. He didn't say how or where to." There was a question in the governor's voice that Demian did not respond to. "I'm glad to know you're all safe. Sorry about your houses and personal belongings."

Demian ignored it completely. "I wanted you to know we're safe. I also wanted to ask how comfortable our friend Canig is in jail."

"I think he would describe his continued torment by all the guards and his interrogations by the attorney general as less than ideal." The governor replied. Demian was sure he was smiling in spite of his matter-of-fact tone.

"Well, there's still at least one assassin at large with one missile. I think some kind of deal might help Canig reconsider his circumstances. Have you found all his money yet?"

"Probably not. Countries like Panama, Grand Cayman, Switzerland, and others just relish how much money can be hidden within their borders. It's great for local businesses. And it's against the law to help foreign governments recover those funds." The governor's voice became tense.

"So, if he's still got money, he's still got clout. I was hoping that if you corralled all the funds he stole, then he wouldn't have any money to pay the attackers. Maybe they would just give up and go home," Demian concluded.

"No such luck. We have ACLU people breathing down our necks when we interrogate Canig. We can't be 'creative.' We'll have to see where we'll get. I keep a running tally on all the money your bunch of hackers has led us to. Over three billion dollars. And counting. Unbelievable, really," the governor responded.

"Well, I'm not sure about a lot of things. I still think you have to keep a careful watch on all your surroundings. There is one more assassin still on the loose. I don't know whom he'll choose to attack first. We finally have Sheriff Todd Wilkins back, but that's only because Captain Green used some 'unorthodox' methods to interrogate one of the prisoners before he had the whole world watching him and he had to go by the book, too. I hope you can use some executive discretion while evaluating that. Or better yet, just stop all the internal processes before they start." Demian hoped the governor would help his friend.

"I'm already on it. While I usually uphold the letter of the law, these are very unusual times. A group of assassins launched missiles on American soil, against Americans. Don't worry about the captain. I need to deal with him carefully and quietly, but rest assured his bravery will be well rewarded." The governor's voice was calm and reassuring.

"I'm really glad to hear that. Watch your back and keep the pressure on Canig. That may be the solution to both our problems." Demian thanked his friend and hung up. He wondered if the secretary would hear about making him wait or not.

Demian found John, Bennie, Gunner and Jane speaking softly in the office of Brud's camps. They stopped talking when he walked in, making him think they were talking about him and didn't want him to know it.

"What's up?" Demian asked.

"We're talking about what it is we need to do. We can't decide. If we stay here, we'll potentially make Brud and Tom and Ellen targets. We don't want to do that to friends." Jane made her point by touching all the fingers of her right hand to the palm of her left hand.

"No. We don't," Demian agreed.

John asked, "What options do we have? Will said, and I think I agree, that we should all stay together. We shouldn't split up so that we can be stronger together. Right?"

"Yes, I agree with that. All the tacticians that I know think that 'united we stand' still makes sense," Demian offered.

"Then what's the answer? We have to have a plan, don't we?" Jane touched her right fingers more forcefully to her left palm, accentuating her prior gesture. This bordered on frantic.

"We all need to rest tonight and consult our sources and meet in the morning. I need to talk to Sheriff Wilkins and see if he has thought of anything too," Demian encouraged.

"Yeah. I need to speak to my guys too," Bennie agreed.

"So do John and me," Demian added.

"Gunner. How are Marion, Catherine, Mason, Madison and the kids doing?" Jane asked.

"I really think they're all fine. They were devastated; now they're angry and want to get on with rebuilding their lives. It's an appropriate response to the shit storm they've lived through." Gunner looked confident that his assessment was correct.

"I'm glad to hear it. I don't know of any way we could have saved their houses. I just don't. We're lucky to be alive," Demian said.

Jane broke in. "That's what we were saying when you came in. We're lucky to have had so much trust and faith in you that we did leave in the middle of the night. We're lucky John came upon a plan to save us. And think about it. The map that Deborah and Gunner found was a little more than just lucky, wouldn't you say?"

Demian chuckled. "I can't believe it, actually."

Bennie asked, "So, why don't we sleep on it tonight? Will and I will take turns watching the drive up here. Tom is watching his place and feels confident he can do so by himself. Then, in the morning, we'll all get with our online friends and see what's new. We'll meet here for breakfast. Seven AM sound OK to everyone?"

They all nodded and turned to leave the office to get some much-needed sleep. Will had found a position to guard the road and would switch off with Bennie later in the night.

60

"Yeah, it's me again," Demian said. His voice was kind and soft. Jane and he had cuddled in their cabin. Demian thought it was nice sharing quiet time and feeling their bodies warm each other.

"We've got to stop this affair, speaking late at night and all. People will begin to talk," Albert replied through a yawn.

"I couldn't wait until a decent hour. And you don't sleep anymore, anyway with your need to smoke continuously, do you?" Demian laid it on too thickly.

"Yeah, you prick. I've saved your hide too many times. And I don't give a shit about how much you pay me even after I overcharge you egregiously, either. What is it now?"

"I wanted to know if there's anything new," Demian said as if he were ordering French fries with ketchup.

"So, that couldn't wait?" The old man coughed and hacked up something Demian didn't want to think about.

"Well, I also think I have an angle to work to find the other assassin. He was head-butted by the sheriff that the group abducted. The officer said he hit the guy squarely on the nose and heard the bones fragment. He would have had to have had that looked at or reset or something. There would have been ER records or plastic surgeon records or something. Pain meds prescribed or something?" Demian waited for the old man to ask questions if he had any.

"Yeah, you would think so. The assassins flew directly to Canada after the abduction?"

"Yes."

"So, I'll wake up the troops and get them to look into the electronic records in southern Quebec. Piece of cake. The hospitals and physicians' offices all use the same system that my guys hacked into when they were still developing it. Gave us a wealth of information to use as we needed, if you know what I mean."

Demian whistled. "You mean you have all Canada's medical records hacked?"

"We just have to ask the right question." Albert coughed again.

"So, I'm thinking…where might he have presented for treatment after nasal trauma? He could have shown up at a hospital, ER or private physician's office. But that's stupid. There aren't any private offices in Canada anymore, are there? The government owns everything up there, right?"

"I'll get my guys right on it," Albert replied. "At least we'll get his alias du jour. That might be of some help. I can't wait to hear his phony address either. These guys are pretty creative."

"And the other thing I want your guys to look at is whether they can find us. Are we leaving any traceable trails? Can you find us? If you can, we're in deep shit and we'll have to make other plans." Demian knew his friend would take that as a solemn responsibility.

"Yeah. I got your back." Albert hung up before he had to cough once more.

Bennie typed quickly on the dark side of the net. "How are you guys doing?"

Scatman 16 answered. "Haven't had this many cups of coffee in a long time. Last time may have been trying to trace whether the Russians had anything to do with the Democratic National Committee and whether it unfairly favored Hilary over Bernie. But that's another story."

"Hairy the Eye" typed, "There were several requests for the maps in question and in the time frame you requested—that is before I made them all seem to look like the day before. One set of maps was a routine request from a grad student doing meteorological studies through the University of Burlington. I guess we can rule him out. He's asked for the same photos every day for three years. Some Ph.D.'s take a while, I guess."

"The other?"

"Well, funny you should ask. The other was from a mister Jack Cousteau. I'm not kidding. Bullshit name if I ever heard one. He got a complete set of the photos."

"Shit. Any address, phone number, email, or anything?" Bennie asked hopefully.

"Yeah. You're going to love it, too. 'One Water Study Lane, Lake Placid, New York.' This guy's a real comedian."

"Great. Just great. Listen. I have another angle to have you look into. The remaining assassin has a badly broken nose. He would have had to have had it looked at and treated. Can you look into southern Quebec? Hospitals, ERs, Doctor's offices, that sort of thing?"

"Sure. No problem. Different country, different language, different healthcare system, different computer operating systems. No problem. Give me a minute. I'll be right back online." Scatman 16's sarcasm rang through even on line with typed words.

"I know that's tough. Can you try? Please?" Bennie begged.

"As long as you asked nice."

They all signed off.

61

"Well, it's only right that I should buy my rescuer a cup of coffee." Sheriff Todd Wilkins and Captain Nicholas Green sat on high bar stools at the Starbucks on Main Street in Lake Placid. "I need to thank you for bulldozing through my rescue. They would never have found me otherwise."

"No problem. I've been getting all kinds of compliments for shooting our captive. Funny that I don't think I deserve them. I only did what I needed to do. And I would have done only what I needed to do in other ways, if the situation was different—if I had more time. All the police training in the world can't really prepare a cop for having to shoot someone. Even a son of a bitch sociopath like him." He stared into his coffee.

"Well, I don't think I would have survived in that remote cabin much longer, chained to the wall. It got pretty cold at night. I would have starved and become dehydrated in a few more days. Nobody was close enough to hear my yells or know I was there. They would have found my body in the spring."

"I know. But it would have been the loss of a really good officer who ran a really clean town. Couldn't have that." He sipped his coffee—plain without any flavorings, cream or sugar. "I'm on 'administrative leave' until further notice. I could get used to it. Time to be with my wife and all—like being retired but still on the payroll. So, I'll delay my real retirement until this is all resolved and keep collecting a paycheck."

"I'm sorry the department is going hard on you." Todd shook his head, looking in his cup. "I'll get more coffee. Scones?" He took both cups and went to the counter to get refills. The berry scones looked too inviting.

"So, I've got all the time in the world to think this out. Anything else you can think of that would be of help trying to find the missing link?" They both laughed at the description of the fourth man with a broken nose. Todd described the assailant as having a very flattened bridge of his nose after being head-butted. This made his brow line appear to jut out even farther. "Did they say anything? Any little thing or clue?"

Todd scowled. "I've been racking my brain about that. I've been trained to be observant. I'm not stupid, but they were really good. They strictly adhered to their confinement techniques and nothing got by."

"I didn't mean to imply you weren't thinking, but sometimes the smallest thing may be enough of a clue to make a difference." The captain put his hand on Todd's forearm.

"I know. I'm also sorry that my freedom means your future may be in jeopardy. I'll make your effort worth the trouble. I'll be there for you if you ever need." He paused. "Looks like I've got a case of survivor's guilt—or something like that. Before this, I never gave that concept any credence at all. But I feel it now."

"I don't think of it that way at all. I had an opportunity. I took it. I'd do it again without a second's hesitation. For you or any of us."

"Well, what do we do, now? I mean, you have time; I have resources. Why don't we catch this assassin before he does any more harm? We'll prevent him from collecting his ill-gotten payday."

"Yeah. Like I haven't thought about that. Here's a foreigner threatening our people—and good people, at that. On our soil. I boil inside when I think about it. I wish I *could* pull a rabbit out of my hat. I wish I could pull off a sleight of hand, deal from the bottom of the deck, make a lateral pass—any of the metaphors. I don't know." The captain sighed.

"Wait. There were four missiles on the helicopter when it tried to assault Will and Mason's houses. They abandoned the chopper on Grand Isle, and then they set it on fire to conceal evidence. Then three missiles were fired and hit the houses. Somewhere between there and here, the other missile was hidden or offloaded."

"Yeah?"

"Why don't we both do some real police work? Take a ride?"

"I am on leave. I don't have other pressing commitments. It might just jar something loose in your brain or we might puzzle this out if we cover that area between Grand Isle and the AuSable River."

"I agree. Also, the truck driver whose rig was hijacked only saw three men. He didn't know anything about the missiles and never heard the attackers speak English. Poor guy doesn't speak any German. That means the other attacker separated from the group somewhere around Grand Isle? Or, at least before the driver was abducted."

"Diplomatic immunity. Bullshit is what that is, for sure. All of those men are being deported next week. That immunity didn't save one of them from needing extensive surgery on his foot." The captain didn't gloat.

"That was brave. You knew you would pay the price for being that aggressive, but you took that on the chin for me. Thank you."

"Until that time, the only thing I had ever shot at was a target. Never even hunted. It came automatically. Just the right thing to do. And it's true what they say. In the moment, I didn't hear the gunfire. I didn't feel the recoil. I didn't hear that prick screaming. I just had to do a job."

A minute passed before Todd asked, "Shall we take a ride? Let's see what might happen if a couple of old cops do some *on the ground* investigating. Shall we?" He rose and motioned to the door.

"Yeah. That's where we're at our best. Let the young kids and the computer geeks do what they do. We'll see what we can put together in the field. That's where we belong."

"My sentiments, exactly. You won't get in trouble with your administrative leave?"

"No. My commander told me to get some rest. Nothing more restful than a nice drive in the country."

62

Deborah sat on the bed in her parents' cabin. "I'm sick of this. I can't stand waiting here. What are we going to do next anyway?"

"Deborah…." Madison used her prosodic voice, accentuating each syllable.

"Yeah. We had to leave it all behind. We're lucky to be alive and kicking." Mason thought better of what he had just said. "I know. We'll rebuild. Even better next time, too."

"I lost all our stuff—even the Scrabble game. We only have the clothes we have on our backs. I'd like to change out of these. I'm all dirty after the climb and horse ride. Can't stand myself."

"We'll be fine. When we can, we'll go shopping. But we have to wait for Uncle Gunner and Demian to tell us when it's safe to do so." Madison switched to her consoling voice. "Maybe you can find Uncle Gunner and Ali? They might be doing something interesting."

"Fine. I'll get out of your hair. You don't want me here. I don't like *anything* anymore. Can't have any fun. Shit if I know."

"Deborah! I've never heard you swear before. I don't want to hear any of that language. Ever again!" Madison looked sternly at her daughter.

"An apology is clearly in order, young lady," Mason said.

"OK. All right…I'm sorry. Whatever. Jeez, after Mom has been on a tear for the last week, I can't even swear. You and everyone else are all against me. Why us? Why bomb us? We didn't do shit to anyone."

Madison stood up, pushed her daughter back down to a sitting position on the bed and looked at her carefully. Deborah's eyes were bloodshot, the veins on her forehead pulsed very rapidly and her complexion was almost a cherry red. "Mason, get Gunner and bring him here as quickly as you can. He should look at Deborah. I think she's been poisoned as well."

Mason raced out the door as Madison tried to calm her daughter. "Have you been drinking any soda? Any coffee or tea?"

"No. And I'm fine. I just figured it out—the world is against me."

"Oh, no. Deborah…I'm so sorry…."

Gunner burst in the room with Mason. He surveyed Deborah, a look of horror taking over his usually robust complexion. "We've got to move. I'll get Brud to drive us to the local hospital or call an ambulance. I'll find Demian to tell him and have him interface with the police. We need poison control. I'll call Dr. Ardane to tell the local docs what to order and do."

"We need to be careful that this doesn't get online. We'll have to involve the local police, but maybe Brud or Tom can help with that," Mason added.

Gunner took a long look at Deborah and said, "'Sgo."

Brud rushed into the parking lot outside his camps. The ambulance loaded up Deborah, with Madison and Mason accompanying. The patrolman who was assigned to accompany the emergency calls stood and wrote on his flip pad. His eyes got larger and larger as Demian told him the whole story. He finally closed the notebook, looked at Brud, who silently confirmed the narrative, and radioed in to the station. He used a code to inform his commander to meet him at the hospital—eyes and ears only. No records of any kind.

"Thanks for listening and believing all this. It's imperative that nothing is written down in any police communiqués. We're running from an international assassin," Demian said. "He's the last member of a group of foreign operatives. They were even bold enough to target the governor of New York State. Thankfully, they were foiled."

At the hospital, the emergency room specialist heard the whole story, and then got on the phone with Dr. Ardane without divulging any information about their location. They spoke at length about what had been found in Madison's case and agreed on a plan for Deborah. Labs would have to be checked, but they proceeded as though she had been poisoned as well.

"All right. So far, so good. The police are cooperating and keeping this very quiet. Bennie and John are online right now with their friends to make sure none of this gets out. If so, they'll know. We still have to patrol and protect Tom and Ellen's place and Brud's camps. The police are making their presence known and will help us." Demian looked relieved to have the locals informed. "Everyone report to me and I'll interface with the police. I must say I'm impressed with their professionalism."

Bennie nodded.

Will said, "We'll get back to the camp and stop and see Tom and Ellen on the way. I'm actually reassured that the Berlin Police are informed and aware."

"Let's keep up our end of this and continue to look out for ourselves," Demian reminded the men.

63

"Nice drive, huh?" Sheriff Todd Wilkins and Captain Nicholas Green rode in a Lake Placid patrol car—lights on the top and large red lettering on the side. They had driven north on Route 87 to Rouse's Point and idled, stopping at a red light that appeared to have no legitimate purpose, ready to cross over to Grand Isle. The captain had driven the area encompassing northern New York State countless times professionally, whereas the sheriff had only been this far north for pleasure on a few occasions that he could recall. Neither of the men had a working knowledge of the island, however.

"Yeah, but we're here to figure out where the other missile and bad guy might be. Not just enjoy the scenery, right?" Nicholas asked.

"So why don't we do just that," Todd fired back. "Listen, we've got to think like the assassins. They were just shot out of the sky, the pilot wounded and we don't know if the chopper was damaged. They were under duress, big time." They turned the corner and crossed the bridge to Grand Isle. "A lot of their prior planning might have had to have been abbreviated or aborted."

"Sounds right. Where would they put an extra missile and where would the other criminal hole up or make his attack from?" They drove on to the island and, after passing through the more populated eastern shore, found the remainder desolate, only a few farm fields, barns, houses and cattle. Captain Green mentally reviewed what he had remembered from his trips to the island in the past. "Likely they would use whatever is at hand. These guys are good and wouldn't be too obvious. They wouldn't cause a ruckus. Let's drive around the island. Make sure we get to see the burned-out chopper remains. Let's see it from their point of view after they landed."

"Fixing to do just that," Todd answered.

They drove the main road around the eastern side of the island and finally got to the southern tip of land. The shoreline turned west and north, looking out over the bay between Plattsburgh and Grand Isle. The water lapped up onto large rocks; the land sloped up sharply and leveled out after only a short distance. A dirt road circled to form a scenic overlook and branched to the lake. Only visible from the access road a short distance from the main highway, the burned-out hulk of the helicopter rested in a roped-off section by the shore. The police and fire investigators had finished but still left the area off-limits to the public in case any further clues might warrant a reexamination of the chopper and grounds.

"Do you think they might have also had a boat?" Todd asked.

"No way. The rocks on the shore would make beaching the boat impossible for most of the shore within a few miles from here. Loading live missiles in a jostling boat would be out of the question."

"We know they must have had the van stashed near here. They likely would have just jumped in, moved the missiles and torched the chopper before they drove off," Todd thought out loud.

"Yeah. And we agree that they would have headed north because going the way we came is way too far out of the way and too public. Right?" Captain Green's instincts kicked in.

"Yup." Todd got out, walked around the yellow taped off area, nodded and got back in the patrol car. He had taken a series of cell phone photos. "They took all the missile tubes off the chopper. I can see a lot of footprints, but, I don't know if they were made by the assassins or the police and firemen. Also, a lot of truck's tire tracks. Ditto there. But I see no reason to think they didn't go north, just like you said." He smiled, knowing they thought along the same lines.

"Drive on," Captain Green motioned.

Todd drove very slowly. He wanted to see and feel the area for himself and imagine what the assassins, especially the wounded man, might be thinking. Their plan had been foiled. Would they split up to increase their odds of success? He thought so.

"Mark this on your GPS." Captain Green pointed to an abandoned farmhouse with surrounding fallow fields and large barn. It showed no signs of life; the fields had not been worked in many years, he suspected. The barn sorely needed a good coat of paint or two. "We'll keep driving by at this speed and see if anything else pops out at us as we circle back to the bridge."

"Yeah. Let's continue, but my radar went off too." They craned their necks as they drove at a constant speed. The location was as remote as they would likely find on this island, abandoned, and offered cover for hiding cars, people, missiles or other conspirators. "You know, a place like that—being abandoned, can quickly become invisible to local police who patrol it every day. They just wouldn't think to consider it because it's been so dormant, so long. Got it?" Todd made his point by tapping his friend on the shoulder.

"That's why it's so damn perfect."

The ride eventually took them back to where they started on the island. Nothing else seemed as appropriate to the villain's purposes. "You know? If I were the bad guy, I would have done anything I needed to do before I got off this island—like unloading missiles, changing cars or picking up new passengers. I wouldn't want to risk doing all that on the mainland. It would likely be a lot busier and more populated," Captain Green thought out loud.

"Shall we turn around?" Todd asked. "Do we need back up? I'd like to call this in to my men at least."

"No. We can't let anything out over the usual police communications. They've already hacked us and found out that Demain and the others weren't injured in the attack." Captain Green's voice left no room for discussion.

"How do we proceed?"

"Got your binoculars?"

"Of course. And night-vision goggles. And all the firepower we might need," Todd answered, pleased to be prepared. He smiled broadly.

"Why don't we get some coffee, wait until dusk and swing by. We can get closer to the farmhouse to see what's going on without being discovered. We'll find a vantage point and see if anything's stirring. If not, we'll approach. If so, I'll call in my SWAT team. They can be here in minutes."

"I should call my men. I've already instituted catchphrases that alert them to unfolding situations. We can communicate without anyone knowing jack about it."

Captain Green smiled as he watched Todd do so.

64

"There's only one road up here, am I right?" Bennie asked Brud after meeting with Will at the camps.

"Yeah."

"Well, then are we setting up in the wrong place to protect us? I mean Tom and Ellen are down the same road a half a mile. If there's no turnoffs between here and there, why don't we deploy down there to also protect them?"

"Makes sense. *If* the bad guys caught the horse tracks, and *if* they could read the lettering on the side of the horse trailers or license plates, and *if* they thought they were connected to our escape and relocation here, then that's where they would show up, right?" Will asked.

"Yeah," Brud sighed. He didn't want to think of his friends being pushed into the line of fire because of a good deed they helped perform.

"You coming, then?" Bennie asked Will and Brud.

"I'll leave that to you younger kids. I'll stay and tend to everyone here. I also need to be by the phone in case the hospital calls with reports or questions about Deborah," Brud replied.

"Good enough. But we'll mosey down the road and speak to Tom and Ellen and set up down there." Bennie nodded to Will. "A half-mile walk will start to clean out the cobwebs, right?"

Will nodded.

They picked up their gear and walked to Tom and Ellen's stables.

"Good to see you, Tom. Are you and Ellen doing all right?" Will asked.

"Sure. Nothing new here," Tom answered.

"We figured that there's only one road to Brud's and you're here alone. We could join forces and protect both places with more manpower?" Bennie suggested.

"Sure. Always happy to have another Special Forces operative here. And I would never refuse help from an officer in the Army, West Point grad and all. Might run out of beer, though. Only have a couple of kegs in back, and there're three of us. Ellen doesn't drink beer, thank God, or I'd have to get on the phone right away to order more." Tom laughed.

"Some things never change—like how much we could drink," Bennie said.

"Or how much we could swear! Dammit!" Tom laughed.

Ellen walked in on the discussion and said, "What did I miss?"

"Nothing dear. Just comparing notes," Tom quickly responded.

"Well, then, how are you doing? Will, was your house one of those that got leveled? How are you doing with that?" she asked in a kind tone.

"Yeah, it was my house. I don't know yet. We escaped and I haven't gotten much time to think about what's next, or whatever." His complexion darkened.

"You know, we've been through the harder things in life, too. It's better to deal with things in the moments they happen. Otherwise, they can fester in the subconscious. They become larger and more hideous with time." Ellen looked at Tom to be sure she didn't overstep herself.

"Yeah. I know. I've got good friends who are healers. They keep after me to be on top of my feelings." Will looked at, and then put his hand on, Bennie's shoulder. "We've done two tours in Iraq."

"Then I did ranger school," Bennie added.

"We both came back and had to relearn who we are and how we fit into society. Not easy at all." Will looked at his friends to see if they followed.

Tom looked at Ellen and said, "It took us a long time after the Balkans. We finally found our way back home and to ourselves because of the horses. Their energies are just so large and encompassing. The horses helped us the most. I drank way too much. Ellen withdrew to a place inside herself. The horses helped her come back to life—and to me. I think she still likes the horses better than people, though."

Ellen laughed, but she didn't disagree.

"So we're here to make sure no more bullshit lands on our friends' doorsteps. We'll guard from here. I don't know what's coming at us, but it won't get through us to harm our tribe. Won't happen here," Bennie said.

"You know, I believe you. You managed to hold off a helicopter armed with missiles with a hunting rifle. Shit, damn, son!" Tom slapped Bennie on the back.

"I just used the tool I had on hand. That's all."

"And you're the only one who thinks that's a small feat. The rest of us are damn impressed," Tom encouraged.

"Well, we'll scout and compare notes on the best vantage points to protect the road on the way up to the house. We'll be back in a few minutes to check in and formulate our plans." Will and Bennie walked down the road.

"I do hope they'll find their way back," Ellen said. She put her arm around Tom's waist and drew herself close to him. "Enough time and effort have been wasted, enough lives ruined."

They walked into the house near the stables and put on a large pot of coffee, knowing it wouldn't be the last they'd brew that day.

65

Jane came back to the cabin she shared with Demian. He lay on the bed, staring at the ceiling. "Hi, honey," she purred. "I visited with Marion and Catherine. They invited me to join them with their afternoon meditations. It was—really different. I can't describe it. I've done meditation under the direction of other teachers and monks, but *this* was really sublime."

"They are something, for sure," he answered and started to smile. "I'm glad they invited you to join them. They didn't offer a healing? They must think that you don't need one. Maybe being around me is rubbing off on you? Something like that?"

"Yeah. It's always about you, somehow. Isn't it?"

"I just meant that they know, without asking, how someone is doing. They offer what they think a person needs. You're very together. *I'm* learning from being with you, that's for sure." He rolled to embrace her, now lying next to him.

"How is Deborah? I sure hope it'll only be a passing thing that she's going to have to put up with," Jane said. "Like let it wear off, like it did with Madison?"

"Well, there's a lot I'm relieved about. Deborah will be fine, at least according to Dr. Ardane. We still need to figure out how they both got poisoned and prevent anyone else from being affected."

"Yeah. And?"

"We told the local police the whole story. They believed us and didn't enter it into any official police communiqués. The emergency room doctors didn't give anything away about our location or the poisoning. Used aliases for the insurance billing and addresses that they made up themselves. They were cool. The doctors looked like they enjoyed entering false information into the computers. They stationed a deputy outside Deborah's room and one here on the beginning of the road up to the camps. Brud told me that Bennie and Will are doing the overlook of the road at Tom and Ellen's to protect both places. There's another couple that we have to thank our lucky stars for. They were willing to believe Brud and go off on a very unusual adventure to come to our rescue. All on faith."

"It is all quite unbelievable, really."

"I also spoke to Sheriff Todd again. He and the state police captain think they're on to something. We'll have to wait until nightfall to know for sure."

"What is it?"

"They wouldn't say, of course, even on a burner. We'll have to wait and see."

"Do you think that being with Marion and Catherine, just being with them, helped me with my meditation? Just sitting in the same room with them? Could they *do* that?"

"I know, for a fact, they can, and they did," Demian replied.

"We're so lucky. As much as I'm impressed with Bennie and Will, I'm impressed with Marion and Catherine. They're so different, but so expert in so different ways."

"Yup."

66

"So. Let's take this slow. This may be my last sting with the force," Captain Green said softly. He and Sheriff Wilkins slowly approached the abandoned farmhouse in their patrol car, stopping about a mile from the property they had marked on their drive that afternoon.

"You remember you promised to call your SWAT team in if anyone is there?" Todd asked. He felt awkward about making his friend repeat his pledge to call in help, if the situation called for it. He did not want to risk handling a dicey situation alone when help was readily available.

"Yeah. And I'll do just that. Shooting one person is enough for me in this lifetime."

"Good. Ready?"

They had put on their dark windbreakers with white lettering announcing sheriff and state police captain. They each carried two Glock pistols, one Remington 870 tactical shotgun, enough ammo, tactical lights, night-vision goggles and a taser. As they rounded the last bend in the road leading to the farm, they ducked through a field and approached from the back of a large, abandoned barn that obscured their advance. They could see many windows in the ancient building had been broken and not replaced. The barn doors stood wide open, providing a clear vantage to the house.

Todd put on the night-vision goggles and looked in the barn. A new SUV with rental plates from Idaho sat in the garage. No one was in the car or garage. He handed the goggles to Nicholas who whistled softly and said, "We only need to confirm that someone is in the house, then I'll call in the troops."

"Shall we go around or through the barn?"

"Let's go around. We'll be quieter," the captain whispered. He led the way, occasionally putting on the goggles to check the grounds for possible obstacles. He stared at the house for a long time. He raised one finger and pointed upstairs.

Todd could make out what looked like a single candle burning in the darkness. He put a hand on the captain's shoulder and gave a slight tug to signal they should retreat.

Reluctantly, the captain and sheriff moved to the rear of the structure, made a short phone call giving GPS coordinates, and waited for the arrival of the SWAT team. It was a very long twenty minutes until the arrival of the helicopter. Todd had advanced to guard one side of the barn while Nicholas took the other. They hid in the shadows near the corners of the barn. They could peak around to see the back door of the house. An old board creaked in the loft of the barn and startled the men. They instinctively crouched down, aimed their pistols and waited. Nothing further happened and they slowly returned to watching the house.

Suddenly, the helicopter approached loudly, from a very low altitude to hide its advance, doing over a hundred and twenty miles an hour. Floodlights panned the grounds. A loudspeaker announced the state police, giving directions to the occupant of the house to come out unarmed. In spite of that, a lone man ran out the back of the house carrying a pistol in one hand and a knapsack in the other. Todd fired a warning shot and ordered the man to get on the ground. The helicopter pilot turned on the siren. The loud wailing could be heard even in the prop wash. Nicholas Green ran from the other side of the barn, aiming his Remington shotgun squarely at the man's face. They held the assassin essentially in a crossfire. He took three long seconds to raise his hands, drop the satchel and hold his pistol with two fingers.

"Too bad you're obviously surrendering. It wouldn't be a waste of time to shoot you. And I don't miss." Nicholas shouted, although no one could have heard him.

At that moment, four ropes were dropped from the stationary helicopter. Four groups of two commandos each slid down and surrounded the man. By this time, Todd was pushing the man on the ground, holding him down with a foot to his back. He removed a German Walther P38 and handed it to Captain Green who closed in from the other side. "Here's your trophy."

It was over as quickly as that. The SWAT members swept the house, barn and fields and found no one else. They did find the missing missile, assorted explosives, pistols, long-range military rifles and ammo. They collected all of that and put it in evidence bags after unloading the firearms. An ordinance specialist disarmed the missile. "Haven't seen one of these since Iraq and Afghanistan," he said. "These aren't so easy to do. There's a trigger for each explosive charge. Making a grand total of thirteen in each missile. Got them all." He smiled broadly as he was slapped on the back by his fellow officers.

The SWAT team members jumped on the assassin, handcuffed him and roughly pulled him to his feet. One SWAT officer looked at the back of the man's jacket, appraising the footprint of Todd boot and said, "Size thirteen and a half, at least. You know what they say, big feet, big—" Todd didn't laugh. Nicholas looked admiringly. An officer picked up the satchel, rifled through it and found a computer, change of clothes and thousands of dollars in small U.S. and German bills.

As soon as the restraints were placed, the man demanded diplomatic immunity in a thick German accent. He was brought inside the farmhouse and chained to a chair in the kitchen where a light powered by a portable generator shone directly and irritatingly in his face. He blinked and tried to avert his eyes but could not do so. He still wore a bandage on his nose from the plastic surgery that repaired a very badly broken nasal septum.

Todd approached him, towered over him and pointed to his nose. "I can break it again. I bet that would be really painful, though. Why don't you save me the trouble and tell us how many of you came, how many missiles you had, any other operatives or anything else I might want to know?"

"Screw you. I have diplomatic immunity," the man replied in a nasal tone.

Captain Green mimicked the man and said, "I already shot one of your men who had immunity. Didn't help him in the least. He'll never walk normally again."

Sheriff Todd broke in, speaking directly to Nicholas. "We've got Bubba in my holding cell. He got drunk last night, and we had to arrest him. Again. He doesn't like anything to do with a foreigner coming here to threaten our people. I know Bubba would gladly show him how much he dislikes foreign invaders while we wait outside the jail, drinking coffee." He pulled out his wallet and put a twenty on the table. "Less than one minute. Less than one minute and this puke will be screaming for us to let him out." Todd and Nicholas never looked at the captive directly again.

The captain took out a fifty and said, "He'll be crying before he even gets there."

Several of the SWAT members threw in bets and started arguing among themselves, ignoring the prisoner who looked confused, and then more and more anxious. He had been interrogated by experts in the past using extreme techniques. He knew he could tolerate torture, but he had never been the focus of a bet about how long it might take to make him scream. A mound of twenty and fifty dollar bills laid on the table in front of him.

Two of the SWAT team members began pushing each other around, arguing about how weak the prisoner looked to them until they jostled each other and bumped into the prisoner, knocking him sideways to the floor, still chained to the chair. They quickly righted the chair and prisoner and resumed arguing.

"Maybe you had better save yourself the trouble and confess. We'll still deport your sorry ass, but we won't subject you to Bubba," Sheriff Todd offered.

"Yeah. What does it matter to me at this point? I'll tell you what you need to know." The prisoner shivered, clearly afraid for his life.

The head IT operative burst into the room, carrying the assassin's computer. "Just tell us your password."

The others left the room after being given multiple passwords, leaving only Todd and Nicholas with the prisoner. The SWAT team members understood the value of "alone time."

Todd walked closer and snapped his middle finger on the bandage over the German's nose. "That's for kidnapping me. I wish I could really demonstrate the anger I feel for you coming to this country to attack us and launch missiles at us. I'm boiling inside." He shook a fist at the man. The captive's nose started to bleed, his eyes tearing.

Captain Green took out his gun and aimed it at the assailant's foot. "I shot one of your men in the foot. What more would they do to me for shooting another in the foot? I don't really give a shit anymore." He pulled back the hammer and leveled it at the assailant's right foot.

Todd slowly covered his ears and waited, watching the beads of sweat grow on the forehead of the captive.

"Piece of shit like him is not worth firing a bullet. They're about seventy-five cents each. Then there's all the paperwork." Nicholas uncocked the pistol, put it in his holster, and quickly slugged the man in the face—a perfect right cross landed square on the man's cheek. Nicholas put his full weight behind the punch and delivered it expertly. Now he had not only shot a prisoner who was clearly defenseless but punched another who was in full restraints.

"Now *that* hurt. I'm sure," Todd said.

"Maybe it is time to retire now that I've done two things I said I never wanted to do."

"I don't know, sounds like you're just getting warmed up to me."

A transport van and state police personnel arrived to take over guarding the prisoner and transporting him to the Plattsburgh station. Three big and very strong looking men roughly escorted him out of the farmhouse in ankle and wrist cuffs chained together, making him hunch over at the waist. The captive shuffled away. He spat a mouth full of blood at Nicholas.

"There's your answer. That piece of shit didn't learn a thing, did he?" Todd asked.

After reviewing the villain's computer correspondence, the computer specialist confirmed that there were only four assassins in this group. He also discovered where and whom they got the missiles and other arms and explosives from. A trail led to Canig, showing that he had ordered international hit men to attack U.S. citizens on U.S. soil. Other useful information for German, Canadian and U.S. law enforcement agencies would be coming as soon as translations of the computer emails could be done. The different governments' agencies would be busy unraveling the webs of illicit supplies, arms sales, international hit squads, and, the men were sure, the revocation of the diplomatic immunity of the assassins.

"You know what this means? Canig can now be tried for treason and claim a cell on death row. Too bad, really. I'm sure the guards would never tire of tormenting him. Now he's got an out," Captain Green said, almost disappointed looking. "His lawyer, too. They'll share accommodations and sentences."

Todd stepped outside. "I'll call Demian."

"I'll call the governor." Nicholas dialed and was quickly connected. The secretary didn't delay him.

67

Demian only had to listen to Todd for a few seconds before he covered the mouthpiece of the phone and said to Jane, "Tell all the others. It's over." He refocused his attention on the phone while Jane ran to the other rooms and, in turn, told them this part of their nightmare was over. As she left the room, she heard quite a few "shit, damns!" and "holy shits!" She quickly came back to Demian. She jumped on him, pushing him down on the bed, and smothered him with kisses.

Marion said to Catherine, "They need our help. Now, more than ever. Now that they're done running, they have to face rebuilding their lives and recover from their trauma. Let's sit and be quiet, as we always have, and show them the compassion and composure that will help them heal."

"Yeah. I know you're right. And in the morning, we can go home—they can't."

"I'll suggest to Demian and the others that they should stay at the healing center. There are a lot of rooms and the environment is just right for them to settle into a daily rhythm."

Catherine smiled. "You're always two steps ahead."

"I have to speak to Demian. I'll be back very quickly." Marion stood and walked out to find Demian.

John and Elisabeth shared a bottle of Brud's raspberry wine, straight out of the bottle. They spoke to Mason, Madison and Ali who had returned from the hospital. The news continued to be very good for Deborah. She would likely be discharged in the morning. Marion overheard John quote Brud who said that the family had lost only their *things* in the missile attack on their houses. They could and would rebuild and become stronger in the process.

Marion caught their attention and in as loud a voice as a man of his age could muster said, "Pass the word to everyone. We'll all meet in Brud's dining area at seven AM tomorrow morning. I don't know how much sleep you can get after these events, but I insist that we all meet there, at that time." After he asked, the others pointed him to Demian's room and watched him shuffle off wondering what that could be about.

Marion knocked on the door and after a moment, it was opened. He went inside to speak to Demian.

68

"Yeah, well I don't know. The house is gone, so anything in the house that might have been poisoned is no longer a threat." Madison and Mason had been trying to piece together the apparent poisonings of Madison and Deborah. Where had they eaten without Mason and Ali? Any new foods or candies in the house? Did the two of them drink different juices? They could not come to any conclusions, no matter how many questions they asked.

"I don't know either," Mason answered. "We just have to start with a clean slate." He looked at his wife for a long time. "Are you really back to normal?"

"Yes. I finally feel OK. I don't think everyone is out to get me. I feel this compassion in my chest that I can use in my work." She looked for the right words. "Yes. I feel like my old self."

"Gunner will be happy. He's been beside himself, worried about you."

"Yeah. I'll talk to him. I was rough on him. I even called him a 'pathetic little man' when I was so paranoid. I owe him an apology. He was with me when I might have been having a stroke and took good care of me. We owe him a lot. He took Deborah to the Beaver Dams, and they found the other map to get us over Death Mountain for our very timely escape."

"Deborah stepped right up and confronted the adults with what she knew was a map, even when we didn't see it at first," Mason said admiringly.

"She's becoming a self-possessed young lady, for sure."

Mason thought, *The apple don't fall far from the tree.* "We should sleep on it tonight. In the morning, things will be clearer and we can get Deborah out of the hospital and go back to Lake Placid. I don't know where, yet."

"We'll figure it all out."

John and Elisabeth looked a little drunk as they finally made their way to their cabin. They fell on the bed and only had the energy to wish each other a good night. "You have to call your guys and tell them we're safe," Elisabeth told John.

"In the morning. We have to go to breakfast at seven AM. Such an odd thing that Marion wants us to do. Any idea about that?"

"No. But I wouldn't miss it. He's been such an important, positive influence on us all," Elisabeth answered.

"So, let's get to sleep before I get the whirlies."

"OK."

"We didn't kill the keg, did we?" Bennie asked. He held out his mug for a refill and couldn't stifle a belch. He looked around sheepishly. "Had to make more room, didn't I?"

Ellen waved it off dismissively.

"Yeah. After I started to feel better about myself, and after Madison, Gunner and Marion did quite a few healings for me, I gave up drinking heavily. Now I only drink like this to celebrate. And this, here, is the best reason I've *ever* had to celebrate." Will's eyes didn't follow as quickly, anymore.

"Well, celebrate to your heart's content. I'll have Ellen put on another pot of coffee. You guys have to get up in the morning for your meeting with Marion, you know," Tom reminded.

"You and Ellen are special invited guests, along with Brud. Fill 'er up, my friend." Will held out the large German style mug Tom and Ellen had loaned him. Bennie followed suit.

Tom asked, "So tell me about you, after you came home, Bennie?"

"I drank too much. For a long time. I got paranoid, angry and I got in fights that I knew I could win just to let off steam." He took a long drink from his mug. When he understood that no one wanted to deflect attention from his story, he continued. "Then I went to rangers' school and finished. It was the hardest training in the world, as you know, Tom. Anyway, the next day, I retired from the Army and drifted. I went way off the grid. No address, no taxes, nobody wanting me. I moved for about six months and met a very rich fellow who was fascinated with my story. He hired me to do odd jobs. Eventually, he persuaded me to 'influence' his political opponents and business rivals to see things his way. You get my drift. It was easy work. He paid me a suitcase full of twenties whenever I asked, and eventually, I ran out of odd jobs to do." He refilled his mug.

The others didn't want to interrupt, so Bennie felt pressured to complete the story.

"Yeah. Maybe it is time to get it all off my chest. Some of those odd jobs included very violent demonstrations of my earnestness." Bennie looked in the eyes of Will, Tom and Ellen. He didn't see shock or horror, only compassion. "I think some of the people I communicated with deserved it. Some didn't. I finally got my last payment and dropped out of sight. I started to spend a large amount of time online in very exclusive chat rooms. There arose occasions that I traveled and dealt with things for friends I connected with online. Those friends are the ones I asked to watch out for us. As I became more comfortable with myself, I did less and less of that work. I eventually helped myself and thought my way through the PTSD. A few weeks ago, Will called me. And here I am."

"Shit, damn, son!" Tom held his mug to clink it with the others.

"How are you right now?" Ellen asked. Her tone was reassuring.

"I feel really good. Catherine did a couple of healing sessions for me and she helped my subconscious to work through misunderstandings I had from a very young age that made me feel unworthy throughout my life. Now that just doesn't cross my mind. I feel no need to be combative—except, of course, when an attack helicopter comes to assault my friends."

Everyone laughed.

"Maybe you can see yourself in a different light, from now on?" Ellen asked. "We had to go through a similar thing. We ended up here. Tom drank himself a river of vodka. Now, I made him promise to stick with beer. I retreated and became depressed. And I wasn't even in any combat at all. But I saw the troops—way too many of them—come back injured, maimed, paralyzed, paranoid, what have you. I tried to make them all whole. It wore on me. Tom and I were shipped home and we drifted until we found these lovely horses. Their spirits exude healing and compassion. Even compassion for people." She didn't laugh.

"So, we've been *there*. And we've been *here* ever since. You've got to find a place to make your stand. This farm and these stables do it for us. I heard Madison talk about the mountains around your house. They do it for her. Part of healing is belonging. And needing," Tom said.

"And being needed by real people who you can see and talk to and be with," Ellen interrupted.

"I agree. Maybe you'll feel you no longer have to hide. Maybe you'll find a place that owns you as much as you own it. Maybe you can use the strength that you've shown us to help others heal and make progress in their lives, however that might be…." Tom's words trailed off.

"The world is full of possibilities when you trust and stop hiding. And the world could use your experience. Your story could help I don't know how many others to come back," Ellen said.

"So. Enough of all that. Do I have to tap the next keg?" Tom looked in his friends' eyes. "Maybe not. We all want to be awake and bright-eyed and bushy-tailed in the morning, don't we?"

Will and Bennie eventually made their way to their cabins to get a short rest before the early meeting.

70

"So, that's it. It's over." Todd had given his friend, Nicholas, a ride home. He had been invited in and asked to open a new bottle of Bombay Sapphire gin while Nicholas got out the ice. The whole bottle disappeared in no time.

The two men just drank, looked at each other wordlessly and occasionally smiled.

The captain's wife had made a full pot of coffee, but it sat unpoured. When they ran out of ice, they realized it was time to call it a day. "I know you boys had an exciting day, but it is late," she said.

"I know. I hope I haven't overstayed my welcome," Todd answered.

"No, but we're not getting any younger," she said, pulling on her husband's shoulder, motioning him towards their upstairs bedroom.

Todd turned to the captain. "I'll do everything I can to make this all square with you. I'll have Demian call the governor."

"He already has called the governor. Demian assured me that he would make this all go my way. I don't know if even he has that much pull, though."

"He sure does. He can work miracles. Just hold on long enough to let it all work out. How about coffee in the morning? You can help me write out the reports. You, being on leave, don't have any unending forms to fill out yourself, do you?"

"No. But I do have to call the right people and explain myself." They both laughed.

"Why don't I swing by at nine and we have coffee as I struggle with the paperwork?"

"Good. Done."

71

"Jesus. It was over that quick, after all that?" Albert croaked when he asked.

Demian had called him before the 7:00 AM meeting with Marion. "Yup. The local sheriff and the state police captain who shot the other prisoner in the foot to make him talk came through. They did real fieldwork on the ground, retraced the path of the assassins and figured out his most likely hiding place on Grand Isle."

"Grand Isle? That's not a rival to Long Island, is it?" Albert joked.

"No. Thankfully. It's a large island in Lake Champlain where the helicopter ditched after Bennie shot at it with a hunting rifle." He paused, letting his friend interrupt, but apparently, this time, Albert chose not to do so. "Anyway, they retraced the likely escape route and found the most deserted property to evaluate further. They approached, concluded that the only remaining villain was there and called in the state police SWAT team."

"Nice."

"I called the captain to congratulate him. He told me the oddest story of how the interrogation went. They offered to let the man tell his story. Of course, he refused and claimed diplomatic immunity."

"Of course. That prick."

"The sheriff went on about how they had 'Bubba' in a holding cell. The sheriff, captain and SWAT team members then started yelling and arguing about their bets over how long it might take for the captive to scream for help. They played it up and jostled around until two of the police pushed into his chair, knocking him over. They picked him up and started arguing among themselves, all over again, completely ignoring him. The prisoner could see piles of bills on the table in front of him. He gave up, surrendered his computer passwords and the other police left the sheriff and captain to have a private discussion."

"Did they plan that out ahead of time?" Albert asked.

"That's the funny thing. The sheriff and captain and other policemen just let it play out organically."

"Beautiful. They didn't threaten him at all; just took bets on how long it would take for him to scream for help?"

"Yup."

"Beautiful." Albert filed that approach away, in case he needed it in the future.

"So, listen. We all owe you a lot. You had our backs. I want to invite you to come to our healing center. As our guest. I'll have the staff treat you like royalty and you can stop your smoking habit if you're ready for that?" Demian offered.

"Yeah. I got this classic black Cadillac. The biggest one ever made. I got chauffeurs to drive me up there. How far is it?" Albert coughed.

"Four to five hours, depending on traffic out of the city."

"You can pay me the last part of my fee when I see you. How about in a couple of weeks?"

"Great. I also want you to meet someone. The woman I mean to stay with for the rest of my life. She's the administrator of the local hospital. If you think you need to make any charity donations for tax purposes, think of donating there. I know you'll find her captivating and a good match for me."

"Yeah. Your last few wives? I knew they wouldn't last." Albert croaked out a laugh.

"I'm really happy that you will come on up and meet her. And take care of your health, most of all."

"Don't tell me you're trying to turn me to the light side, like you?"

"Wouldn't think of it. But you could work on your legacy. What charity work have you done in the last few years?" Demian's voice softened.

"I don't have to think hard and long, for sure."

"Maybe after your visit, you'll feel differently about how you spend your money?"

"Yeah, right."

"Oh, I almost forgot, if your guys are not too pissed at you for abusing them, is there any way that Captain Green will not be punished for shooting his prisoner in the foot to expedite an extremely time-sensitive interrogation? Any way your guys could call in favors for me? That'll be something I would really appreciate."

"Did you forget who you're talking to? That's easy. In fact, I already started the project. And I figure the captain and sheriff should be awarded medals. I have my men speaking to all the right people. I figured if they were to receive medals, it wouldn't look right to reprimand them at the same time."

"Albert, it'll be good to see you again, my friend."

"You left out the 'old' this time? Maybe you've aged a little over the last few weeks?"

"Maybe. And then, maybe I've been associating with all the right people...

"See you in a couple of weeks."

72

Brud had been up for several hours. He had prepared a sumptuous breakfast for the group with special guests—himself, Tom and Ellen. Catherine's offer of help in the kitchen had been quickly accepted. She added her expertise and fashioned small satchels of organic herbs and honey to be steeped in boiling hot water as a special healing tea. Tables were set up, covered with white and pink cloth tablecloths and the silverware handed down from Brud's grandmother was polished and laid out. A small vase of flowers from the planters surrounding the office was placed at each table.

Marion had searched around to find kindling enough to build a fire that would burn for about fifteen minutes. He assembled the smallest sticks, then the progressively larger pieces in a teepee formation. He also collected pencils and paper for each participant. Then he sat in an outdoor chair, closed his eyes and chanted, watching the rising sun crest the mountains to the east. He had chosen 7:00 AM for the ceremony because the sun would have completely cleared the skyline at that time.

"All ready, my friend?" Brud asked, feeling it an unusual experience not to be the oldest person he met.

"Yes. Just clearing my mind for the ceremony," Marion quietly answered.

"If there's anything else, call out to me. I'll be helping Catherine in the kitchen. She is so delicate with the spices and seasonings. I can learn a lot from her."

Marion smiled and sat motionless.

The others had gathered before 7:00 AM. Deborah, the only one absent, hopefully would be released later that morning. Marion started. "Friends, new and old, thank you for getting up earlier than most of you are accustomed to."

Laughs and groans could be heard coming from all quarters.

"And I'm sure some of you have earnestly celebrated last night, so thanks for making the effort." John, Elisabeth, Will and Bennie looked at each other and smiled.

"We have a solemn and joyful ceremony to perform, with each of us participating. But the most important member of our ritual is the earth itself—with all her beings." He started to give each person a sheet of paper and a pencil after he grasped their hands and looked deeply in their eyes, taking several minutes to do so. After this, he said, "Your directions are simple. Write down briefly one of three things—a wish for the future, something you want to get away from or give up or change about yourself, or a prayer for the earth. These can be symbolic, metaphorical, practical or even a small drawing. These are personal and do not need to be shared. Roll or fold up the paper and bring it with you outside. We'll have the fire ceremony out there. No speaking in the meantime." His serious look left no room for controversy.

Some of the group sat at tables; some leaned over the chairs to write; some wrote with the paper in their palms. Everyone was silent. They neatly folded or rolled the papers into long tubes. Ali folded his into a small airplane shape. When they had completed the task, Marion said, "Catherine, will you go first and show the others how to do this? We will all keep silent and do exactly what Catherine does as soon as you're ready. Reverently place the note in the fire to be transformed by the fire and the earth. Gaze at the paper until the fire has consumed it and transformed it all."

They filed out of the office and stood around the fire that Marion started with a single match. He blew on the flames, and a small roaring fire bloomed and crackled. It smelled of the wood fires that Demian had experienced as a youth at the Jay Mountain hunting camp.

Marion chanted softly in an Indian dialect. Even though he was elderly, his voice seemed strong and full. Catherine approached the fire with her paper in her hands. She bowed and gently placed it in the fire and waited until it burned. Her gaze followed the smoke upwards, as she smiled, stood and stepped aside. Marion stood behind Catherine as she approached the fire until she completed her prayer, with his arms spread widely to the side, chanting rhythmically.

One after another, each placed his or her paper in the fire, watched it burn, followed the smoke upwards, smiled, stood aside and silently watched as the others did the same. They all smiled, breathed deeply and knew that, as the notes on the papers had been transformed, so had their wishes become actualized.

Gunner and Demian stood on either side of Marion, their hands resting on his shoulders. "Thank you, old friend," Demian whispered.

Gunner closed his eyes and felt the air clear.

The others kept silent until Ali said, "That food smells good. I can't believe how hungry I feel."

"Well, we better go and fix that. We made a lot of food, and I don't want to deal with any leftovers!" Brud laughed.

Marion, Demian and Gunner stayed and stared at the fire until it completely burned out. They joined the rest for a sumptuous feast. Gunner felt as though something new was taking form in their lives. Sitting at the table, Jane moved her chair to touch Demian's—they shared warmth in their thighs, knees and calves. They smiled and kissed each other on the ear, many times.

Tom and Ellen, seated across the table from Bennie and Will, surveyed their new friends. Tom said, "Remember what I said about finding a place that owns you as much as you own it? The earth spoke to us clearly around that fire." He lowered his eyes when he realized he might have sounded corny.

"Part of the earth is its beings—all of them. The stone people, plant people, two-legged, four-legged, furred, finned, feathered—all of them give us their energy. We're most lucky when they give us their blessings, too," Ellen added.

73

Several days after the houses were destroyed, Brud, Tom and Ellen drove all of the evacuees back to Lake Placid. The trio was welcomed to a hero's dinner at the healing center and a night's stay before they drove back, needing to return quickly to care for the horses and Brud's business. But, before they left, Marion, Catherine, Gunner and Madison held another healing ceremony at the center in the evening, after a sumptuous dinner of local organic meats, vegetables from the gardens, and fruits picked earlier that day.

The staff at the healing center went all out for their co-directors, welcoming them back. They set up small luminaria lining the pathways to and through the extensive gardens Marion had designed and planted. They all held hands, forming a circle in silence and had each member of the celebration stand in the center, receiving energy from the intentions of each of the healers. Mason, Madison and the kids went inside as a group. They stood and felt compassion, kindness and love come to them. It was just what they needed to feel grounded. Their work ahead would not be easy, but, after being in the circle and receiving the healing intentions, they were sure it would be accomplished.

Next, Demian and Jane stood, faced each other, held each other at the waist and started to move slowly. When they felt comfortable, they stepped aside for Will. He stood, bowed his head, slowly looked up and turned in a circle to look at everyone sending him prayers. A final, curt bow of his head, and he stepped out.

Brud, Tom and Ellen held hands, looked into each other's eyes and then closed their eyes to feel the group's unqualified acceptance of them. Although this was a new and unusual experience for them, they understood this was a gift from the heavens and from some of the most experienced healers on earth. They accepted this gift graciously without question.

Bennie waited to be the last one into the ring. He stood, erect, staring at Catherine and Marion, wondering how they did what they did. He finally stepped out of the ring, after feeling "full."

Three weeks later, a very large, shiny black Cadillac slid silently up to the front doors of the healing center. Demian remembered joking that a car like that should have at least three zip codes it's so long. The driver got out, rubbed his low back and opened the rear door. He helped an elderly, grey-haired gentleman step out and waited a few moments until he straightened up completely. He did so slowly and coughed a rattling cough.

Demian greeted the visitor with a warm hug. "Albert, you look good." In fact, the elderly gentleman stood erectly, his eyes were bright and his complexion clear. His grey hair was neatly coiffed, coming down to his ears on the side and to his collar in the back. "You've lost weight? You look completely trim. Excellent."

"Funny thing happened. There I was lying in bed when I suddenly felt warm. I knew, at that instant, that I would never smoke another cigarette again. And, I knew that you and your group had something to do with it. That was right after you called me to tell me your ordeal was over." He paused, "Funny, that. Been almost three weeks and I haven't slipped up yet. I keep finding hidden cigarettes in all kinds of places. I just flush 'em."

Demian smiled and laughed. "All I did was ask our healers to work for you. I only had to tell them your name and that you lived in New York. They did the rest."

"Bullshit."

"The God's truth." Demian raised his right hand to swear to it.

"That's what I thought you would say. So, I thought I really had to meet these healers if they could do that for me. And without even seeing me, or being in the same room or even in the same part of the state. Still, I'm *sure* they did just that for me too."

"Come on in and get settled. Then you can meet everyone. They want to meet you because you had a large hand in saving their lives."

Demian carried Albert's bags to his room, showed him around and left him to rest and shower before dinner.

Mason, Madison, Deborah and Ali had settled into a suite of rooms at the healing center. Madison relayed to Demian that they were doing very well. Mason supervised the demolition and had already begun the rebuilding of the two houses. The demolition only took a day. There were only ashes remaining of what had been two complete houses, furnishings and a large pole barn with tractors and lawn implements. Everything had burned to the ground and become pulverized with the attack and subsequent explosions.

It was Jane who solved the mystery of the poisoning of Madison and Deborah. Mason and Ali never showed any signs of toxicity at all, even though the family had lived together, eaten and drank the same foods and liquids and been exposed to all the same air, water and allergens. Jane had sat bolt upright in bed awakening Demian and said, "I know! I know! It's lipstick." She promptly lay back down, fell asleep, and left Demian to wonder what all that was about— and struggle in vain to get back to sleep himself as she snored away.

After Jane awoke the next morning and had waited until a reasonable hour, she called Madison and asked her, "How about any new lipstick? I think that's the only link between you and Deborah that Mason and Ali wouldn't share."

Madison immediately recalled the "free sample of sunscreen/lipstick" in a beautiful shade of glittered red. It had come with a glossy advertising brochure from Germany announcing, "The best European skin preserving balm with sun protection." Because it was a sample of sunscreen, she permitted Deborah to try a bit. Madison had used it several days in a row. The "miracle from Europe" was destroyed in the bombing. They finally had their answer. "Nothing is free, is it Jane?" The two women laughed until they realized how true that was.

74

Bennie asked Will if he was able to get by without his help, for a few days.

"Sure. What's up?"

"Don't know, really. But, I need to see someone. I hope she'll come back here to meet all of the healers. I know they could help her. I know it."

"Are you OK? Anything I or maybe Demian could do?" Will asked.

"No. I have to get through this myself. But, if I can get her to come, I would ask that all the healers do their earnest best for her."

"You know that's the only thing they do. They don't settle for just a little, or OK," Will said a little worried and a little put off.

"Yeah. I do. I know how powerful they are. They were strong enough to deflate all my energies. Remember? I couldn't take watch?"

"How could I forget?"

"So, do you think you'll need me in the next few days?" Bennie looked expectantly at his dearest friend.

"Get lost. Go and do what *you* need. You've already done your duty here."

Bennie looked at his best friend and knew they would always be there for each other. He bowed slightly, turned and left the room.

He drove to the small motel he occasionally used—he had no place that he felt more permanence, and certainly no place he called "home." He opened the door by jostling the handle and putting his shoulder against the door, giving it just the right force. He didn't want to break off the latches or hinges. He smelled the musty old odors, felt the heat from the lack of air conditioning and knew he would never stay there again. He closed the door behind him. He would call his friend, the owner of the hotel, and tell him later.

He felt differently in a lot of ways. He no longer needed to be *absent*—that was the right word. He could be present. He didn't need to hide. He could fit in. He wasn't sure how, but he would figure that out—he was confident.

He drove to Jenn's. He stopped in the parking lot, got out of his car and approached her apartment. He had not been there for more than a week, missing their customary time of meeting at 11:00 AM. His watch read 2:30 PM. He approached and knocked on the door.

"Hey, Jenn. It's Bennie," he called, hoping she would not refuse to see him.

"What are you coming now for? I need to rest most afternoons, you know that."

"I want to tell you a lot of new things." He waited. "Mostly about how I feel. And how I am."

"Well, you might as well come in. I don't have anything for you, though. You haven't been here for so long." Her voice sounded tired and weaker.

With some reluctance, Bennie entered and closed the door behind him. "Thank you for seeing me."

"What choice do I have and what difference does it make, anyway?" Her voice fell off at the end of her question.

"Are you OK?"

"No. Jesus, you are dense, aren't you? I haven't been OK since I was fourteen. Shit." She wore floppy sweats and slippers. She appeared paler.

"Jesus. Let me get you something to eat and drink, OK?"

"There's nothing here."

"Good. Get in my car and we'll go for food. We can talk on the way." Bennie had already started to help her to her feet.

"Whatever." She didn't have the energy to argue.

They got in Bennie's car and drove to a grocery store nearby that specialized in organic, non-processed foods. He left her in the car to buy soups, bread, soft cheeses, cider and deviled eggs. He brought them to the car in the parking lot and made her drink some cider, eat a few eggs and start on some hearty soup. Her cheeks filled out and her complexion became less transparent and less shiny.

"Where have you been?" There was an edge to her voice—that was all she could muster.

"I was helping my friends who captured the guy who set off the electromagnetic pulse in Lake Placid. Even though he was sitting in prison, he hired two teams of hit men—one from Germany, the other from South Africa. They were assigned to kill all of us who had anything to do with the capture of Gary Canig, including Marion, Catherine, and even the governor of New York."

"Wow. How could he do all that?"

"We think through his lawyer." Bennie took his time and made sure she had had enough to eat and drink. "I saved the lives of myself and eight other people by shooting at a moving helicopter with a hunting rifle. It was armed with four rockets that I recognized from Iraq. I held off an attack that would surely have killed them all. I still can't believe it. I bet it was more than three hundred yards and moving fast."

"Is it true?" she asked disbelievingly.

"Yes," he replied testily.

"Well, you have to admit that you can spin a tale, when you want to." She smiled. She would have laughed at Bennie but didn't have the energy yet, he noticed.

"It's true." Bennie waited again for her to finish eating and drinking. She had started a nice-looking mushroom broth. "Then one team of assassins was captured by John's group of online hackers. The other group of three assassins actually blasted off three missiles and demolished Will's house—he's my life-long friend. They also destroyed Mason and Madison's house and a large pole barn but were captured shortly thereafter. Then, finally, the last assassin was captured by the sheriff I told you about. Now, all my friends have to rebuild their lives, homes—everything, really."

"Jesus. Do you even know reality from fantasy anymore?" Jenn showed her concern for Bennie's mental status.

"Yes. All that is the God's honest truth. I can prove it to you. I can take you there and show you."

"No fucking way!"

"What? Which? That I can take you there, or that I can prove the rest of the story to you?" he questioned.

"Both. I'm not strong enough to make a trip like that. And I don't know what to believe anymore, anyhow."

It became obvious to Bennie that she didn't have the strength to argue. "Can you meet me half way? Can I take you to a spa, get you super nutritious food to help your energy, rest a few days, then take you to Lake Placid? There's the healing center that my friends run. They can help you heal. They owe me. They'll do their best work to heal you. I know they can heal you."

"Bullshit."

"I know it. They've healed me. And no tests, operations, or anything else invasive. I just talked until I understood myself. Then they did their healing rituals. I'm a different person, now." Bennie stopped arguing and started to drive. He arrived at the Saratoga health spa.

At the spa, they checked in. Bennie left off a credit card and discussed the situation with the admissions clerk and then the supervising physician, went to get things for Jenn to make her stay comfortable and checked in himself. He looked forward to doing physical training like he had done with the Special Forces. He would let the nutritionists, physical therapists and counselors care for Jenn until she was well enough to make the trip to Lake Placid. He had openly discussed this plan with the staff and they, having heard such good reports about the healing center, concurred wholeheartedly that it would be the logical next step.

Jenn complied with all the diet recommendations made by the staff. She remained listless and joyless, and simply did what she was told. But she did gain weight and stamina. She walked only with assistance, but she did walk. Bennie's choices for exercise clothes suited her tastes as well, but she remained disengaged. Bennie understood this as Jenn's only way of showing her disapproval. She withdrew.

75

"Hi, Jenn. How are you?" Bennie asked after several days of pampering from the staff at the Saratoga spa. He had thoroughly enjoyed the exercise equipment and jogging trails through town. He felt he had sweated enough to burn off any unwanted calories and regained his peak fitness. He had also run long and hard enough to separate his mind from the everyday, mundane concerns he struggled with. He settled into a rhythm of running and breathing. He began to have intuitions—like the mountains talked directly to him. He took his time to process their messages.

"I'm stronger. The pain is the same. Now, I notice it more. When I didn't eat and drink, my pain would dull a little." She turned away from him, angry.

"Are you mad at me for taking you here?"

"How could I have argued with you? I wasn't strong enough." Now he could clearly see how pissed she was.

"Well, just keep getting better. I'm sorry I had to leave for those few days. I'm sorry you slid backwards when I was away."

"It wasn't your fault."

Bennie knew she had almost failed enough to be irretrievable. "I know that. But from here on, I'll make sure you're gaining. I won't let you flounder."

"Shit."

"I've called Demian. I need to drive up there and see Will and him about an important issue I think can't wait. I've talked with the director here. She'll look after you and make sure you're getting enough to eat, and exercise. You're stronger every day. It's good to see."

Jenn moaned, facing away from him. She couldn't look him in the eye. "You saved me right into more pain."

"No. That's only the first part of saving you. When you're strong enough, I'll take you to Lake Placid. The healers there will help you stop hurting all the time." Now Bennie understood how depressed Jenn had become in just the few days he had been away. "I've got to go and deal with an issue for my friends; then I'll be back. When you're ready, I'll take you there, too."

"Do you really think I'll get better?" she sobbed.

"Yes. No doubt about it." He got up to go to the door of her room. He turned to look back and smile. "I know because I've been there. I've been healed. I know it can happen for you, too."

He had called Demian and Will and asked them to meet him where the houses had been. They both had busy agendas but wouldn't ever refuse their friend. Will had been looking after Deborah and Ali during the day while Madison and Gunner tried to catch up with their patient loads at the healing center. He tried to keep them occupied as Mason started the rebuilding of the two houses. Neither of the children had been back to where the missiles had struck. Will had visited several times to advise Mason on rebuilding. Will wanted to recreate his house as it was before the rocket's destruction, as closely as possible. Mason envisioned many changes to his house. The kids had grown and had different needs. Madison wanted a first-floor bedroom and laundry. Mason made careful note of all of it and would make it all happen.

"Should I bring Deborah and Ali along with us?" Will asked.

"Why don't you ask Madison if she thinks they're ready?" Bennie thought it might be too soon and too difficult for them to see the wreckage.

"Maybe you're right. I was just thinking," Will explained.

"I've called Demian and he'll meet us there. I have something to show you both up at the Beaver Dams."

"What?"

"Maybe it's something, and maybe not. But I want to be there to show you both."

"OK. Then we'll all meet and walk up there."

Bennie drove the three hours, not feeling the need to speed. He enjoyed the scenery. He played out in his head how he should tell his friends what he had been through, and ask Demian about the gold. Nothing solidified as a plan, so he decided to approach the situation as it presented itself to him.

He finally pulled into the area between the bombed-out houses and was surprised that none of the wreckage was visible. It had all been hauled away. The town's people had turned out to help with rakes, shovels and small tractors. As the larger debris was loaded away in dumpsters with large front loaders, they swept away the small bits of the houses that had been blown away with the explosions into small shrapnel chunks. At this point, the lawn between the craters looked well-manicured.

The craters left from the larger demolition now held footers and new basement walls to support the rest of the new construction. Different crews of electricians, plumbers, masons and laborers worked efficiently to help with the projects. The town's people and these crews felt it was incumbent upon them to finish as quickly as possible to let the families get back to their normal lives. It became their way of giving back. Some of this was patriotism—no U.S. citizen should ever be the target of foreign assassins—or for some, a way of repayment for Demian's generosity to the town.

"Man, they're really getting this done, aren't they?" Bennie remarked to Demian and Will.

"Yup. They are," Demian said admiringly.

"I wish they would concentrate on Mason's place to get it done first. They could use their place more than I need mine, having kids and all," Will said.

"Mason has a great sense of fairness. He would truck no favoritism," Demian replied.

"At the rate they're going, they'll get both done shortly. There won't be any need to wish they were completed. They'll be done," Bennie added.

Demian turned to his friends. "I wonder what it is that you've had us come up here to do or see?"

"I wonder, too," Will chimed in.

"Why don't we walk? I need to tell you both something to get it off my chest." Bennie motioned uphill towards the Beaver Dams.

"Lead on. Tell us what you need to tell us," Demian said, trusting his friend to have dragged them all the way up here for a good reason.

As they walked on, Bennie and the others came to the spot where he had shot at the helicopter.

"I've done a lot of shooting. I was a decathlon champion in my twenties. I've hunted on all the continents—big game, small game, with lethal projectiles and tranquilizing darts, but that was one hell of a long shot on a small target moving hundreds of miles an hour. I've had the most experienced marksmen instructing me and I know I couldn't have done it. How did you make the shots?" Demian was obviously impressed.

"Man. That was good shooting. And you didn't even range it with a laser rangefinder, you didn't use a rest, and you didn't adjust for the wind which is considerable up here," Will added. They stood and looked down the slope to the new construction. They imagined the helicopter flying up towards the houses, tried to range it mentally and pretended to shoot at the quick moving target.

"That's part of what I wanted to show you. I don't know how I did it. I think—I think the earth or these mountains helped. You're right. I didn't have time to range the distance, I didn't have a steady rest and couldn't deploy my tripod. I just ran up the road in about twelve minutes, carrying the gear and rifle. I was winded. Shooting like that just shouldn't happen—I don't know." Bennie looked visibly uncertain.

"You did it, though. I'm sure that they would have shot off those missiles and we all would have died—safe room or not. It wouldn't have held up under those missiles." Demian started to tear up.

"I couldn't have lived with all those lives on my conscience," Bennie moaned.

"Why are you questioning all this now?" Will asked.

"I'm not questioning. I know something helped me. These mountains, maybe. I don't know."

"Son. As sure as I'm standing here, we all have confidence in you to do whatever you must do to get the job done. I know you can and will protect your friends at all costs and with any means," Demian commanded.

"It doesn't explain the impossible." Bennie sat down on a log. "I've been struggling with this. So, I went on quite a few long hikes and runs, clearing my mind. What kept coming back to me was the mountains telling me to bring you both up here, to explain this and something else at the dams. I had to clear the air and admit that I had help from sources that are unexplainable."

"We're here to listen. Lead on at your own pace," Demian said, understanding Bennie was still working all of this out in his mind.

"Bennie. You know we're here for you. Tell us the whole story," Will encouraged.

"Yeah. But, let's get to the dams." They turned uphill and walked.

None of the men felt pressured to go quickly. They joked about pulling Catherine and Marion uphill with the deer haulers. Demian laughed at the idea of raking half an acre to hide tracks on his way up. They all related that they still felt that the *whole escape* was beyond belief—the map, the horses, getting out of the houses just in time—all of it. And, it seemed, everyone had a hand in their safe escape, from the children to the most elderly.

They finally came to the Beaver Dams and larger stone stack. Bennie removed his pack. He took out canteens and passed them around. Then he pulled out tracing paper. He cleaned off both stones that had been engraved and traced over the stones as carefully as he could. He superimposed the maps on the same tracing, lining up the two stone pyramids.

"From what Gunner told me, there is a detail that Will didn't tell everyone about when you originally went looking for the gold." He held up the superimposed tracings. They shone clearly in the light. "I don't know if you knew this, it was a ranger thing. The error in the maps points to the direction that's true. Gunner mentioned that you stopped over on that bank, thinking it was the spot where the gold was buried. It's not. It's right here." Bennie had walked to about thirty yards beyond the opposite side of the stone stack.

"Shit, damn, son!" Demian looked bewildered. "I looked up here for weeks after we thought we found the gold, then I gave up. I forgot about it. I went about with trying to live my life, and Marion had done healings on me that made me not care about it after that. I just went about all my business dealings in a new light. I thought that was the gold I was supposed to find."

"Bennie, I never heard about that map detail. I only heard that the image was likely reversed to throw off our enemies. No one ever asked Demian about the gold. We figured it was his business to deal with." Will looked cloudy. "My grandfather, Bill, seemed the most interested in it. He spent a lot of his life looking and never found it. Now he'll never know." Will's eyes teared. "Are you saying you've found the gold?"

"No. I had no permission to be here or dig for gold." Bennie turned to Demian. "So the next step is yours, Demian. I felt, very clearly, that I had to tell you about this. On my forced marches, the land spoke to me and told me to tell you. I couldn't ignore it. I had to bring you here."

"Thank you, Bennie." Demian thought a long while. "I don't know. I don't know what's right. I think you should tell me. What did the earth tell you we should do with the gold?"

"I only got the message to tell you about the quirk in the maps. It surely misled you, didn't it?"

Will offered, "Maybe this is a question for Marion?"

Bennie opened his knapsack again, pulling out his favorite beer. "Guinness, all right?" The six-pack didn't last long among the three friends.

76

"I don't know a thing about how they do what they do. I only know it has worked for me," Bennie said as Jenn packed the few belongings she had in a new knapsack. She had spent a total of ten days under the care of the nutritionists, physical therapists, physicians and therapists at the Saratoga spa. They had reviewed all of Jenn's records and were as baffled as her original physicians and referral consultants. She had regained her strength, put on weight and become more mobile, but her depression persisted, and her pain increased now that she had become more enlivened.

"So, now I'm your prisoner? You can take me anywhere you want to?" she said snidely to Bennie.

"Jesus. Don't lay that on me. I've been a good friend to you and only want what will help you," he fired back.

"Whatever," the resignation is her voice was unmistakable, deflating Bennie's will.

"It simply isn't right to let you flounder. I took you here to save your life. The doctors here think you might have been close to multi-organ failure from malnutrition and dehydration. You were committing suicide if you didn't know it." He tried to explain himself.

"I feel like it's just a game. The better I am physically, the more I feel the pain. I can't continue with that merry-go-round anymore." She finally looked him in the eyes.

"If they don't help you in Lake Placid, I'll let you do what you want to yourself. I promise. But the reason I can promise that is I know you'll improve. And I'll be there to help you all the way."

"Promise me."

"I promise. It's only about a hundred miles from here, but we can stop as often as you like. I'll go slow. I've put the comforter back on your seat. Let's go." He helped her to his car.

Jenn didn't enjoy the ride. Every bump reminded her that she was on a fool's chase. She didn't ask to stop or to have Bennie make up any stories for her. She barely endured the whole ordeal.

They finally pulled into the Jay Mountain Healing Center. Waiting for her were Gunner, Madison, Marion and Catherine. She arrived at her room, was given a dark green smoothie, asked if she needed to rest and left to do so. Bennie discussed what he knew of Jenn's story, as they reviewed the medical history from the Saratoga spa and his impressions of Jenn. He also divulged his relationship with Jenn's father. This helped dispel any fear that Bennie might have had any inappropriate intentions with this vulnerable and much younger woman.

Marion went to his room at the center to meditate and clear his mind. Catherine went to the gardens to collect the specific herbs that she felt might be of help. She went to the kitchen to make a series of teas and smoothies. Madison started her distance healing reiki for Jenn. Gunner cleared his schedule and sat in his treatment room. He needed to devote himself to his rituals of destiny retrieval. He felt he needed to be alone. For Bennie and Jenn, he wanted to do his best work.

Bennie understood how seriously they all undertook their healing practices. He was honored to be a friend of everyone here. He had never felt such a clear connection to anyone other than Will and the troops he commanded. He knew the mountains were speaking to him in this way again. He stopped to sit in the gardens and listen as they allowed him to feel—whole, contented, attached and calm.

"Jane, can I come and pick you up to take you to the healing center? Bennie's brought his friend Jenn today. Gunner asked us to come. Marion actually insists."

"Sure, Demian. But why us? We don't do healing. I just administrate that it should be done. You finance it—both are important, but we don't do the healing part."

"Yeah. I know. Gunner seemed really fixed on the idea, so we should go," he pleaded.

"OK. Six or so OK?"

"I'll pick you up at the hospital then. At your office?"

"That'll be fine." She paused, came to a conclusion, and said, "I think I'm ready to move a few things over to your place. Is that all right?"

"Jane. That's music to my ears. I need you. I love you. I can't get enough of you in my life—but I remember what you said about four seasons, and I won't push you."

"I know. Just a few things."

Jane couldn't see his smile, but she could feel it as plainly as she could see the sun through her windows.

Marion and Catherine met up with Gunner and Madison for their daily debrief. They discussed all their patients' progress, plans and whatever particular issues might have come up in the day's work. Marion said, "I think I should take the lead in Jenn's planning and care. She's in dire distress and can't even see how ill she is herself."

The others nodded, somewhat relieved to allow him to plan for her.

"My destiny retrieval for her didn't go well. It wasn't interference like with the electromagnetic pulse, but, I couldn't find any helpful scenarios to bring back for her. Bleak. Just bleak," Gunner said sadly.

"I felt the distance reiki I did for her was repelled—like she didn't want any help, like she's given up," Madison added.

"This isn't going to be easy. I've called Demian and Jane. Their energies are fairly clear. I want them in the background to be present as a calming force. It may be good for them to see what we do, as well." Marion could see the others agreed with him. "Catherine and I need to start with herbals and acupuncture to build her up enough so that she can even respond to all the other treatments she'll need. And we have to get Bennie to trust that she can heal. He's been shocked that she fell so far, so rapidly, when he came up here to help us. And thank God he did help us." The others nodded.

"So the plan is to fortify her physically and spiritually? Then we can all do our practices for her and we'll be more effective?" Madison asked.

"Yes." Marion was resolute. He commanded such respect from the others that there was no argument. Jenn presented the hardest of cases. They were all glad for his expert guidance. "We'll start with a group healing session tonight. Demian and Jane will be here for dinner and stay to help us by being here."

77

"Jenn, I hope you're rested enough to join a special ceremony for you?" the aid asked. She had opened Jenn's door and found her lying on her bed.

Jenn moaned.

"I'll get a wheelchair for you and push you to the treatment room. Here's some tea made especially for you by Catherine. You'll love her. She takes care of us all," the aid said. She had already positioned a chair next to the bed to swing Jenn into and then get her to the wheelchair in stages.

Jenn took the steaming tea and sipped it as she was pushed to the treatment room. Nothing looked clinical, like in so many hospitals and clinics she had visited. She heard soft music. The hallways had real art work—some of it from the high school art classes, some of it authentic work of the old masters. The carpets were thick, matching the curtains, while a life-sized photograph of the therapists with Groucho Marx eyeglasses with mustaches and eyebrows overlooked the entrance to the main therapy areas. As she entered a large conference room, the group of therapists introduced themselves in turn, stating they were pleased to meet her. This helped to put her at ease. She continued drinking her tea.

"Jenn, I would like to welcome you to our center," Marion said. "I'm the 'old guy' here and we've talked about what we plan to do for you. We plan to help fortify your energies first, then we can deal with your pain." He paused. "That all right?"

"Yes. If you think you can do it?" Jenn answered with some effort.

The others could see how depleted she had become and were horrified at the thought that she was much worse before spending ten days in the Saratoga spa, being cared for, fed special fortifying foods and starting initial therapies. Gunner thought that Bennie had likely saved her life, as well as all of theirs.

"We've reviewed the work done for you at the spa. They're good friends of ours and we respect them and their work," Marion continued.

"They only got me to feel the pain more. What can you do that's any more or different?" She clearly sounded frustrated.

"It's a whole process that maybe you're too tired to make huge decisions about right now. Could I suggest that we go slowly, discuss each treatment we'll do, and you can say yes or no so things are completely in your control?" Marion asked. "We can start right now. All you have to do is to rest, drink a little more tea if you like and wonder what could be next in life for you."

Jenn looked perplexed. She slowly said, "OK?"

Bennie, Demian, Jane, Madison, Gunner and Catherine were seated in chairs around the perimeter of the room. Jenn slowly looked at each one of them and finally said, "Well, we are here. I just can't be touched. It hurts too much."

"We read that in the reports coming from the spa. We know, so we'll just sit and do our meditations or prayers for you. You only have to wait, and maybe drink a little tea, or just rest."

Marion moved a chair to face Jenn and sat across from her and smiled. He looked in her eyes, then focused his eyes through her or behind her. He then quickly looked down on the floor. Jenn's eyes followed, then closed and she rested.

"Yes, that's good," Marion said. He looked to his colleagues and nodded. They closed their eyes and started their own healing rituals for Jenn, knowing Marion had signaled Jenn's subconscious to rest. He had perfected hypnosis without the need for words.

Demian and Jane felt the power in the room. It was soft, but full, warm and tingly. It was the kindness of the universe directed to Jenn in the form of a prayer to manifest what would be in her highest healing good.

Jane closed her eyes. She knew that intuitively she should add what she could and envisioned a beautiful fall day. Jane imagined that she felt the sun on her forehead, heard the birds in the distance, smelled the odor of fresh cut grass and could taste the fresh air. She let these impressions grow and she wished them to Jenn, understanding that she very likely had not had the pleasure of enjoying nature in the recent past or had even felt good enough to notice the beauty around her.

Demian smiled at his friends. He relaxed and did not *do* anything. He envisioned kindness, compassion and joy. He saw those emotions as different colors, swirling around the room. He kept his eyes closed and allowed the energies in the room to work their magic.

After only about ten minutes, Marion summoned the attention of the others. He gently called to Jenn to awaken and feel refreshed. They watched as she opened her eyes, blinking in an exaggerated manner.

She gave an uneasy half-smile. "I did feel something. I don't know what."

"You felt the goodness in the universe, and the brightness of a beautiful fall day." Marion looked at Jane and nodded. "This is all good. We will respect your wishes to go slowly. One small step at a time."

Jenn noticed that her clothes didn't hurt rubbing against her skin as she was wheeled back to her room. Bennie pushed her wheelchair as he gave her a short tour of the healing center on the way.

"You really think they will help me?" she asked, still not confident.

"Of course. Don't you feel at least something different, even as you ride in the chair?" he asked, encouragingly.

"No."

"Yes, you do. But you're having a hard time admitting it to yourself."

They came to her room where she settled in for the night. Marion and Catherine had arranged a special tea to be sipped when only warm—not hot. She did so and slept very well.

78

"Marion, could Bennie, Jane and I speak to you, just for a few minutes?" Demian asked politely, knowing he imposed on the elderly gentleman but that he would not refuse.

"Sure. Catherine is already in her room, resting. I need to get to bed shortly to be at my best, but what could the three of you have in mind?" He answered while taking a seat in another small conference room. He got room-temperature water to drink as he waited.

They all sat around the table in the center of the room. Jane had a curious look on her face. "Do you want me here too?"

"Yes, Jane." He hugged her. "I wonder if you remember that I told you there was something else special about the Beaver Dams area? I didn't get into it on the day that we found out that the sheriff was abducted. We were all too busy worrying about Todd."

"Yes...."

"The answer might surprise us all. Bennie, here, had the answer all the time. Maybe he should tell us about it?" Demian looked expectantly at his friend.

"If you think so." Bennie put down his tea. "About a dozen years ago, Demian, Bill, Will, Gunner and Dr. Crandall found the engravings on two large stones. They rightly deduced that these were maps at the base of the large, pyramidal-shaped stone stack to point out the location of what they thought could be buried gold. The elaborate stacking of the stones, engravings and the very remote location all make us think that this was a very serious undertaking from at least one hundred and fifty years ago. You saw the stones when we escaped the missile attack." He looked around to see that they all followed his description. They nodded, encouraging him to continue.

"Anyway, as Gunner described the maps, and Demian's location of the supposed gold, I realized that one significant fact was either not known by the group or was disregarded."

"What?" Marion asked.

"The two maps were meant to be superimposed, with one map having an obvious error. What the group didn't know was that that error pointed in the direction of what was important. It's an old ruse used at the Military Academy to trick the enemy if the maps were stolen." Bennie took a minute to be sure they all understood. "So, when I looked at the maps and saw the obvious error, I knew the location where Demian originally thought the gold was buried was wrong. He went about fifty yards from the real spot notated on the map."

"I looked for the gold for quite some time, but that was when you treated me," he said, looking at Marion. "After the treatments, I gave up finding the gold, really changed my ways—in all ways—and got to work trying to benefit Lake Placid. I sold the land and house to Will, and I forgot about the gold. I figured it was all a huge hoax," Demian explained.

"Now, you don't know if there's a fortune out there or not? I saw those stacks when we made our escape. I know they're important. They were important to whoever built them," Marion said.

Demian interjected. "The question is whether to dig up the gold—if there is any at all—or to ignore the issue and let it remain an unsolved Adirondack mystery."

"Huh...."

"So, you believe, in the middle of the devastation of the houses, there might be a fortune in buried gold?" Jane's eyes were wide. Demian couldn't be sure if that was excitement or dread showing plainly on her face.

"And, if there is gold, what is the best possible use for it? We researched the old story of the gold. At least four people died associated with its theft." Demian immediately saw the confusion on the faces of his friends. He continued. "That's the story of Sue Ellen, Theron, their unborn baby and the unlucky obstetrician who attended the unfortunate delivery." He paused. "How many more soldiers, train workers, or what not might have been killed during the robberies, as well? We will never know."

"You haven't begun to dig the gold or know how much might be there?" Marion asked.

"No. I wanted your sage advice about how to go about this, or whether to go about this at all. And what would be the best use of the gold?"

"The land belongs to Will, right? Doesn't the gold belong to him, as well? And are there any rights that New York State will try to assert? Or the feds? And then will the town be overrun by hordes of other treasure seekers, completely changing our perfect little village into a Las Vegas of the East? What a mess. And there's nothing like a lot of gold to ruin good friendships." Marion looked bewildered. "I've always managed my affairs to have sufficient assets to look after Catherine and me, and not too much. I've always given away everything else. What a potential mess."

"You see why I asked. I want to do the right thing. I need your help," Demian implored.

"This might take a couple of days of concentrated thought and meditation. Does Madison or anyone else know?"

"Only Gunner and Will. I've asked them not to discuss this with anyone else until we arrive at a decision."

"Good. I need to rest and meditate. Everyone here needs to rest and meditate. Let's meet again when we think we have an answer." Marion stood and left the room.

"Told you there were special things about these mountains," Demian said to Jane.

"I should get some rest too," Bennie said. "I hope you're not too upset hearing about this from me, but I heard clearly from the mountains that you had to make a decision about what to do. I couldn't just leave it alone."

"I know, Bennie. You've been a great friend to all of us here. We all need to decide what, if anything, we have to do."

"I need to get some rest and get back to work tomorrow, early. Always some disaster at the hospital, you know? All those disasters involve funding. Just a thought." Jane kissed Demian on the cheek and left him.

"Bennie, that leaves you and me. How about good bourbon at Bud's?"

"Wouldn't miss it. I can rest tomorrow."

"I'll bring a bottle and meet you there. Bud won't let me buy anything from him, so I bring my own when I have some serious drinking to do."

"Meet you there."

79

Deborah, Ali, and their parents had settled into their suite at the healing center. She introduced herself and her brother to the patients and offered to do small tasks for them, just as a way to pass the time until she could resume school in the fall or move back to their rebuilt house. "Hi, Jenn. I'm Deborah. You're Bennie's friend. We all love Bennie. He saved our lives."

"Yeah. He thinks he's saving me too." Jenn sighed.

"If you let him…."

Deborah pulled up a chair in the dining room after asking Jenn if she could get her anything else for breakfast. "I like it here. It's not like home, though….." Her face showed regret for an instant; then she was embarrassed that she showed remorse for losing possessions while people at the healing center had to deal with far more relevant and devastating chronic pain, life-threatening illnesses or trauma recovery.

"I heard about how Bennie helped save the group, but I also heard about how *you* found the map and recognized it for what it was. That showed you how to escape over the mountain."

"Yeah, it's called Death Mountain, but to us, it's Life Mountain." Deborah smiled and looked into Jenn's eyes. "Can I do anything for you?"

Before she could say something snide, Jenn thought better of it and replied, "I don't know?"

"How about if I roll you to the gardens? They are beautiful. Just being there helps me feel better." Deborah paused. "I would really like to help you too. My mom and the others are so good at what they do; maybe I could just be your friend?"

"Maybe a trip to the garden would be nice."

They wheeled to the lush, flower-filled, covered space. The aromas of the blooming plants and vegetables hung in the air softly. Deborah breathed in deeply, in an exaggerated fashion, hoping Jenn would take the cue to let the aromas come to her.

"Yeah, this smells like the flower gardens my mother used to keep, before she got ill," Jenn said.

"Just breathing the air here seems to calm me down. I don't know how that works, but it does."

"Can we pick any of the flowers?"

"We do, all the time, and they grow right back. Marion designed the gardens to do that. He said that picking a flower perks up our spirits. I know he's right," she answered. "Then we have to appreciate the colors and aromas until the flowers wilt away. I'll get vases and water when we get back to our rooms."

"How about those pink hydrangeas? Just one or two of them is a whole bouquet." Jenn struggled to stand, but she waved off Deborah's offered hand. She wobbled a bit but walked a few steps, picked a couple of the large blooms and sat back down. She breathed in their fragrance deeply. She allowed a timid smile.

"Do you just want to sit here for a while? I can pull up a chair."

"Yes, why don't we breathe this air. And could you tell me about these mountains?" Jenn pointed to the vista to the east.

"That's where I'm from. You can barely see it, but beyond Whiteface Mountain is Jay Mountain, where the missiles blew up our houses." Deborah sniffled a little and was immediately embarrassed again. "Anyway, that mountain is where I grew up. We're rebuilding there, now, and living here until we can move back." Deborah let a few minutes pass. "I miss it. We could play outside, walk in the hills, climb the high peaks, and we never worried about anyone coming around that might be a problem. I still can't believe we were attacked like that."

"You love it there?"

"Yeah. I love the mountains. I haven't been to the really big cities, but I don't want to, either." She looked at the pale, frail woman. "I know that the mountains have helped us. I know they led me to find the map and then the mountains allowed us to get away, before everything was destroyed."

"Maybe they'll help me, too?"

"I know it."

The two sat in the sun for an hour until Deborah noticed Jenn looked tired. "You should get back and rest. You have PT in a while."

"What are they going to do with me? I can't lift weights or even walk. I'm a mess."

"They'll start slow and help you regain everything."

"You have no idea." Jenn burst out in sobs. Deborah got her a Kleenex. "I used to be a gymnast. I used to be able to do a standing backflip on a balance beam. That used to be something—now most gymnasts can do one—but that was my specialty, and I loved it. I'll never do it again."

"Is that what you really miss the most?"

She thought about it for a while and said, "I guess I miss trusting myself, feeling good in my skin. Everything hurts. I don't trust myself, or my muscles, or my balance or my flexibility. I haven't reached down to pick anything up in years."

Deborah started to understand how desperate Jenn felt. She kept handing her Kleenex as she needed for the next few minutes. They wheeled back to Jenn's room without speaking.

"I'll see you tomorrow. I know you'll have a better day. I know my mother and the rest of the healers can help you. The mountains will be there, too." Deborah left Jenn to rest and do the other therapies after arranging all the flowers they picked into a beautiful bouquet. "Maybe this can remind you of the mountains. Maybe you can draw from their strength?"

80

Marion knocked on Jenn's door. "It's Marion, can we come in? I would like to speak to you about our plans and what you think you are able to do."

"OK. Come in."

He opened the door, introduced the head patient care manager who came with him and sat in the easy chairs in Jenn's room. "We wanted to discuss with you that we have a lot to offer you. I do feel that you should choose for yourself in what order you want to do things, but I want to relax you first. Sometimes pain is all about tension in muscles that pull excessively on joints and stiffen them. So, the first order of business is to deal with the tension and pain. That OK?"

"Sure. I just got back from PT. All they could do for me so far was a nice sauna and then moving my arms and legs and neck. They had to slowly move my arms and legs *for* me. I couldn't do it for myself. That's all I could tolerate."

"We know," Valerie said. "We reviewed the report from the PT team. That's a start. We all start from the beginning."

"I propose that I do a very simple and powerful acupuncture and hypnosis for you. With your permission, I can do that with you lying as you are on your bed."

Jenn visibly shuddered.

"I do ask a lot, I know. I can see how traumatized you've been by the medical profession. We do things differently here. Everything we do is with your permission. *For* you. Not *to* you," Marion said.

"I can't take another test, or treatment or torture."

"I know. I can't either. This is not a test. I know exactly what will happen."

"What?" This sounded more like an exclamation than a question. Jenn still looked unconvinced.

"You will be calmed, balanced and feel that you can change. Then you can work with us, with all the modalities we have here, to let you come back to a robust, centered, self-determining person who has dreams, plans for her life and a positive outlook."

"You can do that?"

Valerie quickly interjected. "Every day. It's quite simple and amazing. I'm here because the therapists here are so good at what they do. I've been their patient myself. I maybe wasn't in as much pain as you, but I know what they *can* do, and *do*, every day."

Jenn looked resigned.

"Can I start with six needles? Then, after you relax, I'll speak to you about how healing takes place?"

"Yeah." Jenn sighed. "If I say stop, I mean it."

"I will respect you and your wishes and Valerie promises the same. I brought her with me so that you would know that you are protected and respected."

In a resigned voice, she said, "I am here."

"Can you uncover your feet and hands?" Jenn did so.

"The way acupuncture is done is by me feeling for the points that I will use. It's like a mini massage of the acupuncture points. I imagine that you won't feel the needles much. I've had practice, you know." He had started to gently rub the area between her large toe and second toe, on the top of her left foot. "Good. Thank you for letting me do that. I already have one needle in."

"Yeah. I felt it, but only a little."

"Good. I need to move to your other foot, then your hands, then your forehead and the top of your head." He did so, slowly and gently inserting needles.

"May I speak to you, as well?" Marion asked.

"Yes." Jenn's voice had a distant quality.

"I would like to just speak to you; if you feel that you're tired, you might drift off. Or you can listen to every word. Whatever you choose." He slowed his cadence to match her breathing. Each phrase took one breath cycle to complete.

Valerie looked at Marion with admiration, then closed her eyes and sent silent prayers to Jenn.

"Good. That's right." Marion had seen that Jenn's forehead muscles relaxed. "You might relax the rest of your muscles if you feel that's right for you."

He led her through relaxing her feet, ankles, calves, knees, thighs, hips, back, abdomen, chest, neck, face, arms, hands and fingers.

Valerie shifted to maintain her own alertness, having heard all of the progressive relaxation images given for Jenn. She had to resist being swept along by Marion's voice. Marion smiled at her.

"That's right." He paused longer between each phrase. "I wonder if you've ever really thought, *really thought* about your breathing? Have you ever thought that each breath gently rocks, comforts, consoles and allows all your internal organs to *heal*, and *restore* and become stronger?" He had begun to time his phrases to her breaths. "So, your heart and lungs, stomach, intestines, liver, spleen, all your internal organs are rocked and nourished with gentle breathing, just like rocking a baby in a carriage. Maybe you can feel that right now?"

Valerie smiled, eyes closed.

"Enjoy this moment. Maybe you can feel the *healing* in your organs." He paused.

About a minute later, he continued. "In a breath, or two, or three, you can let yourself gently arouse to full, present awareness. But before you do, remember. We all have an internal healing ability. We carry it with us as we go about our life. We only have to breathe it in." Marion waited.

Jenn slowly opened her eyes and looked at Marion as he took out the needles. "Wow. You didn't hurt me. You didn't assault me."

"That's not what we do here." Marion heard the word "assault," but chose not to respond to it at this time.

"Jenn, please have the confidence that we want the best for you. I wouldn't be here if I didn't truly believe that respect and caring are job one," Valerie said.

"Rest as long as you need to. Catherine has been slow-cooking a special herbal broth for you all day. The aroma is marvelous. We'll join you for dinner after that."

Marion and Valerie left Jenn wondering if there were changes she could experience or whether this was another huge waste of time and effort—or if it would leave her worse off than before.

81

Deborah and Ali had easily befriended most of the patients at the healing center. The others, they had not met as of yet. Their days consisted of walking, biking and playing games with many of the residents—checkers, five hundred, and poker—for the very friendly stakes of ice creams and sodas. They had not been back to their house. They had not asked to do so.

"Come on, let's go and see if Jenn wants to spend some time with us," Deborah said.

"OK, but can she do much? I mean, *can* she do much?" Ali asked.

"I don't know. She's been here for about a week. They've been seeing her and working with her. 'Sgo."

The two walked, skipped and whistled to the other end of the healing center complex. They passed the recreation areas, PT areas, healing rooms, open areas, gardens, and offices. Entering the hall with the patient rooms, they both immediately quieted as a matter of respect. They approached and knocked on Jenn's door.

"Yes?"

"Hi, Jenn. It's me, Deborah. I've got my brother Ali with me. Want to do something?"

The door slowly opened. Jenn stood, looking a little shaky, but let the two in her room. "I'm making progress, they say. I have just as much pain, but I can stand and walk a little. I can't go very far though."

"That's great. You've made a lot of progress, I would say," Deborah encouraged.

"Would you like to do something with us? We like to do everything here. This is a great place. Don't you think?" Ali asked.

"Well, maybe we can go back to the gardens? They were lovely." She turned and sat in her wheelchair. She draped a blanket over her lap.

Ali pushed the wheelchair with Deborah watching him carefully. He negotiated the small bumps caused by thresholds, carpets and rugs, slowing down so as not to jostle Jenn. His passenger didn't whine. Deborah knew Ali took this seriously.

They came to the gardens and noticed that the retractable roofs had been opened to allow the sun to shine in on the plants, orchards and berries. "Shall we pick you some red raspberries?" Deborah asked Jenn.

"Yeah. And I'll pick some for myself, too." Jenn slowly rose, walked a few steps haltingly and ate handfuls of the fresh red berries. She smiled and looked up at the sun. "The last time we were here, the roof was closed. I like it open. It dries up the earth so walking is easier. But I really like the sun on my face. It warms me."

"Does it help with the pain, as well?" Ali asked.

"No. But maybe I don't pay attention to all the pain so much. I let other things distract me. I feel the sun, or hear the birds or think about other things."

"What other things?" Deborah asked, hoping it wasn't too much.

"I've missed so much—like I've been in a horror movie—no way out, only the pain."

"Sorry. I didn't want to bring up bad memories."

"Do you want to do anything else?" Ali quickly asked, hoping to change the subject.

"Like what?"

"We heard you were a famous gymnast. Could you help us with our round-offs?" Ali asked.

Jenn laughed. "Not famous. But I could do a standing backflip on a balance beam." She sat back down in her wheelchair. "Push me over by the lawn and show me your stuff, if you want."

They did so. Deborah did a nice cartwheel. Ali did a summersault. They all laughed.

"OK, so how about those round-offs? Before you do, we have to be safe. Each of you does five pushups so that I know you're strong enough." They did so, looking at each other, making sure they each could do them, urging each other on.

"Have you ever tried a round-off? It's just like a cartwheel, except when you're at the top of the cartwheel, your feet come together and you land facing the opposite direction, feet still together, got it?"

The kids nodded enthusiastically.

"Deborah, can you do a handstand?"

"For a little while."

"Good. Then we'll do a very slow motion round-off to show you how. First, do a handstand. Ali, you spot for her. Bring her feet together and when you come down, turn your body and face me. Real slow." Jenn watched them, giving pointers and laughing as they did exactly as they were told. Next, she directed Deborah to help Ali. He had a lot harder time because he was smaller, younger and not as strong.

"I get it now. I get how to turn my body. I feel it. It's great." Deborah panted between the words, thoroughly tired out from the exertion.

"I'll have to work on mine, but I'll get it, I'm sure." Ali wanted to sound like part of the group.

"It takes time and it's easier when you're older, bigger and stronger. A lot of things are like that," Jenn told them. "But you did make progress today. I'm proud of both of you. And you watched out for each other. You always need to make sure you have a spotter like that. Never take any stupid risks." *Like I did*, she thought.

"We know. Everyone talks about safety. We know." Ali showed just a little bit of irritation.

"Promise me! Promise me!" Jenn's eyes teared as she looked away. "Living is no good if you don't feel good."

Deborah walked in front of her line of sight and said, "We know, and we prom-ise." The two looked each other in the eyes and understood each other completely.

"Ali, why don't we help Jenn back inside to rest? We've been out here for an hour. We don't want to tire her out." Ali carefully pushed her away.

After they left Jenn at her room, Deborah told Ali that she had to speak to Marion and Madison immediately. She found her mother between patients and took her by the hand to Marion's room.

"I think I found out something very important. Ali and I were in the gardens with Jenn. She didn't say it herself, but I know what happened to her. And I think she blames herself for her pain and she can't let it go."

"What do you mean?" Marion asked.

"Ali and I asked her to help us with our round-offs—it's like a cartwheel—and Jenn made us promise, really promise to always be safe and protect each other. Really promise to be safe and use a spotter so we don't get injured."

"Do you think that she might have gotten hurt somehow and blamed herself for all her pain all these years? Is that it?" Madison asked.

"I haven't gotten around to asking her what might have happened to her at age fourteen. I didn't think it was appropriate yet," Marion answered. He looked directly at Deborah and asked, "You're sure? You know this?"

"I could see it in her eyes," she answered, looking directly in Marion's eyes.

Marion turned to Madison. "Well, you've got a very special little girl here." He turned to Deborah and continued. "You found the map that saved us—you recognized it for what it was. Now you've found the golden key to helping Jenn. Your mom and I will see her today, and I'll do a special treatment for someone who blames herself for her own misery. She'll slowly heal, after that—slow, but sure."

"You can do that?" Deborah asked.

"Don't tell her or anyone else about what you think or about what we'll do. It's not proper to speak about another person's problems or treatments unless you're trying to help too."

Deborah nodded.

Marion and Madison laughed. Then they smiled, looking directly in each other's eyes.

82

"You mean it?" Deborah asked while sucking in a breath. She met up with her mom in their rooms that afternoon.

"That's what Marion said. And I've never disagreed with or doubted what he's told me." Madison looked appreciatively at her daughter and wondered what other special abilities she might have beyond what a fine young lady she was becoming.

"OK, but you have to help me and tell me what to do." Deborah jumped up and ran to the door of their suite. "'Sgo."

While they walked to Marion's treatment room, Madison reviewed the only real rules that she lived by—be as quiet as possible, keep your heart full of possibilities and believe that change can happen. "So just be confident that Marion knows that you will be helpful. Don't worry."

Deborah entered after knocking. She saw Marion talking softly to Jenn. Madison motioned to her to sit in a chair near the window overlooking the gardens. Jenn looked at Deborah and her mother and smiled weakly, nodding.

Marion said, "Good, you're both here. Deborah, sit and fill your heart with love and the firm conviction that change is possible."

Because she had not done this before, this puzzled her, but she sat and tried to do so. From the chair, she looked to the garden and saw that the garden was full of love. She could see the flowers and plants sway gently in the soft breezes. The greens of the leaves seemed to dance and merge. She looked back to the treatment room and saw the greens fill the room.

"Good, Deborah." Marion could sense the color and feeling of love Deborah added to their process. As his smile grew, Deborah felt more and more welcome and started to understand why Marion had requested her to come.

Deborah smiled and looked back to the garden. As she watched, the plants began to dance seductively. She stared and let other colors come to her. She passed those colors to the treatment room.

Madison sat next to her, put her hand on her shoulder and smiled. "Be with the flowers and plants. Their energies come from the earth and are grounding. They remind us that we belong to these mountains. Their strength can come to us in colors, or feelings or sounds. Maybe think of the mountains. They've shown you things before, just listen. Let your impressions come to us here in the room."

Deborah took in a deep breath and looked further beyond the gardens to the mountains and understood that the mountains kept the memories of the people who had lived in the area. She saw the sweep of history.

Marion had reassured Jenn that today's treatment would be gentle. He asked her to imagine how her life could change, how she might want to feel after the treatment and to lie down and relax.

Deborah saw her lying comfortably. Marion moved more slowly and deliberately than just his age might account for, she thought. Then she slowed down her own thoughts. She let her mind's concentration center in her own heart. Maybe she could fill her heart with love, and maybe send that to Jenn. She closed her eyes to better study her breathing. It slowed, and she followed the stream of her breath into her lungs. Then she noticed her heart—the pumping organ, but also the center of her being, and the seat of her compassion—begin to fill with love. She thought she could concentrate that feeling and send it to Jenn. She spent the rest of the session doing so in what she conceived of as floating, multi-colored orbs. Deborah could not see Marion's appreciative smile or her mother's pride.

Marion had felt the pulses in both of Jenn's wrists. He nodded to himself and put one small needle below her lower lip, one at each angle of her jaw and one in each palm. Then he put a slightly larger needle near her right ankle and one near her left thumb at her wrist. He opened a window and watched as a dark, misty substance drifted from Jenn out the window. He could see the colors that Deborah sent begin to fill the vacuum in Jenn's heart.

Madison held Jenn's head gently, also sending the goodness of the universal love and compassion to Jenn. She hummed softly. This gave a quiet, ethereal quality to the air in the room.

After ten minutes, Marion removed the needles, closed the window, and Jenn aroused herself. She needed a few minutes to sit and stretch a little. "Can you do that? I mean can you *do* that?" Jenn asked.

"What?" Marion asked. Madison, Deborah and he laughed.

"I don't know how I feel. I can't describe it—I'm lighter. I can breathe easily—I don't have pain at this instant." She looked appreciatively at the trio.

"You don't have to put it in words right now. You might want to walk and stand and see how that feels."

They helped her to her feet. She stood and started to cry. "I don't have pain. My skin and joints move without screaming. I don't get it."

"It took three of us to help you, today. But now you have the most glorious and grand adventure ahead of you—creating your life. We'll all be here to advise you as you need it," Marion concluded.

"I think a nice walk in the gardens, slowly, is just what Jenn and Deborah need right now," Madison insisted. "Then get some rest, and we'll welcome you with a feast tonight with all the patients and staff here. We'll all want to get acquainted with the real you."

Deborah's head was full of questions that she knew that she shouldn't ask in front of Jenn. She said, "'Sgo. We'll see the flowers again and see how much more beautiful they are."

83

"I'm so glad all of you could come here to be with us tonight to make a very important decision." Demian's commanding voice quieted the crowd gathered at his condominium. Bud and his staff had catered the evening meal, served and then cleared the dishes. Bud poured very tasty port in little glasses for all the guests. Demian took his time thanking him and his crew for serving a delightful meal. They all waited until Demian returned to toast the group.

"To all of us. Here's to us. We're missing a few of our group from the old days—Bill and Evan—but the rest of us and newcomers, we welcome." He raised his glass of port and looked around the room to all the guests in turn. He sipped the dark ruby red liquid, blinked and said, "This is really good. We'll work on it slowly." He slipped his arm around Jane's waist.

Dr. Crandall, a retired OB/GYN who had come to Jay Mountain and the old hunting lodge more than a dozen years ago to regain his self-respect, said, "You haven't gathered us all together just to sample your port, have you?" The doctor was the only one in the room who could speak is such a forthright manner to Demian. He had earned the right to do so after being Demian's friend for decades. He had also been among the original group who had found the maps and puzzled through their meanings.

"No, Robert. But let's first remember the members of our group who have passed on. Including my father, my grandfather, Will's grandfather, Will's father, your father and all the old hunters who spent countless hours trying to find the gold on Jay Mountain." Demian closed his eyes for a moment, then took another sip of port. "I called you all here because Marion told me to do so. He is the wisest man I've ever met. Everyone, if you haven't already done so, meet Marion."

The room murmured greetings. No one questioned Demian's assertion about Marion being the wisest person Demian, with his vast travels, had ever met. It became a foregone conclusion.

"The other newcomers to our group are Jane," he gave her a kiss on the cheek, "and Bennie. Bennie has quite a story to tell us. He comes from who knows where, has been off the grid for so long he likely has nowhere to call home and saved all of us using a hunting rifle to fend off a helicopter armed with missiles."

The room murmured gratitude to Bennie and waved to Jane. Dr. Crandall and his wife, Ellen, looked admiringly at Bennie.

"So, Bennie. Could you tell the group what you told us on the mountain the other day?" Demian asked.

"Sure. I told you and Will that a force greater than myself helped me shoot at a helicopter flying at over a hundred and fifty miles an hour, from over three hundred yards away and deflect an attack with missiles that would surely have killed all of the people at the houses—everyone. The thing is, *I* couldn't have done that. *I* must have had help—call it supernatural or whatever. In fact, I hope in the future Marion can tell me how I could possibly have done such a thing." Bennie took a drink of water and quickly put it down as if it was a mistake. He picked up the port, sipped it and smiled contentedly. "Anyway, as I was told the story of all of you guys finding the maps carved in the stones, following the directions and so on, I knew that Demian was in the wrong location to find any gold. So, I took him and Will up the mountain and told him where I thought the gold would be buried. It was an old Special Forces and Military Academy ruse about map making and where the important direction lies. Will didn't know it. So, I had to tell Demian and Will about the gold. I had had several meditations that told me to do so. And, I had to clear the air about me shooting the helicopter out of the sky. That wasn't me. I was told in my meditation that I had to admit that and tell Demian and Will about the real location of the gold."

"So, Demian never found the gold? I assumed he had and kept it to himself," Robert said, looking astonished.

"I looked for it, for sure, but then, Marion did a few healings for me, and I reoriented myself to other purposes. I gave up on it," Demian replied.

"Like building our healing center," Madison added. "We all appreciate that, beyond words."

Gunner added, "We've been at work here and assumed the money to build the center came from digging the gold. We had no idea that Demian must have funded all that by himself, from personal funds."

"No problem." Demian went about refilling the port glasses and opening another bottle.

"Don't blow it off as easily as that. I know you went through some hard times back then. I heard about you selling off your collections. You even sold off the land and the camp." Robert again said something only he could get away with about his long-time friend.

"Marion was right. The more I gave away, the more that came back to me." He turned and smiled at Jane. "Now, I have the love of my life." Demian gave her a kiss.

"It wasn't only the gifts of money. You helped me publish what I think is the definitive work on the local history of OB/GYN. You helped Mason become an endowed instructor at Paul Smith's College. You started the research center for Adirondack studies and got Jim Tower three research assistants to help publish the truth about the Adirondacks and living in the outback regions."

"And you gave a bombastic, hyperbolic fool like me the time of day and the freedom to experience these mountains and learn just how much a fool I was," Gunner interjected. "If you had thrown me out of the old camp, I would certainly have thought it was appropriate, but I would never have changed and become the healer and author that I am right now." Gunner wiped a tear from his eye. "You know it's true. All of you."

"That was then. This is now." Demian paused. "Now we have an even more dangerous path to take if we decide to do so. The problem is whether to dig the gold at all. And if we do, what to do with it? If there is any."

Marion finally stood. "In my life, I've learned the really hard things are acting in good faith, with reverence for all, not taking advantage of anyone or anything and doing the right things. It's never easy."

Will interjected. "I don't want anything to do with the gold. It will only bring us misery if we become possessive of it." He remembered how obssessed his grandfather had become, trying to find the gold.

"Well, you do own it now," Gunner argued.

"Then the balance of things includes the good the gold might do and the danger of what might change around here if word of a gold rush gets out. We might lose all that's good about the small towns around here, especially Lake Placid. And would each of us feel differently or act differently if another huge fortune came to us?" Demian asked after looking around the table. "You see why I had to consult Marion."

There were nods of agreement.

Mason asked, "Is there some kind of law about digging up buried antiquities or treasure?"

"Who knows? Even asking that question out loud would start an avalanche of prospectors. We don't want that," Jane said.

Demian finally asked, "Marion, what is your best advice? We presented this problem to you a few days ago and left you to think it over."

"There are real plusses and minuses. One the one hand, I am sure that all of us would advocate for charitable works to be completed with the gold. On the other hand, the risk of flooding the area with treasure hunters, followed by organized crime, gambling, prostitution and who knows what else, would negate all those good deeds. From the story I've heard about the discovery of the maps, and now the correct interpretation of the maps, you should all have a say in what to do, in that so many of you worked together to find the gold. Sound good?"

Everyone nodded.

"I think I should abstain. I've never spent much time here or been a part of the finding of the gold," Ellen said. Jane and Bennie quickly elected to do the same.

Demian looked at the remaining group who would likely offer opinions. Gunner, Madison, Mason, Will and Dr. Crandall considered their options. Finally, Will started to speak slowly. "I think I want the gold off my land. It's been such a dream—and nightmare—for so many people for so long. The search for the gold nearly consumed my grandfather. The treasure needs to be out in the world, doing some good. The earth needs to heal by letting go of it."

Marion nodded. He looked at Madison.

She answered. "I agree. It's been up there too long. I think the mountains' vibrations will be clearer without that collection of bounty—ill-gotten at that."

Dr. Crandall said, "I can see that."

"Madison speaks for me. And better than me, too," Mason said.

The gathered friends looked at Demian.

"The question is how to use the gold." Demian stared back at the group. "We shouldn't touch it if we don't have rock solid plans."

Marion answered. "In my meditations, I came upon a plan to benefit the community—a community-driven, sponsored and directed foundation to disperse the funds according to need. I think *any* local charitable organization can and should be able to use the funds. We also need very clearly delineated separation of the availability of funds from all of us. No one can know where the money comes from. No one can know we're part of this. That's the only way this will work." Marion saw relief on the faces of all those gathered.

Dr. Crandall and his wife smiled. "I think I'm happy to be rid of the legend, finally and for good. We've spent too much time chasing fools' dreams," he said.

"I lived that fool's dream—until I came here to learn from all of you," Gunner said.

"I'm glad this is where we want to take this project. No self-seeking behaviors here," Marion concluded.

84

It looked like the whole village of Lake Placid had turned out for the celebration and awards ceremony. It had been a long four weeks since the last of the assassins had been captured. The governor, himself, had helicoptered in from Albany to present the awards. Demian scanned the crowd. On the podium with him were Sheriff Todd Wilkins, Captain Nicholas Green, Jane Parker, the mayor of Lake Placid, the commandant of the state police, the two-star general commanding West Point, Bennie, and several other local town leaders.

Demian looked out over the audience. Villagers from Lake Placid and the surrounding small towns joined business owners, workers, hospital staff and tourists wanting to see what the pomp and circumstance might be about. All of the sheriff's staff were on duty to enjoy the day. They knew there would be no disturbances from this crowd. They walked among the people and chatted amiably, understanding that their position in a village that adored them was rare and special.

The presentation ceremony proceeded in the outdoor stadium of the Olympic arena. The crowds filled the field inside the Olympic skating and racing track. The sun shone brightly with a gentle breeze. Demian walked behind the other dignitaries milling about on the stage to stand behind Jane and whisper, "I love you," in her ear.

She smiled the largest smile of her life, turned and kissed him on the cheek. "Hold that thought, will you?"

"Sure. That's a promise."

Demian walked to Bennie and said, "Without you, this wouldn't be happening." Bennie only smiled.

The mayor walked up to the microphone; tapping it caused most of the audience to recoil. He bent to speak and whispered, "I think we can turn this down a couple of notches." After several more tests, he said, "I would like to welcome everyone to the awards ceremony and celebration." He looked at the crowd and those on the podium. He paused, then folded several sheets of paper and put them in his inner suit coat pocket. "I've just made the decision to save you from hearing all the boring things I might have said." The crowd cheered.

"OK, OK. I get it. I was right. Just remember this when election time comes around again." The crowd roared with laughter. When they finally quieted, he slowed his rapid speech and said solemnly, "I have the pleasure of introducing the governor of New York State. Please welcome him in the warm fashion this area is known for." He gestured to the governor, motioning him to the podium. Cheers broke out. Shouts of approval could be heard over the high school band starting to play a Susa tune. The crowd took several minutes to quiet.

The governor approached the podium, but turned to shake the hands of Bennie, Todd, Nicholas and finally Demian. He whispered to Demian, "Your town is so welcoming. Thank you, my friend, for insisting that I come." He turned to Jane, offered his hand, and said, "I've heard a lot about you. Take care of my good friend Demian."

He finally turned to the audience. "I'm no fool. I know all you people came to share in the picnic and beverages after the ceremony. You certainly don't want me to drone on up here forever." He paused to gather his thoughts. "However, I do want to honor our medal recipients. They likely literally saved my life. With no further ado, let's get on with the ceremony and then the eats—they smell irresistible even from here, I can tell you that. Even our congress would *all* have to agree on that!" He stepped aside while the crowd laughed and applauded.

The two-star general stepped up. "Retired Captain Bennie R. Grimm, come up here. You've made us proud. Please accept this medal for Distinguished Valor for a Military Academy Graduate. This may come as a surprise because you have never heard of such a medal. We had to make it up just for you." The crowd roared as the medal was slipped around his neck on a red, white and blue ribbon. Bennie gave the sharpest salute of his life. The general held his salute for a long time. Finally, they both slowly lowered their arms, sharing the moment. Bennie did an about face and sat down.

The governor stood to present medals to Sheriff Todd Wilkins and Captain Nicholas Green, stating that they were public servants, and as such, ultimately worked for him, so he should have the pleasure of presenting the medals. They both accepted their awards, smiled, saluted and sat down.

"Well, it's clear that everyone here knows when to shut up and enjoy the picnic." The governor laughed. "There is one more thing that I have to do. And I'm sure everyone here will agree. I need only a few more minutes." He stood at the podium for dramatic effect. "Demian, come up here. I want to present you with the key to the village of Lake Placid. You deserve the respect, love and admiration of everyone here." The crowd erupted. The band began another Susa tune. Strings of fireworks and firecrackers popped off. Demian made his way to the podium. The governor hugged him in a ferocious bear hug. He whispered, "Be gracious—take the adulation. They need to show their appreciation. And promise never to run for governor against me."

Demian slowly turned to Jane and smiled. Then he faced the audience. "I really appreciate the key to Lake Placid. You all deserve my admiration for living the lives that I've come to think are the closest to Godliness. I've traveled the world and here is where I've chosen to live, to be here with all of you." He clapped his hands in front of himself and then opened his arms to the audience. More fireworks, the band playing and celebratory cheers were heard all around. Demian went to stand by Jane and hold her hand, tears streaming down his face. The governor said again, "Don't you dare run for governor against me!" This time the microphone caught the admonition, and the whole audience laughed.